"WHEN YOU PICK UP A NOVEL BY TREVANIAN, YOU KNOW YOU'VE WITNESSED A PRO AT WORK."
—*Pittsburgh Post-Gazette*

Down in the Main, Montreal's teeming underworld, the dark streets echo with cries in a dozen languages, with the swift footsteps of thieves, with the murmurs of women of pleasure. To the people of the Main, Lieutenant Claude LaPointe is judge and jury, father confessor and avenging angel. And when cold-blooded murder invades LaPointe's territory, it means the beginning of another gripping tale of death and danger, of action and mystery, by the incomparable Trevanian, author of *The Eiger Sanction, The Loo Sanction* and *Shibumi.*

"Trevanian moves . . . with an éclat that Simenon, Hammett and Macdonald might well salute. The plotting is dexterous, the police work realistic, the suspense considerable."

—Barbara A. Bannon,
Publishers Weekly

THE MAIN

TREVANIAN

A JOVE BOOK

This Jove book contains the complete
text of the original hardcover edition.
It has been completely reset in a typeface
designed for easy reading, and was printed
from new film.

THE MAIN

A Jove Book / published by arrangement with
Harcourt Brace Jovanovich, Inc.

PRINTING HISTORY
One previous printing
Harcourt Brace Jovanovich edition published 1976
Jove edition / September 1977
Tenth printing / April 1984

ISBN: 0-515-08096-9

Library of Congress Catalog Card Number: 76-24896

Jove books are published by The Berkley Publishing Group,
200 Madison Avenue, New York, N.Y. 10016.
The words "A JOVE BOOK" and the "J" with sunburst
are trademarks belonging to Jove Publications, Inc.

PRINTED IN THE UNITED STATES OF AMERICA

To Tony Godwin

on behalf of the writers he helped

1

Evening on the Main, and the shops are closing. Display bins have been pulled back off the sidewalks; corrugated shutters clatter down over store windows. One or two lights are kept on as a deterrent to burglary; and empty cash registers are left ajar so that thieves won't smash them open pointlessly.

The bars remain open, and the cafés; and loudspeaker cones over narrow music stalls splash swatches of noise over sidewalks congested with people, their necks pulled into collars, their shoulders tight against the dank cold. The young and the busy lose patience with the crawling, faceless Wad. They push and shoulder their way through, confusing the old, irritating the idle. The mood of the crowd is harried and brusque; tempers have been frayed by weeks of pig weather, with its layers of zinc cloud, moist and icy, pressing down on the city, delaying the onset of winter with its clean snows and taut blue skies. Everyone complains about the weather. It isn't the cold that gets you, it's the damp.

The swarm coagulates at street corners and where gar-

7

bage cans have been stacked on the curb. The crowd surges and tangles, tight-packed but lonely. Tense faces, worried faces, vacant faces, all lit on one side by the garish neon of nosh bars, saloons, cafés.

In the window of a fish shop there is a glass tank, its sides green with algae. A lone carp glides back and forth in narcotized despair.

Schoolboys in thick coats and short pants, bookbags strapped to their backs, snake through the crowd, their faces pinched with cold and their legs blotchy red. A big kid punches a smaller one and darts ahead. In his attempt to catch up and retaliate, the small boy steps on a man's foot. The man swears and cuffs him on the back of the head. The boy plunges on, tears of embarrassment and anger in his eyes.

Fed up with the jams and blockages, some people step out into the street and squeeze between illegally parked cars and the northbound traffic. Harassed truck drivers lean on their air horns and curse, and the braver offenders swear back and throw them the fig. The swearing, the shouting, the grumbling, the swatches of conversation are in French, Yiddish, Portuguese, German, Chinese, Hungarian, Greek—but the lingua franca is English. The Main is a district of immigrants, and greenhorns in Canada quickly learn that English, not French, is the language of success. Signs in the window of a bank attest to the cosmopolitan quality of the street:

HABLAMOS ESPANOL
ΟΜΙ ΟΥΜΕΝ ΕΛΛΗΝΙΚΑ
PARLIAMO ITALIANO
WIR SPRECHEN DEUTSCH
FALAMOS PORTUGUES

And there is a worn street joke: "I wonder who in that bank can speak all those languages?"

"The customers."

Commerce is fluid on the Main, and friable. Again and again, shops open in a flurry of brave plans and hopes;

8

frequently they fail, and a new man with different plans and the same hopes start business in the same shop. There is not always time to change the sign. Retail and wholesale fabrics are featured in a store above which the metal placard reads: PAINTS.

Some shops never change their proprietors, but their lines of goods shift constantly, in search of a profitable coincidence between the wants of the customer and the availability of wholesale bargains. In time, the shopkeepers give up chasing phantom success, and the waves of change subside, leaving behind a random flotsam of wares marking high tides in wholesale deals and low tides in customer interest. Within four walls you can buy camping gear and berets, batteries and yard goods, postcards and layettes, some slightly damaged or soiled, all at amazing discounts. Such shops are known only by the names of their owners; there is no other way to describe them.

And there are stores that find the task of going out of business so complicated that they have been at it for years.

The newspaper seller stands beside his wooden kiosk, his hands kept warm under his canvas change belt. He rocks from foot to foot as he jiggles his coins rhythmically. He never looks up at the passers-by. He makes change to hands, not to faces. He mutters his half of an unending conversation, and he nods, agreeing with himself.

Two people press into a doorway and talk in low voices. She looks over his shoulder with quick worried glances. His voice has the singsong of persuasion through erosion.

"Come on, what do you say?"

"Gee, I don't know. I don't think I better."

"What you scared of? I'll be careful."

"Oh, I better be getting home."

"For crying out loud, you do it for the other guys!"

"Yeah, but . . ."

"Come on. My place is just around the corner."

"Well . . . no, I better not."

9

"Oh, for crying out loud! Go home then! Who wants you?"

An old Chasidic Jew with *peyiss, shtreimel* level on his head, long black coat scrupulously brushed, returns home from work, maintaining a dignified pace through the press of the crowd. Although others push and hurry, he does not. At the same time, he avoids seeming too humble, for, as the saying has it, "too humble is half proud." So he walks without rushing, but also without dawdling. A gentle and moderate man.

Always he checks the street sign before turning off toward his flat in a low brick building up a side street. This although he has lived on that street for twenty-two years. Prudence can't hurt.

"The Main" designates both a street and a district. In its narrowest definition, the Main is Boulevard St. Laurent, once the dividing line between French and English Montreal, the street itself French in essence and articulation. An impoverished and noisy street of small shops and low rents, it naturally became the first stop for waves of immigrants entering Canada, with whose arrival "the Main" broadened its meaning to include dependent networks of back streets to the west and east of the St. Laurent spine. Each succeeding national tide entered the Main bewildered, frightened, hopeful. Each successive group clustered together for protection against suspicion and prejudice, concentrating in cultural ghettos of a few blocks' extent.

They found jobs, opened shops, had children; some succeeded, some failed; and they in turn regarded the next wave of immigrants with suspicion and prejudice.

The boundary between French and English Montreal thickened into a no man's land where neither language predominated, and eventually the Main became a third strand in the fiber of the city, a zone of its own consisting of mixed but unblended cultures. The immigrants who did well, and most of the children, moved away to English-speaking west Montreal. But the old stayed, those who had spent their toil and money on the education of children

10

who are now a little embarrassed by them. The old stayed; and the losers; and the lost.

Two young men sit in a steamy café, looking out onto the street through a window cleared of mist by a quick palm swipe. One is Portuguese, the other Italian; they speak a mélange of Joual slang and mispronounced English. Both wear trendy suits of uncomfortable cut and unserviceable fabric. The Portuguese's suit is gaudy and cheap; the Italian's is gaudy and expensive.

"Hey, hey!" says the Portuguese. "What you think of that? Not bad, eh?"

The Italian leans over the table and catches a quick glimpse of a girl clopping past the café in a mini, platform boots, and a bunny jacket. "Not so bad! *Beau pétard, hein?*"

"And what you think of those *foufounes?*"

"I could make her cry. I take one of those in each hand, eh? Eh?" In robust mime, the Italian holds one in each hand and moves them on his lap. "She would really cry, I'm tell you that." He glances up at the clock above the counter. "Hey, I got to go."

"You got something hot waiting for you?"

"Ain't I *always* got something hot waiting?"

"Lucky son of a bitch."

The Italian grins and runs a comb through his hair, patting down the sides with his palm. Yeah, maybe he's lucky. He's lucky to have the looks. But it takes talent, too. Not everybody's got the talent.

In just over five hours, he will be kneeling in an alley off Rue Lozeau, his face pressed against the gravel. He will be dead.

There is a sudden block in the flow of pedestrians. Someone has vomited on the sidewalk. Chunks of white in a sauce of ochre. People veer to avoid it but there is a comma of smear where a heel skidded.

A cripple plunges down the Main against the flow of pedestrian traffic. Each foot slaps flat upon the pavement

11

as he jerks his torso from side to side with excessive, erratic energy. He lurches forward, then plants a foot to prevent himself from falling. A lurch, a twist, the slack flap of a foot. He is young, his face abnormally bland, his head too large. A harelip contorts his mouth into something between a grin and a sneer. His eyes are huge behind thick iron-rimmed glasses which are twisted on his face so that one eye looks through the bottom of its lens, while the other pupil is bisected by the top of its lens. Coiled back against his chest is a withered, useless hand in a pale blue glove. An incongruous curved pipe is clenched between his teeth, and he sucks it moistly. Sweet aromatic smoke pours over his shoulder and disintegrates in the eddies of his lurching motion.

Pedestrians are startled out of their involute thoughts to see him barging toward them through the crowd. They move aside to make room, eager to avoid contact. Eyes are averted; there is something frightening and disgusting about the Gimp, who drives ahead in his determined, angry way. The human flood breaks at his prow, then blends back in his wake, and people forget him immediately he has passed. They have their own problems, their own plans; each is isolated in and insulated by the alien crowd.

Chez Pete's Place is a bar for the street *bommes;* it is the only place that admits them, and their presence precludes any other clientele. Painted plywood has replaced glass in the window, so it is always night inside. The fat proprietor sits slumped behind the bar, his watery eyes fixed on a skin magazine in his lap. Around a table in the back sits a knot of ragged old men, their hands so filthy that the skin shines and crinkles. They are sharing a half-gallon bottle of wine, and one of the *bommes,* Dirtyshirt Red, is spiking his wine with whisky from a pint bottle screwed up in a brown paper bag. He doesn't offer to share the whisky, and the others know better than to ask.

"Look at that stuck-up son of a bitch, won't ya?" Dirtyshirt Red says, lifting his chin toward a tall, gaunt tramp sitting alone at a small table in the corner, out of the light, his concentration on his glass of wine.

12

"Potlickin' bastard thinks he's too good to sit with the rest of us," Red pursues. "Thinks his shit don't stink, but his farts give him away!"

The other tramps laugh ritually. Ridiculing the Vet is an old pastime for all of them. No one feels sorry for the Vet; he brings it on himself by bragging about a nice snug kip he's got somewhere off the Main. No matter how cold it is, or how hard up a guy is, the Vet never offers to share his kip; he won't even let anybody know where it is.

"Hey, what you dreamin' about, Vet? Thinking about what a hero you was in the war?"

The Vet's broad-brimmed floppy hat tilts up as he raises his head slowly and looks toward the table of jeering *bommes*. His eyebrows arch and his nostrils dilate in a caricature of superiority, then his musings return to his wine glass.

"Oh, yeah! Big hero he was! Captured by the Germans, he was. Left by the Limeys at Dunkirk 'cause they didn't want him stinkin' up their boats. And you know what big hero thing he done when he was in prison camp? He lined his ass with ground glass so the Germans would get castrated when they cornholed him! Big hero! That's why he walks funny! He claims he was wounded in the war, but I heard different!"

There are snickers and nudgings around the table, but the Vet does not deign to respond. Perhaps he no longer hears.

Lieutenant Claude LaPointe crosses Sherbrooke, leaving the somber mass of the Monastère du Bon Pasteur behind. His pace slows to the measured rhythm of the beat-walker. The Main has been his patch for thirty-two years, since the Depression was at its nadir and frightened people treated one another with humanity, even in Montreal, the most impolite city in the world.

LaPointe presses his fists deep into the pockets of his shapeless overcoat to tug the collar tighter down onto his neck. Over the years, that rumpled overcoat has become something of a uniform for him, known by everybody who works on the Main, or who works the Main. Young detectives down at the Quartier Général make jokes about it, saying he sleeps in it at night, and in the summer uses it as a laundry bag. Feelings differ about the man in the overcoat; some recognize a friend and protector, others see a repressive enemy. It depends upon what you do for a living; and even more it depends on how LaPointe feels about you.

When he was young on the street, the Main was French and he its French cop. As the foreigners began to arrive in numbers, there was coolness and distance between them and LaPointe. He could not understand what they wanted, what they were saying, how they did things; and for their part they brought with them a deep distrust of authority and police. But with the wearing of time, the newcomers became a part of the street, and LaPointe became their cop: their protector, sometimes their punisher.

As he walks slowly up the street, LaPointe passes a bakery that is something of a symbol of the change the years have brought to the Main. Thirty-odd years ago, when the Main was French, the bakery was:

PATISSERIE ST. LAURENT

Ten years later, in response to the relentless pressure of English, one word was added to permit the French to use the first two-thirds of the sign and the Anglos the last two-thirds:

PATISSERIE ST. LAURENT *Bakery*

Now there are different breads in the window, breads with odd shapes and glazes. And the women waiting in line gossip in alien sounds. Now the sign reads:

PATISSERIE ST. LAURENT *Bakery*
ΑΡΤΟπΩΛΕΙΟΝ

The throng is thinning out as people arrive at destinations, or give up trying. LaPointe continues north, uphill, his step heavy and slow, his professional glance wandering from detail to detail. The lock on that metal grating over the store window wants replacing. He'll remind Mr. Capeck about it tomorrow. The man standing in that doorway . . . it's all right. Only a *bomme*. The streetlight is out in the alley behind Le Kit-Kat, a porno theatre. He'll report that. Men who get overexcited in the porno house use that alley; and sometimes rollers use it too.

Deep in his pocket, LaPointe's left hand lies lightly over the butt of his stub .38. In summer he carries it in a holster behind his hip, so he can keep his jacket open. In winter he leaves it loose in his left overcoat pocket, so his right hand is free. The pistol is so much a part of him that he releases it automatically when he reaches for something, and takes it up again when his hand returns to his pocket. The weight of it wears out the lining, and at least once each winter he has to sew it up. He is clumsy with a needle, so the pocket becomes steadily shallower. Every few years he has to have the lining replaced.

In more than thirty years on this street of voluble and passionate people, a street on which poverty and greed and despair find expression in petty crime, LaPointe has fired his weapon only seven times. He is proud of that.

A harried child, her eyes down as she gnaws nervously at her lip, bumps into LaPointe and mutters "Excuse me" without looking up, her voice carrying a note of distress. She is late getting home. Her parents will be angry; they will scold her because they love her. The Lieutenant knows the girl and the parents. They want her to become a nurse, and they make her study long hours because she is not good at schoolwork. The girl tries, but she does not have the ability. For her training, for her future, her parents have suffered years of scrimping and self-denial. She is everything to them: their future, their pride, their excuse.

The girl spends a lot of time wishing she were dead.

As he passes Rue Guilbault, LaPointe glances down and sees two young men idling by the stoop of a brownstone. They wear black plastic jackets, and one swings back and forth from the railing. They *chantent la pomme* to a girl of fourteen who sits on the stoop, her elbows resting on the step above, her meager breasts pressed against a thin sweater. She taunts and laughs, and they sniff around like pubescent puppies. LaPointe knows the house. That would be the youngest Da Costa girl. Like her sisters, she will probably be selling ass on the street within two years. Mama Da Costa's dream of the girls following their aunt into the convent is beginning to fade.

LaPointe is walking behind two men who speak a strained English. They are discussing business, and how it's easy for the rich to get richer. One maintains that it's a matter of percentages; if you know the percentages, you're set. The other agrees, but he complains that you've got to be rich to find out what the percentages *are*.

They step apart gingerly to avoid colliding with the cripple who lurches toward them, his pipe smoke trailing a smear in the red neon of a two-for-one bar.

LaPointe stands in the middle of the sidewalk. The cripple stumbles to a stop and wavers before the policeman.

"Say-hey, Lieutenant. How's it going?" The Gimp's speech is blurred by the affliction that has damaged his centers of control. His mother was diseased at the time of his birth. He speaks with the alto, adenoidal whine of a boxer who has been hit on the windpipe too often.

LaPointe looks at the cripple with fatigued patience. "What are you doing at this end of the street, Gimp?"

"Nothing, Lieutenant. Say-hey, I'm just taking a walk, that's all. Boy, you know, this pig weather is really hanging on, ain't it, Lieutenant? I never seen anything like . . ."

LaPointe is shaking his head, so the Gimp gives up his attempt to hide in small talk. Taking one hand from his overcoat pocket, the Lieutenant points toward a narrow passage between two buildings, out of the flow of the crowd. The cripple grimaces, but follows him.

"All right, Gimp. What are you carrying?"

"Hey, nothin', Lieutenant. Honest! I promised you, didn't I?"

LaPointe reaches out; in his attempt to step back, the cripple stumbles against the brick wall. "Hey, please! We need the money! Mama's going to be pissed at me if I don't bring back any money!"

16

"Do you want to go back inside?"

"No! Hey, have a heart, Lieutenant!" the cripple whines. "Mama'll be pissed. We need the money. What kind of work can a guy like me get? Eh?"

"Where's it stashed?"

"I tol' you! I ain't carrying . . ." The Gimp's eyes moisten with tears. His body slumps in defeat. "It's in a tube," he admits sullenly.

LaPointe sighs. "Go up the alley and get it out. Put it inside your glove and give it to me." LaPointe has no intention of handling the tube.

The cripple moans and whimpers, but he turns and lurches up the alley a few steps until he is in the dark. LaPointe turns his back and watches the passing pedestrians. An old man steps toward the mouth of the recess to take a piss, then he sees LaPointe and changes his mind. The cripple comes back, clutching one glove in his withered hand. LaPointe takes it and puts it into his pocket. "All right, now where did this shit come from, and where were you bringing it?"

"Say-hey, I can't tell you that, Lieutenant! Mama'll beat me up for sure! And those guys she knows, they'll beat me up!" His eyes, bisected by the rims of his glasses, roll stupidly. LaPointe does not repeat his question. Following his habit in interrogation, he simply sighs and settles his melancholy eyes on the grotesque.

"Honest to God, Lieutenant, I can't tell you! I don't dare!"

"I'd better call for a car."

"Hey, no! Don't put me back inside. Those tough guys inside like to use me 'cause I'm a cripple."

LaPointe looks out over the crowd with weary patience. He gives the Gimp time to think it over.

". . . Okay, Lieutenant . . ."

In a self-pitying whimper, the cripple explains that the stuff came from people his mother knows, tough guys from somewhere out on the east end of town. It was to be delivered to a pimp named Scheer. The Lieutenant knows this Scheer and has been waiting for a chance to run him off the Main. He has not been able to put a real case together, so he has had to content himself with maintaining constant harassing pressure. For a moment he considers going after Scheer with the Gimp's testimony, then he abandons the thought, realizing what a glib defense lawyer would do to this half-wit in the witness box.

"All right," LaPointe says. "Now listen to me. And tell your mother what I say. I don't want you on my patch anymore. You have one month to find someplace to go. You understand?"

"But, say-hey, Lieutenant? Where'll we go? All my friends are here!"

LaPointe shrugs. "Just tell your mother. One month."

"Okay. I'll tell her. But I hate to piss her off. I mean, after all . . . she's my mother."

LaPointe sits at the counter of a café, his shoulders slumped, his eyes indifferently scanning the passersby beyond the window.

A small white radio on a shelf by the counterman's ear is insisting that

> *Everybody digs the Montreal Rock*
> *Oh, yes! Oh, yes!*
> *Oh, yes! O-o-h YES!*
> *Everybody digs the Montreal Rock!*

LaPointe sighs and digs into his pocket to pay for the coffee. As he rises he notices a sign above the counterman's head. "That's wrong," he says. "It's misspelled."

The counterman gives a sizzling hamburger a definitive slap with his spatula and turns to examine the sign.

APPL PIE—30¢

He shrugs. "Yeah, I know. I complained, and the painter cut his price."

"Samuel?" LaPointe asks, referring to the old man who does most of the sign painting on this part of the Main.

"Yes." The counterman uses the inhaled *oui* typical of Joual.

18

LaPointe smiles to himself. Old Samuel always makes fancy signs with underlinings and ornate swirls and exclamation points, all at no extra cost. He is given to setting things off with quotation marks, inadvertently raising doubts in the customer's mind, as in:

"FRESH" FISH DAILY

He is also an independent artist who spells words the way he pronounces them. The counterman is lucky the sign doesn't read: EPP'L PIE.

Not fifty paces off the Main, down Rue Napoléon, the bustle and press are gone and the noise is reduced to an ambient baritone rumble. The narrow old street is lit by widely spaced streetlamps and occasional dusty shopwindows. Children play around the stoops of three-story brick row houses. Above the roofline, diffused city-light glows in the damp, sooty air. Each house depends on the others for support. They have not collapsed because each wants to fall in a different direction, and there isn't enough room.

It is after eight o'clock and cold, but the children will play until the fourth or fifth two-toned call of an exasperated mother brings them toe-dragging up the stoops and off to sleep, probably on a sofa in a front room, or in a cot blocking a hallway, covered with wool blankets that are gummy to the touch—bingo blankets that absorb body warmth without retaining it.

LaPointe leans against the railing of a deserted stoop, holding on tightly as the tingle rises in his chest. It is a familiar feeling by now, an oddly pleasant sensation in the middle of his chest and upper arms, as though there were carbonated water in his veins. Sometimes pain follows the tingling. His blood fizzes in his chest; he looks up at the light-smeared sky and breathes slowly, expecting to find a little flash of pain at the end of each breath, and relieved not to.

Little kids a few stoops away are playing *rond-rond*, and at the end of each minor-key chant they all fall giggling to the sidewalk. The English-speaking kids play the same game with different words—about a ring of roses. All the children of Europe preserve in their atavistic memory the scar of the Black Death. They reel to simulate the dizziness; they make sounds like the symptomatic sneezing; they sing of bouquets of posies to ward off the miasma of the Plague. Then, giggling, they all fall down.

When LaPointe was a kid in Trois Rivières, he used to play in the streets at night, too. In summer, all the grownups would sit out on the stoops because it was stifling indoors. The men wore only undershirts and drank ale from the bottle. And old lady Tarbieau . . . LaPointe remembers old lady Tarbieau, who lived across the street and who used to tend everybody's onions. She always pretended to care about people's problems in order to find out what they were. LaPointe's mother didn't like old lady Tarbieau. The only off-color thing he ever heard his mother say was in response to Mme. Tarbieau's nosiness. One night when all the block was out on the stoops, old lady Tarbieau called across the street, "Mme. LaPointe? Didn't I see the rent man coming out of your house today? It's only the middle of the month. I always thought you paid your rent the same way I do." And LaPointe's mother answered, "No, Mme. Tarbieau. I don't pay my rent the same way you do. I pay in money."

Poor Mme. Tarbieau, already aged when LaPointe was a boy. He hasn't thought of her for years. He pictures the old busybody in his mind, and realizes that this is probably the first time anybody has remembered her for a quarter of a century. And probably this will be the last time any human memory will hold her. In that case, she is gone . . . really gone.

The tingle in his arms and chest has passed, so he pushes his fists further into his pockets and walks on toward the liquor store, in and out of the cones of streetlight, where kids dart from stoop to stoop, like starlings on a summer evening.

One summer, the summer after his father left home never to come back, LaPointe discovered that playing with the other kids around the stoops had become dull and pointless. In the long evenings, he used to walk alone on the street, looking up at the moon through newly hung electric wires. The moon would follow him, sliding along over the weaving wires. He would turn quickly and go up the street, and the moon followed. He would stop suddenly, then go again, but the moon was never tricked. Once, when he had been running, then stopping, running and stopping, all the time looking up and getting a little dizzy, he was startled to find himself standing only inches from the Crazy Woman who lived down the block. She grinned, then laughed a wheezing note. She pointed a finger at him and said he was a *fou*, like her, and they would sizzle in hell side by side.

He ran away. But for the rest of the week he had nightmares. He was terrified at the thought of going crazy. Maybe he was already crazy. How do you know if you're crazy? If you're crazy, you're too crazy to know you're crazy. What does "crazy" mean? Say the word again and again, and the sense dries out, leaving only a husk of sound. And you hear yourself saying a meaningless noise over and over again.

That was the last summer he played on the streets. The following winter his mother died of influenza. Grandpapa and Grandmama were already dead. He went to St. Joseph's Home. And from the Home, he went into the police.

LaPointe squeezes his eyes closed and pulls himself out of it. He has found himself daydreaming like this a lot of late, remembering old lost things, unimportant things triggered by some little sound or sight on the Main.

He smiles at himself. Now, that *is* crazy.

The middle-aged Greek counterman looks up and smiles as LaPointe enters the deserted liquor store. He has been expecting the Lieutenant, and he reaches up for the bottle of red LaPointe always brings along to his twice-weekly games of pinochle.

"Everything going well?" LaPointe asks as he pays for the wine.

The counterman gulps air and growls, "Oh, fine, Lieu-

tenant." He gulps again. "Theo wrote. Got the letter—"
Another gulp. "—this morning."

"How's he doing?"

"Fine. He's up for parole soon."

It was too bad that LaPointe had to put the son inside
for theft so shortly after the father had an operation for
throat cancer. But that's the way it goes; that is his job.
"That's good," he says. "I'm glad he's getting parole."

The counterman nods. For him, as for others in the
quartier, LaPointe is the law; the good and the bad of it.
He will never forget the evening seven years ago when the
Lieutenant walked in to buy his usual Thursday night bottle of wine. A young man with slick hair had been loitering
in the store, carefully looking over the labels of exotic aperi-
tifs and liqueurs. LaPointe paid for his wine and, in the
same movement of putting his change into his pocket, he
drew out his gun.

"Put your hands on top of your head," LaPointe said
quietly to the young man.

The boy's eyes darted toward the door, but LaPointe
shook his head slowly. "Never," he said.

The young man put his hands on top of his head, and
LaPointe snatched him by his collar and bent him over the
counter. Two swift movements under the boy's jacket, and
LaPointe came up with a cheap automatic. While they
waited for the arrival of a police car, the boy sat on the
floor in a corner, cowed and foolish, his hands still on top
of his head. Customers came and went. They glanced uneasily toward the boy and LaPointe, and they carefully
avoided coming near them, but not one question was
asked, not one comment made. They ordered their wine in
subdued voices, then they left.

There had been several hold-ups in the neighborhood
that winter, and the old man who ran the cleaners down
the street had been shot in the stomach.

It never occurred to anyone to wonder how LaPointe
knew the boy was pumping up his courage for a hold-up.
He was the law on the Main, and he knew everything. Actually, LaPointe had known nothing until the moment he

stepped into the shop and passed by the boy. It was the tense nonchalance he instantly recognized. The Indian blood in LaPointe smelled fear.

The Greek counterman is comforted to know that La-Pointe is always out there in the street somewhere. And yet . . . this is the same man who arrested his son Theo for auto theft and sent him to prison for three years. The good of the law, and the bad. But it could have been worse. LaPointe had put in a good word for Theo.

The Lieutenant continues north on the Main, the bottle of wine, twisted up in a brown paper bag, heavy in his overcoat pocket. He passes a closed shop and automatically checks the padlock on the accordion steel grid covering its window. Once a beat cop . . .

But LaPointe had better get moving along. He doesn't want to be late for his pinochle game.

2

". . . so all the wise men and *pilpulniks* of Chelm get together to decide which is more important to their village, the sun or the moon. Finally they decide in favor of the moon. And why? Because the moon gives light during the night when, without it, they might fall into ditches and hurt themselves. While the sun, on the other hand, shines only during the day, when already it is light out. So who needs it!" David Mogolevski snorts with laughter at his own story, his thick body quaking, his growling basso filling the cramped little room behind the upholstery shop. His eyes sparkle as he looks from face to face, nodding and saying, "Eh? Eh?" soliciting appreciation.

Father Martin nods and grins. "Yes, that's a good one, David." He is eager to show that he likes the joke, but he has never known how to laugh. Whenever he tries out of politeness, he produces a bogus sound that embarrasses him.

David shakes his head and repeats, his eyes tearing with laughter, "The sun shines only during the day! So who needs it!"

Moishe Rappaport smiles over the top of his round glasses and nods support for his partner. He has heard each of David's jokes a hundred times, but he still enjoys them. Most of all, he enjoys the generous vigor of David's laughter; but sometimes he is tense when David starts off on one of his longer tales, because he knows the listener has probably already heard it, and may be unkind enough to say so. There is no danger of that with these pinochle friends; they always pretend never to have heard the stories before, although Moishe and David have been playing cards with the priest and the police lieutenant every Thursday and Monday night for thirteen years now.

The back room is cramped by stacks of old furniture, bolts of upholstery, and the loom on which Moishe makes fabrics for special customers. A space is cleared in the center under a naked light bulb, and a card table is set up. At some time during the night there will be a break, and they will eat sandwiches prepared by Moishe and drink the wine LaPointe brought.

Father Martin contributes only his presence and patience—and this last is no small offering, for he is always David's partner.

Throughout the evening there is conversation. Moishe and Father Martin look forward to these opportunities to examine and debate life and love; justice and the law; the role of Man; the nature of Truth. They are both scholarly men to whom the coincidences of life denied outlets. David injects his jokes and a leavening cynicism, without which the philosophical ramblings of the other two would inflate and leave the earth.

LaPointe's role is that of the listener.

For all four, these twice-weekly games have become oases in their routines, and they take them for granted. But if the games were to end, the vacuum would be profound.

Each would have to search his memory to recall how they got together in the first place; it seems they have always played cards on Thursdays and Mondays. In fact, Father Martin met David and Moishe while he was canvassing the Main for contributions toward the maintenance of

26

his battered polyglot parish. But how that led to his playing cards with them he could not say. LaPointe entered the circle just as casually. One night on his way home after putting the street to bed, he saw a light in the back of the shop and tapped at the window to see if everything was all right. They were playing three-handed cutthroat. Maybe LaPointe was feeling lonely that night without knowing it. In any event, he accepted their invitation to join the game.

They were all in their forties when first they started playing. LaPointe is fifty-three now; and Moishe must be just over sixty.

David rubs his thick hands together and leers at his friends. "Come, deal the cards! The luck has been against me tonight, but now I feel strong. The good Father and I are going to *schneider* you poor babies. Well? Why doesn't somebody deal?"

"Because it's your deal, David," Moishe reminds him.

"Ah! That explains it. Okay, here we go!" David has a flashy way of dealing which often causes a card to turn over. Each time this occurs he says, "Oops! Sunny side up!" His own cards never happen to turn over. He sweeps in his hand with a grand gesture and begins arranging it, making little sounds of surprised appreciation designed to cow adversaries. "Hello, hello, hel-lo!" he says as he slips a good card into place and taps it home with his finger.

David's heritage is rural and Slavic; he is a big man, unsubtle of feature and personality; gregarious, gruff, kind. When he is angry, he roars; when he feels done in by man or fate, he complains bitterly and at length; when he is pleased, he beams. The robust, life-embracing *shtetl* tradition dominates his nature. In business he is a formidable bargainer, but scrupulously honest. A deal is a deal, which- ever way it turns. Although it is Moishe's skill and crafts- manship that make their little enterprise popular with deco- rators from Westmont, the business would have failed a hundred times over without the vigor and acumen of David. His personality is perfectly reflected in the way he plays cards. He tends to overbid slightly, because he finds the game dull when someone else has named trump. When

27

he is taking a run of sure tricks, he snaps each card down with a triumphant snort. When he goes set, he groans and slaps his forehead. He gets bored when Moishe and Father Martin delay the game with their meandering philosophical talks; but if *he* thinks of a good story, he will reach across the table and place his hand upon the cards to stop play while he holds forth.

Moishe, too, is revealed in his cardplaying. He collects his hand and arranges it carefully. Behind the round glasses, his eyes take an interior focus as he evaluates the cards. He could be the best player by far, if he were to concentrate on the game. But winning isn't important to him. The gathering of friends, the talk, these are what matter. Occasionally, just occasionally, he takes a perverse delight in bearing down and applying his acute mind to the job of setting David, particularly if his friend has blustered a little too much that evening.

Slight, self-effacing, Moishe is the very opposite of his business partner. During the days he is to be found in the back room, tacks in his mouth, driving each one precisely into place with three taps of his hammer. Tap . . . TAP . . . tap. The first rap setting the point, the second neatly driving the tack home, the third for good measure. Or he will be working at his small loom, his agile fingers flying with precision. If he is in a repeat pattern requiring little attention, his expression seems to fade as his mind ranges elsewhere, on scenes of his youth, on hypothetical ethical problems, on imagined conversations with young people seeking guidance.

As a young man he lived in Germany in the comfortable old ghetto house where his great-grandfather had been born, a home that always smelled of good cooking and beeswax polish. They were a family of craftsmen in wood and fabric, but they admired learning, and the most revered of their relatives were those who had the gifts and devotion for Talmudic scholarship. As a boy he showed a penchant for study and that mental habit of seeing things simultaneously in their narrowest details and their broadest implications that marks the Talmudic scholar—a gift Moishe calls "intellectual peripheral vision." His mother

28

was proud of him and found frequent opportunities to mention to neighbor ladies that Moishe was up in his room studying again, instead of out playing and wasting his time. She would lift her hands helplessly and say that she didn't know what she would do with that boy—all the time studying, learning, saying brilliant things. Maybe in the long run it would be better if he were a common ordinary boy, like the neighbors' sons.

Moishe's adoring sister used to bring up little things for him to eat when he was studying late. His father also supported his intellectual inclination, but he insisted that Moishe learn the family craft. As he used to say, "It doesn't hurt a brilliant man to know a little something."

When the Nazi repression began, the Rappaports did not flee. After all, they were Germans; the father had fought in the 1914 war, the grandfather in the Franco-Prussian; they had German friends and business associates. Germany, after all, was not a nation of animals.

Moishe alone survived. His parents died of malnutrition and disease in the ever-narrowing ghetto; and his sister, delicate, shy, unworldly, died in the camp.

He came to Montreal after two years in the anonymous cauldron of a displaced persons camp. Occasionally, and then only in casual illustration of some point of discussion, Moishe mentioned the concentration camp and the loss of his family. LaPointe never understood the tone of shame and culpability that crept into Moishe's voice when he spoke of these experiences. He seemed ashamed of having undergone so dehumanizing a process; ashamed to have survived, when so many others did not.

Claude LaPointe sorts his cards into suits, taps the fan closed on the table, then spreads it again by pinching the cards between thumb and forefinger. He re-scans his hand, then closes it in front of him. He will not look at it again until after the bidding is over. He knows what he has, knows its value.

For the third time, Father Martin sorts his cards. The diamonds have a way of getting mixed up with the hearts. He pats the top of his thinning hair with his palm and looks at the cards mournfully; it is the kind of hand he

29

dreads most. He doesn't mind having terrible cards that no one could play well, and he rather enjoys having so strong a hand that not even he can misplay it. But these cards of middle power! Martin admits to being the worse cardplayer in North America. Should he fail to admit it, David would remind him.

When first he came to the Main, an idealistic young priest, Martin had affection for his church, nestled in a tight row of houses, literally a part of the street, a part of everyone's life. But now he feels sorry for his church, and ashamed of it. Both sides have been denuded by the tearing down of row houses to make way for industrial expansion. Rubble fields flank it, exposing ugly surfaces never meant to be seen, revealing the outlines of houses that used to depend on the church for structural support, and used to defend it. And the projects he dreamed of never quite worked out; people kept changing before he could really get anything started. Now most of Father Martin's flock are old Portuguese women who visit the church at all times of day, bent women with black shawls who light candles to prolong their prayers, then creep down the aisle on painful legs, their gnarled fingers gripping pew ends for support. Father Martin can speak only a few words of Portuguese. He can shrive, but he cannot console.

When he was a young man in seminary, he dared to dream of being a scholar, of writing incisive and illuminating apologetics that applied the principles of the faith to modern life and problems. He would sometimes wake up at night with a lucid perception of some knotty issue—a perception that was always just beyond the stretch of his memory the next morning. Although his mind teemed with ideas, he lacked the knack of setting his thoughts down clearly. Prior considerations and subsequent ramifications would invade his thinking and carry him off to the left or right of his main thesis, so he did not shine in seminary and was never considered for that post he so desired in a small college where he could study and write and teach. There was a joke in seminary: publish or parish.

But Father Martin's mind still runs to ethics, to the

nature of sin, to the proper uses of the gift of life; so, while being David's bungling partner is mortifying, the conversations with Moishe make it worthwhile. And there is something right about that, too. A payment in humiliation for the opportunity to learn and to express oneself.

"Come on! Come on!" David says. "It's your bid, Claude. Unless, of course, you and Moishe have decided to save face by throwing in your hands."

"All right," LaPointe says. "Fifteen."

"Sixteen." Father Martin says the word softly, then sucks air in through his teeth in an attempt to express the fact that he has a fair playing hand but no meld to speak of.

"Ah-ha!" David ejaculates.

Father Martin catches his breath. David is going to plunge after the bid, dragging the uncertain priest after him to a harrowingly narrow victory or a crushing defeat.

Moishe studies his cards, his gentle eyes seeming to pass over the number indifferently. He purses his lips and hums a soft ascending note. "Oh-h-h. Seventeen, I suppose."

"Eighteen!" is David's rapid reply.

Father Martin winces.

LaPointe taps the top of the face-down stack before him. "All right," he says, "nineteen, then."

"Pass," says Father Martin dolefully.

"Pass," says Moishe, looking at his partner slyly from behind his round glasses.

"Good!" David says. "Now let's sort out the men from the sheep. Twenty-two!"

LaPointe shrugs and passes.

"Prepare to suffer, fools," David says. He declares spades trump, but he has only a nine and a pinochle to meld.

Gingerly, apologetically, Father Martin produces a king and queen of hearts.

David stares at his partner, hurt and disbelief flooding his eyes. "That's all?" he asks. "This is what you meld? One marriage?"

31

"I . . . I was bidding a playing hand."

LaPointe objects. "Why don't you just show one another your hands and be done with it?"

Moishe sets down his cards and rises. "I'll start the sandwiches."

"Wait a minute!" David says. "Where are you going? The hand isn't over!"

"You are going to play it out?" Moishe asks incredulously.

"Of course! Sit down!"

Moishe looks at LaPointe with operatic surprise. He spreads his arms and lifts his palms toward the ceiling.

Roaring out his aces in an aggressive style that scorns the effeminate trickery of the finesse, David takes the first four tricks. But when he tries to cross to his partner, he is cut off by LaPointe, who manages to finesse a ten from Father Martin, then sends the lead to Moishe, who finishes the assassination.

At one point, Father Martin plays a low club onto a diamond trick.

"What?" cried David. "You're out of trump?"

"Aren't clubs trump?"

David slumps over and softly bangs his forehead against the table top. "Why me?" he asks the oilcloth. "Why *me?*"

Too late, the lead returns to David, who slams down his last five cards, collecting impoverished and inadequate tricks.

He stares heavily at the tabletop for a few seconds, then he speaks in a low and controlled voice. "My dear Father Martin. I ask the following, not in anger, but in a spirit of humble curiosity. Please tell me. Why did you bid when *you had nothing in your hand but SHIT!*"

Moishe removes his glasses and lightly rubs the red dents on the bridge of his nose. "There was nothing Martin could have done to save you. You overbid your hand and you went set. That's all there is to it."

"Don't tell me that! If he had come out with his ten earlier—"

"You would have won one more trick. Not enough to save you. You had two clubs left; I had the ace, Claude the ten. And if you had returned in diamonds—at that time you still had the queen—Martin would have had to trump it with his jack, and I would have overtrumped with the king." Moishe continues to rub his nose.

David glares at him in silence before saying, "That's wonderful. That is just wonderful!" The tension in David's voice causes Martin to look over at him, his breathing suspended. "Listen to the big scholar, will you? If my jack of hearts has its fly unbuttoned, he remembers! But when it comes to accounts, suddenly he's a *luftmensh*, too busy with philosophical problems to worry about business! Oh, yes! Taking care of the business is too commonplace for a man who spends all his time debating does an ant have a *pupik!* For your information, Moishe, I was talking to the priest! So butt out for once! Just butt out!"

David jumps up, knocking the table with his knees, and slams out of the room.

In the ensuing silence, Father Martin looks from Moishe to LaPointe, upset, confused. LaPointe draws a deep breath and begins desultorily to collect the cards. The moment David began his abuse, Moishe froze in mid-action; and now he replaces his glasses, threading each wire temple over its car.

"Ah . . . listen," he says quietly. "You must forgive David. He is in pain. He is grieving. Yesterday was the anniversary of Hannah's death. He's been like a balled-up fist all day."

The others understand. David and Hannah had been children together, and they had married young. So close, so happy were they that they dared express their affection only through constant light bickering and quarreling, as if it were unlucky to be blatantly happy and in love in a world where others were sad and suffering. After they immigrated to Montreal, Hannah's world was focused almost totally on her husband. She never learned French or English and shopped only in Jewish markets.

During the pinochle games, David used to talk about

Hannah constantly; complaining, of course. Bragging about her in his negative way. Saying that no woman in the world was so fussy about her cooking, such a nuisance about his health. She was driving him crazy! Why did he put up with it?

Then, six years ago, Hannah died of cancer. Sick less than a month, and she died.

For weeks afterward, the card games were quiet and uncomfortable; David was distant, uncharacteristically polite and withdrawn, and no one dared console him. His eyes were hollow, his face scoured with grief. Sometimes they would have to remind him that it was his play, and he would snap out of his reverie and apologize for delaying the game. David apologizing! Then, one evening, he mentioned Hannah in the course of conversation, grumbling that she was a nag and a pest. And moreover she was fat. *Zaftig* young is fat old! I should have married a skinny woman. They're cheaper to feed.

That was how he would handle it. He would continue complaining about her. That way, she wouldn't be gone completely. He could go on loving her, and being exasperated beyond bearing by her. Occasionally the sour void of grief returned to make him desperate and mean for a day or two, but in general he could handle it now.

The complicated double way he thought of his wife was expressed precisely one night when he happened to say, "Should Hannah, *alshasholm,* suddenly return, *cholilleh,* she would have a fit!"

"So just pretend nothing happened when he comes back," Moishe says. "And whatever you do, don't try to cheer him up. A man must be allowed to grieve once in a while. If he avoids the pain of grieving, the sadness never gets purged. It lumps up inside of him, poisoning his life. Tears are a solvent."

Father Martin shakes his head. "But a friend should offer consolation."

"No, Martin. That would be the easy, the comfortable thing to do. But not the kindest thing. Just as David is not grieving for Hannah—people only grieve for themselves,

34

for *their* loss—so we wouldn't be consoling him for his own sake. We would be consoling him because his grief is awkward for *us.*"

LaPointe feels uncomfortable with all this talk of grief and consolation. Men shouldn't need that sort of thing. And he is about to say so, when David appears in the doorway.

"Hey!" he says gruffly. "I went out to make the sandwiches, and I can't find anything. What a mess!"

Moishe smiles as he rises. David has never made the sandwiches in his life. "You find some glasses for the wine. I'll make the sandwiches, for a change."

As David rummages about grumpily for the glasses, Moishe steps to a narrow table against the wall on which are arranged cold cuts and a loaf of rye bread. He cuts the bread rapidly, one stroke of the knife for each thin, perfect slice.

"It's amazing how you do that, Moishe," Father Martin says, eager to get the conversation rolling.

"Agh, that's nothing," David pronounces proudly. "Have you ever seen him cut fabric?" He spreads two fingers like scissors and makes a rapid gesture that narrowly misses Father Martin's ear. "Psh-sh-sht! It's a marvel to watch!"

Moishe chuckles to himself as he continues slicing. "I would call that a pretty modest accomplishment in life. I can just see my epitaph: 'Boy! Could he cut cloth!' "

"Yeah, yeah," David says, fanning his hand in dismissal of Moishe's modesty. "Still, think what a surgeon you would have made."

Father Martin has a funny idea. "Yes, he'd make a great surgeon, if my appendix were made of damask!"

David turns and looks at him with heavy eyes. "What? What's this about your appendix being damask?"

"No . . . I was just saying that . . . well, if Moishe were a surgeon . . ." Confused, Martin shrugs and drops it.

"I still don't get it," David says flatly. He is embarrassed about his recent loss of control, and Father Martin is going to feel the brunt of it.

"Well . . . it was just a joke," Martin explains, deflated.

"Father," David says, "let's make a deal. *You* listen to confessions from old ladies too feeble to make interesting sins. *I'll* tell the jokes. To each according to his needs; from each according to his abilities."

"Look who's the communist," Moishe says, trying to attract some of the fire away from Martin.

"Who said anything about being a communist?" David wants to know.

"Forget it. Did you manage to find the glasses?"

"What glasses? Oh. The glasses."

Moishe puts a plate of sandwiches on the table, while David brings three thick-bottomed water glasses and a handleless coffee mug, which he gives to Father Martin. The wine is poured, and they toast life.

David drains his glass and pours another. "Tell me, Father, do you know the meaning of *aroysgevorfeneh verter?*"

Father Martin shakes his head.

"That's Yiddish for 'advice given to a priest about how to play pinochle.' But that's all right. I forgive you. I understand why you overbid."

"I don't believe I overbid . . ."

"The *reason* you overbid was because you had a marriage of hearts. And who can expect a priest to know the value of a marriage? Eh?"

Father Martin sighs. David always delights in little digs at celibacy.

"Now *me!*" David gestures broadly with his sandwich. "I know the value of a marriage. My wife Hannah was Ukrainian. Take my advice, Father. Never marry a Ukrainian. *Nudzh, nudzh, nudzh!* When she was born, she complained about the midwife slapping her on the ass, and she never got out of the habit. There is an old saying about Ukrainian women. It is said that they never die. Their bodies get smaller and smaller through wind erosion until there is nothing left but a complaining voice by the side of the fireplace. Me, I know the value of a marriage. I would have bid nothing!"

LaPointe laughs. "I'd like to see the hand you wouldn't bid on."

David laughs too. "Maybe so. Maybe so. Hey, tell me, Claude. How come you never married, eh?"

Father Martin glances uneasily at LaPointe.

When Martin was a young priest on the Main, he had known LaPointe's wife. He was her confessor; he was with her when she died. And later, after the funeral, he happened upon LaPointe, standing in the empty church. It was after midnight, and the big uniformed cop stood alone in the middle of the center aisle. He was sobbing. Not from grief; from fury. God had taken from him the only thing he loved, and after only a year of marriage. More urbane men might have lost their faith in God; but not LaPointe. He was fresh from downriver, and his Trifluvian belief was too fundamental, too natural. God was a palpable being to him, the flesh-and-blood man on the cross. He still believed in God. And he hated His guts! In his agony he shouted out in the echoing church, "You son of a bitch! Rotten son of a bitch!"

Father Martin didn't dare approach the young policeman. It chilled him to realize that LaPointe wanted God to appear in the flesh so he could smash His face with his fists.

After that night, LaPointe never came to church again. And over the years that followed, the priest saw him only in passing on the Main, until they happened to come together in the card games with David and Moishe. Because LaPointe never mentioned his wife, Father Martin didn't dare to.

That was how LaPointe handled it. One great howl of sacrilegious rage; then silence and pain. He did not grieve for Lucille, because to grieve was to accept the fact of her death. There were a muddled, vertiginous few months after the funeral, then work began to absorb his energy, and the Main his ragged affection. Emotional scar tissue built up around the wound, preventing it from hurting. Preventing it, also, from healing.

37

"How come you never married, Claude?" David asks. "Maybe with all the *nafka* on the streets you never needed a woman of your own. Right?"

LaPointe shrugs and drinks down his wine.

"Not that there would be many working the street in this pig weather," David continues. "Have you ever seen the snow hold off so long? Have you ever seen such ugly weather? Jesus Christ! Forgive me, Father, but I always swear in Catholic so if God overhears, He won't understand what I'm saying. Anyway, what's so bad about swearing? Is it a crime?"

"No," Father Martin says quietly. "It's a sin."

Moishe glances up. "Yes, Martin. I like that distinction." He presses his palms together and touches his lips with his forefingers. "I don't know how many times I have considered this difference between crime and sin. I am sure that sin is worse than crime. But I've never been able to put my finger exactly on the difference."

"Oh boy," David says, rising and looking under a shelf for the schnapps bottle. "*I* should have problems that trivial."

"For instance," Moishe continues, ignoring David, "to throw an old woman out of her apartment because she cannot pay her rent is not a crime. But surely it is a sin. On the other hand, to steal a loaf of bread from a rich baker to feed your starving family is obviously a crime. But is it a sin?"

David has returned with half a bottle of schnapps and is pouring it around into the empty wine glasses. "Let me pose the central question here," he insists. *"Who cares?"*

Father Martin flutters his fingers above his glass. "Just a little, thank you, David. Take this case, Moishe. Let us say your man with the starving family breaks into a grocery store and steals only the mushrooms, the caviar, the expensive delicacies. What do you have? Sin or crime?"

Moishe laughs. "What we have then is a priest with a subtle mind, my friend."

"Who ever heard of such a thing?" David demands. "Tell me, Claude. You're the expert on crime here. Who

38

breaks into a grocery store and steals the mushrooms and the caviar only?"

"It happens," LaPointe says. "Not exactly that, maybe. But things like that."

"Who does it?" Moishe asks, pouring out more schnapps for himself. "And why?"

"Well . . ." LaPointe sniffs and rubs his cheek with his palm. He'd really rather be the listener, and this is a hard one to explain. "Well, let's say a man has gone hungry often. And let's say it doesn't look like things are going to change. He's hungry now, and he'll be hungry again tomorrow, or next week. That man might break into a grocery and steal the best foods to have a big gorge—even if he doesn't like the taste of mushrooms. Because . . . I can't explain . . . because it will be something to remember. You know what I mean? Like the way people who can't keep up with their debts go out and splurge for Christmas. What's the difference? They're going to be in debt all their lives. Why not have something to remember?"

Moishe nods reflectively. "I see exactly what you mean, Claude. And such a robbery is a crime." He turns to Father Martin. "But a sin?"

Father Martin frowns and looks down. He isn't sure. "Ye-e-s. Yes, I think it's a sin. It's perfectly understandable. You could sympathize with the man. But it's a sin. There is nothing remarkable about a sin being understandable, forgivable."

David is passing the bottle around again, but Martin puts his hand firmly over his glass. "No, thank you. I'm afraid it's time for me to go. I suppose the world will have to wait until next Monday for us to sort out the difference between sin and crime."

"No, wait. Wait." Moishe prevents him from rising with a gesture. He has drunk his schnapps quickly, and his eyes are shiny. "I think we should pursue this while it's on our minds. I have a way to approach the problem practically. Let's each of us say what he considers to be the greatest sin or the greatest crime."

"That's easy," David says. "The greatest crime in the

world is for four *alter kockers* to talk philosophy when they could be playing cards. And the greatest sin is to bid when you have nothing in your hand but a lousy marriage."

"Come on, now. Be serious." Moishe takes up the almost empty schnapps bottle and shares it equally around, attempting to anchor his friends to the table with fresh drinks. He turns to the priest. "Martin? What in your view is the greatest sin?"

"Hm-m-m." Father Martin blinks as he considers this. "Despair, I suppose."

Moishe nods quickly. He is excited by the intellectual possibilities of the problem. "Despair. Yes. That's a good one. Clearly a sin, but no kind of crime at all. Despair. A seed sin. A sin that supports other sins. Yes. Very good."

David gulps down his drink and declares, "I'll tell you the greatest crime!"

"Are you going to be serious?" Moishe asks. "Your playing the *letz* nobody needs."

"But I am serious. Listen. The only crime is theft. Theft! Do you realize that a man spends more time in prison for grand larceny than for manslaughter? And what is murder to us but the theft of a man's life? We punish it seriously only because it's a theft that no one can make restitution for. And rape? Nothing but the theft of something a woman can use to make her living with, like prostitutes . . . and wives. It's all theft! All we really worry about is our possessions, and all our laws are devoted to protecting our property. When the thief is bold and obvious, we make a law against him and send someone like Claude here to arrest him. But when the thief is more cowardly and subtle—a landlord, maybe, or a used-car salesman—we can't make laws against him. After all, the men in Ottawa *are* the landlords and the used-car salesmen! We can't threaten them with the law, so we tell them that what they are doing is sinful. We say that God is watching and will punish them. The law is a club brandished in the fist. Religion is a club held behind the back. There! Now tell me, is that talking serious or what?"

"It's talking serious," Moishe admits. "But it's also talking shallow. However, for you it's not a bad try."

"Forget it, then!" David says, peeved. "What's the use of all this talk anyway? It helps the world *vi a toyten bankes.*"

Moishe turns to LaPointe. "Claude?"

LaPointe shakes his head. "Leave me out of this. I don't know anything about sin."

"Ah!" David says. "The man who has known no sin! Dull life."

"Well, crime then," Moishe pursues. "What's the greatest crime?"

LaPointe shrugs.

"Murder?" Father Martin suggests.

"No, not murder. Murder is seldom . . ." LaPointe searches for a word and ends up with a silly-sounding one. "Murder is seldom *criminal.* I mean . . . the murderer is not usually a criminal—not a professional. He's usually a scared kid pulling a holdup with a cheap gun. Or a drunk who comes home and finds his wife in bed with someone. Sometimes a maniac. But not often a real criminal, if you see what I mean. What about you, Moishe?" LaPointe asks, wanting to shunt the questions away from himself. "What do you think is the greatest sin?"

Moishe is feeling the effects of the schnapps. He fixes his eyes on the tabletop, and he speaks of something he very seldom mentions. "I thought a lot about crime, about sin, when I was in the camps. I saw great crimes—crimes so vast they lose all sense of human misery and can be expressed only in statistics. A man who has seen this finds it easy to shrug off a single beating outside a bar, or a theft, or one killing. The heart and the imagination, like the hands, can grow calluses, can become insensitive. That's what it means to be brutalized. They brutalized us, and by that I don't mean being beaten or tortured by brutes. No. I mean being beaten until you *become* a brute. Until, in fact, you become such an animal that you *deserve* to be beaten." Moishe looks up and sees expressions of concern and close attention in the faces of his friends. Even David does not offer a flip remark. It always happens, when they drink a little more than usual, that Moishe gets tipsy first. The priest is abstemious, and the other two have thick bodies to

41

absorb the alcohol. He feels foolish. He smiles wanly and shrugs. The shrug says: I'm sorry; let's forget it.

But Father Martin wants to understand. "So you make the greatest sin the brutalizing of a fellow man? Is that it, Moishe?"

Moishe runs his fingers through his long, thin hair. "No, it is not that simple. Degree of sin is not based upon the act. It's more complicated than that." He is not sure he can say it neatly. Often Moishe brings the card talk around to some point he has rehearsed and rephrased again and again during his workday. But this evening it is not like that. When he speaks, he does so hesitantly, with pauses and searches for words. For once he is not sharing with his friends the results of thought; he is sharing the process.

"Yes, I suppose brutalizing could be one of the great sins. You see . . . how do I put this? . . . it isn't the *act* that determines the degree of sin. And it isn't the motive. It's the *effect*. To my mind, it is much worse to chop down the last tree in the forest than to chop down the first. I think it is much worse to kill a good husband and father than to kill a sex maniac. In both cases the act and the motive could be identical, but the effect would be different.

"So, yes. Brutalizing a man could be a great sin, because a man who has become a brute can never love. And sins against love are the greatest sins, and deserve the greatest punishments. Theft is a crime, often a sin; but it only operates against money or goods. Murder is a crime, often a sin; but the degree of sin depends upon the value of the life, which might not be worth living, or which might have brought pain and misery to others. But love is always good. And sins against love are always the worst, because love is the only . . . the only especially *human* thing we have. So, rape is the greatest sin, greater than murder, because it is a sin against love. And I don't only mean violent rape. In fact, violent rape is perhaps the least sinful kind of rape because the perpetrator is not always responsible for his acts. But the subtler kinds of rape are great sins. The businessman who makes getting a job dependent on having sex with him, he is a rapist. The man who takes a plain girl out for dinner and an expensive evening because he knows she will feel obliged to make love with him, he is a rapist. The young man who finds a girl starving for affection and who talks of love in order to get sex, he is a rapist. All these crimes against love. And without love . . . my God, without love . . . !" Moishe looks around helplessly, knowing he is making a fool of himself. He is perfectly motionless for a moment, then he chuckles and shakes his head. "This is too ridiculous, my friends. Four old men sitting in a back room and talking of love!"

"*Three* men," David corrects, "and a priest. Come on! One last hand of cards! I feel the luck coming to me."

LaPointe fetches a cloth and wipes the table.

David deals quickly, then picks up his hand, making little sounds of appreciation as he slips each card into place. "Now, my friends, we shall see who can play pinochle!"

The bidding goes rather high, but David prevails and names trump.

He goes set by four points.

LaPointe, Moishe, and Father Martin are grouped around the door of the shop, buttoning their overcoats against the cold wet wind that moans down the almost empty street. David lives in the apartment above the shop, so did not accompany them to the door. He said good night and began clearing things away for the next day's business, all the while muttering about how nobody could win a game while schlepping a priest on his back.

As he shakes hands good night, Father Martin is shivering, and his eyes are damp with the cold. Moishe asks why he isn't wearing a scarf, and he says he lost it somewhere, making a joke of being absent-minded. He says good night again and walks up the street, bending against the wind to protect his chest. LaPointe and Moishe walk together in the other direction, the wind pushing them along. They always walk together the three blocks before Moishe's turnoff, sometimes chatting, sometimes in silence, depending upon their moods and the mood of the evening. Tonight they walk in silence because the mood of the evening has been uncommonly tense and . . . personal. It is

43

just after eleven and, although their block is almost deserted, the action on the lower Main will be in full flow. LaPointe will make one last check, putting the street to bed before returning to his apartment. Once a beat cop . . .

Moishe chuckles to himself. "Agh, too much schnapps. I made a fool of myself, eh?"

LaPointe walks several steps before saying, "No."

"Maybe it's the weather," Moishe jokes. "This pig weather is enough to wear anyone down. You know, it's amazing how weather affects personalities. It'll be better when the snow comes."

LaPointe nods.

They cross the street and start down a block that is lit by saloon neon and animated by the sound of jukeboxes. A girl is walking on the other side of the street. She is young and unnaturally slim, her skinny legs bent as she teeters on ridiculous, fashionably thick clog soles. She wears no coat, and her short skirt reveals a parenthesis between her meager thighs. She is not more than seventeen, and very cold indeed.

"See that girl, Moishe?" LaPointe says. "Do you believe she is committing the greatest sin?"

Moishe glances at the girl as she passes a bar and looks in the window for prospects who don't seem too drunk. He turns his eyes away and shakes his head. "No, Claude. It's never the girls I blame. They are the victims. It would be like blaming the man who gets run over by a bus because, if he hadn't been there, there wouldn't have been an accident. No, I don't blame them. I feel sorry for them."

LaPointe nods. Prostitution is the least violent crime on the Main and, if it doesn't involve rolling the mark and isn't controlled by pimps protected by the heavies from the Italian Main, LaPointe habitually overlooks it. He feels particularly sorry for the whores who don't have the money to work out of apartments or hotels—the young ones fresh in from the country, broke and cold, or the old ones who can only score drunks and who have to take it standing in a back alley, their skirts up, their asses pushed up against a cold brick wall. He feels pity for them, but disgust, too. Other crimes make him feel anger, fear, rage, helplessness;

44

but this kind of scratch prostitution produces in him as much disgust as pity. Maybe that's what Moishe means by a sin against love.

They stop at the corner and shake hands. "See you Monday," Moishe says, turning and walking down his street.

LaPointe thrusts his hands deep into the pockets of his baggy overcoat and walks down the Main.

As he passes a deep-set doorway, a slight motion catches the tail of his eye. His hand closes down on the butt of his revolver.

"Step out here."

At first there is no movement. Then a grinning, ferret-thin face appears around the corner. "Just keeping out of the wind, Lieutenant."

LaPointe relaxes. "Got no kip tonight?" He speaks English because Dirtyshirt Red has no French.

"I'm okay, Lieutenant," the *bomme* says, reaching under his collar to adjust the thickness of newspaper stuffed beneath his shirt to keep out the cold. "I sleep here lots of times. Nobody cares. I don't bother nobody. I won't get too cold." Dirtyshirt Red grins slyly and shows LaPointe a bottle wrapped in a brown paper bag. "It's half full."

"What are you going to do when the snow comes, Red? You got something lined up?" There are seven *bommes* whom LaPointe recognizes as living on the Main and having rights based on long residence. He takes care of them on their level, just as he takes care of the prostitutes on theirs, and the shopkeepers on theirs. There used to be eight recognized tramps, but old Jacob died last year. He was found frozen to death between stacks of granite slabs behind the monument-maker's shop. He drank too much and crawled in to sleep it off. It snowed heavily that night.

"No, I don't have anything lined up, Lieutenant. But I ain't worried. Something will come along. That's one thing you can say: I've always been lucky."

LaPointe nods and walks on. He doesn't like Dirtyshirt Red, a sneak thief, bully, and liar. But the *bomme* has been on the Main for many years, and he has his rights.

45

It is past midnight, and the street is beginning to dim and grow quiet. Thursday is a slow night on the Main. LaPointe decides to leave St. Laurent and check out the tributary streets to the east. He passes through the darkened Carré St. Louis, with its forgotten statue of the dying Cremazie:

Pour Mon Drapeau
Je Viens Ici Mourir

The fountain no longer works, and on the side of the empty basin someone has written in black spray paint: LOVE. Next to that there is a peace sign, dried rivulets of paint dripping down from it, like the blood that used to drip from the swastikas in anti-Nazi posters. And under the peace sign there is: FUCK YO . . . then the spray can ran out.

That would be young Americans who have come to Montreal to avoid the Vietnam draft. They have a special flair for spray paint. LaPointe is not fond of the young, bearded boys from the States who hang around dimly lit coffee bars filled with eerie music and odd-smelling incense, brandishing their battered guitars, singing in nasal groans, cadging drinks from sympathetic college girls, or practicing their more-tragic-than-thou stares into space. Most of them live off federal dole, cutting into funds already inadequate for the needs of the poor of east Montreal.

But they will pass, and they are no real trouble, aside from the nuisance of marijuana and other kiddie shit. They bring yet another alien accent to the Main, with their hard "r's" and their odd pronunciation of "out" and "house" and "about," but LaPointe assumes he will get used to them, as he got used to all the others.

In general, his feelings toward Americans are benevolent, for no better reason than that when he went on his brief honeymoon—now thirty-one years ago—he found the thoughtfulness of road signs in French as far south as Lake George Village; while in his own country, the French signs stopped abruptly at the Ontario border.

46

At least these young draft avoiders are quiet. Not like the American businessmen from the convention quarters of the Expo site on Ile Ste. Hélène. Those types are a real nuisance. They get drunk in their chrome-and-leatherette hotel bars, and small bands of them come up to the Main, seeking a little action, mistaking poverty for vice. They flash too much money and bargain childishly with the whores. As often as not they get rolled or punched up. Then LaPointe has to respond to complaints lodged with the Quartier Général, has to listen to diatribes about tourism and its value to Montreal's economy.

Always turning toward the darkest streets, LaPointe picks his way through the tangle of back lanes until he comes out again onto the Main, quiet now and nearly closed up.

As he passes the narrow alley that runs beside the Banque de Nova Scotia, he feels a slight rush of adrenalin in his stomach. Even after all these years, his nerves, quite independent of his conscious mind, take a systemic jolt whenever he passes that alley. It's become automatic, and he is used to it. It was in that alley that he got hit; it was there that he sat awaiting death, expecting it. And once a man loses his sense of immortality, he never regains it.

He had put the street to bed, like tonight; and he was on his way home. There was a tinkle of glass down the alley. A figure dropped down to the brick pavement from a window at the back of the bank. Three of them, running toward LaPointe. He fired into the air and called to them to stop. Two of them fired at once, two flashes of light, but he had no memory of the sound because a slug took him square in the chest and slammed him against the metal door of a garage. He slid down the door, sitting on one twisted foot, the other leg straight out in front of him. They fired again, and he *heard* the slug slap into the meat of his thigh. Holding his gun in both hands, he returned fire. One went down. Dead, he later learned. The other two ran.

After the shots, there was no sound in the alley, save for the sigh of wind around the corner of the garage. He sat there, slipping in and out of consciousness, staring at his

47

own foot, and thinking how silly he would look when they found him, one foot under his butt, the other straight out in front of him. A long time passed. A minute, perhaps. A very long time. He opened his eyes and saw a yellow cat crossing before him. Its tail was kinked from an ancient break. It stopped and looked at him, one forepaw poised, not touching the ground. Its eyes were wary, but frigid. It tested the ground with its paw. Then it walked on, indifferent.

The wound in his chest felt cold. He put his hands over it to keep the wind out. His last conscious thought was a stupid, drunken one. Must keep the wind out. Mustn't catch cold. Catch cold at this time of year, and you don't get rid of it until spring.

He knew he was going to die. He was absolutely sure. The fact was more sad than terrifying.

He was four and a half weeks in the hospital. The leg wound was superficial, but the slug in his chest had grazed the aorta. The doctors said things about his being lucky to have the constitution of an *habitant* peasant. After leaving the hospital he had a period of recuperation, lounging around his apartment until he couldn't stand it any longer. Even though he wasn't technically back on active service yet, he began making rounds of the Main at night, putting the street to bed. Once a beat cop . . .

Soon he was back in his office, doing his regular duties. He received his third commendation for bravery and, a year later, his second Police Medal. Down at the Quartier Général, the myth of the indestructible LaPointe was even more firmly established.

Indestructible maybe, but altered. Something subtle but significant had shifted in his perception. He had accepted the fact of his death so totally, had surrendered to it with such calm, that when he did not die, he felt unfinished, open-ended, off balance.

For the first time since he had cauterized his emotions with hate after the death of his wife, he felt lonely, a loneliness expressed in a kind of melancholy gentleness toward the people of his patch, particularly toward the old, the children, the losers.

It was shortly after he was hit in the alley that he met and began to play pinochle with Moishe, David, and Martin—his friends.

Only one rectangle of dingy neon breaks the dark of Rue Lionais, a beer bar that is a hangout for loudmouths and toughs of the *quartier*. LaPointe mentally runs down a list of its usual clientele and decides to drop in. The barman greets him loudly and with a bogus grin. Knowing the loud greeting is a warning signal for the customers, LaPointe ignores the owner and looks about the dim, fuggy room. One man catches his eye, a dandy dresser with the thin, mobile face of a hustler. The dandy is sitting with a group of middle-aged toughs whose faces record a lot of cheap hooch and some battering. LaPointe stands in the arched entranceway and points at the dandy. When the man raises his eyebrows in a mask of surprise, LaPointe crooks his finger once.

As the dandy rises, one of the toughs, a penny-and-nickle arm known as Lollipop, gets to his feet as if to protect his mate. LaPointe looks at the tough, his eyes calm and infinitely bored; he shake his head slowly. For a face-saving moment, the tough does not move. Then LaPointe points a stabbing finger toward their booth, and the tough sits down, grumbling to himself.

The dandy flashes a broad smile as he approaches La-Pointe. "Good to see you, Lieutenant. Now isn't that coincidence? I was just telling—"

"Cut the shit, Scheer. I ran into the Gimp on the street."

"The Gimp?" Scheer frowns and blinks as he pretends to search his memory. "Gee, I don't think I know anybody by—"

"What day is this, Scheer?"

"Pardon me? What day?"

"I'm busy."

"It's Thursday, Lieutenant."

"Day of the month."

"Ah . . . the ninth?"

"All right, I want you to stay off the street until the ninth of next month. And I don't want to see any of your girls working."

"Now look, Lieutenant! You don't have any right! I'm not under arrest!"

LaPointe's eyes open with mock surprise. "Did I hear you say I don't have any right?"

"Well . . . what I meant was . . ."

"I'm not interested in what you meant, Scheer. LaPointe is giving you a punishment. One month off the street. And if I see you around before that, I'm going to hurt you."

"Now, just a minute—"

"Do you understand what I just said to you, asshole?" LaPointe reaches out with his broad stubby hand and pats the dandy's cheek firmly enough to make his teeth click. "Do you understand?"

The dandy's eyes shine with repressed fury. "Yes. I understand."

"How long?"

"A month."

"And who's giving you the punishment?"

Scheer's jaw muscles work before he says bitterly, "Lieutenant LaPointe."

LaPointe tilts his head toward the door. "Now, get out."

"I'll just tell the guys I'm going."

LaPointe closes his eyes and shakes his head slowly. "Out."

The dandy starts to say something, then thinks better of it and leaves the bar. LaPointe turns to follow him, but he stops and decides to visit the booth. By standing up aggressively, this Lollipop has challenged his control. That is dangerous, because if LaPointe ever lets these types build up enough courage, they could beat him to a pulp. His image must be kept high in the street because the shadow of his authority covers more ground than his actual presence can. He approaches the booth.

The three toughs pretend not to see him coming. They stare down at their bottles of ale.

"You. Lollipop," LaPointe says. "Why did you stand up when I called your friend over?"

The big man doesn't look up. He sets his mouth in determined silence.

"I think you were showing off, Lollipop," LaPointe says quietly.

The brute shrugs and looks away.

LaPointe picks up the tough's half-finished bottle of ale and pours it into his lap. "Now you sit there awhile. I wouldn't want you going out into the street like that. People would think you pissed your pants."

As LaPointe leaves the bar, he hears two of the toughs laughing while the third growls angrily.

That's just fine, LaPointe thinks. It's the kind of story that will get around.

He turns up Avenue Esplanade toward his second-floor apartment in a row of bow-windowed buildings facing Parc Mont Royal. Above the park, a luminous cross stands atop the black bulk of the Mont. The wind gusts and flaps the tails of his overcoat. His legs are heavy as he mounts the long wooden stoop of number 4240.

He closes the door of his apartment and flicks on the slack toggle switch. Two of the four bulbs are burnt out in the red-and-green imitation Tiffany lamp. He tugs off his overcoat and hangs it over the wooden umbrella stand. Then, by habit, he goes into the narrow kitchen and sets water to boil. The stove's pilot light is blocked with ancient grease and has to be lit with a match. The circle of blue flame pops on and singes his fingers, as always. He snaps his hand back and swears without passion, as usual.

While the water is heating, he goes into the bedroom and sits heavily on the bed. The only light is the upward-lancing beam of a streetlamp below his window, illuminating the ceiling and one wall but leaving the floor and the furniture in darkness. He grunts as he pulls off his shoes and wriggles his toes before stepping into his carpet slippers. He loosens his tie, pulls his shirt out from under his belt and scratches his stomach.

By now the water will be boiling, so back he goes into the unlit kitchen, his slippers slapping against his heels. His coffee-maker is an old-fashioned pressure type, with a handle to force the water through the grounds. His cup is always on the counter, its bottom always wet because he never wipes it, just rinses it out and turns it upside down on the drainboard.

Coffee cup in hand, he pads into the living room, where he settles into his overstuffed armchair by the bow window. Over the years, the springs and stuffing of the chair have shifted and bunched until it fits him perfectly. Holding the saucer under his chin in the way of workingclass men from Trois Rivières, he sips noisily. Four long sips and the cup is empty, save for the thick dregs. He believes that his routine cup of coffee before bed helps him to sleep. He sets the cup aside and turns to look out of the window. Beyond the limp curtain is the park, and above the dark hump of Mont Royal, the sky is a smudged gray-black, dim with cityglow. Within the park's iron fence, lamp-posts lay vague patterns of light along the footpath. The street is empty; the park is empty.

He scrubs his matted hair with the palm of his hand and sighs, comfortable and half anesthetized by the platitudes of routine that comprise his life in the apartment. Sitting slumped like this, wearing slippers, his shirt over his belly, he does not look like the tough cop who has become something of a folk hero to young French Canadian policemen because of his personal, only coincidentally legal style of handling the Main, and because of his notorious indifference to administrators, regulations, and paper work. Rather, he looks like a middle-aged man whose powerful peasant body is beginning to sag. A man who has come to prefer peace to happiness; silence to music.

He stares out the window, his mind almost empty, his face slack. He no longer really sees the apartment he and Lucille rented a week before their marriage. Since her death only a year later, he has changed nothing. The frumpy furniture in the catalogue styles of the thirties stands now where it ended up after a flurry of arrangement and rearrangement under Lucille's energetic, but vacillating, inspiration. When at last it was done and things had ended up pretty much where they began, they sat together on the bright flowered sofa, her head on his shoulder, until very late at night. They made love for the first time there on the sofa, the night before their marriage.

Of course, the apartment was to be only temporary. He would work hard and go to night school to learn English better. He would advance on the force, and they would save their money to buy a house, maybe up toward Laval, where there were other young couples from Trois Rivières.

Over the years, the gaudy flowers on the sofa have faded, more on the window end than the other, but it has happened so slowly that LaPointe has not noticed. The cushions are still plump, because no one ever sits on them.

He blinks his eyes, and presses his thumb and forefinger into the sockets. Tired. With a sigh, he pushes himself out of the deep chair and carries his cup back to the kitchen, where he rinses it out and puts it on the drainboard for morning.

Dressed only in his shorts, he shaves over the rust-stained washbasin in the small bathroom. He acquired the habit of shaving before going to bed during his year with Lucille. His thick, blue-black whiskers used to irritate her cheek. It was several months before she told him about it, and even then she made a joke of it. The fact that in the mornings he always appears at the Quartier Général with cheeks blue with eight hours of growth has given rise to another popular myth concerning the Lieutenant: LaPointe owns a magic razor; he always has a one-day growth of beard. Never two days of growth, never clean-shaven.

After scraping the whiskers off his flat cheeks, his straight razor making a dry rasping sound even with the grain, he rinses his mouth with water taken from the tap in cupped hands. He straightens up and leans, his elbows locked, on the basin, looking in the mirror. He finds himself staring at his thick chest with its heavy mat of graying hair. He can see the slight pulse of his heart under the ribs. He watches the little throb with uncertain fascination. It's in there. Right there.

That's where he's going to die. Right there.

The very efficient young Jewish doctor with a cultured voice and a tone of mechanical sincerity had told him that he was lucky, in a way.

Inoperable aneurism.

Something like a balloon, the doctor explained, and too close to the heart, too distended for surgery. It was a miracle that he had survived the bullet that had grazed the artery in the first place. He was lucky, really. That scar tissue had held up pretty well, it had given him no trouble for twelve years. Looked at that way, he was lucky.

As he sat listening to the young doctor's quiet, confident voice, LaPointe remembered the yellow cat with the kinked tail and one forepaw off the ground.

The doctor had handled many situations like this; he prided himself on being good at this sort of thing. Keep it factual, keep it upbeat. Once the doctor permits a little hole in the dike of emotion, he can end up twenty minutes— even half an hour—behind in his appointments. "In cases like this, when a man doesn't have any immediate family, I make it a habit to explain everything as clearly and truthfully as I can. To be frank, with a mature man, I don't think a doctor has the right to withhold anything that might delay the patient's attending to his personal affairs. You understand what I mean, M. Dupont?"

LaPointe had given him a false name and had said he was retired from the army, where he had received the wound in combat.

"Now, your first question, quite naturally, is what kind of time do I have? It's not possible to say, M. Dupont. You see, we doctors really don't know everything." He smiled at the admission. "It could come tomorrow. On the other hand, you could have six months. Even eight. Who knows? One thing is sure; it will happen like that." The doctor snapped his fingers softly. "No pain. No warning. Really just about the best way to go."

"Is that right?"

"Oh, yes. To be perfectly honest, M. Dupont, it's the way I would like to go, when my time comes. In that respect, you're really quite lucky."

54

There was a young receptionist with a fussy, cheerful manner and a modish uniform that swished when she moved. She made an appointment for the next week and gave LaPointe a printed reminder card. He never returned. What was the point?

He walked the streets, displaced. It was September, Montreal's beautiful month. Little girls chanted as they skipped rope; boys played tin-can hockey in the narrow streets, spending most of their energy arguing about who was cheating. He wanted to—expected to—feel something different, dramatic; but he did not, except that he kept getting tangled up in memories of his boyhood, memories so deep that he would look up and find that he had walked a long way without noticing it.

Evening came, and he was back on the Main. Automatically, he chatted with shopkeepers, took coffee in the cafés, reaffirmed his presence in the tougher bars. Night came, and he strolled through back streets, occasionally checking the locks on doors.

The next morning he woke, made coffee, carried down the garbage, and went to his office. Everything felt artificial; not because things were different, but because they were unchanged. He was stunned by the normalcy of it all; a little dazed by a significant absence, as a man going down a flight of stairs in the dark might be jolted by reaching the bottom when he thought there was another step to go.

And yet, he had guessed what was wrong before he went to the doctor. For a couple of months there had been that effervescence in his blood, that constriction in his upper arms and chest, those jagged little pains at the tops and bottoms of breaths.

In the middle of that first morning, there was one outburst of rage. He was pecking away at an overdue report, looking up the spelling of a word, when suddenly he ripped the page from his dictionary and threw the book against the wall. What the fucking use is a fucking dictionary! How can you look up the spelling of a fucking word when you don't know how to spell the fucking thing?

He sat behind his desk, stiff and silent, his fingers interlaced and the knuckles white with pressure. His eyes stung with the unfairness of it. But he couldn't push through to feeling sorry for himself. He could not grieve for himself. After all, he had not grieved for Lucille.

He insulated himself from his impending death by accepting it only as a fact. Not a real fact, like the coming of autumn; more like . . . the number of feet in a mile. You don't do anything about the number of feet in a mile. You don't complain about it. It's just a fact.

With great patience, he mended the torn page in his dictionary with transparent tape.

LaPointe pulls the string of the bathroom ceiling light and goes into the bedroom. The springs creak as he settles down on his back and looks up at the ceiling, glowing dimly from the streetlamp outside.

His breathing deepens and he finds himself vaguely considering the problem of worn-out water hosing. Last Sunday he spent a lazy morning sitting in his chair by the window, reading *La Presse*. There was a do-it-yourself article describing things you could make around the house with old water hosing. He has a house; a fantasy house in Laval, where he lives with Lucille and the two girls. Whenever he passes shops that have garden tools, he daydreams about working in his garden. Several years ago he put in a flagstone patio from the plans in a special section of the paper devoted to Fifteen Things You Can Do to Improve the Value of Your House. That patio figures often in his reveries just before sleep. He and Lucille are having lemonade under a sun umbrella he once saw in a hardware store window—Clearance!!! Up to 2/3 Off!!! The girls are off somewhere, and they have the house to themselves for a change. Sometimes, in his imaginings, his girls are kids, sometimes teen-agers, and sometimes already married with children of their own. During the first years after Lucille's death, the number and sex of their children shifted around, but it finally settled on two girls, three years apart. A pretty one, and a smart one. Not that the pretty one is what you would call a dummy, but . . .

He turns over in bed, ready to sleep now. The springs creak. Even when it was new, the bed had clacked and creaked. At first, the noise made Lucille tense and apprehensive. But later, she used to giggle silently at the thought of imagined neighbors listening beyond the wall, shocked at such carryings-on. . . .

3

The phone rings.

Half of the sound blends into the eddy of a dream; half is jagged and real, still echoing in the dark room.

The phone rings again.

He swings out of bed and gropes into the dark living room. The floor is icy.

The phone ri—

"Yes! LaPointe."

"Sorry, Lieutenant." The voice is young. "I hate to wake you up, but—"

"Never mind that. What's wrong?"

"A man's been killed on your patch." The caller's French is accurate, but it has a continental accent. He is an Anglophone Canadian.

"Murdered?" LaPointe asks. Stupid question. Would they call him for an automobile accident? He still isn't fully awake.

"Yes, sir. Knifed."

"Where?"

"Little alley near the corner of Rue Lozeau and St. Dominique. That's just across from—"

"I know where it is. When?"

"Sir?"

"When did it happen?"

"I don't know. I just got here with Detective Sergeant Gaspard. We took an incoming from a patrol car. The Sergeant asked me to call you."

"All right. Ten minutes." LaPointe hangs up.

He dresses quickly, with fumbling hands. As he leaves he remembers to take the paper bag of garbage with him. He may not get back in time for the collection.

It is three-thirty, the coldest part of the night. Following the pattern of this pig weather, the overcast has lifted with the early hours of morning, taking with it the smell of city soot. The air is still and crystalline, and the exhaust from a patrol car parked halfway up the narrow alley shoots a long funnel of vapor out into the street. A revolving roof light skids shafts of red along the brick walls and over the chests and faces of the half-dozen policemen and detectives working around the corpse. Bursts of blue-white glare periodically fill the alley, freezing men in mid-gesture, as the forensic photographer takes shots from every angle. Two uniformed officers stand guard at the mouth of the alley, tears of cold in their eyes, their gloved fingers under their armpits for warmth.

Despite the cold and the hour, a small knot of rubbernecks has gathered at the mouth of the alley. They move about and stand on tiptoe to catch glimpses, and they talk to one another in hushed, confidential tones, instant friends by virtue of shared experience.

LaPointe crosses the street just as an ambulance pulls up. He stands for a time on the rim of the knot of onlookers, unobtrusively joining them. Some maniac killers, like some arsonists, like to blend with the crowd and experience the effects of their actions.

There is a street *bomme* in conversation with a small uncertain man whose chin is buried in a thick wrap of scarf. This latter looks out of place here, like a bank clerk, or an accountant. LaPointe lays his hands on the shoulder of the *bomme*.

"Oh, hi-ya, Lieutenant."

"What are you doing up at this end of the street, Red?"

"It got too cold in that doorway. The wind shifted. It was better walking around."

LaPointe looks into the tramp's eyes. He is not lying. "All the same, stay around. Got any *fric*?"

"None I can spend." Like most *clochards,* Dirtyshirt Red always keeps a dollar or two stashed back for really hard times.

"Here." LaPointe gives him a quarter. "Get some coffee." With a jerk of his head he indicates the all-night Roi des Frites joint across the street.

The clerk, or accountant, or pederast, moves away from the *bomme*. Anyone on talking terms with a policeman can't be perfectly trustworthy.

LaPointe looks up and down the street. The air is so cold and clear that streetlights seem to glitter, and the corners of buildings a block away have sharp, neat edges, like theatrical sets. Everyone's breath is vapor, twin jets when they exhale through their noses. From somewhere there comes the homey, yeasty smell of bread. The bakeries would be working at this hour, men stripped to the waist in hot back rooms, sweating with the heat of ovens.

As LaPointe turns back toward the alley, it starts. A light, rather pleasant tingle in his chest, as though his blood were carbonated. God damn it. A rippling fatigue drains his body and loosens his knees. A constriction swells in his chest, and little bands of pain arc across his upper arms. He leans against the brick wall and breathes deeply and slowly, trying to appear as nonchalant as possible. There are dark patches in his vision, and bright dots. The flashing red light atop the police car begins to blur.

"Lieutenant LaPointe?"

The chest constrictions start to ebb, and the stabs of pain in his arms become duller.

"Sir?"

Slowly, his body weight returns as the sense of floating deflates. He dares a deep breath taken in little sucks to test for pain.

"Lieutenant LaPointe?"

"What, for Christ's sake!"

The young man recoils from the violence of the response. "My name's Guttmann, sir."

"That's *your* problem."

"I'm working with Detective Sergeant Gaspard."

"That's his problem."

"I was the one who telephoned you." The young officer-in-training's voice is stiff with resentment at LaPointe's uncalled-for sarcasm. "Sergeant Gaspard is down the alley. He asked me to keep an eye out for you."

LaPointe grunts. "Well?"

"Sir?"

LaPointe settles his heavy melancholy eyes on the OIT. "You say Gaspard is waiting for me?"

"Yes, sir. Oh. Follow me, sir."

LaPointe shakes his head in general criticism of young policemen as he follows Guttmann into the alley where a bareheaded photographer from the forensic lab is packing up the last of his equipment.

"That you, LaPointe?" Gaspard asks from the dark. Like a handful of the most senior men on the force, Gaspard *tutoyers* LaPointe, but he never uses his first name. In fact, most of them would have to search their memories to come up with his first name.

LaPointe lifts a hand in greeting, then drops the fist back into the pocket of his rumpled overcoat.

The forensic photographer tells Gaspard that he is going back to the Quartier Général with the film. He will get it into an early batch, and it will be developed by mid-morning. He sniffs back draining sinuses and grumbles, "Colder than a witch's *écu!*"

"Titon," Gaspard corrects absent-mindedly, as he shakes hands with LaPointe.

"We haven't searched the body yet. We've been waiting for Flash Gordon here to take the class pictures." Gaspard addresses the photographer. "Well? If you're through, I'll let my men move the bundle."

The victim is a young male dressed in a trendy suit with belled trousers, a shirt with a high rolled collar, and shoes of patent leather. He had dropped to his knees when stabbed, then he had fallen forward. LaPointe has never seen a corpse in that posture: on its knees, its buttocks on its heels, its face pressed into the gravel, its arms stretched out with the palms down. It looks like a young priest serving High Mass, and showing off with excessive self-abasement.

LaPointe feels sorry for it. A corpse can look ugly, or peaceful, or tortured; but it's too bad to look silly. Unfair.

Guttmann and another detective turn the body over to examine the pockets for identification. A piece of gravel is embedded in the boy's smooth cheek. Guttmann flicks it off, but a pink triangular dent remains.

LaPointe mutters to himself, "Heart."

"What?" Gaspard asks, tapping out a cigarette.

"Must have been stabbed through the heart." Without touching each of the logical steps, LaPointe's experience told him that there were only two ways the body could have ended up in that comic posture. Either it had been stabbed in the heart and died instantly, or it had been stabbed in the stomach and had tried to cover up the cold hole. But there was no smell of excrement, and a man stabbed in the stomach almost always soils himself through sphincter convulsion. Therefore, heart.

To turn the body over, the detectives have to straighten it out first. They lift it from under its arms and pull it forward, unfolding it. When they lower it to the pavement, the young face touches the ground.

"Careful!" LaPointe says automatically.

Guttmann glances up, assuming he is being blamed for something. He already dislikes the bullying LaPointe. He doesn't have much use for the old-time image of the tough cop who uses fists and wisetalk, rather than brains and understanding. He has heard about LaPointe of the Main from admiring young French Canadian cops, and the Lieutenant is true to Guttmann's predicted stereotype.

Sergeant Gaspard pinches one of his ears to restore feeling to the lobe. "First time I've ever seen one kneeling like that. Looked like an altar boy."

For a moment, LaPointe finds it odd that they had similar images of the body's posture. But, after all, they share both age and cultural background. Neither of them is a confessing Catholic any longer, but they were brought up with a simple fundamentalist Catholicism that would define them forever, define them negatively, as a mold negatively defines a casting. They are non-Catholics, which is a very different thing from being a non-Protestant or a non-Jew.

The detectives go through the pockets routinely, one putting the findings into a clear plastic bag with a press seal, while Guttmann makes a list, tipping his note pad back awkwardly to catch the light from the street.

"That's it?" Gaspard asks as Guttmann closes his notebook and blows on his numb fingers.

"Yes, sir. Not much. No wallet. No identification. Some small change, keys, a comb—that sort of thing."

Gaspard nods and gestures to the ambulance attendants who are waiting with a wheeled stretcher. With professional adroitness and indifference, they turn the body onto the stretcher and roll it toward the back doors of the ambulance. The cart rattles over the uneven brick pavement, and one arm flops down, the dead hand palsied with the vibrations.

They will deliver it to the Forensic Medicine Department, where it will be fingerprinted and examined thoroughly, together with the clothes and articles found in the pockets. The prints will be telephoned to Ottawa, and by morning Dr. Bouvier, the department pathologist, should have a full report, including a make on the victim's identity.

"Who found the body?" LaPointe asks Gaspard.

"Patrol car. Those two officers on guard."

"Have you talked to them?"

"No, not yet. Did you recognize the stiff?" It is generally assumed that LaPointe knows by sight everyone who lives around the Main.

"No. Never saw him before."

"Looked Portuguese."

LaPointe thrusts out his lower lip and shrugs. "Or Italian. The clothes were more Italian."

As they walk back to the mouth of the alley, the ambulance departs, squealing its tires unnecessarily. LaPointe stops before the uniformed men on guard. "Which of you found the body?"

"I did, Lieutenant LaPointe," says the nearest one quickly. He has the rectangular face of a peasant, and his accent is Chiac. It is a misfortune to speak Chiac, because there is a tradition of dour stupidity associated with the half-swallowed sound; it is a hillbilly accent used by comics to enhance tired jokes.

"Come with us," LaPointe says to the Chiac officer, and to his disappointed partner, "You can wait in the car. And turn that damned thing off." He indicates the revolving red light.

LaPointe, Gaspard, Guttmann, and the Chiac officer cross the street to the Roi des Frites. The policeman left behind is glad to get out of the cold, but he envies his partner's luck. He would give anything to take coffee with LaPointe. He could just see the faces of the guys in the locker room when he dropped casually, "Lieutenant LaPointe and I were having a coffee together, and he turns to me and says . . ." Someone would throw a towel at him and tell him he was full of shit up to his eyebrows.

Dirtyshirt Red rises when the policemen enter the bright interior of the all-night coffee place, but LaPointe motions him to sit down again. Quite automatically, he has already taken over the investigation, although Gaspard from homicide is technically in charge of it. It is an unspoken law in the department that what happens on the Main belongs to LaPointe. And who else would want it?

The four men sit at a back table, warming their palms on the thick earthenware cups. The Chiac officer is a little nervous—he wants to look good in front of Lieutenant LaPointe; even more, he doesn't want to seem a boob in relation to this Anglo tagging along with Sergeant Gaspard.

"By the way, have you met my Joan?" Gaspard asks LaPointe.

"I met him." LaPointe glances at the big-boned young man. Must be a bright lad. You only get into the OIT apprentice program if you are in the top 10 percent of your academy class, and then only after you have done a year of service and have the recommendation of your direct superior.

When LaPointe began on the force, there were almost no Anglo cops. The pay was too low; the job had too little prestige; and the French Canadians who made up the bulk of the department were not particularly kind to interlopers.

"He's not a bad type, for a Roundhead," Gaspard says, indicating his apprentice, and speaking as though he were not present. "And God knows it's not hard to teach him. There's nothing he already knows."

The Chiac officer grins, and Guttmann tries to laugh it off.

Gaspard drinks off the last of his coffee and taps on the window to get the attention of the counterman for a refill. "Robbery, eh?" he says to LaPointe.

"I suppose so. No wallet. Only change in the pockets. But . . ."

Gaspard is an old-timer too. "I know what you mean. No signs of a fight."

LaPointe nods. The victim was a big, strong-looking boy in his mid-twenties. Well built. Probably the kind who lifts weights while he looks darkly at himself in a mirror. If he had resisted the theft, there would have been signs of it. On the other hand, if he had simply handed over his wallet, why would the mugger knife him?

"Could be a nut case," Gaspard suggests.

LaPointe shrugs.

"Christ, we need that sort of thing like the Pope needs a Wassermann," Gaspard says. "Thank God there was a robbery."

The Chiac patrolman has been listening, maintaining a serious expression and making every effort to participate intelligently. That is, he has been keeping his mouth shut and nodding with each statement made by the older men. But now his cold-mottled forehead wrinkles into a frown. Why is it fortunate that there was a robbery? He lacks the experience to sense that there was something not quite right about the killing . . . something about the position of the body that makes both LaPointe and Gaspard intuitively uncomfortable. If there had been no robbery, this might have been the start of something nasty. Like rape mutilations, motiveless stabbings are likely to erupt in patterns. You get a string of four or five before the maniac gets scared or, less often, caught. It's the kind of thing the newspapers love.

"I'll walk it around for a few days," LaPointe says. "See what Bouvier's report gives us. You don't mind if I take it on, do you?" The question is only pro forma. LaPointe feels that all crime on his patch belongs to him by right, but he is careful of the feelings of the other senior men.

"Be my guest," Gaspard says with a wave of his arm that indicates he is happy to be rid of the mess. "And if I ever get the clap, you can have that, too."

"I'll route the paper work through you, so we don't upset the Masters."

Gaspard nods. That is the way LaPointe usually works. It avoids direct run-ins with the administration. There is nothing official about LaPointe's assignment to the Main. In fact, there is no organizational rubric that covers him. The administration slices crime horizontally into categories: theft, bunco, vice, homicide. LaPointe's responsibility is a vertical one: all the crime on the Main. This assignment was never planned, never officially recognized, it just developed as a matter of chance and tradition; and there are those in authority who chafe at this rupture of the organizational chain. They consider it ridiculous that a full lieutenant spends his time crawling around the streets like a short timer. But they console themselves with the realization that LaPointe is an anachronism, a vestige of older, less efficient methods. He will be retiring before long; then they can repair the administrative breach.

LaPointe turns to the uniformed policeman. "You found the body?"

Caught off guard, and wanting to respond alertly, the Chiac cop gulps, "Yes, sir."

67

There is a brief silence. Then LaPointe lifts his palms and opens his eyes wide as if to say, "Well?"

The young officer glances across at Guttmann as he tugs out his notebook. The leather folder has a little loop to hold a pen. It's the kind of thing a parent or girlfriend might have given him when he graduated from the academy. He clears his throat. "We were cruising. My partner was driving slowly because I was checking license plates against the watch list of stolen cars—"

"What did you have for breakfast?" Gaspard asks.

"Pardon me, sir?" The Chiac officer's ears redden.

"Get on with it, for Christ's sake."

"Yes, sir. We passed the alley at . . . ah . . . well, let's see. I wrote the note about ten minutes later, so that would put us at the alley at two-forty or two-forty-five. I saw a movement down the alley, but we had passed it by the time I told my partner to stop. He backed up and I got a glance of a man hopping down the alley. I jumped out and started to chase him, then I came across the body."

"You gave pursuit?" LaPointe asks.

"Well . . . yes, sir. That is, after I discovered that the guy on the ground was dead, I ran to the end of the alley after the other one. But he had disappeared. The street was empty."

"Description?"

"Not much, sir. Just caught a glimpse as he hopped away. Tallish. Thin. Well, not fat. Hard to tell. He had on a big shabby overcoat, sort of like . . ." The officer quickly looks away from LaPointe's shapeless overcoat. ". . . you know. Just an old overcoat."

LaPointe seems to be concentrating on a rivulet of condensed water running down the steamy window beside him. *"Il a clopiné?"* he asks without looking at the officer. "That's twice you said the man 'hopped' off. Why do you choose that word?"

The young man shrugs. "I don't know, sir. That's what he seemed to do . . . sort of hobble off. But quick, you know?"

"And he was dressed shabbily?"

"I had that impression, sir. But it was dark, you know."

LaPointe looks down at the tabletop as he taps his lips with his knuckle. Then he sniffs and sighs. "Tell me about his hat."

"His hat?" The young officer's eyebrows rise. "I don't remember any . . ." His expression seems to spread. "Yes! His hat! A big floppy hat. Dark color. I don't know how that could have slipped my mind. It was kind of like a cowboy hat, but the brim was floppy, you know?"

For the first time since they entered the Roi des Frites, Guttmann speaks up in his precise European French, the kind Canadians call "Parisian," but which is really modeled on the French of Tours. "You know who the man is, don't you, Lieutenant? The one who ran off?"

"Yes."

Gaspard yawns and rubs his legs. "Well, there it is! You see, kid? You're learning from me how to solve cases. Just talk people into committing their crimes on the Main, and turn them over to LaPointe. Nothing to it. It's all in the wrist." He speaks to LaPointe. "So it's routine after all. The guy was stabbed for his money, and you know who . . ."

But LaPointe is shaking his head. It's not that simple. "No. The man this officer saw running away is a street *bomme*. I know him. I don't think he would kill."

"How do you know that, sir?" Guttmann's young face is intense and intelligent. "What I mean is . . . anyone can kill, given the right circumstances. People who would never steal might kill."

With weary slowness, LaPointe turns his patient fatigued eyes on the Anglo.

"Ah . . ." Gaspard says, "did I mention that my Joan here had been to college?"

"No, you didn't."

"Oh, yeah! He's been through it all. Books, grades, long words, theories, raise your hand to go to the bathroom—one finger for pee-pee, two for ca-ca." Gaspard turns to Guttmann, who takes a long-suffering breath.

"One thing I've always wondered, kid," Gaspard pursues. "Maybe you can tell me from all your education. How come a man grins when he's shitting a particularly hard turd? I mean, it isn't all that much fun, really."

Guttmann ignores Gaspard; he looks directly at La-Pointe. "But what I said is true, isn't it? People who would never steal might kill, under the right circumstances?"

The kid's eyes are frank and vulnerable and they shine with suppressed embarrassment and anger. After a second, LaPointe answers, "Yes. That's true."

Gaspard grunts as he stands and stretches his settled spine. "Okay, it's your package, LaPointe. Me, I'm going home. I'll collect the reports in the morning and send them over to you." Then Gaspard gets an idea. "Hey! Want to do me a favor? How about taking my Joan here for a few days? Give him a chance to see how you do your dirty work. What do you say?"

The Chiac officer's mouth opens. These goddamned Roundheads get all the luck.

LaPointe frowns. They never assign Joans to him, just as they never give him committee work. They know better.

"Come on," Gaspard persists. "He can sort of be liaison between my shop and yours. Take him off my back for a few days. He cramps my style. How can I pick up a quick piece of ass with him hanging around all the time, taking notes?"

LaPointe shrugs. "All right. For a couple of days."

"Great," Gaspard says. As he buttons his overcoat up to the neck, he looks out the window. "Look at this goddamned weather, will you! It's already socking in again. By dawn the clouds will be back. Have you ever seen the snow hold off so long? And every night it gets cold as a witch's tit."

LaPointe's mind is elsewhere. He corrects Gaspard thoughtlessly. "*Écu*. Cold as a witch's *écu*."

"You're sure it's not tit?"

"*Écu*."

Gaspard looks down at Guttmann. "You see, kid? You're going to learn a lot with LaPointe. Okay, men, I'm off. Keep crime off the streets and in the home, where it belongs."

The Chiac officer follows Gaspard out into the windy night. They get into the patrol car and drive off, leaving the street totally empty.

"Thanks, Lieutenant," Guttmann says. "I hope you don't feel railroaded into taking me on."

But LaPointe has already crooked his finger at Dirty-shirt Red, who shuffles over to the table. "Sit down, Red." LaPointe shifts to English because it's Red's only language, the language of success. "Have you seen the Vet tonight?"

Dirtyshirt Red makes a face. Over the years he has fostered a fine hatred for his fellow *bomme,* with all his blowing off about being a war hero, and always bragging about his great kip—a snug sleeping place he has hidden away somewhere. A comforting idea strikes Dirtyshirt Red.

"Is he in trouble, Lieutenant? He's a badass, believe you me. I wouldn't put nothin' past him! What's he done, Lieutenant?"

LaPointe settles his melancholy eyes on the *bomme.*

"Okay," Red says quickly. "Sorry. Yeah, I seen him. Down Chez Pete's Place, maybe 'bout six, seven o'clock."

"And you haven't seen him since?"

"No. I left to go down to the Greek bakery and get some toppins promised me. I didn't want that potlickin' son of a bitch hanging around trying to horn in. He's harder to shake than snot off a fingernail."

"Listen, Red. I want to talk to the Vet. You ask around. He could be holed up somewhere because he probably got a lot of drinking money tonight."

The thought of his fellow tramp coming into a bit of luck infuriates Dirtyshirt Red. "That wino son of a bitch, the potlickin' splat of birdshit! *Morviat!* Fartbubble! Him and his snug pad off somewheres! I wouldn't put nothin' past him. . . ."

Dirtyshirt Red continues his flow of bile, but it is lost on LaPointe, who is staring out the window where beads of condensation make double rubies of the taillights of pre-

71

dawn traffic. Trucks, mostly. Vegetables coming into market. He feels disconnected from events; a kind of generalized déjà vu. It's all happened before. Some different kid, killed in some different way, found in some different place; and LaPointe sorting it out in some other café, looking out some other window at some other predawn street. It really doesn't matter very much anymore. He's tired.

Without seeming to, Guttmann has been examining LaPointe's reflection in the window. He has, of course, heard tales about the Lieutenant, his control over the Main, his dry indifference to authorities within the department and to political influences without, improbable myths concerning his courage. Guttmann is intelligent enough to have discounted two-thirds of these epic fables as the confections of French officers seeking an ethnic hero against the Anglophonic authorities.

Physically, LaPointe satisfies Guttmann's preconceptions: the wide face with its deep-set eyes that is practically a map of French Canada; the mat of graying hair that appears to have been combed with the fingers; and of course the famous rumpled overcoat. But there are aspects that Guttmann had not anticipated, things that contradict his caricature of the tough cop. There is a quality that might be called "distance"; a tendency to stay on the outer rim of things, withdrawn and almost daydreaming. Then too, there is something disturbing in LaPointe's patient composure, in the softness of his husky voice, in the crinkling around his eyes that makes him seem . . . the only word that Guttmann can come up with is "paternal." He recalls that the young French policemen sometimes refer to him as "Papa LaPointe," not that anyone dares to call him that within his hearing.

". . . and that potlickin' cockroach—that gnat—tells everybody what a hero he was in the war! That pimple on a whore's ass—that wart—tells everybody what a nice private kip he's got! That son of a bitch gnat-wart tells—"

With the lift of a hand, LaPointe cuts short Dirtyshirt Red's flow of hate, just as he is getting up steam. "That's enough. You ask around for the Vet. If you locate him, call down to the QG. You know the number." With a tip of his

72

head, LaPointe dismisses the *bomme,* who shuffles to the door and out into the night.

Guttmann leans forward. "This Vet is the man with the floppy hat?"

LaPointe frowns at the young policeman, as though he has just become aware of his presence. "Why don't you go home?"

"Sir?"

"There's nothing more we can do tonight. Go home and get some sleep. I'll see you at my office tomorrow."

Guttmann reacts to the Lieutenant's cool tone. "Listen, Lieutenant. I know that Gaspard sort of dumped me on you. If you'd rather not . . ." He shrugs.

"I'll see you tomorrow."

Guttmann looks down at the Formica tabletop. He sucks a slow breath between his teeth. Being with LaPointe isn't going to be much fun. "All right, sir. I'll be there at eight."

LaPointe yawns and scrubs his matted hair with his palm. "You're going to have a hell of a wait. I'm tired. I won't be in until ten or eleven."

After Guttmann leaves, LaPointe sits looking through the window with unfocused eyes. He feels too tired and heavy to push himself up and trudge back to the cold apartment. But . . . he can't sit here all night. He rises with a grunt.

Because the streets are otherwise empty, LaPointe notices a couple standing on a corner. They are embracing, and the man has enclosed her in his overcoat. They press together and sway. It's four-thirty in the morning and cold, and their only shelter is his overcoat. LaPointe glances away, unwilling to intrude on their privacy.

When he turns the corner of Avenue Esplanade, the wind flexes his collar. Litter and dust swirl in miniature whirlwinds beside iron-railed basement wells. LaPointe's body needs oxygen; each breath has the quality of a sigh.

A slight movement in the park catches his eye. A shadow on one of the benches at the twilight rim of a lamplight pool. Someone sitting there. At the foot of his long wooden stoop, he turns and looks again. The person has not moved. It is a woman, or a child. The shadow is so thin it doesn't seem that she is wearing a coat. LaPointe climbs a step or two, then he turns back, crosses the street, and enters the park through a creaking iron gate.

Though she should be able to hear the gravel crunching under his approaching feet, the young girl does not move. She sits with her knees up, her heels against her buttocks, arms wrapped around her legs, face pressed into her long paisley granny gown. Beside her, placed so as to block some of the wind, is a shopping bag with loop handles. It is not until LaPointe's shadow almost touches her that she looks up, startled. Her face is thin and pale, and her left eye is pinched into a squint by a bruise, the bluish stain of which spreads to her cheekbone.

"Are you all right?" he asks in English. The granny gown makes him assume she is Anglo; he associates the new, the modern, the trendy with the Anglo culture.

She does not answer. Her expression is a mixture of defiance and helplessness.

"Where do you live?" he asks.

Her chin still on her knees, she looks at him with steady, untrusting eyes. Her jaw takes on a hard line because she is clenching her teeth to keep them from chattering. Then she squints at him appraisingly. "You want to take me home with you?" she asks in Joual French, her voice flat; perhaps with fatigue, perhaps with indifference.

"No. I want to know where you live." He doesn't mean to sound hard and professional, but he is tired, and her direct, dispassionate proposition took him unawares.

"It's none of your business."

Her sass is a little irritating, but she's right; it's no business of his. Kids like this drift onto the Main every day. Flotsam. Losers. They're no business of his, until they get into trouble. After all, he can't take care of them all. He shrugs and turns away.

"Hey?"

He turns back.

"Well? Are you going to take me home with you, or

not?" There is nothing coquettish in her tone. She is broke and has no place to sleep; but she does have an *écu*. It's a matter of barter.

LaPointe sighs and scratches his hairline. She appears to be in her early twenties, younger than LaPointe's day-dream children. It's late and he's tired, and this girl is noth-ing to him. A skinny kid with a gamine face spoiled by that silly-looking black eye, and anything but attractive in the oversized man's cardigan that is her only protection against the wind. The backs of her hands are mottled with cold and purple in the fluorescent streetlight.

Not attractive, probably dumb; a loser. But what if she turned up as a rape statistic in the Morning Report?

"All right," he says. "Come on." Even as he says it, he regrets it. The last thing he needs is a scruffy kid cluttering up his apartment.

She makes a movement as though to rise, then she looks at him sideways. He is an old man to her, and she knows all about old men. "I don't do anything . . . special," she warns him matter-of-factly.

He feels a sudden flash of anger. She's younger than his daughters, for Christ's sake! "Are you coming?" he asks impatiently.

There is only a brief pause before she shrugs with pro-tective indifference, rises, and takes up her shopping bag. They walk side by side toward the gate. At first he thinks she is stiff with the cold and with sitting all huddled up. Then he realizes that she has a limp; one leg is shorter than the other, and the shopping bag scrapes against her knee as she walks.

He opens his apartment door and reaches around to turn on the red-and-green overhead lamp, then he steps aside and she precedes him into the small living room. Be-cause the putty has rotted out of the big bow windows, they rattle in the wind, and the apartment is colder than the hallway.

As soon as he closes the door, he feels awkward. The room seems cramped, too small for two people. Without taking off his overcoat, he bends down and lights the gas in the fireplace. He squats there, holding down the lever until the limp blue flames begin to make the porcelain nipples glow orange.

Oddly, she is more at ease than he. She crosses to the window and looks down at the park bench where she was sitting a few minutes ago. She rubs her upper arms, but she prefers not to join him near the fire. She doesn't want to seem to need anything that's his.

With a grunt, LaPointe stands up from the gas fire. "There. It'll be warm soon. You want some coffee?"

She turns down the corners of her mouth and shrugs.

"Does that mean you want coffee, or not?"

"It means I don't give a shit one way or the other. If you want to give me coffee, I'll drink it. If not . . ." Again she shrugs and squeeks a little air through tight lips.

He can't help smiling to himself. She thinks she's so goddamned tough. And that shrug of hers is so downriver.

The French Canadian's vocabulary of shrugs is infinite in nuance and paraverbal articulation. He can shrug by lifting his shoulders, or by depressing them. He shrugs by glancing aside, or by squinting. By turning over his hands, or simply lifting his thumbs. By sliding his lower lip forward, or by tucking down the corners of his mouth. By closing his eyes, or by spreading his face. By splaying his fingers; by pushing his tongue against his teeth; by tightening his neck muscles; by raising one eyebrow, or both; by widening his eyes; by cocking his head. And by all combinations and permutations of these. Each shrug means a different thing; each combination means more than two different things at the same time. But in all the shrugs, his fundamental attitude toward the role of fate and the feebleness of Man is revealed.

LaPointe smiles at her tough little shrug, a smile of recognition. While he is in the kitchen putting the kettle on, she moves over to the mantel, pretending to be interested in the photographs arranged in standing frames. In this way she can soak up warmth from the gas fire without appearing to need or want it. As soon as he returns, she steps away as nonchalantly as possible.

"Who's that?" she asks, indicating the photographs.

"My wife."

Her swollen eye almost closes as she squints at him in disbelief. The woman in the photos must be twenty-five or thirty years younger than this guy. And you only have to look around this dump to know no woman lives here. But if he wants to pretend he has a wife, it's no skin off her ass.

He realizes the room is still cold, and he feels awkward to be wearing a big warm overcoat while she has nothing but that oversized cardigan. He tugs off the coat and drops it over a chair. It occurs to him to give her his bathrobe, so he goes into the bedroom to find it, then he steps into the bathroom and starts running hot water in the deep tub with its claw feet. He notices how messy the bathroom is. He is swishing dried whiskers out of the basin when he realizes that the coffee water must have dripped through by now, so he starts back, forgetting the robe and having to go back for it.

Christ, it's complicated having a guest in your house! Who needs it?"

"Here," he says grumpily. "Put this on." She regards the old wool robe with caution, then she shrugs and slips it on. Enveloped in it, she looks even smaller and thinner than before, and clownlike, with that frizzy dustmop of a hairstyle that the kids wear these days. A clown with a black eye. A child-whore with a street vocabulary in which *foutre* and *fourrer* do most of the work of *faire*, and with everything she owns in a shopping bag.

LaPointe is in the kitchen, pouring out the coffee and adding a little water from the kettle because it is strong and she is only a kid, when he hears her laugh. It's a vigorous laugh, lasting only six or. eight notes, then stopping abruptly, still on the ascent, like the cry of a gamebird hit on the rise.

When he steps into the living room, carrying her cup, she is standing before the mirror that hangs on the back of the door; her face is neutral and bland; there is no trace of the laugh in her eyes. He asks, "What is it? What's wrong? Is it the robe?"

"No." She accepts the coffee. "It's my eye. It's the first time I've seen it."

"You find it funny, your eye?"

77

"Why not?" She brings her cup over to the sofa and sits, her short leg tucked up under her buttock. She has a habit of sitting that way. She finds it comfortable. It has nothing to do with her limp. Not really.

He sits in his overstuffed chair opposite as she sips the hot coffee, looking into the cup as a child does. That laugh of hers, so total and so brief, has made him feel more comfortable with her. Most girls would have expressed horror or self-pity to see their faces marred. "Who hit you?" he asks.

She shrugs and blows a puff of air in a typically Canadian gesture of indifference. "A man."

"Why?"

"He promised me I could spend the night, but afterward he changed his mind."

"And you raised hell?"

"Sure. Wouldn't you?"

He leans his head back and smiles. "It's a little hard to imagine being in the situation."

She stops in mid-sip and sets the cup down, looking at him levelly. "What the hell's that supposed to mean?"

"Nothing."

"Why'd you say it then?"

"Forget it. You're from out of town, aren't you?"

She is suddenly wary. "How'd you know that?"

"You have a downriver accent. I was born in Trois Rivières myself."

"So?" She picks up her cup again and sips, watching him closely, wondering if he's trying to get something for nothing with all this friendly talk.

He makes a sudden movement forward, remembering the bath he is running.

Her cup rattles as she jerks back and lifts an arm to protect herself.

Then he realizes the tub won't be half full yet. Water runs slowly through the old pipes. He sits back in his chair. "I didn't mean to startle you."

"You didn't startle me! I'm not afraid of you!" She is angry to have cowered so automatically after her swaggering talk.

Is this the same kid who just now was laughing at herself in the mirror? *Pauvre gamine.* Tough; sassy; vulnerable; scared. "I thought the tub might be overflowing. That's why I jumped up. I'm drawing a bath for you."

"I don't want any goddamned bath!"

"It will warm you up."

"I'm not even sure I want to stay here."

"Then finish your coffee and go."

"I don't even want your fucking coffee!" She stares at him, her narrow chin jutting out in defiance. Nobody bosses her around.

He closes his eyes and sighs deeply. "Go on. Take your bath," he says quietly.

In fact, the thought of a deep hot bath . . . All right. She would take a bath. To spite him.

Steam billows out when she opens the bathroom door. The water is so hot that she has to get in bit by bit, dipping her butt tentatively before daring to lower herself down. Her arms seem to float in the water above her small breasts. The heat makes her sleepy.

When she comes back into the living room, dressed only in his robe, he is sitting in the armchair, his chin down and his eyes closed. Heat from the gas burner has built up in the room, and she feels heavy and very drowsy. Might as well get it over with and get some sleep.

"Are you ready?" she asks. "If you're not, I can help you." She lets the front of the robe hang open. That ought to get him started.

He blinks away the deep daydream about his daughters and the Laval house, and turns his head to look at her. She's so thin that there are hollows in her pelvis. The black tangle of hair at the *écu* has a wiry look. One knee is slightly bent to keep the weight on both feet. The breasts are so small that there is a flat of chestbone between them.

"Cover yourself up," he says. "You'll catch cold."

"Now just a minute," she says warily. "I told you in the park that I don't do anything special—"

"I know!"

She takes his anger as proof that he had hoped for some kind of old man's perversion.

He stands up. "Look, I'm tired. I'm going to bed. You sleep here." While she was in the bath, he had made up the sofa, taking one of the pillows from his bed and pulling down two Hudson Bay blankets from the shelf in the closet. They smelled a little of dust, but there is nothing as warm as a Hudson Bay. There is no sheet. He owns only four, and he hasn't picked up his laundry yet this week. He thought of giving her his, but they are not clean. Nothing in the apartment is prepared for visitors. Since Lucille's death, there have never been any.

She slowly closes the robe. So he really hadn't meant for them to sleep together at all. Maybe it's the leg. Maybe he doesn't like the thought of screwing a cripple. She's met others like that. Well, to hell with him. She doesn't care.

While he is rinsing out the cup and emptying the coffee-maker in the kitchen, she makes herself comfortable on the sofa and pulls the heavy blankets over her. Only when the delicious weight is pressing on her does she realize how tired she is. It almost hurts her bones to relax.

On his way to the bedroom, he turns off the gas. "You don't need it while you're sleeping. It's bad for the lungs."

Who the hell does he think he is? Her father?

When he turns off the overhead light, the windows that seemed black become gray with the first damp light of dawn. He pauses at the bedroom door. "What's your name, by the way?"

Sleepiness already rising in the dry wick of her fatigue, she mutters, "Marie-Louise."

"Well . . . good night then, Marie-Louise."

She hums, half annoyed by the fact that he keeps talking. It doesn't occur to her to ask his name.

4

Even before he opens his eyes, he knows it is late. Something in the quality of the sounds out in the street is wrong for getting-up time. He sits on the edge of his bed and groggily reaches for his bathrobe. It is not there. Only then does he remember the girl sleeping in his robe out in the living room.

He tiptoes through on his way to the kitchen, fully dressed, although he usually takes his coffee before dressing. He doesn't want her to see him padding around in his underwear.

She lies on her side, curled up, the blankets so high that only her mop of frizzed hair is visible. From the line of her body beneath the blankets, he can tell that her hands are between her legs, the palms touching the sides of her thighs. He remembers sleeping like that when he was a kid.

His cup is on the drainboard, where it always is, but he has to rummage about in the cupboard to find another. He puts too little water in the kettle, underestimating the amount needed for two cups, but he decides not to boil more because the coffee already made will get cold. Pouring from one cup to another to make equal shares doesn't work out well, and he loses about a quarter of a cup. He grumbles *"Merde"* with each accident or miscalculation. It's really a nuisance having someone living with you. Staying with you, that is.

Because the cups are only half full, he has no difficulty balancing them as he carries them into the living room.

She is still asleep as he places the cups carefully on the table by the window. The worn springs of his chair clack; he grimaces and settles down more slowly. Maybe he shouldn't wake her; she is sleeping so peacefully. But what's the point of making coffee for two if you don't give it to her? But, no. It's best to let the poor kid sleep.

"Coffee?" he asks, his voice husky.

She doesn't move.

All right. Let her sleep, then.

"Coffee?" he asks louder.

She half hums, half groans, and her head turns under the blankets.

Poor kid's worn out. Let her sleep.

"Marie-Louise?"

A hand slips out and tugs the blanket from her cheek. Her eyelids flutter, then open. She blinks twice and frowns as she tries to remember the room. How did she get here?

"Your coffee will get cold," he explains.

She looks at him blearily, not recognizing him at first. "What?" she asks, her voice squeaky. "Oh . . . you." She presses her eyes shut before opening them again. The puffiness of her black eye has gone down, and the purplish stain has faded toward green.

"Your coffee's ready. But if you'd rather sleep, go ahead."

"What?"

"I said . . . you can go back to sleep, if you want."

She frowns dazedly. She can't believe he woke her up to tell her that. She puts her hand over her eyes to shade them from the cold light as she recollects, then turns and looks at him, wondering what he is up to. He didn't want it last night, so he's probably after a little now.

But he's just sitting there, sipping his coffee.

When she sits up, she notices that her robe is open to the nipples; she tugs it back around her. She accepts the cup he hands her and looks into it bleakly. "Do you have any milk?"

"No. Sorry."

She sips the thick dark brew. "How about sugar?"

"No. I don't keep sugar in the house. I don't use it, and it attracts ants."

She shrugs and drinks it anyway. At least it's hot.

They don't talk, and instead of looking at one another, they both look out the window at the park across the street. A woman is pushing a pram along the path while a spoiled child dangles from her free hand, twisting and whining. She gives it a good shake and a splat on the bottom that seems to improve its humor.

Marie-Louise can see the bench where he found her. It's going to be cold and damp again today, and she won't be able to make a score until dark, if then. Maybe he would let her stay. No, probably not. He'd be afraid she might steal something. Still, it's worth a try.

"You feel better this morning?" she asks.

"Better?"

"If you don't have to rush off, we could . . ." Palm up, her hand saws the air between them horizontally in an eloquent Joual gesture.

"Don't worry about it," he says.

"It won't cost you. Just let me stay until dark." She produces a childish imitation of a sexy leer that is something between the comic and the grotesque, with that black eye of hers. "I would be good to you." When he does not respond, another thought occurs to her. "I'm all right," she promises. "I mean . . . I'm healthy."

He looks at her calmly for several seconds. Then he rises. "I have to go to work. Would you like more coffee?"

"No. No, thank you."

"Don't you like coffee?"

"Not really. Not without milk and sugar."

"I'm sorry."

She lifts her shoulders. "It's not your fault."

He pulls out his wallet. "Look . . ." He doesn't know exactly how to say this. After all, it doesn't matter to him one way or the other if she stays or goes. "Look, there's a store around the corner. You can buy things for your breakfast. The . . . the stove works." What a stupid thing to say. Of course the stove works.

She reaches up and takes the offered ten-dollar bill. This must mean she can stay until night.

He takes up his overcoat. "Okay. Good, then." He goes to the door. "Oh, yes. You'll need a key to get back in after your shopping. There's one on the mantel." It occurs to him that it must seem stupid to leave the extra key on the mantel, because you would have to be in the apartment to get it. And if you're already in the apartment . . . But Lucille had always left it there, and he never misplaced his own key, so . . .

As he is leaving, she asks, "May I use your things?"

"My things?"

"Towel. Deodorant. Razor."

Razor? Oh, of course. He has forgotten that women shave under their arms. "Certainly. No, wait a minute. I use a straight razor."

"What's that?"

"You know . . . just a . . . straight razor."

"And you don't want me using it?"

"I don't think you can. Why don't you buy yourself a razor? There's enough money there." He closes the door behind him and gets halfway down the stairs before something occurs to him.

"Marie-Louise?" He has opened the door again.

She looks up. She has been pawing through her shopping bag of clothes, planning to take this chance to wash out a few things and dry them in front of the gas heater before he comes back. She acts as though she's been caught at something. "Yes?"

"The stove. The pilot light doesn't work. You have to use a match."

"Okay."

He nods. "Good."

When he arrives at the Quartier Général, the workday is in full swing. The halls outside the magistrate's courts are crowded with people standing around or waiting on benches of dark wood, worn light in places by the legs and buttocks of the bored, or the nervous. One harassed woman has three children with her, separated in age by only the minimal gestation period. She hasn't made up that day; perhaps she has given up making up. The youngest of her kids clings to her skirt and whimpers. Her tension suddenly cracking, she screams at it to shut up. For an instant the child freezes, its eyes round. Then its face crumples and it howls. The mother hugs and rocks it, sorry for both of them. Two young men lounge against a window frame, their slouching postures meant to convey that they are not impressed by this building, these courts, this law. But each time the door to the courtroom opens, they glance over with expectation and fear. There are a few whores, victims of a street sweep somewhere. One is telling a story animatedly; another is scratching under her bra with her thumb. A girl in her late teens, advanced pregnancy dominating her skinny body, chews nervously on a strand of hair. An old man rocks back and forth in misery, rubbing his palms against the tops of his legs. It's his last son; his last boy. Youngish lawyers in flowing, dusty black robes and starched collars crossed at the throat, their smooth foreheads puckered into self-important frowns, stalk through the crowd with long strides calculated to give the impression that they are on important business and have no time to waste.

LaPointe scans automatically for faces he might recognize, then steps into one of the big, rickety elevators. Two young detectives mumble greetings; he nods and grunts. He gets out on the second floor and goes down the gray corridor, past old radiators that thud and hiss with steam, past identical doors with ripple-glass windows. His key doesn't seem to work in his lock. He mutters angrily, then the door opens in his hand. It wasn't locked in the first place.

"Good morning, sir."

Oh, shit, yes. Gaspard's Joan. LaPointe has forgotten

all about him. What was his name? Guttmann? LaPointe notices that Guttmann has already moved in and made himself at home at a little table and a straight-backed chair in the corner. He hums a kind of greeting as he hangs his overcoat on the wooden coat tree. He sits heavily in his swivel chair and begins to paw around through his in-box.

"Sir?"

"Hm-m."

"Sergeant Gaspard's report is on your desk, along with the report he forwarded from the forensic lab."

"Have you read it?"

"No, sir. It's addressed to you."

LaPointe is following his habit of scanning the Morning Report first thing in his office. "Read it," he says without looking up.

It seems strange to Guttmann that the Lieutenant seems uninterested in the report. He opens the heavy brown interdepartmental envelope, unwinding the string around the plastic button fastener. "You'll have to initial for receipt, sir."

"*You* initial it."

"But, sir—"

"Initial it!" This initialing of routing envelopes is just another bit of the bureaucratic trash that trammels the ever-reorganizing department. LaPointe makes it a practice to ignore all such rules.

What's this? A blue memo card from the Commissioner's office. Look at this formal crap:

FROM: Commissioner Resnais

TO: Claude LaPointe, Lieutenant

SUBJECT: Morning of 21 November: appointment for

MESSAGE: I'd like to see you when you get in.

Resnais

(dictated, but not signed)

LaPointe knows what Resnais wants. It will be about the Dieudonné case. That weaselly little turd of a lawyer is threatening to lodge a 217 assault charge against LaPointe

86

for slapping his client. We must protect the civil rights of the criminal! Oh, yes! And what about the old woman that Dieudonné shot through the throat? What about her, with her last breaths whistling and flapping moistly through the hole?

LaPointe pushes the memo card aside with a growl.

Guttmann glances up from the report on the kid they found in the alley. "Sir? Something wrong?"

"Just read the report." He must be tired this morning. Even this kid's careful continental French annoys him. And he seems to take up so goddamned much room in the office! LaPointe hadn't noticed last night how big the kid was. Six-two, six-three; weighs about 210. And his attempt to fit himself into as little space as possible behind that small table makes him seem even bigger and bulkier. This isn't going to work out. He'll have to turn him back over to Gaspard as soon as possible.

LaPointe shoves the routine papers and memos away and rises to look out his office window toward the Hôtel de Ville. There are scaffolds clinging to the sides of the Victorian hulk, and above the scaffolds the sandblasters have cleaned to a creamy white a façade that used to bear the comfortable patina of soot with water-run accents of dark gray. For months now, they have been sandblasting the building, and the roaring hiss has become a constant in LaPointe's office, replacing the rumble of traffic as a base line for silence. It is not the noise that bothers LaPointe, it is the change. He liked the Hôtel de Ville the way it was, with its stained and experienced exterior. They change everything. The law, rules of evidence, acceptable procedure in dealing with suspects. The world is getting more complicated. And younger. And all these new forms! This endless paper work that he has to peck out with two fingers, hunched over his ancient typewriter, growling and smashing at the keys when he makes an error . . .

. . . It's strange to think of her using his Mum. Putting his Mum under her arms. He supposes young girls don't use Mum. They probably prefer those fancy sprays. He shrugs. Well, that's just too bad. Mum is all he has. And if it's not good enough for her . . .

"No identification," Guttmann says, mostly to himself.

"What?"

"The forensic lab report, sir. No identification of that man in the alley. And no make on the fingerprints."

"They checked with Ottawa?"

"Yes, sir."

"Hm-m." The victim looked like the type who ought to have a record, if not for petty arrests, at least as an alien. No fingerprints. One possibility immediately occurs to LaPointe. The victim might have been an unregistered alien, one of those who slip into the country illegally. They are not uncommon on the Main; most of them are harmless enough, victims of the circular paradox of having no legal nationality, and therefore no passports and no means of legitimate immigration, therefore, no legal nationality. Several of the Jews who have been on the street for years are in this category, particularly those who came from camps in Europe just after the war. They cause no trouble; anyway, LaPointe knows about them, and that's what counts.

"What else is in the report?"

"Not much, sir. A technical description of the wound . . . angle of entry and that sort of thing. They're running down the clothing."

"I see."

"So what do we do now?"

"We?" LaPointe looks at the daunting pile of back work, of forms and memos and reports on his desk. "Tell me, Guttmann. When you were in college, did you learn to type?"

Guttmann is silent for fully five seconds before saying, "Ah . . . yes, sir?" The rising note says it all. "You know, sir," he adds quickly, "Sergeant Gaspard had me filling out reports for him when I was assigned as his Joan. It struck me that was a sort of perversion of the intention of the apprentice program."

"A what?"

"A perversion of the . . . That was one of the reasons I was glad when he let me work with you."

88

"It was?"

"Yes, sir."

"I see. Well, in that case, you start working on this junk on my desk. Whatever requires a signature, sign. Sign my name if you have to."

Guttmann's face is glum. "What about Commissioner Resnais?" he asks, glad to have a little something to pique back with. "There was a memo about him wanting to see you."

"I'll be down in Forensic Medicine, talking to Bouvier, if anyone calls."

"And what should I tell the Commissioner's office, if they call?"

"Tell them I'm perverting your intentions . . . that was it, wasn't it?"

As LaPointe steps out of the elevator on the basement level, he is met by a medley of odors that always brings the same incongruous image to his mind: a plaster statue of the Virgin, her bright blue eyes slightly strabismic through the fault of the artist, and a small chip out of her cheek. With this mental image always comes a leaden sensation in his arms and shoulders. The stale smells of the Forensic Medicine Department are linked to this odd sensation of weight in his arms by a long organic chain of association that he has never attempted to follow.

The odor in these halls is an olio of chemicals, floor wax, paint cooking on hot radiators, dusty air, the sum of which is very like the smells of St. Joseph's Home, where he was sent after the pneumonia took his mother. (In Trois Rivières, it wasn't pneumonia; it was *the* pneumonia. And it didn't kill one's mother; it *took* her.)

The smells of St. Joseph's: floor wax, hot radiators, wet hair, wet wool, brown soap, dust, and the acrid smell of ink, dried and caked on the sides of the inkwell.

Inkwell. The splayed nib scrapes over the paper. You have to write it a hundred times, perfectly, without a blemish. That will teach you to daydream. Your mind slips away from the exercise for a second, and the point of the nib digs into the cheap paper on the upstroke. A splatter of ink makes you have to start all over again. It's a good thing for you that Brother Benedict didn't find the *moue* on you. You'd get something worse than a hundred lines for that. You'd get a *tranche*.

Moue. You make *moue* by pressing bread into a small tin box and moistening it with a little water and spit. In a day or two, it begins to taste sweet. It is the standard confection of the boys at St. Joseph's, and is munched surreptitiously during classes, or is traded for favors, or gambled in games of "fingers" in the dormitory after lights out, or given to the big boys to keep from being toughed up. Because the bread is stolen from the dinner line, *moue* is illegal in St. Joseph's, and if you're found with it on you, you get a *tranche*. You can pick up *tranches* for other sins too. For talking in line, for not knowing your lessons, for fighting, for sassing. If you haven't worked off all your *tranches* by the end of the week, you don't eat on Sunday.

A *tranche* is a fifteen-minute slice of time spent in the small chapel the boys call the Glory Hole, where you kneel before the plaster Mary, your arms held straight out in cruciform, under the supervision of old Brother Jean who seems to have no other duties than to sit in the second row of the Glory Hole and record the boys' punishments. You kneel there, arms straight out. And for five minutes it's easy. By the end of the first fifteen minutes, your arms are like lead, your hands feel huge, and the muscles of your shoulders are trembling with effort. Maybe you shouldn't try for your second *tranche*. Anything less than a full fifteen-minute slice doesn't count at all. You can do as much as fourteen minutes before your arms collapse, and it's as though you hadn't even tried. Oh, to hell with it! Go for a second one. Get the goddamned thing over with. Halfway through the second *tranche* you know you're not going to make it. You squeeze your eyes shut and grit your teeth. Everyone says that Brother Jean cheats, makes the second slice longer than the first. You ball up your fists and fight against the numbness in your shoulders. But inevitably the arms sag. "Up. Up," says Brother Jean gently. With a sneer of pain, you pull your arms back up. You take deep breaths. You try to think of something other than the pain. You stare at the face of the plaster Virgin, so calm, so pure, with her slightly crossed eyes and her goddamned stupid chipped cheek! The hands fall, clapping to the sides of the legs, and you grunt with the sudden change in the timbre of the pain. Brother Jean's voice is flat and soft. "LaPointe. One *tranche.*"

Every time he steps off the elevator into the basement and breathes these particular odors, LaPointe's arms feel heavy, for no reason he can think of.

For a second, he attributes the sensation to his heart, his aneurism. He awaits the rest of it—the bubbles in his blood, the constriction, the exploding lights behind the eyes. When these do not come, he smiles at himself and shakes his head.

The door to Dr. Bouvier's office is open, and he is talking to one of his assistants while he examines a list on a clipboard, holding the board close to his right eye, huge behind a thick lens. His left eye is hidden behind a lens the color of nicotine. It must be an ugly eye, for he takes pains to prevent anyone from seeing it. He tells his assistant to make sure something is done by this afternoon, and the young man leaves. Bouvier scratches his scalp with the back of his pencil, then cocks his head toward the door. "Who's that?" he demands.

"LaPointe."

"Ah! Come in. For God's sake, don't hover. How about some coffee?"

LaPointe sits in a scrofulous old leather chair beneath one of the high wire-screened windows that let a ghost of daylight into the basement rooms. Bouvier feels along the ledge behind him until he touches a cup. He puts his finger down into it and, finding it wet, deduces it is his. He feels for another, finds it, and brings it close to his right eye to be sure he has not butted cigarettes in it. His minimal standards of sanitation satisfied, he fills the cup and thrusts it in LaPointe's direction.

In his own way, Bouvier is as much an epic figure in

the folklore of the department as LaPointe. He is famous, of course, for his coffee. Imaginations strain in efforts to account for the taste and texture of this ghastly brew. He is famous also for his desk, which is piled with letters, forms, memos, requisitions, and files to a height that is an offense to the law of gravity. Bouvier also possesses, both in legend and in fact, a remarkable memory for minute details of past cases, a memory that has developed porportionately as he descended toward blindness. By means of this memory, he is sometimes able to reveal a linking *modus operandi* between what appear to be unrelated events or cases. His "interesting little insights" have occasionally led to solutions, or to the discrediting of facile solutions already in hand. But these "interesting little insights" are not always welcome, because they sometimes reopen files everyone would rather leave closed.

Like LaPointe, Bouvier is a bachelor, and he puts in a prodigious amount of time down in the bowels of the QG, where his duties have spread far beyond those normally assigned to a staff pathologist. His authority has expanded into each vacuum created by a departing man or a new reorganization, until, by his own admission, his domain is so wide that the department would collapse two days after he left.

Not that he's ever likely to leave. From medical school he went directly into the army, where he served through the Second World War. When he got out, money was tight and he took a temporary job with the police until he could set up in practice. Time passed, and his eyesight began to fail. He stayed on with the department because, as he used to say himself, a patient's confidence might be eroded a bit if, as a brain surgeon, Bouvier had to begin by saying: "Now, sir, if you would please direct my hands toward your head."

He sits in the straight-backed kitchen chair behind his heaped-up desk, sniffing as he pushes up the glasses that continually slip down his stubby nose. He broke them a few years ago, and they are patched at the bridge with dirty adhesive tape. He intends to get new ones one of these days. "Well?" he asks, as LaPointe presses his refilled cup into his hand, "I assume you're here on behalf of that kid who got reamed on your patch. Anything special about the case?"

LaPointe shrugs. "I doubt it."

"Good. Because I don't think you will close this one. If you took the time to read my report, written in crisp but lucid professional language, you would know that there were no fingerprints on record with Ottawa. And we all appreciate the heavy significance of that."

Bouvier reveals his bitterness at ending up a police pathologist by his sarcasm and cynicism, and by a style of speech that mixes swatches of erudition with vulgarity and gallows humor. To this he adds a jerky, non sequitur conversational tactic that dazzles many and impresses some.

LaPointe long ago learned to handle the technique by simply waiting until Bouvier got around to the point.

"Can you tell me anything that is not in the report?" LaPointe asks.

"A great deal, of course. I could tell you things ranging through aesthetics, to thermodynamics, to conflicting theories concerning the functions of Stonehenge; but I suspect your interests are more restricted than that. Informational tunnel vision: an occupational hazard. All right, how about this? Your young man used hair spray, if that's any help."

"None at all. Is the press release out?"

"No, I've still got it here in my out-box." Bouvier waves vaguely toward the heaped tabletop. By departmental practice, information concerning murder, suicide, or rape cases is not released to the newspapers until Bouvier has finished his examination and the next of kin are informed. "You want me to hold it?"

"Yes. For a couple of days." When pressure from newspapers or family allows, LaPointe likes to start his inquiries before the press release is out. He prefers to make the first mention of the crime, to watch for qualities of surprise or anticipation.

"I could probably block it up here forever," Bouvier

says. "I doubt that anyone will be around inquiring after this one. Except maybe a woman claiming breach of promise, or a pregnancy suit, or both. He made love shortly before his death."

"How do you know that?"

Bouvier sips his coffee, makes a face, and cocks his nicotine lens at the cup. "This is terrible. I think something's fallen into the pot. I'll have to empty it one of these days and take a look. On second thought, maybe I don't want to know. Say, I hear you've broken down and taken on a Joan."

Three-quarters blind and never out of his den in the bowels of the building, Dr. Bouvier knows everything that is going on in the Quartier Général. He makes a point of letting people know that he knows.

"Gaspard sent his Joan over to me for a few days."

"Hm-m. I can't help feeling sorry for the kid. He's an interesting boy, too. Have you read his file?"

"No. But I suppose you have."

"Of course. Did very well in college. Excellent grades. The offer of a scholarship to do graduate study in social work, but he chose instead to enter the force. Another instance of a strange demographic pattern I have observed. Year by year, the force is attracting a better class of young men. On the other hand, what with kids bungling their way through amateur holdups to get a fix, crime is attracting a lower class than it once did. It was simpler in our day, when the men on both sides were of the same sociological, intellectual, and ethical molds. But what you *really* wanted to know was how I divined that the young man in the alley made love shortly before he was killed. Simple really. He failed to wash up afterwards, in direct contradiction to the sound paternal advice given in army VD films. I wonder if they ever consider how carefully they're going to be examined after they get themselves gutted, or in some other way manage to shuffle their mortal coils off to Buffalo. I remember my mother always telling me to wear clean shorts, in case I got hit by a truck. For much of my youth I entertained the belief that clean shorts were a totemic protection against trucks—in much the same way that apples keep doctors away. When I think of the daring and dangerous things I used to do in the middle of heavy traffic to amuse my friends, all in the belief that I was invulnerable because I had just changed my shorts! So tell me, what are the gods up to these days? Is our anointed Commissioner Resnais still driving toward a brilliant future in politics, as he drives the rest of us toward dreams of regicide?"

"Every day they dream up a new form, a new bit of paper work. We've got paper work coming out of our ears."

"Hm! Have you talked to your doctor about that? I just read in a medical journal about a man who drank molten iron and pissed out telephone wire. Something of an exhibitionist, I suspect. Even more to the point, we haven't finished checking out your stiff's clothing. The analysis of dust and lint and crap in pockets and cuffs isn't quite done. I'll contact you if anything comes up. Matter of fact, I'll give the case a bit of thought. Might even come up with one of my 'interesting little insights.' "

"Don't do me any favors."

"Wouldn't dream of it. And to prove that, how about another cup of coffee?"

Guttmann is typing out an overdue report when La-Pointe enters. He has taken the liberty of going through the Lieutenant's desk and clearing out every forgotten or overlooked report and memo he could find. He tried to organize them into some kind of sequence at first, but now he is taking them in random order and bungling through as best he can.

LaPointe sits at his desk and surveys the expanse of unlittered surface. "Now, that looks better," he says.

Guttmann looks over the piles of paper work on his little table. "Did you find out anything from Dr. Bouvier, sir?"

"Only that you're supposed to be a remarkable young man."

"Remarkable in what way, sir?"

"I don't remember."

"I see. Oh, by the way, the Commissioner's office called again. They're pretty upset about your not coming right up when you got in."

"Hm-m. Any call from Dirtyshirt Red?"

"Sir?"

"That *bomme* you met last night. The one who's looking for the Vet."

"No, sir. No call."

"I don't imagine the Vet will be out on the streets before dark anyway. He has drinking money. What time is it?"

"Just after one, sir."

"Have you had lunch?"

"No, sir. I've been doing paper work."

"Oh? Well, let's go have lunch."

"Sir? Do you realize that some of these reports are six months overdue?"

"What does that have to do with getting lunch?"

"Ah . . . nothing?"

They sit by the window of a small restaurant across Bonsecours Street from the Quartier Général, finishing their coffee. The decor is a little frilly for its police clientele, and Guttmann looks particularly out of place, his considerable bulk threatening his spindly-legged chair.

"Sir?" Guttmann says out of a long silence. "There's something I've been wondering about. Why do the older men on the force call us apprentices 'Joans'?"

"Oh, that comes from long ago, when most of the force was French. They weren't called 'Joans' really. They were called '*jaunes*.' Over the years it got pronounced in English."

"*Jaunes?* Yellows? Why yellows?"

"Because the apprentices are always kids, still wet behind the ears . . ."

Guttmann's expression says he still doesn't get it.

". . . and yellow is the color of baby shit," LaPointe explains.

Guttmann's face is blank.

LaPointe shrugs. "I suppose it doesn't really make much sense."

"No, sir. Not much. Just more of the wiseass ragging the junior men have to put up with."

"That bothers you, eh?"

"Sure. I mean . . . this isn't the army. We don't have to break a man's spirit to get him to conform."

"If you don't like the force, why don't you get out? Use that college education of yours."

Guttmann looks quickly at the Lieutenant. "That's another thing, sir. I guess I'm supposed to be sorry that I got a little education. But I'm afraid I just can't cut it." His ears are tingling with resentment.

LaPointe rubs his stubbly cheek with the palm of his hand. "You don't have to cut it, son. Just so long as you can type. Come on, finish your coffee and let's go."

Leaving Guttmann waiting on the sidewalk, LaPointe returns to the restaurant and places a call from the booth at the back. Five times . . . six . . . seven . . . the phone rings, unanswered. He shrugs philosophically and sets the receiver back into its cradle. But just as he hangs up, he thinks he hears an answering click on the other end. He dials again quickly. This time the phone is answered on the first ring.

"Yes?"

"Hello. It's me. Claude."

"Yes?" She does not place the name.

"LaPointe. The man who owns the apartment."

"Oh. Yeah." She has nothing more to say.

"Is everything all right?"

"All right?"

"I mean . . . did you buy enough for breakfast and lunch?"

"Yes."

"Good."

There is a silence.

She volunteers, "Did you call just now?"

"Yes."

"I was in the bathroom. It stopped ringing just when I answered."

"Yes, I know."

"Oh. Well . . . why did you call?"

"I just wanted to know if you found everything you need."

"Like what?"

"Like . . . did you buy a razor?"

"Yes."

"That's good."

A short silence.

Then he says, "I won't be back until eight or nine tonight."

"And you want me out by then?"

"No. I mean, it's up to you. It doesn't matter."

A short silence.

"Well? Should I go or stay?"

A longer silence.

"I'll bring some groceries back with me. We can make supper there, if you want."

"Can you cook?" she asks.

"Yes. Can't you?"

"No. I can do eggs and mince and things like that."

"Well, then, I'll do the cooking."

"Okay."

"It'll be late. Can you hold out that long?"

"What do you mean?"

"You won't get too hungry?"

"No."

"Well then. I'll see you tonight."

"Okay."

LaPointe hangs up, feeling foolish. Why call when you have nothing to say? That's stupid. He wonders what he'll buy for supper.

The dumb twit can't even cook.

The secretary's skirt is so short that modesty makes her back up to file cabinets and squat to extract papers from the lower drawers.

LaPointe sits in a modern imitation-leather divan so deep and soft that it is difficult to rise from it. On a low coffee table are arranged a fine political balance of back-

98

dated *Punch* and *Paris Match* magazines, together with the latest issue of *Canada Now*. The walls of the Commissioner's reception room are adorned with paintings that have the crude draftsmanship and flat perspective of fashionable Hudson Bay Indian primitive; and there is a saccharine portrait of an Indian girl with pigtails and melting brown comic-sad eyes too large for her face, after the style of an American husband-and-wife team of kitsch painters. The size of the eyes, their sadness, and the Oriental upturn of the corners make it look as though the girl's mother plaited her braids too tightly.

Along with the popular Indian trash on the walls, there are several framed posters, examples of the newly established Public Relations Department. One shows a uniformed policeman and a middle-aged civilian male standing side by side, looking down at a happy child. The slogan reads: *Crime Is Everybody's Business.* LaPointe wonders what crime the men are contemplating.

The leggy secretary squats again, her back to the file cabinet, to replace a folder. Her tight skirt makes her lose her balance for a second, and her knees separate, revealing her panties.

LaPointe nods to himself. That's smart; to avoid showing your ass, you flash your crotch.

The door behind the secretary's desk opens and Commissioner Resnais appears, hand already out, broad smile in place. He makes it a habit to greet senior men personally. He brought that back with him from a seminar in the States on personnel management tactics.

Make the men who work FOR you think they work WITH you.

"Claude, good to see you. Come on in." Just the opposite of Sergeant Gaspard, Resnais uses LaPointe's first name, but does not *tutoyer* him. The Commissioner's alert black eyes reveal a tension that belies his facile camaraderie.

Resnais' office is spacious, its furniture relentlessly modern. There is a thick carpet, and two of the walls are lined with books—and not only lawbooks. There are titles dealing with social issues, pyschology, the history of Canada, problems of modern youth, communications, and the arts and crafts of Hudson Bay Indians. No civilian visitor could avoid being impressed by the implication of social concern and modern attitudes toward the causes and prevention of crime. No ordinary cop, this Commissioner. A liberal intellectual working in the trenches of quotidian law enforcement.

Nor is it easy to dismiss Resnais as a bogus political man. He has in fact read each of the books in his office. He in fact does his best to understand and respond to modern community needs. He does in fact see himself as a liberal; as a policeman by vocation, and a politician by necessity. Resnais is not the man to attract devotion and affection from those under him, but the majority of the force respect him, and many of the younger men admire him.

Like LaPointe, Resnais began by patrolling a beat. Then he went to night school; perfected his English; married into one of the reigning Anglo families of Montreal; took leaves of absence, without pay, to finish his college education; made a career of delicate cases involving people and events that required protection from the light of newspaper exposure. Finally, he became the first career policeman to occupy the traditionally civilian post of commissioner. For this reason, he thinks of himself as a cop's cop. Few of the older men on the force share his view. True, he has been on the force for thirty years, but he was never a cop in the rough-and-tumble sense. He never shook information out of a pimp he despised. He never drank coffee at two in the morning out of a cracked mug, sleeplessness irritating his eyes, his overcoat stinking of wet wool. He never had to use the cover of a car door when returning fire.

LaPointe notices his personnel file on Resnais' desk, otherwise bare save for a neat stack of pale blue memo cards, an open note pad, and two perfectly sharpened pencils.

Men who look busy are often only disorganized.

Resnais stations himself in front of the floor-to-ceiling window, the glare of the overcast skies making it difficult to look in his direction without squinting.

"Well, how have you been, Claude?"

LaPointe smiles at the accent. Resnais is really trilingual. He speaks continental French; perfect English, although with the growled "r" of the Francophone who has finally located that difficult consonant; and he can revert to a Joual as twangy as the next man's when he is addressing a group from east Montreal, or speaking to senior French Canadian officers.

"I think I'll make it through the winter, Commissioner." LaPointe never uses his first name.

Resnais laughs. "I'm sure you will! Tough old son of a bitch like you? I'm sure you will!" There is something phony and condescending in his use of profanity, just like one of the guys. He clasps his hands behind his back and rocks up on his toes, a habit born of being rather short for a policeman. His body is thick, but he keeps in perfect trim by jogging with neighbors, swimming with members of his exclusive athletic club, and playing handball in the police league, for which he signs up just like any other cop, and where he accepts defeat at the hands of younger officers with laughing good grace. His expensive suits are closely cut, and he could pass for ten years younger than he is, despite the gleaming pate with its wreath of coal-black hair. Suntanning under lamps has given him a slightly purplish gleam. "Still living in the old place on Esplanade?" he asks offhandedly.

"Yes. Just like it says in my dossier," LaPointe responds.

Resnais laughs heartily. "I can't get away with anything with you, can I?" It is true that he makes a practice of looking over a man's file just before seeing him, for the purpose of refreshing himself on an intimate detail or two—number of children and their sexes, the wife's name, awards or medals. He drops these bits of information casually, as though he knows each man personally and holds in his memory details of his life. He once read somewhere that this was a trick used by a popular American general in the Second World War, and he adopted it as a good management tactic.

An employee gives of his TIME, a buddy gives of HIMSELF.

Unfortunately, there wasn't much in LaPointe's life to comment upon. No children, a wife long since dead, citations for merit and bravery all earned years ago. You're scraping the bottom of the barrel when you have to mention the street a man lives on.

"I don't want to waste too much of your time, Commissioner," LaPointe says, "So, if there's something . . ." He raises his eyebrows.

Resnais does not like that. He prefers to control the timing and flow of conversation when it involves delicate personnel problems like this one. To do so is an axiom of Small Group and One-to-One Communication Technique.

If you're not IN control, you're UNDER control.

"I was expecting you this morning, Claude."

"I was on a case."

"I see." The Commissioner again rocks onto his toes and squeezes his hands behind his back. Then he sits down in his high-backed desk chair and turns it so that he is looking not at LaPointe, but past him, out of the window. "Frankly, I'm afraid I have to give you what in the old days was called an ass-chewing."

"We still call it that."

"Right. Now look, Claude, we're both old-timers . . ." LaPointe shrugs.

". . . and I don't feel I have to pull any punches with you. I've been forced to talk to you about your methods before. Now, I'm not saying they're inefficient. I know that sometimes going by the book means losing an arrest. But things have changed since we were young. Greater emphasis is placed today upon the protection of the individual than upon the protection of the society." There seem to be invisible quotation marks around this last sentence. "I'm not calling these changes good, and I'm not calling them bad. They are facts of life. And facts of life that you continue to ignore."

"You're talking about the Dieudonné case?"

Resnais frowns. He doesn't like being rushed. "That's

102

the case in point right now. But I'm talking about more than this one instance. This isn't the first time you've gotten information by force. And it's not the first time I've told you that this is not the way things happen in my department." He instantly regrets having called it *his* department. Make every man feel a part of the organization.

He works best who works for himself.

"I don't think you know the details of the case, Commissioner."

"I assure you that I know the case. I've had every bit of it rammed down my throat by the public prosecutor!"

"The old woman was shot for seven dollars and some change! Not even enough for the punk to get a fix!"

"That's not the point!" Resnais' jaw tightens, and he continues with exaggerated control. "The point is this. You got information against Dieudonné by means of force and threat of force."

"I knew he did it. But I couldn't prove it without a confession."

"How did you know he did it?"

"The word was out."

"What, *exactly,* does that mean?"

"It means the word was out. It means that he's a bragging son of a bitch who spills his guts when he takes on a load of shit."

"You're telling me he admitted to others that he killed the old woman . . . whatshername?"

"No. He bragged about having a gun and not being afraid to use it."

"That's hardly admission of murder."

"No, but I *know* Dieudonné. I've known him since he was a wiseassed kid. I know what he's capable of."

"Believe it or not, your intuition does not constitute evidence."

"The slugs from his gun matched up, didn't they?"

"The slugs matched up, all right. But how did you get the gun in the first place?"

"He told me where he had buried it."

"*After* you beat him up."

"I slapped him twice."

"*And* threatened to lock him up in a room and let him suffer a cold-turkey withdrawal! Christ, you didn't even have any hard evidence to connect him with the old woman . . . whatshername!"

"Her *name*, goddamn it, was Mrs. Czopec! She was seventy-two years old! She lived in the basement of a building that doesn't have plumbing. There's a bit of sooty dirt in front of that building, and in spring she used to get free seed packets on boxes of food, and plant them and water them, and sometimes a few came up. But her basement window was so low that she couldn't see them. She and her husband were the first Czechs on my patch. He died four years ago, but he wasn't a citizen, so she didn't have much in benefits coming in. She clung to her purse when that asshole junkie tried to snatch it because the seven dollars was all the money she had to last to the end of the month. When I checked out her apartment, it turned out that she lived on rice. And there was evidence that toward the end of the month, she ate paper. Paper, Commissioner."

"That's not the point!"

LaPointe jumps up from his chair, "You're right! That's not the point. The point is that she had a right to live out her miserable life, planting her stupid flowers, eating her rice, spending half of every day in church where she couldn't afford to light a candle! *That's* the point! And that hophead son of a bitch shot her through the throat! *That's the point!*"

Resnais lifts a denying palm. "Look, I'm not defending him, Claude. . . ."

"Oh? You mean you aren't going to tell me that he was underprivileged? Maybe his father never took him to a hockey game!"

Resnais is off balance. What's wrong with LaPointe? It isn't like him to get excited. He's supposed to be the big professional, so coldblooded. Resnais expected chilly insubordination, but this passion is . . . unfair. To regain control of the situation, Resnais speaks flatly. "Dieudonné is getting off."

LaPointe is stopped cold. He can't believe it. "What?"

"That's right. The public prosecutor met with his lawyers yesterday. They threatened to slap you with a two-seventeen assault, and the newspapers would love that! I have my—I have the department to think of, Claude."

LaPointe sits down. "So you made a deal?"

"I don't like that term. We did the best we could. The lawyers could probably have gotten the case thrown out, considering how you found the gun. Fortunately for us, they are responsible men who don't want to see Dieudonné out on the street any more than we do."

"What kind of deal?"

"The best we could get. Dieudonné pleads guilty to manslaughter; they forget the two-seventeen against you. There it is."

"Manslaughter?"

"There it is." Resnais sits back in his high-backed desk chair and gives this time to sink in. "You see, Claude, even if I condoned your methods—and I don't—the bottom line is this: they don't work anymore. The charges don't stick."

LaPointe is lost and angry. "But there was no other way to get him. There was no hard evidence without the gun."

"You keep missing the point."

LaPointe stares straight ahead, his eyes unfocused. "You'd better get word to Dieudonné that if he ever sets foot on the Main after he gets out . . ."

"For Christ's sake! Don't you ever listen? Does a truck have to drive over you? You've embarrassed . . . the department long enough! I've worked like a son of a bitch to give this shop a good image in the city, and all it takes . . . ! Look, Claude. I don't like doing this, but I'd better lay it on the line for you. I know the reputation you have among the guys in the shop. You keep your patch cool, and I know that no other man, probably no team of men, could do what you do. But times have changed. And you haven't changed with them." Resnais fingers LaPointe's personnel file. "Three recognitions for merit. Twice awarded the Police Medal. Twice wounded in the line of duty—once very seriously, as I recall. When we heard about that bullet grazing your heart, we kept an open line to the hospital all night long. Did you know that?"

LaPointe is no longer looking at the Commissioner; his eyes are directed out the window. He speaks quietly. "Get on with it, Commissioner."

"All right. I'll get on with it. This is the last time you embarrass this shop. If it happens one more time . . . if I have to go to bat for you one more time . . ." There is no need to finish the sentence.

LaPointe draws his gaze back to the Commissioner's face. He sighs and rises. "Is that all you wanted to talk to me about?"

Resnais looks down at LaPointe's file, his jaw tight. "Yes. That's all."

The slam of the office door rattles the glass, and LaPointe brushes past Guttmann without a word. He sits heavily in his desk chair and stares vacantly at the Forensic Medicine report on that kid found in the alley. Instinct for self-preservation warns Guttmann to keep his head down over his typing and not say a word. For half an hour, the only sound in the room is the tapping of the typewriter and the hiss of the sandblasting across the street.

Then LaPointe takes a deep breath and rubs his mat of hair with his palm. "Did I get a call from Dirtyshirt Red?"

"No, sir. No calls at all."

"Hm-m." LaPointe rises and comes to Guttmann's little table, looking over his shoulder. "How's it going?"

"Oh, it's going fine, sir. It's lots of fun. I'd rather type out reports than anything I can think of."

LaPointe turns away, grunting his disgust for all paper work and all who bother with it. Outside the window, the city is already growing dark under the heavy layers of stationary cloud. He tugs down his overcoat from the wooden rack.

"I'm going up onto the Main. See what's happening."

Guttmann nods, not lifting his eyes from the form he is retyping, for fear of losing his place again.

"Well?"

The younger man puts his finger on his place and looks up. "Well what, sir?"

"Are you coming or not?"

A minute later, the door is locked, the lights off, and the unfinished report is still wound into the machine.

5

By the time they cross Sherbrooke, the last greenish light is draining from sallow cloud layers over the city. Streetlights are already on, and the sidewalks are beginning to clog with pedestrians. A raw wind has come up, puffing in vagrant gusts around corners and carrying dust that is gritty between the teeth. The cold makes tears stand in Guttmann's eyes, and the skin of his face feels tight, but it doesn't seem to penetrate the Lieutenant's shaggy overcoat hanging to his mid-calves. Guttmann would like to pace along more quickly to heat up the blood, but LaPointe's step is measured, and his eyes scan the street from side to side, automatically searching out little evidences of trouble.

As they pass a shop, LaPointe takes his hand from his pocket and lifts it in greeting. A bald little man with a green eyeshade waves back.

Guttmann looks up at the sign overhead:

S. KLEIN — BUTTONHOLES

"Buttonholes?" Guttmann asks. "This guy makes buttonholes? What kind of business is that?"

LaPointe repeats one of the street's ancient jokes. "It would be a wonderful business, if Mr. Klein didn't have to provide the material."

Guttmann doesn't quite get it. He has no way of knowing that no one on the Main quite gets that joke either, but they always repeat it because it has the *sound* of something witty.

Each time they pass a bar, the smell of stale beer and cigarette smoke greets them for a second before it is blown away by the raw wind. Halfway up St. Laurent, LaPointe turns in at a run-down bar called Chez Pete's Place. It is fuggy and dark inside, and the proprietor doesn't bother to look up from the girlie magazine in his lap when the policemen enter.

Three men sit around a table in back, one a tall, boney tramp with a concave chest who has the shakes so badly that he is drinking his wine from a beer mug. The other two are arguing drunkenly across the table, pounding it sometimes, to the confused distress of the third.

"Floyd Patterson wasn't shit! He never . . . he couldn't . . . he wasn't shit, compared to Joe Louis."

"Ah, that's your story! Floyd Patterson had a great left. He had what you call one of your world's great lefts! He could hit . . . anything."

"Ah, he couldn't . . . he couldn't punch his way out of a wet paper bag! I used to know a guy who told me that he wasn't shit, compared to Joe Louis. You know . . . do you know what they used to call Joe Louis?"

"I don't care what they called him! I don't give a big rat's ass!"

"They used to call Joe Louis . . . Gentleman Joe. Gentleman Joe! What do you think of that?"

"Why?"

"What?"

"Why did they call him Gentleman Joe?"

"Why? Why? Because . . . because that Floyd Patterson couldn't punch worth shit, that's why. Ask anybody!"

LaPointe crosses to the group. "Has anyone seen Dirty-shirt Red today?"

They look at one another, each hoping the question is directed to someone else.

"You," LaPointe says to a little man with a narrow forehead and a large, stubbly Adam's apple.

"No, Lieutenant. I ain't seen him."

"He was in a couple hours ago," the other volunteers. "He asked around about the Vet." The name of this universally detested tramp brings grunts from several *bommes* at other tables. No one has any stomach for the Vet, with his uppity ways and his bragging.

"And what did he find out?"

"Not much, Lieutenant. We told him the Vet come in here late last night."

"How late?"

The proprietor lifts his head from the skin magazine and listens.

"Well?" LaPointe asks. "Was it after closing time?"

One of the tramps glances toward the owner. He doesn't want to get in trouble with the only bar that will let *bommes* come in. But nothing is as bad as getting in trouble with Lieutenant LaPointe. "Maybe a *little* after."

"Did he have money?"

"Yeah. He had a wad! His pension check must of come. He bought two bottles."

"Two bottles," another sneers. "And you know what that cheap bastard does? He gives one bottle to all of us to share, and he drinks the other all by hisself!"

"Potlickin' son of a bitch," says another without heat.

LaPointe crosses to the bar and speaks to the owner. "Did he seem to have money?"

"I don't sell on the cuff."

"Did he flash a roll?"

"He wasn't *that* drunk. Why? What did he do?"

LaPointe looks at the owner for a second. There is something disgusting about making your money off *bommes*. He reaches into his pocket and takes out some change. "Here. Give them a bottle."

111

The proprietor counts the change with his index finger. "Hey, this ain't enough."

"It's our treat. Yours and mine. We're going fifty-fifty."

The arrangement does not please the owner, but he reaches under the bar and grudgingly gets out a bottle of muscatel. By the time it touches the counter, one of the *bommes* has come over and picked it up.

"Hey, thanks, Lieutenant. I'll tell Red you're lookin' for him."

"He knows."

They have been wandering for an hour and a half, threading through the narrow streets that branch out from the Main, LaPointe stopping occasionally to go into a bar or café, or to exchange a word with someone on the street. Guttmann is beginning to think the Lieutenant has forgotten about the Vet and that young man stabbed in the alley last night. In fact, LaPointe is still on the lookout for Dirty-shirt Red and the Vet, but not to the exclusion of the rest of his duties. He never pursues only one thing at a time on his street, because if he did, all the other strings would get tangled, and he wouldn't know what everyone was up to, or hoping for, or worried about.

At this moment, LaPointe is talking with a fat woman with frizzy, bright orange hair. She leans out of a first-story window, her knobby elbows planted on the stone sill over which she has been shaking a dust mop in fine indifference to passers-by. From the tenor of their conversation, Guttmann takes it that she used to work the streets, and that she and LaPointe have a habit of exchanging bantering greetings on the basis of broad sexual baiting and suggestions on both sides that if they weren't so busy, they would each show the other what real lovemaking is. The woman seems well informed on events on the Main. No, she hasn't heard anything of the Vet, but she'll keep her ears open. As for Dirtyshirt Red, yes, that sniping bastard's been around, also looking for the Vet.

Guttmann can't believe she ever made a living selling herself. Her face is like an aged boxer's, a swollen, pulpy

112

look that is more accented than masked by thick rouge, a lipstick mouth larger than her real one, and long false eyelashes, one of which has come unstuck at the corner. As they walk on, he asks LaPointe about her.

"Her pimp did that to her face with a Coke bottle," LaPointe says.

"What happened to him?"

"He got beat up and warned to stay off the Main."

"Who beat him up?"

LaPointe shrugs.

"So what did she do after that?"

"Continued to work the street for a couple of years, until she got fat."

"Looking like that?"

"She was still young. She had a good-looking body. She worked drunks mostly. Hooch and hard-ons blind a man. She's a good sort. She does cleaning and scrubbing up for people. She takes care of Martin's house."

"Martin?"

"Father Martin. Local priest."

"*She* is the priest's housekeeper?"

"She's a hard worker."

Guttmann shakes his head. "If you say so."

Back on St. Laurent, they are slowed by the last of the pedestrian tangle. Snakes of European children with bookbags on their backs chase one another to the discomfort of the crowd. Small knots of sober-faced Chinese kids walk quickly and without chatting. Workingmen in coveralls stand outside their shops, taking last deep drags from cigarettes before flicking them into the gutter and going back to put in their time. Young, loud-voiced girls from the dress factory walk three abreast, singing and enjoying making the crowd break for them. Old women waddle along, string bags of groceries banging against their ankles. Clerks and tailors, their fragile bodies padded by thick overcoats, thread diffidently through the crowd, attempting to avoid contact. Traffic snarls; voices accuse and complain. Neon, noise, loneliness.

"Now that is something," Guttmann says, looking up at a sign above a shop featuring women's clothes:

The business is new, and it is located where a pizzeria used to be. The owners are greenhorns newly arrived on the Main. Older, established merchants refer to the shop as "the shmatteria."

"Shmatteria?" asks Guttmann.

"Yes. It's sort of a joke. You know . . . a pizzeria that sells *shmattes?*"

"I don't get it."

LaPointe frowns. That's the second time this kid hasn't gotten a street joke. You have to have affection for the street to get its jokes. "I thought you were Jewish," he says grumpily.

"Not in any real way. My grandfather was Jewish, but my father is a one-hundred-percent New World Canadian, complete with big handshake and a symbolic suntan he gets patched up twice a year in Florida. But what's this about . . . how do you say it?"

"Shmatteria. Forget it."

LaPointe does not remember that twenty-five years ago, when the now-established Jews first came to the Main, he did not know what a *shmatte* was either.

They climb up a dark flight of stairs with loose metal strips originally meant to provide grips for snow-caked shoes, but now a hazard in themselves. They enter one of the second-floor lounges that overlook St. Laurent. It is still early for trade, and the place is almost empty. An old woman mumbles to herself as she desultorily swings a mop into a dark corner by the jukebox. The only other people in the place are the bartender and one customer, a heavily rouged woman in white silk slacks.

LaPointe orders an Armagnac and sips it, looking down upon the street, where one-way northbound traffic is still heavy and the pedestrian flow is clogged. He has got off the street for a few minutes to give this most congested time of evening a chance to thin out. Friday night is noisy in the Main; there is a lot of drinking and laughter, some fighting, and the whores do good business. But there will be a quieter time between six and eight, when everyone seems to go home to change before coming back to chase after fun. Most people eat at home because it's cheaper than restaurants, and they want to save their money to drink and dance.

Guttmann sips his beer and glances back at the customer in conversation with the bartender. She seems both young and middle-aged at the same time, in a way Guttmann could not describe. A dark wig falls in long curls to the middle of her back. He particularly notices her hands, strong and expressive, despite the big dinner rings on every finger. There is something oddly attractive about those hands—competent. Periodically, the customer glances away from her talk and looks directly at Guttmann, her eyes frankly inquisitive without being coy.

As they walk back down the long stairs to the street, Guttmann says, "Not really what you'd call a bird."

"What?" LaPointe asks, his mind elsewhere.

"That barfly back there. Not exactly the chick type."

"No, I guess not. Women never go to that bar."

"Oh," Guttmann says, as soon as he figures it out. He blushes slightly when he remembers the expressive, competent hands covered with dinner rings.

It is nearing eight o'clock, and the pedestrian traffic is thickening again. Blocking the mouth of a narrow alley is a knife sharpener who plies his trade with close devotion. The stone wheel is rigged to his bicycle in such a way that the pedals can drive either the bicycle or the grinding stone. Sitting on the seat, with the rear wheel up on a rectangular stand, he pedals away, spinning his stone. The noise of the grinding and the arc of damp sparks attract the attention of passers-by, who glance once at him, then hurry on. The knife sharpener is tall and gaunt, and his oily hair, combed back in a stony pompadour, gives him the look of a Tartar. His nose is thin and hooked, and his eyes under their brooding brows concentrate on the knife he is working, on the spray of sparks he is making.

He pedals so hard that his face is wet with sweat, despite the cold. His thin back rounded over his work, his knees pumping up and down, his attention absorbed by the knife and the sparks, he does not seem to see LaPointe approaching.

"Well?" LaPointe says, knowing he has been noticed.

The Grinder does not lift his head, but his eyes roll to the side and he looks at LaPointe from beneath hooking eyebrows. "Hello, Lieutenant."

"How's it going?"

"All right. It's going all right." Suddenly the Grinder reaches out and stops the wheel by grabbing it with his long fingers. Guttmann winces as he sees the edge of the stone cut the web of skin between the Grinder's thumb and forefinger, but the old tramp doesn't seem to feel the pain or notice the blood. "It's coming, you know. It's coming."

"The snow?" LaPointe asks.

The Grinder nods gravely, his black eyes intense in their deep sockets. "And maybe sleet, Lieutenant. Maybe sleet! Nobody ever worries about it! Nobody thinks about it!" His eyebrows drop into a scowl of mistrust as he stares at Guttmann, his eyes burning. "You've never thought about it," he accuses.

"Ah . . . well, I . . ."

"Who knows," LaPointe says. "Maybe it won't snow this year. After all, it didn't snow last year, or the year before."

The Grinder's eyes flick back and forth in confusion. "Didn't it?"

"Not a flake. Don't you remember?"

The Grinder frowns in a painful bout of concentration. "I . . . think . . . I remember. Yes. Yes, that's right!" A sudden kick with his leg, and the wheel is spinning again. "That's right. Not a flake!" He presses the knife to the stone and sparks spray out and fall on Guttmann's shoes.

LaPointe drops a dollar into the Grinder's basket, and the two policemen turn back down the street.

Guttmann squeezes between two pedestrians and catches up with LaPointe. "Did you notice that knife, Lieutenant? Sharpened down to a sliver."

LaPointe guesses what the young man is thinking. He thrusts out his lower lip and shakes his head. "No. He's

116

been on the Main for years. Used to be a roofer. Then one day when the slates were covered with snow, he took a bad fall. That's why he fears the snow. People on the street give him a little something now and then. He's too proud to beg like the other *bommes*, so they give him old knives to sharpen. They never get them back. He forgets who gave them to him, and he sharpens them until there's nothing left." LaPointe cuts across the street. "Come on. One more loop and we'll call it a night."

"Got a heavy date?" Guttmann asks.

LaPointe stops and turns to him. "Why do you ask that?"

"Ah . . . I don't know. I just thought . . . Friday night and all. I mean, I've got a date tonight myself."

"That's wonderful." LaPointe turns and continues his beat crawl, occasionally making little detours into the networks of side streets. He tests the locks on iron railings. He taps on the steamy window of a Portuguese grocery and waves at the old man. He stops to watch two men carrying a trunk down a long wooden stoop, until it becomes clear that they are helping a young couple move out, to the accompaniment of howls and profanity from a burly hag who seems to think the couple owe her money.

They are walking on an almost empty side street when a man half a block ahead turns and starts to cross the street quickly.

"Scheer!" LaPointe shouts. Several people stop and look, startled. Then they walk on hurriedly. The man has frozen in his tracks, but there is a kinesthetic energy in his posture, as though he would run . . . if he dared. LaPointe raises a hand and beckons with the forefinger. Reluctantly, Scheer crosses back and approaches the Lieutenant. In the forced swagger of his walk, and in his mod clothes, he is very much the dandy.

"What did I tell you when I saw you in that bar last night, Scheer?"

"Oh, come on, Lieutenant . . ." There is an oily purr to his voice.

"All right," LaPointe says with bored fatigue. "Get on that wall."

With a long-suffering sigh, Scheer turns to the tenement wall and spread-eagles against it. He knows how to do it; he's done it before. He tries to avoid letting his clothes touch the dirty brick.

Guttmann stands by, unsure what to do, as LaPointe kicks out one of Scheer's feet to broaden the spread, then runs a rapid pat down. "All right. Off the wall. Take off your overcoat."

"Listen, Lieutenant . . ."

"Off!"

Three children emerge from nowhere to watch, as Scheer tugs his overcoat off and folds it carefully before holding it out to LaPointe, each movement defiantly slow.

LaPointe chucks the coat onto the stoop. "Now empty your pockets."

Scheer does so and holds out the comb, change, wallet, and bits of paper to LaPointe.

"Drop all that trash down into the basement well there," LaPointe orders.

His mouth tight with hate, Scheer lets his belongings fall into the well fenced off by a wrought-iron railing. The wallet makes a splat because the bottom of the well is covered with an inch of sooty water.

"Now take out your shoelaces and give them to me."

By now the onlookers have grown to a dozen, two of them girls in their twenties who giggle as Scheer hops to maintain balance while tugging the laces out of the last pair of grommets. Petulantly, he hands them to LaPointe.

The Lieutenant puts them into his pocket. "All right, Scheer. After I leave, you can climb down and get your rubbish. I'll keep the shoelaces. It's for your own good. I wouldn't want you to get despondent over being embarrassed in public and try to hang yourself with them."

"Tell me! Tell me, Lieutenant! What have I ever done to you?"

"You're on the street. I told you to stay off it. I wasn't giving you a vacation, asshole. It was a punishment."

"I know my rights! Who are you, God or something? You don't *own* the fucking street!" He would never have

118

gone that far if there hadn't been the pressure of the crowd and the need to save face.

LaPointe's eyes crinkle in a melancholy smile, and he nods slowly. Then his hand flashes out and his slap sends Scheer spinning along the railing. One of the loose shoes comes off.

LaPointe turns and strolls up the street, followed after a moment by the stunned and confused Guttmann.

"What was all that about, Lieutenant?" Guttmann asks. "Who is that guy?"

"No one. A pimp. I ordered him off the street."

"But . . . if he's done something, why don't you pick him up?"

"I have. Several times. But his lawyers always get him off."

"Yes, but . . ." Guttmann looks over his shoulder at the small knot of people around the pimp, who is just climbing out of the dirty basement well. The girls laugh as he tries to walk with his loose shoes flopping. He takes them off and carries them, walking tenderly in his stocking feet.

"But, sir . . . isn't that harassment?"

LaPointe stops and looks at the young officer appraisingly, his glance shifting from eye to eye. "Yes. It's harassment."

They walk on.

Guttmann sits alone in a small Greek café on Rue Cerat, cramped in a space that would be adequate for a man of average size. The place has only two oilcloth-covered tables crowded against the window, across from a glass-fronted display case containing cheese, oil, and olives for sale. A fly-specked sign on the wall says:

7-UP—CA RAVIGOTE

While LaPointe is telephoning from a booth attached to the outside of the café, Guttmann is trying to work out a problem in his mind. He knows what he has to do, but he

119

doesn't know how to do it. He has been withdrawn since the incident with Scheer half an hour before. Everything he believes in, everything he has learned, combine to make LaPointe's treatment of that pimp intolerable. Guttmann cannot accept the concept of the policeman as judge—much less as executioner—and he knows what he would have to do should Scheer bring a complaint against the Lieutenant. Further, his sense of fair play demands that he warn LaPointe of his decision, and that will not be easy.

When the Lieutenant returns from the telephone booth a girl of eighteen or nineteen comes from the back room to serve them little cups of strong coffee, her eyes always averted with a shyness that advertises her awareness of men and of her own sexual attractiveness. She has long black lashes and the comfortable beauty of a Madonna.

"How's your mother?" LaPointe asks.

"Fine. She's in back. Want me to call her?"

"No. I'll see her next time I drop by."

The girl lets her damp brown eyes settle briefly on Guttmann, who smiles and nods. She glances away sidewards, lowers her eyes, and returns to the back room.

"Pretty girl," Guttmann says. "Pity she's so shy."

LaPointe grunts noncommittally. Years ago, the mother was a streetwalker on the Main. She was a lusty, laughing woman always in good spirits, always with a coarse joke to tell, pushing her elbow into your ribs with the punch line. When, every month or two, LaPointe felt the need for a woman, she was usually the one he went with.

Then suddenly she was off the street. She had got pregnant; by a lover, of course, not a customer. With the birth of the child, she changed completely. She began to dress less flashily; she looked for work; she started attending church. She didn't often laugh, but she smiled a lot. And she devoted herself to her baby girl, like a child playing dolls. She borrowed a little money from LaPointe, who also countersigned her note, and she put a down payment on this back-street café. At five dollars a week, she paid LaPointe back, never missing a payment except around Christmas, when she was buying presents for her girl.

They never made love again, but he made it a habit to drop in occasionally during quiet times. They used to sit together by the window and talk while they drank cups of thick Greek coffee. He would listen as she went on about her daughter. It was amazing what that child could do. Talk. Run. And draw? An artist! The mother had plans. The girl would go to university and become a fashion designer. Have you ever seen her drawings? How can I tell you? Taste? You wouldn't believe it. Never pink and red together.

While in high school, this girl became pregnant. At first the mother couldn't understand . . . couldn't believe it. Then she was crazy with fury. She would kill that boy! She had an acrimonious shout-down with the boy and his parents. No, the boy would not marry her. And here's why . . .

The next time LaPointe dropped in, the woman had changed. She was lifeless, dull, vacant. They took coffee together in the empty café, the woman looking out the window as she talked, her voice flat and tired. The girl had a reputation in high school for being a hot box. She made love with anybody, any time, anywhere—down in the boiler room, once in the boys' lavatory. Everybody knew about it. She was a slut. She wasn't even a whore! She gave it away!

LaPointe tried to comfort her. She'll get married one of these days. Everything will be all right.

No. It was a punishment from God. He's punishing me for being a whore.

"Good-looking girl," Guttmann says. "Pity she's so shy."

"Yes," LaPointe says. "A pity." He swirls his cup to suspend the thick coffee dust and finishes it off, sucking it through a cube of sugar pressed against the roof of his mouth. "Look, I just called in to the QG to have them pick up the Vet."

"Lieutenant . . . ?"

"We can't wait forever for Dirtyshirt Red. When they find him, they'll call you. When they do, get down there

121

immediately. If he's not too drunk to talk, call me and I'll come down."

"You told them to call *me?*"

"Sure. You're here to get experience, aren't you?"

"Well, yes, but . . ."

"But what?"

"I have a date tonight. I told you."

"That's too bad."

Guttmann takes a deep breath. "Lieutenant?"

"Yes?"

"About that pimp back there?"

"Scheer? What about him?"

"Well, if I'm going to be working with you . . ."

"I wouldn't say you're working with me. It's more like you're following me around."

"Okay. Whatever. But I'm here, and I feel I have to be straight with you." Guttmann feels awkward looking into LaPointe's hooded, paternal eyes. He's sure he's going to end up making an ass of himself.

"If you have something to say, say it," LaPointe orders.

"All right. About the pimp. It's not right to harass a civilian like that. It's not legal. He has rights, whoever he is, whatever he's done. Harassment is the kind of stuff that gives the force a bad name."

"I'm sure the Commissioner would agree with you."

"That doesn't make me wrong."

"It goes a ways."

Guttmann nods and looks down. "You're not going to give me a chance to say what I want to say, are you? You're making it as hard as possible."

"I'll say it for you if you want. You're going to tell me that if this asshole brings charges against me, you feel that you would have to corroborate. Right?"

Guttmann forces himself not to look away from La-Pointe's eyes with their expression of tired amusement. He knows what the Lieutenant is thinking: he's young. When he gets some experience under his belt, he'll come around. But Guttmann is sure he will never come around. He would quit the force before that happened. "That's right,"

122

he says, no quaver at all in his voice. "I'd have to corroborate."

LaPointe nods. "I told you he was a pimp, didn't I?"

"Yes, sir. But that's not the point."

That was what Resnais kept saying: that's not the point.

"Besides," Guttmann continues, "there are lots of women working the streets. You don't seem to hassle them."

"That's different. They're pros. And they're adults."

Guttmann's eyes flicker at this last. "You mean Scheer uses . . ."

"That's right. Kids. Junk-hungry kids. And if I deny him the use of the street, he can't run his kids."

"Why don't you take him in?"

"I *have* taken him in. I told you. It doesn't do any good. He walks back out again the same day. Pimping is hard to prove, unless the girls give evidence. And they're afraid to. He's promised that if they talk, they'll get their faces messed up."

Guttmann tips up his cup and looks into the dark sludge at the bottom. Still . . . even with a pimp who runs kids . . . a cop can't be a judge and executioner. Principles don't change, even when the case in hand makes it tough to maintain them.

LaPointe examines the young man's earnest, troubled face. "What do you think of the Main?" he asks, lifting the pressure by changing the subject.

Guttmann looks up. "Sir?"

"My patch. What do you think of it? You must realize that I've been dragging you around, giving you the grand tour."

"I don't know what I think of it. It's . . . interesting."

"Interesting?" LaPointe looks out the window, watching the passers-by. "Yes, I suppose so. Of course, you get a warped idea of the street when you walk it as a cop. You see mostly the hustlers, the *fous*, the toughs, the whores, the *bommes*. You get what Gaspard calls a turd's-eye view. Ninety percent of the people up here are no worse than anywhere else. Poorer, maybe. Dumber. Weaker. But not worse." LaPointe rubs his hair with his palm and sits back in his chair. "You know . . . a funny thing happened eight or ten years ago. I was doing the street, and I happened to be walking behind a man—must have been seventy years old—a man who moved in a funny way. It's hard to explain; I felt I knew him, but I didn't, of course. It wasn't *how* he looked at things; it was *what* he looked at. You know what I mean?"

"Yes, sir," lies Guttmann.

"Well, he stopped off for coffee, and I sat down next to him. We started talking, and it turned out that he was a retired cop from New York. *That* was what I had recognized without knowing it—his beatwalker's way of looking at things only an old cop would look at: door locks, shoes, telephone booths with broken panes, that sort of thing. He had come up here because his granddaughter was marrying a Canadian and the wedding was in Montreal. He got tired of sitting around making small talk with people he didn't know, so he wandered off, and he ended up on the Main. He told me that he felt a real pang, walking these streets. It reminded him of New York in the twenties—the different languages, the small shops, workers and hoods and chippies and housewives and kids all mixed up on the same street but not afraid of one another. He said it used to be like that in New York when the immigrants were still coming in. But it isn't like that anymore. It's a closed-up frightened city at night. Not even the cops walk around alone. We're about thirty years behind New York in that way. And as long as I'm on the Main, we are never going to catch up."

Guttmann imagines that all this has something to do with the harassment of that pimp, but he doesn't see just how.

"Okay," LaPointe says, stretching his back. "So if Scheer makes a complaint, you'll back him up."

"Yes, sir. I would have to."

LaPointe nods. "I suppose you would. Well, I have some grocery shopping to do. You'd better get home and get something to eat. Chances are they'll pick up the Vet tonight, and we may be up late."

LaPointe rises and tugs on his overcoat, while Guttmann sits there feeling—not defeated exactly in this business of Scheer, but undercut, bypassed.

"What's wrong?" LaPointe asks, looking down at him.

"Oh . . . I was just thinking about this date I've got for tonight. I hate to break it, because it's the first time we've been out together."

"Oh, she'll understand. Make up some lie. Tell her you're a cop."

LaPointe braces one of the grocery bags against the wall of the hall and gropes in his pocket for his key. Then it occurs to him that he ought to knock. There is no answer. He taps again. No response.

His first sensation is a sinking in his stomach, like a fast down elevator stopping. Almost immediately, the feeling retreats and something safer replaces it: ironic self-amusement. He smiles at himself—dumb old man—and shakes his head as he inserts his key in the slack lock and pushes the door open.

The lights are on. And she is there.

She is wearing Lucille's pink quilted dressing gown, which she must have gotten from the closet where Lucille's things still hang.

Lucille's dressing gown.

She is sitting on the sofa, one foot tucked up under her butt, sewing something, the threaded needle poised in the air. Her mouth is slightly open, her eyes alert.

"Oh, it's you," she says. "I didn't answer because I thought it might be the landlord. I mean . . . he might not like the idea of your having a girl in your apartment."

"I see." He carries the groceries into the narrow kitchen. She sets her sewing down and follows him.

"Here," he says. "Unwrap the cheese and let the air get to it."

"Okay. I've been walking around quietly so no one would hear me."

"You don't have to worry about that. Just set the cheese on a plate."

"Which plate?"

"Any one. It doesn't matter."

"Doesn't the landlord care if you have girls up here?"

LaPointe laughs. "I *am* the landlord." This is true, although he never thinks of himself as a landlord. Seven years after Lucille's death, he heard that the building was going to be sold. He was used to living there, and he could not quite grasp what it would mean to move away from their home, Lucille's and his—what that would imply. Because there was nothing to spend it on, he had saved a little money, so he arranged a long-term mortgage and bought the building. Just two years ago, he made the last payment. He had become so used to making out the mortgage check each month that he was surprised when it was returned to him with the notification that the mortgage was paid off. The other tenants—there are three—do not know he owns the building, because he arranged to have the bank receive their rents and credit them to his debt. He did this out of a kind of shame. His concept of "the landlord" was fashioned in the slums of Trois Rivières, and he doesn't care for the thought of being one himself.

Marie-Louise sits at the kitchen table, her elbow on the oilcloth, her chin in her hand, watching him tear up the lettuce for their salad. He has planned a simple meal: steak, salad, bread, wine. And cheese for dessert.

"It's funny seeing a man cook," she says. "Do you always cook for yourself?"

"I eat in restaurants, mostly. On Sundays I cook. I enjoy it for a change."

"Hm-m." She doesn't know what to make of it. She never met anybody who enjoyed cooking. God knows her mother didn't. It occurs to her that this old guy might be a queer. Maybe that's why he didn't make love to her last night. "What kind of work do you do?"

"I'm with the police." He says this with a shrug meant to shunt away any fear she might have of the police.

"Oh." She's not very interested in what he does.

He puts the salad bowl on the table before her. "Here. Make yourself useful. Mix this." The skillet is smoking, and the steaks hiss and sizzle as he drops them in. "What did you do today?" he asks, his voice strained because he is standing tiptoe, looking in the cupboard for an extra plate and glass.

"Nothing. I just sat around. Mended some things. And I took another bath. Is that all right?"

"Of course. No, you don't stir a salad. You toss it. Like this. See?"

"What difference does it make?" There is annoyance in her voice. She could never do anything right in her mother's kitchen either.

"It's the way it's done, that's all. Here, let's see." He lifts her chin with his palm. "Ah. That eye is looking better. Swelling's gone." She is not a pretty girl, but her face is alert and expressive. "Well." He takes his hand away and turns to cut the bread. "So you sat around and mended all day?"

"I went out shopping. Made breakfast. I borrowed that coat from your closet when I went out. It was cold. But I put it back again."

"Did it fit?"

"Not bad. You should have seen the man at the grocery look at me!" She laughs, remembering what she looked like in that coat. Her laughter is enthusiastic and vulgar. As before, it stops suddenly in mid-rise and is gone.

"Why did he look at you?" LaPointe asks, smiling along with her infectious laughter.

"I guess I looked funny in an old woman's coat."

He pauses and frowns, not understanding. She must mean an old-fashioned coat. It is not an old woman's coat; it was a young woman's coat. He attends to the steaks.

"There isn't much to do around here," she says frankly. "You don't have any magazines. You don't have TV."

"I have a radio."

"I tried it. It doesn't work."

"You have to jiggle the knob."

"Why don't you get it fixed?"

"Why bother? I know how to jiggle the knob. Okay, let's eat. I think everything's ready."

She eats rapidly, like a hungry child, but twice she

127

remembers her manners and tells him it's good. And she drinks her wine too fast.

"I'll do the dishes," she offers afterwards. "That's something I know how to do."

"You don't have to." But the thought of her puttering around in the kitchen is pleasant. "All right, if you want to. I'll make the coffee while you're washing up."

There isn't really enough room for two in the narrow kitchen, and three times they touch shoulders. Each time, he says, "Excuse me."

". . . so I thought I might as well try Montreal. I mean, I had to go somewhere, so why not here? I was hoping I could get a job . . . maybe as a cocktail waitress. They make lots of money, you know. I had a girlfriend who wrote me about the tips."

"But you didn't find anything?"

She is curled up on the sofa, Lucille's pink quilted robe around her; he sits in his comfortable old chair. She shakes her head and looks away from him, toward the hissing gas fire. "No, I didn't. I tried everywhere for a couple of weeks, until I ran out of money. But the cocktail bars didn't want a cripple. And my boobs are small." She says this last matter-of-factly. She knows how it is in the world. Yet there is some wistfulness in it, or fatigue.

"So you started working the street."

She shrugs. "It was sort of an accident, really. I mean, I never thought of screwing for money. Of course, I had screwed men before. Back home. But just friends and guys who took me out on dates. Just for fun."

"Don't use that word." LaPointe knows that no daughter of his would ever use that word.

Marie-Louise cocks her head thoughtfully, trying to think back to the offending word. With her head cocked and her frizzy mop of hair, she has the look of a Raggedy Ann doll. "Screw?" she asks, uncertain. "What should I say?"

"I don't know. Making love. Something like that."

She grins, her elastic face impish. "That sounds funny. *Making love.* It sounds like the movies."

128

"But still . . ."

"Okay. Well, I never thought of . . . doing it . . . for money. I guess I didn't think anyone would pay for it."

LaPointe shakes his head. *Doing it* sounds worse yet.

"Well, I stayed with some people for a while. All people of my age, sort of living together in this big old house. But then I had a fight with the guy who sort of ran everything, and I moved to a room. Then I ran out of money and they kicked me out. They kept most of my clothes and my suitcase. That's why I don't have a coat. Anyway, I was kicked out, and I was just walking around. Scared, sort of, and trying to think of what to do . . . where I could go. See, it was cold. Well, I ended up at the bus station and I sat around most of the night, trying to look like I was waiting for a bus, so they wouldn't kick me out. But this guard kept eyeing me. I only had that shopping bag for my clothes, so I guess he knew I wasn't really waiting for a bus. And then this guy comes up to me and just straight out asks me. Just like that. He said he would give me ten dollars. He was sort of . . ." She decides not to say that.

"Sort of what?"

"Well . . . he wasn't young. Anyway, he brought me to his apartment. He came in his pants while he was feeling me up. But he paid anyway."

"That was good of him."

"Yeah," she agrees with a frankness that undercuts his irony. "It *was* sort of good of him, wasn't it? I didn't know that at the time, because I hadn't been around, and I thought everyone was like him. Nice, you know. He let me stay the night; and the next morning he bought me breakfast. Most of the others weren't like that. They try to cheat you out of your money. Or they say you can spend the night, but when they've had all they want, they kick you out. And if you make a fuss, sometimes they try to beat you up. Some of them really get a kick out of beating you up." She touches her eye with her fingertips. The swelling is gone, but a faint green stain remains. "You know what you have to do?" she confides seriously. "You have to get your money before he starts. A girl I went around with for a while told me that. And she was right."

"That was how long ago? When this old man picked you up?"

She thinks back. "Six weeks. Two months, maybe."

"And since then you've been getting along by selling yourself?"

She grins. That sounds even funnier than *making love*. "It's not so bad, you know? Guys take me to bars and I eat in restaurants. And I go dancing." She tucks her short leg up under her. "You might not think it, but I can dance real well. It's funny, but I can dance better than I can walk, you know what I mean? I like dancing more than anything. Do you dance?"

"No."

"Why not?"

"I don't know how."

She laughs. "Everyone knows how! There's nothing to know. You just sort of . . . you know . . . *move*."

"It sounds like you had nothing but fun on the streets."

"You say that like you don't believe it. But it's true. Most of the time I had fun. Except when they got rough. Or when they wanted me to do . . . funny things. I don't know why, but I'm just not ready for that. The thought makes me gag, you know? Hey, what's wrong?"

He shakes his head. "Nothing."

"Does it bother you when I talk about it?"

"Nothing. Never mind."

"Some guys like it. I mean, they like you to talk about it. It gets them going."

"Forget it!"

She ducks involuntarily and lifts her arms as though to fend off a slap. Her father used to slap her. When the adrenalin of sudden fright drains off, it is followed by offense and anger. "What the hell's wrong with you?" she demands.

He takes a deep breath. "Nothing. I'm sorry. It's just . . ."

Her voice is stiff with petulance. "Well, Jesus Christ, you'd think a cop would be used to that sort of thing."

"Yes, of course, but . . ." He rolls his hand. "Tell me. How old are you?"

She readjusts herself on the sofa, but she doesn't relax. "Twenty-two. And you?"

"Fifty-two. No, three." He wants to return to the calm of their earlier conversation, so he explains unnecessarily, "I just had a birthday last month, but I always forget about it."

She cannot imagine anyone forgetting a birthday, but she supposes it's different when you're old. He is acting nice again. Her instinct tells her that he is genuinely sorry for frightening her. This would be the time to take advantage of his regret and make some arrangements.

"Can I stay here again tonight?"

"Of course. You can stay longer, if you want."

Push it now. "How much longer?"

He shrugs. "I don't know. How long do you want to stay?"

"Would we . . . make love?" She cannot help saying these last words with a comic, melodramatic tone.

He doesn't answer.

"Don't you like women?"

He smiles. "No, it isn't that."

"Well, why do you want me to stay, if you don't want to sleep with me?"

LaPointe looks down at the park, where a tracery of black branches intersects the yellow globes of the streetlamps. This Marie-Louise is the same age as Lucille—the Lucille of his memory—and she speaks with the same downriver accent. And she wears the same robe. But she is younger than the daughters he daydreams about, the daughters who are sometimes still little girls, but more often grown women with children of their own. Come to think of it, the daughters of his daydreams are sometimes older than Lucille. Lucille never ages, always looks the same. It never before occurred to him that the daughters are older than their mother. That's crazy.

"What's wrong?" she asks.

"I'll tell you what. I'll look around and see if I can find you a job."

"In a cocktail bar?"

"I can't promise that. Maybe as a waitress in a restaurant."

She wrinkles her nose. That doesn't appeal to her at all. She has seen lots of waitresses, running around and being shouted at during rush times, or standing, tired and bored, and staring out of windows when the place is empty. And the uniforms always look frumpy. If it weren't for this damned pig weather, and if the men never tried to beat you up, she'd rather go on like she is than be a waitress.

"I'll try to find you a job," he says. "Meanwhile you can stay here, if you want."

"And we'll sleep together?" She wants to get the conditions straight at the beginning. It is something like making sure you get your money in advance.

He turns from the window and settles his eyes on her. "Do you really want to?"

She shrugs a "why not?" Then she discovers a loose thread on the sleeve of the dressing gown. She tries to break it off.

He clears his throat and rubs his cheek with his knuckles. "I need a shave." He rises. "Would you like another coffee before we go to bed?"

She looks up at him through her mop of hair, the errant thread between her teeth. "Okay," she says, nipping off the thread and spitting out the bit.

He is shaving when the phone rings.

He has to wipe the lather from his cheek before putting the receiver to his ear. "LaPointe."

Guttmann's voice sounds tired. "I just got down here."

"Down where?"

"The Quartier Général. They called me at my apartment. They've picked up your Sinclair, and he's giving them one hell of a time."

"Sinclair?"

"Joseph Michael Sinclair. That's the real name of your bum, the Vet. He's in a bad way. Raving. Screaming. They're talking about giving him a sedative, but I told

132

them to hold off in case you wanted to question him to-night."

"No, not tonight. Tomorrow will do."

"I don't know, sir . . ."

"Of course you don't know. That's part of being a Joan."

"What I was going to say was, this guy's a real case. It's taking two men to hold him down. He keeps screaming that he can't go into a cell. Something about being a claustrophobic."

"Oh, for Christ's sake!"

"Just thought you ought to know."

LaPointe's shoulders slump, and he lets out a long nasal sigh. "All right. You talk to the Vet. Tell him nobody's going to lock him up. Tell him I'll be down in a little while. He knows me."

"Yes, sir. Oh, and sir? Terribly sorry to disturb you at home."

What? Sarcasm from a Joan? LaPointe grunts and hangs up.

Marie-Louise is mending the paisley granny dress she was wearing when he found her in the park. She looks up questioningly when he enters the living room.

"I have to go downtown. What are you smiling at?"

"You've got soap on one side of your face."

"Oh." He wipes it off.

As he tugs on his overcoat, he remembers the coffee water steaming away on the stove. "Shall I make you a cup before I go?"

She shakes her head. "I don't really like coffee all that much."

"Why do you always drink it then?"

She shrugs. She doesn't know. She takes what's offered.

133

6

By the thermometer it is not so cold as last night, but that
was a dry cold, crystallizing on surfaces, and this is a damp
cold, the serrate edge of which penetrates to LaPointe's
chest as he walks down the deserted Main. He does not
find a cruising taxi until Sherbrooke.

LaPointe's footfalls clip hollowly along the empty,
half-lit halls outside the magistrates' courts. The sound is
oddly loud and melancholy, without the covering envelope
of noise that fills the building during the day.

The elevator doors open, and he walks down the
brightly lit corridor of the Duty Office. There is sound and
life here: the stuttering clack of a typewriter in clumsy
hands; the hum of fluorescent lights; and somewhere a
transistor radio plays popular music.

Guttmann steps into the hall at the sound of the elevator. He looks unkempt and haggard; more like a real cop,
LaPointe thinks.

"Good morning, sir. He's in here." Guttmann's tone is
flat and unfriendly.

"What the hell's wrong with you?" LaPointe asks.

135

"Sir?"

"Your attitude, tone of voice. What's wrong?"

"I didn't know it showed, sir."

"It shows. I warned you to cancel that date of yours."

"I did, sir. She went to a film with a friend. But she dropped by later for a drink. We live in the same apartment building."

"And the call got you out of bed?"

"Something like that."

"At an awkward time?"

"As awkward as it gets, sir."

LaPointe laughs. Guttmann recognizes the comic possibilities of the situation, but he doesn't find this particular case funny.

LaPointe enters the Duty Office, Guttmann following. Joseph Michael "the Vet" Sinclair is sitting on a wooden bench against the wall. His long arms are wrapped around his legs, his face is pressed against his knees, and he still wears his ridiculous floppy-brimmed hat. He rocks himself back and forth in misery, humming or moaning one note over and over again. His grip on reality seems fragile. Occasionally he looks around the room, bewildered and frightened, and his teeth begin to chatter, his breath comes in canine sniffs, and he struggles against screaming.

LaPointe's nostrils dilate with the stench of urine. Joseph Michael Sinclair has wet himself.

The symptoms resemble withdrawal. LaPointe has seen this once before. The Vet is a victim of claustrophobia. The Duty Office is a big room, so that isn't what is eroding his sanity. It was the trip down in a police car and, even more, the thought of being locked up in a cell. The Vet is trapped in the classic terrible cycle facing the claustrophobic: he is almost mad with the fear of being shut up, and if he gives way to his madness, they will lock him up.

"Where did you pick him up?" LaPointe asks one of the officers getting coffee at the dispensing machine, a tough Polish old-timer who never bothered to take his sergeant's examinations because he doesn't want the hassle of responsibility. Although his French is thin and badly accented, he has always been accepted by the French Canadian cops as one of them, because he so obviously is not one of the others.

The coffee is hot, and the Polish cop winces as he changes the paper cup from hand to hand, looking for a place to set it down. His gestures are comically delicate, because the paper cup is fragile. He manages to balance it on a ledge and snaps his fingers violently. "Jesus H. Christ! We picked him up on St. Urbain, just south of Van Horne. Somebody named Red phoned in the tip. He gave us one hell of a chase. Took off across Van Horne, hopping like a gimpy rabbit! Right through the traffic! Cars and trucks hitting their brakes! Scared the shit out of the drivers. Their assholes must of bit chunks out of the car seats. And there I am, right after him, dancing and dodging through the traffic. Then your friend here climbs the fence and is halfway down the bank into the freight yard before I get to him. Look at that, will you?" He reaches around and tugs out the slack in the seat of his pants, showing a triangular rip. "Got that climbing the goddamned wire fence after the son of a bitch! Twenty-seven bucks shot in the ass!"

"Literally," Guttmann says.

"What?" the Polish cop demands.

"Did he give you any trouble?" LaPointe asks.

"Any trouble? Wild as a cat crapping razor blades, that's all! You wouldn't know it to see him now, but it took both of us to get him into the car. Kick? Wriggle? Scream? You'da thought we were gang-banging the Mother Superior."

LaPointe looks over at the miserable *bomme* whose eyes are now squeezed shut as he rocks back and forth, with each movement moaning a high, thin note that stops short in his throat. He is right on the limen of sanity.

"You didn't give him anything to calm him down, did you?"

"No, Lieutenant. Your Joan told us not to. Anyway, it wasn't necessary. As soon as we told him you were coming down, he settled right down. Just started moaning and rocking like that. A real nut case. Twenty-fucking-seven bucks! And not a month old!"

LaPointe crosses to the Vet and places his hand on his

shoulder. "Hey?" He gives him a slight shake. "Hey, Vet?"

The tramp does not look up; he is lost in the treacherous animal comfort of his rocking and moaning. His own motion and his own sound surround and protect him. He doesn't want penetrations from the outside.

LaPointe has seen men go inside themselves like this before. He is afraid he'll lose the Vet if he doesn't bring him out right now. He takes off the wide-brimmed hat and lifts up the head by the hair. "Hey!"

The *bomme* tries to pull away, but LaPointe holds the hair tighter. "Vet? Vet!" The smell of urine is strong.

The Vet's vague humid eyes focus slowly on La-Pointe's face. The slack, unshaven cheeks quiver. As he opens his mouth to speak, a bubble of thick spit forms between the lips and bursts with the first word.

"Lieutenant?" It is a pitiful, mendicant whine. "Don't let them lock me up. You know what I mean? I can't be locked up! I can't! I . . . I . . . I . . . I . . . I . . ." With each repetition, the voice rises a note as the Vet plunges toward panic.

LaPointe snatches the greasy hair. He mustn't lose him. "Vet! No one's going to lock you up!"

"No, you don't! I can't go inside! I can't!"

"Listen to me!"

"No! No! No!"

LaPointe slaps the tramp's cheek hard.

The Vet catches his breath and holds it, his cheeks bulging, his eyes wide open and staring up obliquely at the Lieutenant.

"Now listen," LaPointe says more quietly. "Just listen," he says softly. "All right?"

The Vet lets his breath escape slowly and remains silent, but his eyes still stare, and there are rapid little pupillary contractions.

LaPointe speaks very slowly and clearly. "No one is going to lock you up. Do you understand that? No one is going to put you inside."

The *bomme*'s squinting left eye twitches as he struggles to comprehend. As understanding comes, his body, so long rigid, droops with fatigue; his jaw slackens; his breathing slows; and the bloodshot eyes roll up as though in sleep.

LaPointe releases the hair, and the tramp's chin drops back into his chest. LaPointe lays his hand protectively on the nape of the Vet's neck as he turns to Guttmann. "Get some coffee down him."

Guttmann looks around for a coffeepot.

"The machine!" LaPointe says with exasperation, pointing to the coin-operated dispenser.

The two uniformed cops leave the Duty Office, the Polish old-timer fiddling with the back of his pants to see if he can hide the triangular rip, and his partner assuring him that nobody wants to look at his ass.

LaPointe leans against the wall and presses down his hair with his palm. "After you get a few cups of coffee down him," he tells Guttmann, "dunk his head in cold water and clean him up a little. Then bring him to my office."

Guttmann fumbles in his pocket as he looks with distaste at the heap of rags stinking of stale wine and urine. "I'm sorry, sir. I don't seem to have a dime."

"The machine takes quarters."

"I don't have any change at all."

With infinite patience, LaPointe produces a quarter from the depths of his overcoat pocket and holds it up between thumb and forefinger. "Here. This is called a quarter. It makes vending machines work. It also makes telephones work. What would you do if you had to make an emergency call from a public phone and you had no change on you?"

"I just threw on my clothes and came over when they called. I didn't even—"

"*Always* carry change for the phone. It could save somebody's life."

Guttmann takes the quarter. "All right, sir. Thanks for the advice."

"That wasn't advice."

Guttmann shoves the quarter into the slot brusquely. What the hell is bugging the Lieutenant? After all, *he* wasn't the one who was called away from a night with a bird to come down and wet-nurse a drunk who has pissed his pants!

As he starts to leave the Duty Office for his own floor above, LaPointe pauses at the door. He sniffs and rubs his cheek. He is shaven on only one side. "Look. I'm sorry, I . . . I'm tired, that's all."

"Yes, sir. We're probably all tired."

"Did you say it was your first time with that young lady of yours?"

"First for sure. And probably last." Guttmann is still angry and stung.

"Well, I hope not."

"Yes, sir. Me too."

It is fully half an hour before the door to LaPointe's office opens and Guttmann enters, bringing the Vet along by the arm. The old *bomme* looks pale and sick, but sober. Sober enough, at least. The shapeless old overcoat has been left behind, along with the wide-brimmed hat, and the collar and front of his shirt are wet from the dunking Guttmann has given him in a washbowl of the men's room. The hair is wet and dripping, and it has been raked back with fingers that left greasy black ropes. There is a small bruise over the eyebrow, half covered by a hank of hair plastered on the forehead.

"You hit him?" LaPointe asks.

"No, sir. He clipped his head on the edge of the washbowl."

"Do you have any idea what a lawyer would make of that? A lot more than harassment." LaPointe turns his attention to the *bomme*. "Okay, sit down, Vet."

The old tramp obeys sullenly. Now that his first panic is over, something of his haughty sassiness returns, and he attempts to appear indifferent and superior, despite the stink of urine that moves with him.

"Feeling better?" LaPointe asks.

The Vet does not answer. He lifts his head and looks unsteadily at LaPointe down his thin, bent nose. The intended disdain is diluted by an uncontrollable wobbling of the head.

LaPointe has never liked the Vet. He pities him, but the Vet is one of those men toward whom feelings of pity are always mixed with contempt, even disgust.

"Got a smoke?" the Vet asks.

"No." Once the Vet begins to feel safe, he'll be impossible to deal with. It's best to keep him from getting too confident. "I told you we weren't going to put you inside," LaPointe says, leaning back in his chair. "I'd better be straight with you. It's not really settled yet. You may be locked up, and you may not."

With almost comic abruptness, the tramp's composure shatters. His eyes flicker like a rodent's, and his breath starts to come in short gasps. "I can't go into a cell, Lieutenant. I thought you understood! I was wounded in the army."

"I'm not interested in that."

"No, wait! I was captured! A prisoner of war! For four years I was locked up! You know what I mean? I couldn't stand it. One day . . . one day, I began to scream. And I couldn't stop. You know what I mean? I knew I was screaming. I could hear myself. And I wanted to stop, but I didn't know how! You know what I mean? That's why I can't go to jail!"

"All right. Calm down."

The Vet is eager to obey, to put himself in LaPointe's good graces. He stops talking, shutting his teeth tight. But he cannot halt the humming moan. He begins to rock in his chair. Mustn't let the moan out. Mustn't start screaming.

Guttmann clears his throat. "Lieutenant?"

"Hm-m?"

"I think he may be a user. There's a fresh mark on his arm, and a couple of old tracks."

"No, he's not a user, are you, Vet? Between pension checks, he sells his blood illegally for wine money. That's right, isn't it, Vet?"

The *bomme* nods vigorously, still keeping his teeth clenched. He wants to be cooperative, but he doesn't dare speak. He's afraid to open his mouth. Afraid he'll start screaming, and they will put him into a room. Like the

141

English army doctors did after he was liberated from prison camp. They put him into a room because he kept screaming. He was screaming because they locked him in a room!

The Vet breathes nasally, in short puffs, humming with each exhalation. The hum strokes his need to scream just enough to keep it within control, like lightly rubbing a mosquito bite that you mustn't scratch for fear of infection.

"Take it easy, Vet. Answer every question truthfully, and I'll make sure you get back on the street. All right?"

The tramp nods. With great effort, he forces his breathing to slow. Then he carefully unclenches his teeth. "I'll do . . . whatever . . . anything."

"Good. Now, last night you took a wallet from a man in an alley."

The Vet bobs his head once.

"I don't care about the money. You can keep it."

The Vet forces himself to speak. "Money . . . gone."

"You drank it up?"

He nods once.

"It's the wallet I want. If you can give me the wallet, you're free to go."

The Vet opens his mouth wide and takes three rapid, shallow breaths. "I have it! I have it!"

"But not on you."

"No."

"Where?"

"I can get it."

"Good. I'll come along with you."

The Vet doesn't want this. His eyes flick about the room. "No. I'll bring it to you. I promise."

"That's not good enough, Vet. You'd promise anything right now. I'll go with you."

The Vet's upper lip spreads flat over his teeth and his nostrils dilate. "I can't!" He begins to sob.

LaPointe scrubs his hair and sighs. "Is it your kip? You don't want me to find out where it is?"

The *bomme* nods vigorously.

"I'm sorry. But there's nothing for it. It's late, and I'm tired. Either we go right now to get the wallet, or you start ten days of a vag charge."

The tramp looks at Guttmann, his eyes pleading for intervention. The young man frowns and stares at the floor.

LaPointe stands up. "Okay, that's it. I don't have time to fool around with you."

"All right!" The Vet jumps to his feet and shouts into LaPointe's face. "All right! All right!"

LaPointe puts his hands on the tramp's shoulders and presses him back into his chair. "Take it easy." He turns to Guttmann. "Go down and check us out a car and driver."

Before leaving, Guttmann glances again at the Vet, who has retreated into the comfort of rocking and humming.

No sooner has the police car carried them three blocks from the Quartier Général and the threat of being locked up than the Vet's whimpering dread evaporates and he reverts to his cocky, egoistic self. He does not deign to talk to Guttmann, who sits beside him because LaPointe got in front to avoid the alkaline smell of urine. Instead, he leans forward and talks to the Lieutenant's back, explaining what happened in a loud voice because the windows of the car are open to avoid an onset of claustrophobia, and the bitter wind whistles through the car.

"I was just coming down the street, Lieutenant, when I happened to look up the alley and see this mark. He was kneeling down . . . low, you know? With his forehead on the bricks. I figures he's a drunk or maybe high on something. Maybe he's sick, I says to myself. I got first-aid training in the army. You can make a tourniquet with your belt. Did you know that? Sure. Easy as pie, if you know how. This riffraff on the street don't know anything. They never been in the army. They don't know shit from Shinola. Well, I walks up the alley. He don't move. There's nobody around. It's real cold and everybody's off the Main. Now, I wasn't thinking of rolling him or nothing. Honest to God, Lieutenant. I just thought he might be sick or something. Need a tourniquet, maybe. When I get close to him, I could see he was real well-dressed. He looks funny. I mean, you know, ridiculous. Kneeling there with his ass in the air. Then I notice his wallet's half out of his pocket.

143

So . . . I just . . . took it. I mean, if I didn't take it, one of those street tramps was sure to. So why not? First come, first served; that's what we used to say in the army."

"You didn't know he was dead?"

"Honest to God, I didn't. There wasn't any blood or anything."

That is true. The bleeding was largely internal.

"So, anyway, it comes to me that I might as well lift his poke. Share the wealth, like we used to say in the army. So I reach over and pull it out. It comes out hard, what with him squatting over like that and the ass of his pants so tight, you know. And just as I got it, all of a sudden this cop car stops down to the end of the alley, and this cop shouts at me!" The Vet's breath begins to shorten as he relives his fear. "So I takes off! I was a-scared he might run me in! I can't be locked up, Lieutenant! If I'm in a closed place, I start to scream. You know what I mean? You know what I mean?"

"All right! Take it easy."

"Did I tell you that the army doctors kept me locked up after they liberated the camp?"

"You mentioned it. Where are we going?"

"Just straight up the Main. Up to Van Horne. I'll show you when we get there. Yeah, the army doctors kept me locked up in a hospital ward especially for fruitcakes. They didn't understand. I might have been there forever. But then this young doctor—Captain Ferguson, his name was—he says why don't they give me a chance on the outside. See how it would work. Well, I got out, and I stopped screaming just like that. They warned me not to get a job where I was cooped up, and I never did. I didn't have to. I'm a ninety percent disability. Ninety percent! That's a lot, ain't it? Hey, you got a cigarette?"

"No."

The driver twists to get a pack out of his pocket. "Give him one of mine, Lieutenant. We sure could use the smell of smoke in here."

As they near the intersection of Van Horne and St. Laurent, LaPointe becomes curious about this famous snug kip the Vet has always boasted about. It is generally known on the street that the Vet drinks up his pension check within two weeks and has to sell blood to keep alive after that. Like other tramps, winos, addicts, and hippie types *in extremis,* he lies about how long it has been since he gave blood, as he lies about diseases he has had. There is always a need for his uncommon type—another source of his endless bragging. Whenever he gets money, he buys a couple of bottles, but he never drinks much on the Main. He brings it off with him to his hideaway.

Following the Vet's directions, they turn left on Van Horne. The tramp's voice softens toward confidentiality as he speaks to LaPointe. "You can tell him to stop here at the corner. Just you come with me, Lieutenant. I don't want anyone else to come. Okay? Okay?"

"I'll leave the driver here. The young man is attached to me."

Guttmann glances over, uncertain whether or not LaPointe is sending him up.

The car pulls over to the curb, and LaPointe instructs the driver to wait for them.

An unlit side street of storage companies and warehouses ends abruptly at a woven wire fence that screens off a little-used freight shunt yard, the tracks of which glow dimly down in a black depression below and beyond the fence. LaPointe and Guttmann follow the Vet down the steep embankment, glissading dangerously over cinders, braking to prevent a headlong run that would precipitate them into the darkness below.

At the base of the slope, the Vet begins to cut across the tracks with the kind of familiarity that does not require light. LaPointe tells him to wait a minute, and he closes his eyes to speed up the dilation of his pupils. The smudgy dark gray cityglow has the effect of moonlight through mist, obscuring details, yet providing too much light to permit the eyes to adjust to the dark. Eventually, however, LaPointe can make out the parallel sets of rails and the glisten of tar on the ties. He tells the Vet to go on, but more slowly. He feels uncomfortable and out of his element, walking through this broken ground of cinder and weeds that is neither city terrain nor country, but a starved and sooty wasteland that the city has not occupied and the country cannot reclaim.

They cross over half a dozen sets of rails, then turn west, parallel to the tracks. Soon rust mutes the shine of the rails, and ragged black weeds indicate that they are in an unused wing of the shunt yard. One by one, the pairs of tracks end against heavy metal bumpers, until they are following the last along a wide curve close to a dark embankment. Without warning, the Vet turns aside and scrambles down a slope and along a faint trail through dead burrs, and stunted, hollow-stalked weeds brittle with the frost. Wind swirls in this declivity of the freight yard, one minute pushing LaPointe's overcoat from behind, and the next pressing against his chest and leaking in through the collar. The only sounds are the moan of the wind and the harsh rustle of their passage over frosted ground and through the weeds. They are isolated in this vast island of silence and dark in the midst of the city. All around them, but at a distance, the lights of traffic crawl in long double rows. A huge beer sign half a mile away at the far end of the freight yard flashes red-yellow-white, red-yellow-white. And from somewhere afar comes the wailing of an ambulance siren.

The Vet's pace slackens and he stops. "It's right over there, Lieutenant." He points toward the cliff, looming black against the dark gray of the cityglow sky. "I'll go get the wallet for you."

LaPointe peers through the gloom, but he can see no shelter, no shack.

"I'll go with you," he decides.

"I won't run off. Honest."

"Come on, come on! It's cold. Let's get it over with."

The Vet still hesitates. "All right. But he doesn't have to come, does he?""

Guttmann presses back his hair, which the wind is standing on end. "I'll wait here, Lieutenant."

LaPointe nods, then follows the Vet along the dim path.

Guttmann watches the vague figures blend into the dark, then disappear as they pass close to the embankment. He catches a bit of motion later, out of the corner of his eye where peripheral night vision is better. He strains to see, but he loses them. After several minutes, he hears the distant clank and scraping of metal—a heavy sheet of metal, from the sound of it. He hugs his coat around him and tucks his chin into his collar.

In about ten minutes he hears the crackle of dead, frozen stalks, then he sees them returning. The Vet's body is stooped and slack; he seems deflated. For the fourth time that night, the *bomme*'s personality and manner have changed abruptly. The conditions of his life long ago ground away any pretensions of dignity, but there remains the husk of pride, and that has been damaged: the Lieutenant has seen his snug little kip. He passes Guttmann without a glance, and leads the policemen back through the field of frozen weeds, along the single unused track with its rusted rails, back over the pairs of glistening rails, to the base of the embankment, just below the wire fence and the light of the city.

"We can find our way from here," LaPointe tells the tramp.

Without a word, the Vet turns and starts back the way they came.

"Vet?" LaPointe calls.

The *bomme* stops in his tracks, but he doesn't turn to face them.

"You know I won't tell any of them about your kip, don't you?"

The Vet's voice is listless. "Yeah." He clutches the brim of his floppy hat against the wind and trudges back across the tracks.

LaPointe looks after him for a second. "Come on," he says. They scramble up the cinder embankment, over the wire fence, and soon they are back in the light, on the truncated street of warehouses. As Guttmann walks on, LaPointe stands for a moment and looks back over the shunt yard, a matte-black hole ripped out of the map of Montreal's streets and city lights. His sense of reality is upset. Somehow this street with its warehouses and the noise and light of passing traffic down at the corner seems artificial, temporary. That dark, desolate freight yard with its faint

147

paths crowded in by black frozen burrs, with its silence in the midst of the city's noise, its dark in the midst of the city's light—that was real. It was not pleasant, but it was real . . . and inevitable. It is what the whole city would be six months after man was gone. It is the seed of urban ruin.

Oh, he's just tired; feeling a little *cafard*. There is vertigo in his sense of reality because he's been awake too long, because of the hard scramble up the cinder embankment, and because of the pleasant, terrifying tingle, this effervescence in his blood. . . .

Guttmann is cold, and he walks quickly toward the waiting police car with its dozing driver and its radio, against regulations, tuned to music. Then he realizes that LaPointe is not with him. He turns impatiently and sees the Lieutenant standing against the wire fence, his eyes closed. As Guttmann approaches, LaPointe opens his eyes and rubs his upper arms as though to restore circulation. Before Guttmann can ask what's wrong, the Lieutenant growls, "Come on! Let's not stand around here all night! It's cold, for Christ's sake!"

They sit in a back booth, the only customers of the A-One Café. When they came in, LaPointe greeted the old Chinese owner: "How's it going, Mr. A-One?"

The Chinese cackled and responded, "Yes, you bet. That's a good one!"

Guttmann assumed the greeting and response were ancient and automatic, a ritual joke they have shared for years.

Without asking what they wanted, the old man brought them two cups of coffee, thick and brackish, the lees from an afternoon pot. Then he returned to stand by the front window, motionless, his arms folded across his chest, his eyes focused on a mid-distance beyond his window.

The naked bulb above his head produces an oblique angle of light which deepens the furrows and rivulets of his face. His eyes do not blink.

LaPointe sits huddled in his coat, frowning meditatively as he slowly stirs his coffee, although he has not put sugar into it.

On the wall beside Guttmann's head is a gaudy embroidered hanging featuring a long-tailed bird resting on the branch of a tree bearing every kind of flower. And tacked up next to it is a picture of a very healthy girl in a swimsuit coyly considering the commitment involved in accepting the bottle of Coke thrust toward her by an aggressive male fist.

Guttmann stifles a yawn so deep that it brings tears. "Not much business," he says irrelevantly. "Wonder why he stays open all night."

LaPointe looks up as though he has forgotten the young man's presence. "Oh, you don't need much sleep when you're old. He has no wife. It helps to shorten the nights, I suppose."

For the first time, Guttmann wonders if LaPointe has a wife. He cannot imagine it; cannot picture him taking a Sunday afternoon walk in some park, a middle-aged matron on his arm. Then the image starts to form in Guttmann's mind of LaPointe in bed with a woman. . . .

"What is it?" LaPointe asks. "What are you smiling at?"

"Oh, nothing," Guttmann lies. "It's just that . . . I don't know what in hell I'm doing here. I don't know why I didn't take the car back to the Quartier Général." He pushes out a sigh and shakes his head at himself. "I must be getting dopey with lack of sleep."

LaPointe nods. "You've got what Gaspard calls 'the sits.' "

"What?" Guttmann is thrown off track by the unexpected shift to English.

"The sits. That's when you're so tired and numbheaded that you don't have the energy to get up and go home."

"That's what I've got all right. The sits. That's a good name for it. I wish I were in bed right now."

LaPointe glances at him, a smile in his down-sloping eyes.

"No," Guttmann laughs. "She's back in her own

149

apartment by now. But maybe all is not lost. We have a date for tomorrow."

"We're going to have to do some work tomorrow."

"But tomorrow's Saturday."

LaPointe put his elbow on the table and his forehead in his palm. "That's right. You see? Your college education wasn't a waste after all. You know the days of the week. After Friday, Saturday. Come to think of it, tomorrow's Sunday."

"What?"

"What time is it?"

"Ah, it's . . ." Guttmann tips his wrist toward the light. "Christ, it's almost two."

"Want some more coffee?"

"No, sir. After spending the day with you, I don't think I'll ever want another cup of coffee in my life." Guttmann glances toward the motionless Chinese. "Is that all he does? Just stand there looking inscrutable?"

"What does that mean? Inscrutable?"

"Inscrutable means . . . hell, sir, I don't know. My brain's gone to sleep. It means . . . ah . . . of or pertaining to the inability to scrute? Je scrute, tu scrutes, il scrute . . . shit, I don't know." He sits back, and his eyes settle on the Chinese again. "He must be lonely."

LaPointe shrugs. "I doubt it. He's past that."

This simple bit of human understanding from the Lieutenant disturbs Guttmann. He can't peg LaPointe in his mind. Like most liberals, he assumes that all thinking men are liberals. On the one hand, LaPointe is the classic old-timer who rags his juniors, pokes fun at education, harasses and bullies the civilians—the prototypical tough cop. On the other hand, he is a friend to ex-whores with bashed-up faces, a paternal watchdog who chats with people on the street, knows the bums, understands his patch . . . seems to have affection for it. Pride, even. Guttmann knows better than to think that people are black or white. But he expects to find them gray shades, not alternately black *then* white. Lieutenant LaPointe: Your Friendly Neighborhood Fascist.

150

"He should find some old duffers to play pinochle with," Guttmann says.

"Who?"

"The old Chinese who runs this place."

"Why pinochle?"

"I don't know. That's what old farts do when they don't know what else to do with themselves, isn't it? Play pinochle? I mean . . ." Guttmann stops and closes his eyes. He slowly shakes his head. "No, don't tell me. You play pinochle, don't you, sir?"

"Twice a week."

Guttmann hits his forehead with the heel of his hand. "I should have known. You know, sir, it just seems that fate doesn't want us to hit it off."

"Don't blame fate. It's your big mouth."

"Yes, sir."

"What have you got against pinochle?"

"Believe it or not, I don't have anything against pinochle. My grandfather used to play pinochle with his cronies late into the night sometimes."

"Your grandfather."

"Yes, sir. That's mostly what I remember him doing; sitting with his friends until all hours. Playing. Pretending it mattered who won and who lost. I just came to associate it with lonely old men, I guess."

"I see."

"I have nothing against the game. I'm a pinochle player myself, sir. My grandfather taught me."

"Are you any good?"

"Sir, excuse me. But doesn't it strike you as odd that we are sitting in a Chinese all-night coffee shop at two in the morning talking about pinochle?"

LaPointe laughs. The kid's okay. "Let's see what we've got here," he says, taking from his overcoat pocket the wallet the Vet gave him, and emptying the contents onto the table. There is a scrap of paper with two girls' names written in different hands, evidently by the girls themselves. First names only; not much help. There is a little booklet the size of a commemorative stamp, containing a dozen pictures of various sex positions and combinations: the kind of thing shown to objecting but giggling girls by a man who believes the myth that seeing the act automatically brings a woman to the point of panting necessity. In an accordion-pleated change pocket there are two contraceptives of the sort sold in vending machines in the toilets of cheap bars: guaranteed to afford maximum protection with minimum loss of sensation. Sold only for the prevention of disease. One of them features a "tickler"; the other is packed in a liquid lubricant. No money; the Vet got that. No driver's license. The wallet is cheap imitation alligator, quite new. There is a card in one of the plastic windows with places for the owner to provide particulars. Childishly, the dead man had felt impelled to fill it in. La-Pointe passes the wallet over to Guttmann, who reads the round, infantile printing:

NAME	*Tony Green*
ADDRESS	*17 Mirabeau Street*
PHONE	*Apmt. 3B*
BLOOD TYPE	*Hot !!!!!!!!!!!*

"So the victim's name was Tony Green," Guttmann says.

"Probably not." There is a businesslike, mechanical quality to LaPointe's voice. "The printing is European. See the barred seven? The abbreviation for 'apartment' is wrong. That seems to give us a young alien. And the kid had a Latin look—probably Italian. But not a legal entrant, or his fingerprints would have been on file with Ottawa. He picked the name Tony Green for himself. If he runs true to form for Italian immigrants, his real name would be something like Antonio Verdi—something like that."

"Does the name mean anything to you? You know him?"

LaPointe shakes his head. "No. But I know the house. It's a run-down place near Marie-Anne and Clark. We'll check it out tomorrow morning."

"What do you expect to turn there?"

152

"Impossible to say. It's a start. It's all we have in hand."

"That, and the fact that the victim was a little hung up on sex. Oh, God!"

"Why 'Oh, God'?"

"You know that girl I had to leave tonight? Well, I promised her we'd go out tomorrow morning. Take coffee up on the Mount. Maybe drop in at a gallery or two. Have dinner maybe. Now I'll have to beg off again."

"Why do that? There's no real point in your coming along with me tomorrow, if you don't want to."

"Why do you say that, sir?"

"Well . . . you know. All this business of the apprentice Joans learning the ropes from the old-timers is a lot of crap. Things don't work that way. There's no way in the world that you're going to end up a street cop like me. You have education. You speak both languages well. You have ambition. No. You won't end up in this kind of work. You're the type who ends up in public relations, or handling 'delicate' cases. You're the type who gets ahead."

Guttmann is a little stung. No one likes to be a "type." "Is there anything wrong with that, sir? Anything wrong with wanting to get ahead?"

"No, I suppose not." LaPoint rubs his nose. "I'm just saying that what you might learn from me won't be of much use to you. You could never work the way I work. You wouldn't even want to. Look at how you got all steamed up about the way I handled that pimp, Scheer."

"I only mentioned that he has his rights."

"And the kids he bashes around? Their rights?"

"There are laws to protect them."

"What if they're too dumb to know about the laws? Or too scared to use them? A girl hits the city on a bus, coming from some farm or village, stupid and looking for a good time . . . excitement. And the first thing you know, she's broke and scared and willing to sell her ass." LaPointe isn't thinking of Scheer's girls at this moment.

"All right," Guttmann concedes. "So maybe something has to be done about men like Scheer. Stiffer laws,

153

maybe. But not stopping him on the street and making an ass of him in front of people, for God's sake."

LaPointe shakes his head. "You've got to hit people where they're tender. Scheer is a strutting wiseass. Embarrass him in public and he'll keep off the street for a while. It varies with the man. Some you threaten, some you hurt, some you embarrass."

Guttmann lifts his palms and looks about with round eyes, as though calling upon God to listen to this shit. "I don't believe what I'm hearing, sir. Some you hurt, some you threaten, some you embarrass—what is that, a Nazi litany? Those are supposed to be tactics for keeping the peace?"

"They didn't tell you about that in college, I suppose."

"No, sir. They did not."

"And, of course, you'd play everything by the book."

"I'd try. Yes." This is simply said; it is the truth. "And if the book was wrong, I'd do what I could to change it. That's how it works in a democracy."

"I see. Well—by the book—the Vet was guilty of a crime, wasn't he? He took money from this wallet. Would you put him inside? Let him scream for the rest of his life?"

Guttmann is silent. He isn't sure. No, probably not.

"But that would be playing it by the book. And do you remember that *fou* who sharpens knives and worries about the snow? He'd make a great suspect for a knife murder. You almost sniffed him yourself. And do you know what would happen if you brought him in for questioning? He'd get confused and frightened, and in the end he would confess. Oh, yes. He'd confess to anything you wanted. And the Commissioner would be happy, and the newspapers would be happy, and you'd get promoted."

"Well . . . I didn't know about him. I didn't know he was . . ."

"That's the point, son! You don't know. The *book* doesn't know!"

Guttmann's ears are reddening. "But *you* know?"

"That's right! I know. After thirty years, I know! I know the difference between a harmless nut and a murderer. I know the difference between shit tracks on a

154

man's arm and the marks left by selling blood to stay alive!" With a guttural sound and a wave of his hand LaPointe dismisses the use of explaining anything to Guttmann's type.

Guttmann sits, silently pushing his spoon back and forth between his fingers. He isn't cowed. He speaks quietly, without looking up. "It's fascism, sir."

"What?"

"It's facism. The rule of a man, rather than the rule of law, is fascism. Even when the man has been around and thinks he knows what's best . . . even if the man is trying to do good things . . . to be fair. It's still fascism."

For a moment, LaPointe's melancholy eyes rest on the young man, then he looks over his head to the gaudy Chinese hanging and the Coke advertisement.

Guttmann expects a denial. Anger. An explanation.

That's not what comes. After a silence, LaPointe says, "Fascism, eh?" The tone indicates that he never thought of it that way. It indicates nothing more.

Once again, Guttmann feels undercut, bypassed.

LaPointe presses his eye sockets with his thumb and forefinger and sighs deeply. "Well, I think we'd better get some sleep. You can get the sits in your brain, as well as in your ass." He sniffs and rubs his cheek with his knuckles.

Guttmann delays their leaving. "Sir? May I ask you something?"

"About fascism?"

"No, sir. Back there in the freight yard. That *bomme* didn't want me to come with you and see his kip. And later you said something to him about not telling the others. What was that all about?"

LaPointe examines the young man's face. Could you explain something like this to a kid who learned about people in a sociology class? Where would it fit in with his ideas about society and democracy? There is something punitive in LaPointe's decision to tell him about it.

"You remember Dirtyshirt Red last night? You remember how he had nothing good to say about the Vet? All the *bommes* on the Main sleep where they can: in doorways, in alleys, behind the tombstones in the monument-maker's yard. And they all envy the nice snug private kip the Vet's always bragging about. They hate him for having it. And that's just the way the Vet wants it. He wants to be despised, hated, bad-mouthed. Because as long as the other tramps despise and reject him, he isn't one of them; he's something special. That make sense to you?"

Guttmann nods.

"Well—" LaPointe's voice is husky with fatigue, and he speaks quietly. "After we left you back there on the path, I followed him along a trail I could barely see. But there wasn't anything around. No shack, no hut, nothing. Then the Vet went behind a patch of bush and bent over. I could hear a scrape of metal. He was sliding back a sheet of corrugated roofing that covered a pit in the ground. I went over to the edge of it as he jumped down, sort of skidding on the muddy sides of the hole. It was about eight feet deep, and the bottom was covered with wads of rag and burlap sacking that squished with seep water when he walked around. He had a few boxes down there, to sit on, to use as a table, to stash stuff in. He fumbled around in one of these boxes and found the wallet. It was all he could do to get out of the pit again. The sides were slimy, and he slipped back twice and swore a lot. He finally got out and handed over the wallet. Then he slid the sheet of metal back over the hole. When he stood up and looked at me . . . I don't know how to explain it . . . there was sort of two things in his eyes at the same time. Shame and anger. He was ashamed to live in a slimy hole. And he was angry that somebody knew about it. We talked about it for a while. He was proud of himself. I know that sounds nuts, but it's how it was. He was ashamed of his hole, but proud of having figured it all out. I guess you could say he was proud of having made his hole, but ashamed of needing it. Something like that, anyway.

"One night a few years ago, he was drunk and looking for a place to hide, where the police wouldn't run him in for D and D. He found this cave-in hidden away among some bushes. Later on he thought about it, and he got a bright idea. He went back there at night with a spade he pinched somewhere, and he worked on the hole. He made

156

it deeper and made the sides vertical. And whenever the sides crumble from him scrambling in and out, he works on it again. So his hole is always getting bigger. Rain gets in, and water seeps up from the slime, so he keeps adding rags and bags he picks up here and there. It's a clever little trap he's made for himself."

"Trap, sir?"

"That's what it is. That's how he uses it. He's afraid of being picked up drunk and put in a cell and left to scream. So every time he thinks he's got enough wine inside him to be dangerous, he buys another bottle and brings it back to his kip. Down there in the hole, he can drink until he's wild and raving. He's safe down there. Even when he's sober, it's hard for him to climb up those slimy sides. When he's drunk, it's impossible. He traps himself down there to save himself from being arrested and put inside. Of course, he's a claustrophobic, so sometimes he gets panicky down there. When his brain's soggy with wine, he thinks the walls are caving in on him. And he's terrified that a big rain might fill his pit with water when he's too drunk to get out. It's bad down there, you know. When he's drunk, he can't get out to shit or piss, so it's . . . bad down there."

"Jesus Christ," Guttmann says quietly.

"Yeah. He lives in a small hole in the ground *because* he's a claustrophobic."

"Jesus Christ."

LaPointe leans back·in the booth and presses his mat of cropped hair hard with the palm of his hand. "And what do you do if you have to live in a slimy, stinking hole? You brag about it, of course. You make the other *bommes* despise you. And envy you."

Guttmann shakes his head slowly, his mouth agape, his eyes squeezed in pity and disgust. LaPointe's punitive intent in telling him about this has been effective.

"Tell you what," LaPointe says. "Don't come by to pick me up tomorrow until around noon. I need some sleep."

Without turning on the lights, he closes the door behind him and hangs his overcoat on the wooden rack. He flinches when the revolver in his pocket thuds against the wall; he doesn't want to wake her.

There is a crackling hiss in the room, and the crescent dial of the old Emerson glows dim orange. The station has gone off the air. Why didn't she turn the radio off? Ah. He forgot to tell her that you also have to jiggle the knob to turn it off. Then why didn't she pull out the plug? Dumb twit.

The ceiling of the bedroom is illuminated by the streetlamp beneath the window, and he can make out Marie-Louise's form in the bed, although she is below the shadow line. She sleeps on her side, her hands under her cheek, palms together, and her legs are in a kind of running position that takes up most of the bed.

He undresses noiselessly, teetering for a moment in precarious balance as he pulls off his pants. When he aligns the creases to fold the pants over the back of a chair, some change falls out of his pocket, and he grimaces at the sound and swears between his teeth. He tiptoes around to the other side of the bed and lifts the blankets, trying to slip in without waking her. If he curves his body just right, there is enough room to lie next to her without touching her. For five long minutes he remains there, feeling the warmth that radiates from her, but it is impossible to sleep when the slightest movement would either touch her or make him fall out of bed. Anyway, he feels ridiculous, sneaking into bed with her. He rises carefully, but the springs clack loudly in the silent room.

. . . at first the creaking bed had made Lucille tense. But later she used to giggle silently at the thought of imagined neighbors listening beyond the wall, shocked at such carryings-on. . . .

At the noise, Marie-Louise moans in confused irritation. "What's the matter?" she asks in a blurred, muffled voice. "What do you want?"

He lays his hand lightly on her mop of frizzy hair. "Nothing."

7

"Hey?"

He does not move.

"Hey?"

"Ugh!" LaPointe wakes with a start, blinking his eyes against the watery light coming through the window. It is another gray day with low skies and diffused, shadowless brightness. He squeezes his eyes shut again before finally opening them. His back is stiff from sleeping on the narrow sofa, and his feet stick out from below the overcoat he has used as a blanket. "What time is it?" he asks.

"A little before eleven."

He nods heavily, still drugged with sleep. He sits up and scratches his head, grinning stupidly. These last two nights have taken their toll—his joints are stiff and his head cobwebby.

"I've got water boiling," she says. "I was going to make some coffee, but I don't know how to work your pot."

"Yes. It's an old-fashioned kind. Just a minute. Give me a chance to wake up. I'll do it." He yawns deeply. His overcoat covers him from the waist down, but his thick chest is exposed. He rubs the graying hair vigorously because it itches. *"Tabernouche!"* he grunts.

"Hard night?" she asks.

"Long, anyway."

She is wearing Lucille's pink quilted dressing gown again, but she has been up long enough to brush out her hair and put on eye make-up. There is a slight smell of gas in the room. She must have had some difficulty lighting the gas fire.

In his sleep, his penis has come out of the fly of his undershorts. He manages to tuck it back in with the same gesture as that with which he pulls up his overcoat and puts it on in place of a robe. Barefooted, he goes into the kitchen to make coffee.

She laughs half a dozen ascending notes, then stops short.

"What's wrong?"

"Oh, nothing. You look funny with your bare legs coming out of the bottom of your overcoat."

He looks down. "Yes, I suppose I do."

While he is pressing hot water through the fine grounds, it occurs to him that only one thing triggers her peculiar, interrupted laugh: people looking ridiculous. She laughed at her black eye, at him with soap on his cheek, at herself wearing Lucille's coat, and now at him again. It's a cruel sense of humor, one that doesn't even spare herself as a possible victim.

He gives her a cup of coffee and carries one with him to the bathroom, where he washes up and dresses.

Later, he fries eggs and toasts bread over the gas ring, and they take their breakfast in the living room, she coiled up on the sofa, her plate balanced on the arm, he in his chair.

"Why did you sleep out here?" she asks.

"Oh . . . I didn't want to disturb you," he explains, partially.

"Yeah, but why didn't you use the blankets I used last night?"

"I didn't really mean to sleep. I was just going to rest. But I dozed off."

"Yeah, but then why did you take your clothes off?"

"Why don't you just eat your eggs?"

"Okay." She spoons egg onto a bit of toast and eats it that way. "Where did you go last night?" she asks.

"Just work."

"You said you work with the police. You work in an office?"

"Sometimes. Mostly I work on the streets."

That seems to amuse her. "Yeah. Me too. You enjoy being a cop?"

He tucks down the corners of his mouth and shrugs. He never thought of it that way. When she changes the subject immediately, he assumes she isn't really interested anyway.

"Don't you get bored living here?" she asks. "No magazines. No television."

He looks around the frumpy room with its 1930's furniture. Yes, he imagines it would be dull for a young girl. True, there are no magazines, but he has some books, a full set of Zola, whom he discovered by chance twenty years ago, and whom he reads over and over, going down the row of novels by turn, then starting again. He finds the people and events surprisingly like those on his patch, despite the funny, florid language. But he doesn't imagine she would care to read his Zolas. She probably reads slowly, maybe even mouths the words.

Well, if she's bored, then she'll probably leave soon. No reason for her to stay, really.

"Ah . . . why don't we go out tonight?" he offers. "Have dinner."

"And go dancing?"

He smiles and shakes his head. "I told you I don't dance."

This disappoints her. But she is resourceful when it comes to getting her way with men. "I know! Why don't we go to a whisky à go-go after dinner. People can dance by themselves there."

He doesn't care much for the thought of sitting in one of those cramped, noisy places with youngsters hopping all around him. But, if it would please her . . .

She presses her tongue against her teeth and decides to gamble on pushing this thing to her advantage. "I . . . I really don't have the right clothes to go out," she says, not looking up from her cup. "I only have what I could sneak out in the shopping bag."

His eyes crinkle as he looks at her. He knows exactly what she's up to. He doesn't mind giving her money to buy clothes, if that's what she wants, but he doesn't like her thinking he's a dumb mark.

He sets down his cup and crosses to the large veneered chest. He has a habit of putting his housekeeping money into the top drawer every payday, and taking out what he needs through the month. He knows it's a bad habit, but it saves time. And who would dare to steal from Claude LaPointe? He is surprised at how many twenties have accumulated, crumpled up in the drawer; must be five or six hundred dollars' worth. Ever since the mortgage on the house was paid off, he has more money than he needs. He takes out seven twenties and flattens them with his hand. "Here. I'll be working today. You can go out and buy yourself a dress."

She takes the bills and counts them. Maybe he doesn't know how much a dress costs. So much the better for her.

"There's enough there to buy yourself a coat too," he says.

"Oh? All right." Before falling asleep last night, she thought about asking him for money, but she didn't know quite how to go about it. After all, they hadn't screwed. He didn't owe her.

While she sits looking out the window, thinking about the dress and coat, LaPointe examines her face. The green eye shadow she uses disguises what is left of her black eye. It's a nice pert face. Not pretty, but the kind you want to hold between your palms. It occurs to him that he has never kissed her.

"Marie-Louise?" he says quietly.

She turns to him, her eyebrows raised interrogatively.

162

He looks down at the park, colorless under yeasty skies. "Let's make a deal, Marie-Louise. For me, I like having you here, having you around. I suppose we'll make love eventually, and I'll enjoy that. I mean . . . well, naturally, I'll enjoy that. Okay. That's for me. For you, I suppose being here is better than sitting out your nights in some park or bus station. But . . . you find it dull here. And sooner or later you'll go off somewhere. Fine. I'll probably be tired of having you around by then. You can have money to buy some clothes. If you need other things, I don't mind giving you money. But I'm not a mark, and I wouldn't like you to think of me as one. So don't try to con me, and don't bullshit me. That wouldn't be fair, and it would make me angry. Is it a deal?"

Marie-Louise looks steadily at him, trying to understand what he's up to. She's not used to this kind of frankness, and she doesn't feel comfortable with it. She really wishes they had screwed and he had paid his money. That's neat. That's easy to understand. She feels as if she's being accused of something, or trapped into something.

"I knew there was money in that drawer," she says defensively. "I was looking around last night, and I found it."

"But you didn't take it and run off. Why not?"

She shrugs. She doesn't know why not. She's not a thief, that's all. Maybe she should have taken it. Maybe she will, someday. Anyway, she doesn't like this conversation. "Look, I better get going. Or did you want to come shopping with me?"

"No, I have work—" LaPointe hears a car door slam down in the street. He half rises from his chair and peers down from the second-story window. Guttmann has just gotten out of a little yellow sports car and is looking along the row for the house number.

LaPointe tugs his overcoat on rapidly. He doesn't want Guttmann to see Marie-Louise and ask questions or, worse yet, pointedly avoid asking questions. The sleeve of his suit coat slips from his grasp, and he has to fish up through the arm of the overcoat to tug it down. "Okay," he says. "I'll see you this evening."

"Okay."

"What time will you be through shopping?"

"I don't know."

"Five? Five-thirty?"

"Okay."

As he clumps down the narrow stairs he grumbles to himself. She's too passive. There's nothing to her. Want some coffee? Okay. Even though she doesn't like coffee. Shall we eat at five? Okay. Do you want to stay with me? Okay. Do you want to leave? Okay. Shall we make love? Okay. How about screwing out on the hall landing? Okay.

She doesn't care. Nothing matters to her.

Guttmann has his finger on the buzzer when the front door opens with a jerk and LaPointe steps out.

"Morning, sir."

LaPointe buttons up his overcoat against the damp chill. "Your car?" he asks, indicating with a thrust of his chin the new little yellow sports model.

"Yes, sir," Guttmann says with a touch of pride, turning to descend the steps.

"Hm-m!" Obviously the Lieutenant doesn't approve of sports cars.

But Guttmann is in too good a mood to care about LaPointe's prejudices. "That's to say, the car belongs to me and the bank. Mostly the bank. I think I own the ashtray and one of the headlights." His buoyancy is a result of a rare piece of good luck. When he called the girl this morning to tell her he would have to cancel their date, she beat him to it, telling him she had one hell of a head cold, and she wanted to sleep in to see if she could shake it off. He managed to sound disappointed, and he arranged to look in on her that evening.

LaPointe finds the tiny car difficult to get into, and he grunts as he slams the door on his coattail and has to open it again. In fact, he feels silly, riding around in a little yellow automobile. He would rather walk. Give him a chance to check on the street. Guttmann, for all that he is bigger than LaPointe, slips in quite easily. With a popping baritone roar, the car starts up and pulls away from the curb.

LaPointe cranes his neck to see if Marie-Louise is watching from the window. She is not.

They find a parking space on Clark, only half a block up from the rooming house. Opening the door, LaPointe scrapes it against the high curb; Guttmann closes his eyes and winces. LaPointe mutters something about stupid toy cars as he squeezes out and angrily slams the door behind him. Because it is Saturday, the street is full of kids, and one of them has paused in his game of "ledgey" to remark aloud that old men shouldn't ride around in little cars. LaPointe raises the back of his hand to him, but the boy just stares in sassy defiance as he wipes his nose gravely on the sleeve of a stretched-out sweater. LaPointe cannot repress a grin. A typical pugnacious French Canadian kid. A *'tit coq.*

The rooming house is like others around the Main. Dull brick in need of paint; dirty windows with limp curtains of grayish fabric that hangs as though it is damp; a fly-specked card in the window of first floor front advertising rooms to let. This doesn't necessarily mean there is a vacancy. The concierge is probably too lazy to put the card in and take it out each time a short-time vagrant comes or goes. LaPointe climbs the wooden stoop and twists the old-fashioned bell, which rattles dully, broken. When there is no answer, he bangs on the door. Guttmann has joined him on the landing, looking back nervously at the small group of ragged kids that has gathered around his car. LaPointe bangs more violently, making the window rattle.

Almost immediately the door is snatched open by a slovenly woman who pushes back a lock of lank gray hair and snaps, "Hey! What the hell's wrong with you? You want to break down the door?" Her lower lip is swollen and cracked where someone hit her recently.

"Police," LaPointe says, not bothering to show identification.

She looks from LaPointe to Guttmann quickly, then stands back from the doorway. They enter a hall that smells of Lysol and boiled cabbage. The woman's attitude has changed from anger to tense uncertainty. "What do you want?" she asks, touching two fingers gingerly to the split lip.

The tentative tone of the question gives LaPointe his cue. She's frightened about something. He doesn't know what it is, and he doesn't care, but he'll push it a little to give her a scare and make her cooperative. "Routine questions," he says. "But not here in the hall."

She shrugs and enters her apartment, not inviting them to come in, but leaving the door open behind her. LaPointe follows and looks around as Guttmann, a little nervous, smiles politely and closes the door behind him. Without a warrant, you're supposed to await an invitation before entering a home.

The small room is crowded with junk furniture, and hot from an oversized electric heater she uses because it doesn't cost her anything. It just goes on the landlord's monthly bill. She keeps the place too hot because otherwise she'd feel she was losing money. LaPointe knows her type, knows how to handle her. He unbuttons his overcoat and turns to the woman just as she is glancing nervously out the window. She is expecting someone; someone she hopes will not come while the police are there. She adjusts the curtain, as though that is why she went to the window in the first place. "What do you want?" she asks sullenly.

For a moment, LaPointe does not answer. He looks levelly at her, draws a deep, bored breath and says, "You know perfectly well. I don't have time to play games with you."

Guttmann glances at him, confused.

"Look," the woman says. "Arnaud doesn't live here anymore. I don't know where he is. He moved out a month ago, the lazy son of a bitch."

"That's your story," LaPointe says, tossing a pillow out of the only comfortable chair and sitting down.

"It's the truth! Do you think I'd lie for him?" She touches her split lip. "The bastard gave me this!"

LaPointe glances at the fresh bruise. "A month ago?"

"Yes . . . no. I met him on the street yesterday."

"And he said good morning, and hit you in the mouth?"

The woman shrugs and turns away.

LaPointe watches her in silence.

She glances quickly toward the window, but does not dare to go and look out.

LaPointe sighs aloud. "Come on. I don't have all day."

For another minute, she remains tight-lipped. Then she gives in, shrugging, then letting her shoulders drop heavily. "Look, officer. The TV was a present. It doesn't even work good. He gave it to me, like he gave me this fat lip, and once the clap, the no-good bastard!"

So that's it. LaPointe turns to Guttmann, who is still hovering near the door. "Take down the serial number of the TV."

The young man squats behind the set and tries to find the number. He doesn't know why in hell he is doing this, and he feels like an ass.

"You know what it means if the set turns out to be stolen?" LaPointe asks the woman.

"If Arnaud stole it, that's his ass. I don't know anything about it."

LaPointe laughs. "Oh, the judge is sure to believe that." That's enough, LaPointe thinks. She's scared and ready to cooperate now. "Sit down. Let's forget the TV for now. I want to know about one of your roomers. Tony Green."

Confused by the change of topic, but relieved to have the questioning veer away from herself, the concierge instantly becomes confidential and friendly. "Tony Green? Honest, officer—"

"Lieutenant." It always surprises LaPointe to find people on the Main who don't know of him.

"Honest, Lieutenant, there's no one by that name staying here. Of course, they don't always give their right names."

"Good-looking kid. Young. Mid-twenties. Probably Italian. Stayed out all night last night."

"Oh! Verdini!" She makes a wide gesture and her lips flap with a puff of breath. "It's nothing when he stays out all night! It's women with him. He's all the time after it. Chases every *plotte* and *guidoune* on the street. Sometimes they even come here looking for him. Sometimes he has them in his room, even though it's against the rules. Once there were two of them up there at the same time! The neighbors complained about all the grunting and groaning." She laughs and winks. "His thing is always up. He wears those tight pants, and I can always see it bulging there. What's wrong? What's he done? Is he in trouble?"

"Give me the names of the women who came here."

She shrugs contemptuously and tucks down the corners of her mouth. The gesture opens the crack in her lip, and she licks it to keep it from stinging. "I couldn't be bothered trying to remember them. They were all sorts. Young, old, fat, skinny. A couple no more than kids. He's a real *sauteux de clôtures*. He puts it into all kinds."

"And you?"

"Oh, a couple of times we passed on the stairs and he ran his hand up under my dress. But it never went further. I think he was afraid of—"

"Afraid of this Arnaud you haven't seen in a month?"

She shrugs, annoyed with herself at her slip.

"All right. How long has this Verdini lived here?"

"Two months maybe. I can look at the rent book if you want."

"Not now. Give me the names of the women who came here."

"Like I told you, I don't know most of them. Just stuff dragged in off the street."

"But you recognized some of them."

She looks away uncomfortably. "I don't want to get anybody into trouble."

"I see." LaPointe sits back and makes himself comfortable. "You know, I have a feeling that if I wait here for half an hour, I may be lucky enough to meet your Arnaud. It'll be a touching scene, you two getting together after a month. He'll think I waited around because you told me about the TV. That will make him angry, but I'm sure he's the understanding type." LaPointe's expressionless eyes settle on the concierge.

For a time she is silent as she meditatively torments her cracked lip with the tip of her finger. At last she says, "I think I recognized three of them."

LaPointe nods to Guttmann, who opens his notebook.

The concierge gives the name of a French Canadian chippy whom LaPointe knows. She doesn't know the name of the second woman, but she gives the address of a Portuguese family that lives around the corner.

"And the third?" LaPointe asks.

"I don't know her name either. It's that woman who runs the cheap restaurant just past Rue de Bullion. The place that—"

"I know the place. You're telling me that *she* came here?"

"Once, yes. Not to get herself stuffed, of course. After all, she's a butch."

Yes, LaPointe knows that. That is why he was surprised.

"They had a fight," the concierge continues. "You could hear her bellowing all the way down here. Then she slammed out of the place."

"And you don't know any of the other people who visited this Verdini?"

"No. Just *plottes*. Oh . . . and his cousin, of course."

"His cousin?"

"Yes. The guy who rented the room in the first place. Verdini didn't speak much English and almost no French at all. His cousin rented the room for him."

"Let's hear about this cousin."

"I don't remember his name. I think he mentioned it, but I don't remember. He gave me an address too, in case there were any problems. Like I said, this Verdini didn't speak much English." She is growing more tense. Time is running out against Arnaud's return.

"What was the address?"

"I didn't pay any attention. I got other things to do with my time than worry about the bums who live here."

"You didn't write it down?"

"I couldn't be bothered. I remember it was somewhere over the hill, if that's any help."

By "over the hill" she means the Italian stretch of the Main, between the drab little park in Carré Vallières at the top of the rise and the railroad bridge past Van Horne.

"How often did you see this cousin?"

"Only once. When he rented the room. Oh, and another time, about a week ago. They had a row and—hey! Chocolate!"

"What?"

"No . . . not chocolate. That's not it. For a second there I thought I remembered the cousin's name. It was right on the tip of my tongue. Something to do with chocolate."

"Chocolate?"

"No, not that. But something like it. Cocoa? No, that's not it. It's gone now. Something to do with chocolate." She cannot help drifting to the window and peeking through the curtains.

LaPointe rises. "All right. That's all for now. If that 'chocolate' name comes back to you, telephone me." He gives her his card. "And if I don't hear from you, I'll be back. And I'll talk to Arnaud about it."

She takes the card without looking at it. "What's the wop kid done? Some girl knocked up?"

"That's not your affair. You just worry about the TV set."

"Honest to God, Lieutenant—"

"I don't want to hear about it."

They sit in the yellow sports car. LaPointe appears to be deep in thought, and Guttmann doesn't know where to go first.

"Sir?"

"Hm-m?"

"What's a *plotte*?" Guttmann's school French does not cover Joual street terms.

"Sort of a whore."

"And a *guidoune*?"

"Same kind of thing. Only amateur. Goes for drinks."

Guttmann says the words over in his mind, to fix them. "And a . . . *sauteux de* . . . what was it?"

"A *sauteux de clôtures*. It's an old-fashioned term. The concierge probably comes from downriver. It means a . . . sort of a man who runs after women, but there's a sense that he chases young women more than others. Something like a cherry-picker. Hell, I don't know! It means what it means!"

"You know, sir? Joual seems to have more words for aspects of sex than either English or French-French."

LaPointe shrugs. "Naturally. People talk about what's important to them. Someone once told me that Eskimos have lots of words for snow. French-French has lots of words for 'talk.' And English has lots of—ah, there she goes!"

"What?"

"That's what I've been waiting for. The concierge just took the 'To Let' sign out of the window. She was trying to get at it all the time we were there. It's a warning to her Arnaud to stay away. I'd bet anything it'll be put back as soon as we drive away."

Guttmann shakes his head. "Even though he bashes her in the mouth."

"That's love for you, son. The love that rhymes with 'forever' in all the songs. Come on, let's go."

They run down the two leads given them by the concierge. The first girl they catch coming out of her apartment as they drive up. LaPointe meets her at the bottom of the stoop and draws her aside to talk, while Guttmann stands by feeling useless. The girl doesn't know anything, not even his name. Just Tony. They met in a bar, had a couple of drinks, and went up to his room. No, she hadn't charged him for it. He was just a good-looking guy, and they had a little fun together.

LaPointe gets back into the car. Not much there. But at least he learned that Tony Green's English was not all that bad. Obviously he had been taking lessons during the two months he stayed at the rooming house.

Guttmann is even more out of it at the second girl's house. Not a girl, really; a Portuguese woman in her thirties with two kids running around the place and a mother in a black dress who doesn't speak a word of French, but who hovers near the door of an adjoining bedroom, visible only to the standing Guttmann. From time to time, the

171

mother smiles at Guttmann, and he smiles back out of politeness. The timing of the old woman's smile is uncanny in conjunction with the daughter's confession. She seems to punctuate each sexual admission with a nod and a grin. Guttmann is put in mind of his deepest secret dread when he was a kid: that his mother could read his thoughts.

The young woman is scared, and she talks to LaPointe in a low, rapid voice, glancing frequently toward her mother's room, not wanting her to hear, even though she doesn't have two words of French. Just having her mother listen to the incomprehensible noise that carries this kind of confession is daunting.

Her husband left her two years ago. A person has to have some fun in life. *The mother nods and grins.* Yes, she met Tony Green at a cabaret where she went with a girlfriend to dance. Yes, she did go to his room. *The mother nods.* No, not alone. She is embarrassed. Yes, the other woman, her friend, was with them. Yes, all three together in the same bed. *The mother grins and nods; Guttmann smiles back.* It wasn't her idea—all three in the same bed—but that's the way this Tony wanted it. And he was such a good-looking boy. After all, a person has to have some fun in life. It's rough, being left with two kids to bring up all by yourself, and a mother who is just about useless. *The mother nods.* It's rough, working eight hours a day, six days a week. The oldest girl goes to convent school. Uniforms. Books. It all costs money. So you have to work six days a week, eight hours a day. And nobody's getting any younger. It's a sin, sure, but a person has to have some fun. *The mother smiles and nods.*

LaPointe slides into the car beside Guttmann, and for a while sits in silence while he seems to sort through what the women have told him.

Guttmann can't help being impressed by LaPointe's manner as he talked to this woman and that girl in the street. At first they were afraid because he was a cop, but soon they seemed to be chatting away, almost enjoying unburdening themselves to someone who understood, like a priest. LaPointe asked very few questions, but he had a way of nodding and rolling his hand that requested them to

go on . . . And what next? . . . And then? The Lieutenant's attitude was very different from his tough, bullying
manner with the concierge. Guttmann remembers him saying something about using different tactics with different
people: some you threaten, some you hit, some you embarrass.

And some you understand? Is understanding a tactic
too?

"Let's go have a cup of coffee," LaPointe says.

"That's a wonderful idea, sir." Guttmann's stomach is
still sour with all the coffee he drank yesterday. "I was
hoping we'd have a chance to get some coffee."

The Le Shalom Restaurant is bustling with customers
from the small garment shops of the district: young women
with only half an hour off push and crowd to get carry-out
orders; boisterous *forts* from the loading docks push sandwiches into their mouths and ogle the girls; intense young
Jewish men in suits lean over their plates, talking business.
There are few older Jews because most of them are first
generation and still keep *Shabbes*.

Even though it's afternoon, most of the orders involve
breakfast foods, because many of the people only had time
for a quick cup of coffee that morning. And besides, eggs
are the best food you can buy for the money. This area of
Mont Royal Street is the center of the garment service
industry, where labor from undereducated French Canadian girls is cheap. There are no big important companies
in the district, but dozens of small, second-story operations
that receive specialty orders from the bigger houses.

WORLDWIDE TUCKING & HEMSTITCHING
Nathan Z. Pearl, President

Two telephones behind the serving counter ring constantly. While three distraught girls hustle raggedly to clear
and serve the tables, most of the real work is done by one
middle-aged woman behind the counter. She does all the
checks, serves the whole counter, answers all phone orders,
keeps short orders rolling, argues and jokes with the cus-

tomers, and wages a long-running feud with the harassed Greek cook.

To a customer: This your quarter? No? Must be for the coffee. Couldn't be a tip. Who around here would tip a quarter? *To the cook:* Two meat sandwiches. And lean for once! Where's my three orders of eggs? Like hell I didn't! What use are you? *To a customer:* Look, darling, keep your shirt on. I got only two hands, right? *To the phone:* Restaurant? Two Danish? Right. Coffee. One double cream. Right. One no sugar. What's the matter? Someone getting fat up there? Hold on one second, darling. . . . *To a customer:* What's your problem, honey? Here, give me that. Look, it's added up right. Nine, sixteen, twenty-five and carry the two makes fourteen, carry the one makes two. Check it yourself. And do me a favor, eh? If I ever ask you to help me with my income tax—refuse. *Back to the phone:* Okay, that was two-Danish-two-coffee-one-double-cream-one-no-sugar . . . and? One toast, right. One ginger ale? *C'est tout?* It'll be right up. What's that? Look, darling, if I took time to read back all the orders, I'd never get anything done. Trust me. *To a customer:* Here's your eggs, honey. Enjoy. *To a customer:* Just hold your horses, will you? Everyone's in a hurry. You're something special? *To the cook:* Well? You got those grilled cheese? *What* grilled cheese? Useless! Get out of my way! *To the phone:* Restaurant? Just give me your order, darling. We'll exchange cute talk some other time. Yes. Yes. I got it. You want that with the toast or instead of? Right. *To a customer:* Look, there's people standing. If you want to talk, go hire a hall. *To LaPointe:* Here we go, Lieutenant. Lean, like you like it. So who's the good-looking kid? Don't tell me he's a cop too! He looks too nice to be a cop. *To a customer:* I'm coming already! Take it easy; you'll live longer. *To herself:* Not that anybody cares how long you live.

The woman behind the counter is Chinese. She learned her English in Montreal.

The high level of noise and babble in the restaurant insulates any given conversation, so LaPointe and Guttmann are able to talk as they eat their plump hot meat sandwiches and drink their coffee.

"He's turning out to be a real nice kid," Guttmann says, "our poor helpless victim in the alley."

LaPointe shrugs. Whether or not this Tony Green was a type who deserved being stabbed is not the question. What's more important is that someone was sassy enough to do it on LaPointe's patch.

"Well, there's one thing we can rule out," Guttmann says, sipping his milky coffee after turning the cup so as to avoid the faint lipstick stain on the rim. "We can rule out the possibility of Antonio Verdini being a priest in civilian clothes."

LaPointe snorts in agreement. Although he remembered a case in which . . .

"Do you feel we're getting anywhere, sir?"

"It's hard to say. Most murders go unsolved, you know. Chances are we'll learn a lot about this Tony Green. Little by little, each door leading to another. We tipped the Vet because he has a funny hop to his walk. From him we got the wallet. The wallet brought us to the rooming house, where we learned a little about him, got a couple of short leads. From the girls we learned a little more. We'll keep pushing along, following the leads. Another door will lead us to another door. Then suddenly we'll probably come up against a wall. The last room will have no door. With a type like that—rubbers with ticklers, two women at a time, 'blood type: hot!'—anybody might have put him away. Maybe he got rough with some little *agace-pissette* who decided at the last moment that she didn't want to lose her *josepheté* after all, and maybe he slapped her around a little, and maybe her brother caught up with him in that alley, maybe . . . ah, it could be anybody."

"Yes, sir. There's also the possibility that we've already touched the killer. I mean, it could be the Vet. You don't seem to suspect him, but he did take the wallet, and he's not the most stable type in the world. Or, if Green was playing around with that concierge, her boyfriend Arnaud might have put him away. I mean, we have reason to suspect he's no confirmed pacifist." Guttmann finishes his sandwich and pushes aside the plate with its last few greasy *patates frites*.

"You know, you're right there," LaPointe says. "At some point or other in this business, the chances are we'll touch the killer. But we probably won't know it. We'll probably touch him, pass over him, maybe come back and touch him again. Or her. That doesn't mean we'll ever get evidence in hand. But you never know. If we keep pressing, we might get him, even blind. He might get jumpy and do something dumb. Or we might flush out an informer. That's why we have to go through the motions. Right up until we hit the blank wall."

"What do we do now?"

"Well, you go home and see if you can make up with that girl of yours. I'm going to have a talk with someone. I'll see you Monday at the office."

"You're going to question that woman who runs a restaurant? The lesbian the concierge mentioned?"

LaPointe nods.

"I'd like to come along. Who knows, I might learn something."

"You think that's possible? No. I know her. I've known her since she was a kid on the street. She'll talk to me."

"But not if I was around?"

"Not as openly."

"Because I'm a callow and inexperienced youth?"

"Probably. Whatever callow means."

As LaPointe turns off the Main, he passes a brownstone that has been converted into a *shul* by members of one of the more rigid Jewish sects—the ones with sidelocks—he can never remember its name. A voice calls to him, and he turns to see a familiar figure on the Main, walking slowly and with dignity, his *shtreimel* perfectly level on his head. LaPointe walks back and asks what the matter is. Their janitor is home sick with a cold, and they need a *Shabbes goy* to turn on the lights. LaPointe is glad to be of help, and the old Chasidic gentleman thanks him politely, but not excessively, because after all the Lieutenant is a public servant and everyone pays taxes. Too much

176

thanks would give the appearance of artificial humility, and too humble is half proud.

He turns the corner of a side street to face a stream of damp wind as he walks toward La Jolie France Bar-B-Q, the café nearest the Italian boy's rooming house. It is the kind of place that does all its business at mealtimes, mostly from single workingmen who take their meals there at a weekly rate. So the place is empty when he enters, meeting a wall of pleasant heat after the penetrating cold. Almost immediately, the steamy windows and the thick smell of hot grease from *patates frites* make him open his overcoat and tug it off. He has his pick of tables, all of which are still littered with dishes and crumbs and slops. He sits instead at the counter, which is clean, if wet with recent wiping. Behind the counter a plump young girl with vacant eyes rinses out a glass in a sink of water that is not perfectly clear. She looks up and smiles, but her voice is vague, as though she is thinking of something else. "You want?" she asks absently.

Just then a short, sinewy woman with her hair dyed orange-red and a Gauloise dangling from the corner of her mouth bursts through the back swinging door, hefting a ten-gallon can of milk on her hip. "I'll take care of the Lieutenant, honey. You get the dishes off the tables." With a grunt and a deft swing, she hoists the heavy can into place in the milk dispenser, then she threads its white umbilical cord down through the hole in the bottom. "What can I do for you, LaPointe?" she asks, not stopping her work, nor taking the cigarette from her mouth.

"Just a cup of coffee, Carrot."

"A cup of coffee it is." She takes up a butcher knife and with a quick slice cuts off the end of the white tube. It bleeds a few drops of milk onto the stainless-steel tray. "Aren't you glad that wasn't your *bizoune?*" she asks, tossing the knife into the oily water and taking down a coffee mug from the stack. "Not that you'd really miss it all that much at your age. Black with sugar, isn't it?"

"That's right."

177

"There you go." The mug slides easily over the wet counter. "Come to think of it, even if you don't chase the buns anymore, you were probably a pretty good *botte* in your day. God knows you're coldblooded enough." She leans against the counter as she speaks, one fist on a flat hip, the smoke of her fat French cigarette curling up into her eyes, which are habitually squinted against the sting of it. She is one of the few people who *tutoyer* LaPointe. She *tutoyers* all men.

"She's new, isn't she?" LaPointe asks, nodding toward the plump girl who is lymphatically stacking dishes while gazing out the window.

"No, she's used. Goddamned well used!" Carrot laughs, then a stream of raw smoke gets into her lungs and she coughs—a dry wheezing cough, but she does not take the cigarette from her lips. "New to you, maybe. She's been around for about a year. But then, I haven't seen you around here since I had that last bit of trouble. That makes a fellow wonder if your coming around means she's in trouble." She watches him, one eye squinted more than the other.

He stirs the unwanted coffee. "*Are* you in trouble, Carrot?"

"Trouble? Me? No-o-o. A middle-aged lesbian with rotten lungs, a bad business, a heavy mortgage, two shots in prison on her record, and the laziest bitch in North America working for her? In trouble? No way. I won't be in trouble until they stop making henna. *Then* I'm in trouble. That's the problem with being nothing but a pretty face!" She laughs hoarsely, then her dry cough breaks up the rising thread of gray cigarette smoke and puffs it toward LaPointe.

He doesn't look up from his coffee. "There was a good-looking Italian boy named Verdini, or Green. You went to his place."

"So?"

"You had a fight."

"Just words. I didn't hit him."

"No threats?"

She shrugs. "Who remembers, when you're mad. I

probably told him I'd cut off his hose if he didn't stop sniffing around my girl. I don't remember exactly. You mean the son of a bitch reported me?"

"No. He didn't report you."

"Well, that's a good thing for him. Whatever I said, it must have scared him good. He hasn't been back here since. Do you know what that son of a bitch wanted? He used to come in here once in a while. He sized up the situation. I mean . . . just look at her. Look at me. You don't have to be a genius to size up the situation. So, while I'm waiting on the counter, this asshole is singing the apple to my girl. Well, he's a pretty boy, and she owns all the patents on stupid, so pretty soon she's ga-ga. But it isn't just her he wants. He thought it would be a kick to have us both at the same time! Sort of a round robin! He talked the dumb bitch into asking me if I'd be interested. Can you believe that? He gave her his address and told her we could drop in anytime. I dropped in, all right! I went over there and dropped on him like a ton of shit off a rooftop! Hey, what's all this about? If he didn't report me, why are you asking about him?"

"He's dead. Cut."

She reaches up slowly and takes the cigarette from the corner of her mouth. It sticks to the lower lip and tugs off a bit of skin. She touches the bleeding spot with the tip of her tongue, then daubs at it with the knuckle of her forefinger. Her eyes never leave LaPointe's. After a silence, she says simply, "Not me."

He shrugs. "It's happened before, Carrot. Twice. And both times because someone was after one of your girls."

"Yeah, but Jesus Christ, I only beat them up! I didn't kill them! And I did my time for it, didn't I?"

"Carrot, you have to realize that with your record . . ."

"Yeah. Yeah, I guess so. But I didn't do it. I wouldn't shit you, LaPointe. I didn't shit you either of those other times, did I?"

"But it wasn't a matter of murder then. And there were witnesses, so it wouldn't have done you any good to shit me."

Carrot nods. That's true.

The plump girl comes back to the counter carrying only four plates and a couple of spoons. She hasn't heard the conversation. She hasn't been paying attention. She has been humming a popular song, repeating certain passages until she thinks they sound right.

"That's good, honey," Carrot says maternally. "Now go get the rest of the dishes."

The girl stares at her vacantly, then, catching her breath as though she suddenly understands, she turns back and begins to clear the next table.

Carrot's face softens as she watches the girl, and La-Pointe remembers her as a kid, a fresh-mouthed tomboy in knickers, flipping war cards against a wall—gory cards with pictures of the Sino-Japanese war. She was loud and impish, and she had the most vulgar tongue in her gang. The hair she tucked up into her cap used to be genuinely red. LaPointe recalls the time she smashed her toe when she and her gang were pushing a car off its jack for the hell of it. They brought her to the hospital in a police car. She didn't cry once. She dug her fingernails into LaPointe's hand, but she didn't cry. Any boy of her age would have wailed, but she didn't dare. She was never a girl; just the skinniest of the boys.

After a silence, LaPointe asks, "You figure she's worth it?"

"What do you mean?" Carrot lights another Gauloise and sucks in the first long, rasping drag, then she lets it dangle forgotten between her lips.

"A dummy like that? Is she worth the trouble you're in now?"

"Nobody says she's a genius. And talking to her is like talking to yourself . . . but with dumber answers."

"So?"

"What can I say? She's fantastic in the rack. The best *botte* I ever had. She just stares up at the ceiling, squeezing those big tits of hers, and she comes and comes and *comes*. There's no end to it. And all the time she's squirming all over the bed. You have to hang on and ride her, like fighting a crocodile. It makes you feel great, you know what I

180

mean? Proud of yourself. Makes you feel you're the best lover in the world."

LaPointe looks over at the bovine, languid girl shuffling aimlessly to the third table. "And you would kill to keep her?"

Carrot is silent for a time. "I don't know, LaPointe. I really don't. Maybe. Depends on how mad I got. But I didn't kill that wop son of a bitch, and that's the good Lord's own truth. Don't you believe me?"

"Do you have an alibi?"

"I don't know. That depends on what time the bastard got himself cut."

That's a good answer, LaPointe thinks. Or a smart one. "He was killed night before last. A little after midnight."

Carrot thinks for only a second. "I was right here."

"With the girl?"

"Yeah. That is, I was watching television. She was up in bed."

"You were alone, then?"

"Sure."

"And the girl was asleep? That means she can't swear you didn't go out."

"But I was right here, I tell you! I was sitting right in that chair with my feet up on that other one. Last customer was out of here about eleven. I cleaned up a little. Then I switched on the TV. I wasn't sleepy. Too much coffee, I guess."

"Why didn't you go up to bed with her?"

Carrot shrugs. "She's flying the flag just now. She doesn't like it when she's flying the flag. She's just a kid, after all."

"What did you watch?"

"What?"

"On TV. What did you watch?"

"Ah . . . let's see. It's hard to remember. I mean, you don't really watch TV. Not like a movie. You just sort of stare at it. Let's see. Oh, yeah! There was a film on the English channel, so I changed over to the French channel."

181

"And?"

"And . . . shit, I don't remember. I'd been working all day. This place opens at seven in the morning, you know. I think I might have dropped off, sitting there with my feet up. Wait a minute. Yes, that's right. I did drop off. I remember because when I woke up it was cold. I'd turned off the stove to save fuel, and . . ." Her voice trails off, and she turns away to look out the window at the empty street, somber and cold in the zinc overcast. A little girl runs by, screeching with mock fright as a boy chases her. The girl lets herself be caught, and the boy hits her hard on the arm by way of caress. Carrot inhales a stream of blue smoke through her nose. "It doesn't sound too good, does it, LaPointe?" Her voice is flat and tired. "First I tell you I was watching TV. Then when you ask me what was on, I tell you I fell asleep "

"Maybe it was all that coffee you drank."

She glances at him with a gray smile. "Yeah. Right. Coffee sure knocks you out." She shakes her head. Then she draws a deep breath. "What about *your* coffee, pal? Can I warm it up for you?"

LaPointe doesn't want more coffee, but he doesn't want to refuse her. He drinks the last of the tepid cup, then pushes it over to her.

While pouring the coffee, her back to him, she asks with the unconvincing bravado of a teen-age tough, "Am I your only suspect?"

"No. But you're the best."

She nods. "Well, that's what counts. Be best at whatever you do." She turns and grins at him, a faded imitation of the sassy grin she had when she was a kid on the street. "Where do we go from here?"

"Not downtown, if that's what you mean. Not now, anyway."

"You're saying you believe me?"

"I'm not saying that at all. I'm saying I don't know. You're capable of killing, with that temper of yours. On the other hand, I've known you for twenty-eight years, ever since I was a cop on the beat and you were a kid always getting into trouble. You were always wild and snotty, but

182

you weren't stupid. With a day and a half to think up an alibi, I can't believe you'd come up with a silly story like that. Unless . . ."

"Unless what?"

"Unless a couple of things. Unless you thought we'd never trace the victim to here. Unless you're being doubly crafty. Unless you're covering for someone." LaPointe shrugs. He'll see. Little by little, he'll keep opening doors that lead into rooms that have doors that lead into rooms. And maybe, instead of running into that blank wall, one of the doors will lead him back to La Jolie France Bar-B-Q. "Tell me, Carrot. This Italian kid, did he have any friends among your customers?"

She gives him his coffee. "No, not friends. The only reason he ate here sometimes was because some of the guys talk Italian, and his English wasn't all that good. But he always had money, and a couple of my regulars went bar crawling with him once or twice. I heard them groaning about it the next morning, so sick they couldn't keep anything but coffee down."

"What bars?"

"Shit, I don't know."

"Talk to your customers tomorrow. Find out what you can about him."

"I'm closed on Sundays."

"Monday then. I want to know what bars he went to. Who he knew."

"Okay."

"By the way, does chocolate mean anything to you?"

"What kind of question is that? I can take it or leave it alone."

"Chocolate. As a name. Can you think of anybody with a name like chocolate or cocoa or anything like that?"

"Ah . . . wasn't there somebody who used to be on TV with Sid Caesar?"

"No, someone around here. Someone this Tony Green knew."

"Search me."

"Forget it, then." LaPointe swivels on his counter stool and looks at the plump girl. She has given up clearing the tables, or maybe she has forgotten what she was supposed to be doing, and she stands with her forehead against the far window, staring vacantly into the street and making a haze of vapor on the glass with her breath. She notices the haze and begins to draw X's in it with her little finger, totally involved in the activity. LaPointe cannot help picturing her squirming all over the bed, kneading her own breasts. He stands up to leave. "Okay, Carrot. You call me if you find out anything about this kid's bars or friends. If I don't hear from you, I'll be back."

"And maybe you'll be back anyway, right?"

"Yes, maybe." He buttons up his overcoat and goes to the door.

"Hey, LaPointe?"

He turns back.

"The coffee? That's fifteen cents."

8

On the way to his apartment, LaPointe passes the head-
quarters of the First Regiment of the Grenadier Guards of
Canada. Two young soldiers with automatic rifles slung
across their combat fatigues pace up and down before the
gate, their breath streaming from their nostrils in widening
jets of vapor, and their noses and ears red with the cold.
They are watching a little group of hippies across the
street. Three boys and two girls are loading clothes and
cardboard boxes into a battered, flower-painted VW van,
moving from a place where they haven't paid their rent to
a place where they won't. A meaty girl who is above the
social subterfuges of make-up and hair-washing is doing
most of the work, while another girl sits on a box, staring
ahead and nodding in tempo with some inner melody. The
three boys stand about, their hands in their pockets, their
faces somber and pinched with the cold. They have fled
from establishment conformity, taking identical routes toward individuality. They could have been stamped from the
same mold, all long-legged and thin-chested, their shoulders round and huddled against the cold.

By contrast, the guards keep their shoulders unnaturally square and their chests boldly out. LaPointe assumes that once the hippies have driven away, the guards will relax and round their shoulders against the wind. He smiles to himself.

Before mounting the wooden stairs, LaPointe looks up at the windows of his apartment. No lights. She must still be out shopping.

The static cold of the apartment is more chilling than the wind, so he immediately lights the gas heater, then sets water to boil, thinking to have a nice hot cup of coffee waiting for her when she comes back.

The water comes to a boil, and she has still not returned. He empties the kettle, refills it, and replaces it on the gas ring. As though putting on the water is a kind of sympathetic magic that will bring her home to the coffee.

It doesn't work.

He sits in his armchair and looks across the deserted park, drab in the winter overcast. Perhaps she's left for good. Why shouldn't she? She owes him nothing. Maybe she has met somebody . . . a young man who knows how to dance. That would be best, really. After all, she can't go on living with him indefinitely. In fact, he doesn't want her to. Not really. She'd be a pain in the neck. Then too, someday soon . . .

Without thinking, he slips his hand up to his chest, as he has come to do by habit each time he thinks of his aneurism . . . that stretched balloon. He feels the regular heartbeat. Normal. Nothing odd in it. Yes, he decides. It would be best if she's found somebody else to live with. It would be ghastly for her to wake up some morning and find him beside her, dead. Maybe cold to the touch.

Or what if he were to have an attack while they were making love?

Good, then. That's just fine. She has found a young man on the street. Somebody kind. It's better that way.

He grunts out of the chair and goes into the kitchen to take off the kettle before the water boils away. He will enjoy a quiet, peaceful night. He will take off his shoes, put on his robe, and sit by the window, listening to the hiss of the gas fire and reading one of his Zola novels for the third or fourth time. He never tires of reading around and around his battered set of Zola. Years ago, he bought the imitation-leather books from an old man who ran a second-hand bookstore, a narrow slot of a shop created by roofing over an alley between two buildings on the Main. The old man never did much business, and buying the books was a way of helping him out without embarrassing him.

For several years the books sat unread on the top of his bedroom chest. Then one evening, for lack of something to do, he opened one and scanned it over. Within a year he had read them all. It wasn't until the first time through that he realized there was a sort of order to some of them: heroines of one book were the daughters of heroines of another, and so on. Thereafter he always read them in order. His favorite novel is *L'Assommoir*, in which he was able to predict, in his first reading, the inevitable descent of the characters from hope to alcoholism to death. The books feel good in his hand, and have a friendly smell. It is the 1906 *Edition Populaire Illustrée des Oeuvres Complètes de Émile Zola*, with drawings of substantial heroines, their round arms uplifted in supplication and round eyes raised to heaven, the line of dialogue beneath never lacking in exclamation points. Such men as appear in the plates stand back, amongst the dripping shadows, and look mercilessly down on the fallen heroines. The men are not individuals; they are part of the environment of poverty, despair, and exploitation to which futile hope gives edge.

The novels are populated by people who, if they spoke in Joual dialect and knew about modern things, could be living on the Main. It seems to LaPointe that you have to know the street, to have known the parents of the young chippies back when they were young lovers, in order to enjoy or even understand Zola.

Yes, he'll put on his robe and read for a while. Then he'll go to bed. He is looking for his robe when he notices in the corner of the bedroom Marie-Louise's shopping bag with its burden of odds and ends.

She will be back after all. The shopping bag is a hostage. He returns to the living room feeling less tired. She will surely be back within half an hour.

She is not. Evening imperceptibly deepens the sky to dusty slate as details down in the park retire into gloom. The novel is still on his lap, but it is too dark to read. The gas fire hisses, its orange-nippled ceramic elements an insubstantial glow, the room's only light. Twice, when cars stop outside, he rises to look down from the window. And once he starts up with the realization that the kettle must be burning. Then he remembers that he took it off long ago.

The air becomes hot and thick with the oxygen-robbing gas heater, which he knows he should turn down, but he is too tired and heavy to feel like moving.

As always, his daydreams stray to his wife . . . and his girls. It is late evening in their home in Laval. Lucille is doing dishes in the kitchen fixed up with modern appliances he has seen in store windows on the Main. Logs are burning in the fireplace, and he is fussing with them more than they need, because he enjoys poking at wood fires. He goes up to the girls' room—they are young again, and they are disobeying orders to get right to sleep. He finds them jumping on the bed, their long flannel nightgowns billowing out and entangling them when they land in a heap. He kisses them good night and teases them by scrubbing his whiskery cheek against their powdery ones. They complain and struggle and laugh. Lucille calls up that it is late and the girls need their sleep. He answers that they are already asleep, and the girls put their hands over their mouths to suppress giggles. He tucks them in with a final kiss, and they want a story and he says no, and they want the light left on and he says no, and they want a glass of water and he says no, and he turns out the light and leaves them and goes back down the stairs—he must get around to fixing the one that squeaks. He knows every detail of the house, the layout of the rooms, the wallpaper, the pencil marks on the kitchen doorframe that record the growth of the girls. But he never pictures a bedroom for Lucille and him. After all, Lucille is dead. No . . . gone. To the house in Laval.

He wakes with a sweaty throat and a wet mouth, and

with a confused feeling that something is going on. Then he hears the sound of a key in the lock. The door opens with a slant of pale yellow light from the naked hall bulb, and Marie-Louise enters.

"My God, it's hot in here! What are you doing, sitting in the dark?"

As he gropes out of sleepiness, she finds the switch and turns on the lights. She is loaded down with parcels, which she dumps on the sofa, then holds her hands out to the gas fire. "Boy, it's cold tonight. Well? What do you think of it? Cute, eh?" She turns around to model an ankle-length cloth coat of burnt orange. "It was on sale. Well?"

She walks a couple of steps and does a comic little turn, parodying the models she has seen on television. She doesn't bother to conceal her limp, and LaPointe notices it as though for the first time. The detail had dropped from his mind. "It's . . . ah . . . fine," he says dopily. "Very nice." He wonders what time it is.

She hugs herself and rubs her upper arms vigorously. "Boy, it's the kind of cold that goes right through you. I was hoping you might have some hot coffee ready."

"I'm sorry," he says. "It didn't occur to me."

He is uneasy about the babbling quality of her speech. She's trying to say everything at once, as though she has something to hide and doesn't want to leave him space to question her. She says it's too hot in the room, yet she warms herself at the heater. Something's wrong.

"What have you been doing with yourself?" she asks lightly.

"Taking a nap." He looks at the mantel clock. Eight-thirty. "You've been shopping all this time?"

"Yes," she says with the inhaled Joual affirmative that means either yes or no.

"Take a cab home?"

She pauses for a second, her back to him. "No. I walked." Her hollow tone tells him there is something in the way of a confession coming. He wishes he hadn't asked.

"No cabs?" he asks, affording her a facile excuse.

She sits on the sofa and looks directly at him for the first time. She might as well get it over with. "No money," she says. "I'm sorry, but I spent all you gave me. I got other things besides the coat and dress."

That is the confession? He smiles at himself, aware that he has been acting and thinking like a kid. "It doesn't matter," he says.

She turns her head slightly to the side and looks at him uncertainly out of the sides of her eyes. "Really?"

He laughs. "Really."

"Hey! Look at what I got!" Instantly she is up from the sofa, tearing open bags. "And I shopped around for bargains, too. I didn't waste money. Oh, did you see these?" She parts her long cloth coat and shows him thick-soled boots that go to the knee. They are a wet red plastic that clashes with the burnt orange of the coat. She rips open a bag and draws out a long dress that looks as though it were made of patchwork. She holds it up to herself by the shoulders and kicks out at the hem. "What do you think?"

"Nice. It looks . . . warm."

"Warm? Oh, I suppose so. The girl told me it's the in thing. Oh, and I got a skirt." She opens her coat again to show him the mini she is wearing. "And I got this blouse. There was another one I really liked. You know, one of those frilled collars like you see on old-time movies on TV? You know the kind I mean?"

"Yes," he lies.

"But they didn't have my size. And I got . . . let's see . . . oh, a sweater! And . . . I guess that's about it. No! I got some panties and things . . . there must have been something else. Oh, the coat! That's what cost the most. And I guess that's it!" She plunks down on the sofa amongst the clothes and ravished bags, her hands pressed between her knees, her elation suddenly evaporated. "You don't like them, do you?" she says.

"What? No, sure. I mean . . . they're fine."

"It's all the money, isn't it?"

"Don't worry about it."

"You know, we don't *have* to go out to dinner tonight like you promised. We could just stay home. That would save money."

190

There is a quality of pimpish insinuation in the way the proprietor of the Greek restaurant finds them a secluded table, in the way he keeps refilling her glass with raisin wine, in the way he grins and nods to the Lieutenant from behind her chair. LaPointe resents this, but Marie-Louise seems to be enjoying the special attention, so he lets it go.

Greek food is alien to her, but she eats with relish, unfolding the cooked grape leaves to get at the rice and lamb within. She doesn't eat the leaves, considering them to be only wrappings.

A candle set in red glass lights her face from a low angle that would be unkind to an older woman, but it only accents her animation as she recounts her shopping trip, or comments on the other patrons of the restaurant. He has chosen to sit with his back to the room so she can have the amusement of looking at the people and the pleasure of having the people look at her. It is a deliberate and uncommon gesture on the part of a man who normally keeps his back to walls and rooms open before him.

She doesn't really like the Greek wine, but she drinks too much of it. By the time the meal is over, she is laughing a little too loudly.

He enjoys watching the uncensored play of expression over her face. She has not yet developed a mask. She is perfectly capable of lying, but not yet of dissimulating. She is capable of wheedling, but not yet of treachery. She is vulgar, but not yet hardened. She is still young and vulnerable. He, on the other hand, is old and . . . tough.

As they finish their coffee—that Turkish coffee with thick dregs that Greeks think is Greek—she hums along with jukebox music coming from the floor above the restaurant.

"What's up there?" she asks, looking toward the stairs.

"A bar of sorts."

"With dancing?"

He shrugs. "Oh, there's a dance floor. . . ." He really feels like going home.

"Could we dance there?"

"I don't dance."

"Didn't you ever? Even when you were young?"

He smiles. "No. Not even then."

"How old are you anyway?"

"Fifty-three. I told you before."

"No, you didn't."

"I did. You forgot."

"You're older than my father. Do you realize that? You are older than my father." She seems to think that is remarkable.

It is so obvious a tactic that it would be unkind not to let it work. So they climb the stairs and enter a large dark room with a bar lit by colored bulbs behind ripple glass and a jukebox that glows with lights of ever-changing hues. They take one of the booths along the wall. The only other people there are the barmaid and a group of four young Greek boys at the next booth but one, sharing a bottle of ouzo that has been iced until it leaves wet rings on the tabletop. One of the boys leaves the booth and goes to the bar, where he lightheartedly sings the apple to the barmaid. She is wearing a short dress, and her thighs are so thick that her black hose squeaks with friction when she walks to serve the tables.

"What would you like?" LaPointe asks.

"What are they having?" She indicates the group of young men.

"Ouzo."

"Would I like that?"

"Probably."

"Do you like it?"

"No."

She feels there is a mild dig in that, so she orders ouzo defiantly. He has an Armagnac.

While the barmaid squeaks away to fetch the drinks, Marie-Louise rises and goes to the jukebox to examine its selections, slightly bending the knee of her good leg to make her limp imperceptible. LaPointe knows she doesn't care if he notices it, so the caution must be for the young Greek boys. As she leans over the jukebox, its colored light is caught in the frizzy mop of her hair, and she looks very

192

attractive. Her bottom is round and tight under the new mini-skirt. He is proud of her. And the Greek boys do not fail to notice her and exchange appreciative looks.

She is the same age as his imaginary daughters sometimes are. She is the same age as his real wife always is. He feels two things simultaneously: he is proud of his attractive daughter, jealous of his attractive wife. Stupid.

There is some playful nudging among the Greek boys, and one of them—the boldest, or the clown—gets up and joins her, leaning close to study the record offerings. He puts a coin into the slot and gestures to her to make a selection. She smiles thanks and pushes two buttons. When he asks her to dance, she accepts without even looking at LaPointe. The music is modern and loud, and they dance without touching. Despite the jerky, primitive movements of the dance, she seems strong and controlled and graceful, and the dancing completely camouflages her limp. It is easy to see why she enjoys it so much.

The record stops without ending, like all modern music, a fade-out concealing its inability to resolve, and the dance is over. The young man says something to her, and she shakes her head, but she smiles. They return, each to his own table. As he passes, the Greek boy salutes LaPointe with a sassy little wave.

Marie-Louise slides into the booth a little out of breath and exuberant. "He's a good dancer."

"How can you tell?" LaPointe asks.

"Oh, the drinks are here. Well, 'bottoms up.'" She speaks the toast in English so accented that the second word sounds like "zeup." "Hey, this is good. Like licorice candy. But hot." She finishes it off. "May I have another one?"

"Sure. But it might make you sick."

She thrusts out her lower lip and shrugs.

He signals the waitress.

A party of older men clatters up the stairs, half drunk from celebrating a wedding. They drag out the tables from two booths and put them together, collecting chairs from everywhere. One man slaps his hand on the table and clamors for ouzo, and they are served two ice-cold bottles and a tray of glasses. One rises and proposes a toast to the father of the bride, who is the drunkest and happiest of the lot. The toaster is long-winded and somewhat incoherent; the others complain that they will never get a chance to drink, and finally they shout him down and slap back the first glasses.

One of the young men has put money into the jukebox. As the music starts he saunters toward LaPointe's booth.

"You don't mind, do you?" Marie-Louise asks.

He shakes his head.

The proprietor comes up from the restaurant to check on things. When he notices the boy dancing with Marie-Louise, he frowns and crosses to the booth with the three young men. There is a short conversation during which one of the boys stretches his neck to take a look at LaPointe. As he passes the booth to offer insincere congratulations to the father of the bride, the proprietor nods and winks conspiratorially at the Lieutenant. He has taken care of everything. The young men won't be horning in on his girl again.

Marie-Louise finishes her ouzo and wants a third. For some minutes she sits, swaying her shoulders in tempo to a melody she is humming. She doesn't understand why the boys don't play more records and ask her to dance.

LaPointe is about to suggest that they go home, when one of the wedding party rises and navigates an arcing course to the jukebox. He pushes in a coin with operatic thoroughness, then presses first one button, then another. In a moment there comes the first twanging note of a stately traditional song. The old man lifts his arms slowly; his head is turned to one side and his eyes are closed; his fingers snap crisply to every second beat of the music.

The boys in the booth groan over the old-fashioned selection.

The old man looks directly at them, his eyes smiling and clever, and he slowly shuffles toward them, snapping his fingers and dipping gracefully with every third step.

"No way!" says one of the boys. "Forget it!"

But the old man advances confidently. These kids may be modern and may speak English, but their blood is Greek, and he will win.

Three other members of the wedding party are now on the dance floor, their arms around one another's shoulders, the outside two snapping their fingers to the compelling tempo, and dipping with each third step. Too drunk to walk perfectly, they dance with balance, grace, and authority.

There is a friendly scuffle in the young men's booth and one of them is pushed out onto the floor. With peevish reservation, he begins to snap his fingers mechanically, making it perfectly clear that this old-country shit is not for him. But the old man dances directly in front of him, looking him steadily in the eye and insisting silently on their common heritage. And when he puts his arm around the boy's shoulders, the peevishness evaporates and he falls into step. After all, he is a man.

The tempo of the music increases relentlessly. The five link up. Two other old men join the end of the line, one of them brandishing an ouzo bottle in his free hand. It is two steps to the side, then a strong dip forward. Marie-Louise watches with fascination. She is surprised when she notices that LaPointe is clapping his hands in time with the music, then she sees that the men at the double table are clapping also. When she starts to rise to join the dancing, LaPointe shakes his head.

"It's a men's dance."

"Oh, they won't mind."

He shrugs. Perhaps they won't. After all, she is not a Greek girl. In fact, they part to make a place for her in the line, and from the first step she is native to the simple, inevitable dance. She adds to it a flair of her own, dipping very low and bowing her head almost to the floor, then whipping it back as she snaps up again.

With this the other three young men run out to join the dance.

When the music ends, there are yelps of joy and

everyone applauds his own performance. Instantly another coin is in the machine. LaPointe is recognized, and an envoy of two old men come to invite him to join the larger table. He signals for a bottle of ouzo as his contribution and brings his glass along. The instant he sits down, the glass is filled to overflowing with ouzo. He had not finished the Armagnac, and the mixture is ugly, so he downs it quickly to be rid of it. And his glass is instantly filled again.

Because she is Greek, the barmaid does not join the dancing, but she sits at the common table between two old men, one of whom complains drunkenly that nobody let him finish the toast he had rehearsed all day long. The other occasionally slips his hand between her legs where the thick thighs touch. She laughs and rolls her eyes, sometimes slapping the hand away and sometimes giving it a hard squeeze with her thighs that makes the old man whoop with naughty pleasure.

After the fourth or fifth dance, Marie-Louise is exhausted, and she sits one out, pulling up a chair across from LaPointe, between one of the boys and an old man. The old man is very drunk and insists on telling her a very important story that he cannot quite remember. She listens and laughs, despite the fact that he speaks only Greek. LaPointe knows that the boy has his hand in her lap under the table. His extravagant nonchalance gives him away.

An hour and a half later, Marie-Louise is dancing with one of the boys, while one of the old men clings to LaPointe, his hand gripping the nape of his neck, and explains that all cops are bastards, except of course LaPointe, who is a good man . . . so good that he is almost Greek. Not quite, but almost.

By the end of the night, the table is awash with water that has condensed from the icy bottles, and with spilled ouzo.

When he finds the problem of getting his key into the lock both fascinating and amusing, LaPointe realizes that he is drunk for the first time in years. Drunk on ouzo. A sick drunk. Stupid.

It is hot in the room because he forgot to turn the fire

off when they left. He does it now, while she slips through to the bathroom, humming one of the Greek songs and occasionally snapping her fingers.

"Did you have a good time?" she calls when he comes into the bedroom and sits heavily on the bed. She is on the toilet, with the door wide open, talking to him without embarrassment while she pisses.

She doesn't wait for his answer. "I had a great time!" she says. "Best time of my life. I wish you could dance. Can we go there again?" As he tugs off his shoes, she wipes herself and stands up, shaking down her skirt as the toilet flushes.

LaPointe, drunk, is touched by the marital intimacy of it. It is as if they had been together for years. She must like me, he thinks. She must feel safe with me, if she doesn't mind pissing in my presence.

Now he *knows* he is drunk. He laughs at himself. Come on, LaPointe! Is that an act of love? A gesture of confidence? Pissing in your presence? With sodden seriousness, he confirms that, yes, it is. How long was it after your marriage before Lucille lost her embarrassment with you? She didn't even like to brush her teeth in your presence at first.

But . . . it could be something other than confidence, this pissing while chatting. It could be indifference.

Who cares?

Stupid, stupid. Drunk on ouzo. And you shouldn't drink with that aneur . . . anor . . . whateverthehell it is!

She undresses quickly, leaving things where they fall, and slips under the covers. The sheets are cold and she shudders as her naked legs touch them. "Hurry up. Get into bed. Make me warm."

He turns off the light before taking off his pants, then he gets in beside her. She clings to him, putting her leg over his for warmth. Soon their body heat warms the bed enough that one dares to move a leg to virgin parts of the sheet. She slips her knee between his legs and turns over, half upon him. The streetlight beneath the window makes her face visible in the dark. "What's wrong?" she asks, running her hand over his chest. She laughs at him. "Hey, I'm not your daughter, after all."

What? What put that into her head? What's wrong with her?

They make love.

9

He wakes to dazzling sunlight streaming through the bedroom window, and to a heavy block of pain lodged behind his eyes. Ouzo.

The sunlight is unexpected after three weeks of leaden skies. It might mark the end of the pig weather, or it might be nothing more than one of those occasional wind shifts that bring diamond-hard winter cold for a few hours, like the night that Italian kid was found in the alley.

He puffs out a little breath and is not surprised to see it make a shallow cone of vapor. It will be sparkling and frigid out in the park. He slips out of bed, trying not to let cold air in to disturb Marie-Louise. When he bends forward to fish around for his slippers, he discovers the clot of ouzo pain behind his eyes is loose and jagged-edged. One eye closes involuntarily with the ache of it.

He pads into the living room muttering to himself: an ouzo hangover. Stupid, stupid, stupid. Giddiness overwhelms him briefly as he stoops down to light the gas fire. The last time he had a hangover like this was from drinking caribou, that most lethal of all liquids, with an old friend from Trois Rivières. But that was years and years ago.

As the bathtub fills, he cups his hands and drinks tap water from the sink. So desiccated is he that the water seems never to reach his stomach, being absorbed by parched tissue on its way down. He almost gags trying to swallow several aspirin with water from cupped hands. In the tub, his eyes closed, he sits a long time with steam rising all about him. The water and the heat and the aspirin combine to melt some of the ouzo out of his system; the nausea retreats, but the headache persists. Why did he drink so much? Why did he want to get drunk? He thinks about the love he and Marie-Louise made last night. It was good, and very gentle, particularly that long time he held her, between lovemakings. He believes it was good for her too. She wouldn't have faked all that. Why should she?

He did not shave last night before bed, as is his custom, but he doesn't dare try just now. He would probably cut his throat with the straight razor, shaky as he is.

While he makes coffee, he suddenly feels guilty about Marie-Louise. My God. If he feels this bad, what will *she* feel like? Poor kid.

The poor kid chatters with animation as she sits on the sofa, curled up in Lucille's pink robe. He answers in monosyllables, turning his head to look at her; it hurts when he moves his eyes.

"What was that licorice stuff we drank?" she asks. "It was good."

"Ouzo," he mutters.

"What?"

"Ouzo!"

"Hey, what's wrong? Are you mad about something?"

"No."

"You're sure you're not mad? I mean, you seem . . ."

"I'm fine."

"Say . . . you're not sick, are you?"

"Sick? Me?" He manages a chuckle.

"I just thought . . . I mean, you told me to watch out for that . . . what's it called again?"

"Ou-zo. Look, I'm fine. Just a little tired."

200

She looks at him sideways with a childish leer. "I don't blame you. You have a right to feel tired."

He smiles wanly. He cannot quite forgive her for being so healthy and buoyant, but she does look pretty with the sunlight in her hair like that.

She goes into the bedroom to find her hairbrush. When she returns, she is humming one of the Greek songs, doing a little sliding step and dipping down, then snapping her head up on the rise. One of his eyes closes involuntarily with the snap of her head. She plunks down on the sofa and begins to brush her hair. "Hey, we'll have to go out for breakfast. I told you that I didn't buy any groceries. I spent all the money on clothes. Where will we go?"

"I'm not particularly hungry; are you?"

"Hm-m! I could eat a horse! And look what a beautiful day it is!"

The glitter of the park stings his eyes. But yes, it is a beautiful day. Perhaps a walk in the cold air would help.

With few places open on a Sunday morning, they take breakfast in one of the *variété* shops common to this *quartier,* although slowly disappearing with the invasion of large cut-rate establishments. Such shops sell oddments and orts: candy, bagels, teddy bears, Chap Stick, ginger ale, jigsaw puzzles, aspirin, newspapers, cigarettes, contraceptives, kites, everything but what you need at any given moment. Its window is piled with dusty, fly-specked articles that are never sold and never rearranged. In the jumble, knitted snow caps and suntan lotion rest side by side, one or the other always out of season, except in spring, when they both are.

The proprietor moves a stack of newspapers to the floor to make room for them at the short, cracked marble counter. He has a reputation in the district for being a "type," and he works at maintaining it. Although his counter service is usually limited to stale, thick coffee in the winter and soft drinks in summer, he can accommodate light orders, if he happens to have cheese or eggs in the refrigerator of his living space behind the shop. They ask for eggs, toast, and coffee, which the proprietor fixes up

201

on his stove in the back room, all the while singing to himself and maintaining an animated conversation in English, his voice raised, from the other room.

"Is it sunny enough for you, Lieutenant? But I'd bet you a million bucks it won't last. If it don't snow tonight, then tomorrow will be the same as yesterday—shitbrindle clouds and no sun." He sticks his head out through the curtain. "Sorry, lady." He disappears back and calls, "Hey, do you want these sunny side up?

Keep your sunny side up, up . . .

Hey, you remember that one, Lieutenant? Oh-oh! I broke one. How about having them scrambled? They're better for you that way, anyway. Egg whites ain't good for your heart. I read that somewhere.

My heart is a hobo,
Loves to go out berry picking,
Hates to hear alarm clocks ticking.

You've *got* to remember that one, Lieutenant. Bing Crosby." He comes from the back room, carefully balancing two plates, which he sets down on the cracked counter. "There you go! Two orders of scrambled. Enjoy. Yeah, Bing Crosby sang that in one of his films. I think he was a priest. Say, do you remember Bobby Breen, Lieutenant?

There's a rainbow on the river . . .

That was a great movie. He sang that sitting on a hay wagon. You know, that ain't easy, singing while you're on a hay wagon. Yeah, Bobby Breen and Shirley Temple. Wonder whatever became of Shirley Temple. They don't make movies like that any more. All this violence shit. Sorry, lady. Hey! You don't have any forks! No wonder you ain't eating. Here! Geez! I'd forget my ass if it wasn't tied on. Sorry, lady. Here's your coffee. Hey, did you read this morning about that guy getting stabbed in an alley just off the Main? How about that? It's getting so you can't take a walk around the block anymore without getting stabbed by some son of a bitch. Sorry, lady. Things ain't what they used to be. Right, Lieutenant? And the prices these days!

The moon belongs to everyone
The best things in life are free . . .

Don't you believe it! What can you get free these days? Advice. Cancer maybe. It's a miracle a man can stay in business with the prices. Everybody out to fuck his neighbor . . . oh, lady, I *am* sorry! Geez, I'm really sorry."

As they walk slowly along a gravel path through the park, her hand in the crook of his arm, she asks, "What was that *mec* jabbering about?"

"Oh, nothing. It never occurred to him that you don't speak English."

The crisp air has cleared LaPointe's headache away, and the little food has settled his stomach. The thin wintery sunshine warms the back of his coat pleasantly, but he can feel a sudden ten- or fifteen-degree drop in temperature when he steps into a shadow. The touch of this sun, dazzling but insubstantial, reminds him of winter mornings on his grandparents' farm, the soil of which was so rocky and poor that the family joke said the only things that grew there were potholes, which one could split into quarters and sell to the big farmers to be driven into the ground as post holes. All the LaPointes, aunts, cousins, in-laws, came to the farm for Christmas. And there were a lot of La-Pointes, because they were Catholic and part Indian, and you can't lock the door of a teepee. The children slept three or four to a bed, and sometimes the smaller ones were put across the bottom to fit more in. Claude LaPointe and his cousins fought and played games and pinched under the covers, but if anyone cried out with joy or pain, then the parents would stop their pinochle games downstairs and shout up that someone was going to get his ass smacked if he didn't cut it out and go to sleep! And all the kids held their breath and tried not to laugh, and they all sputtered out at once. One of the cousins thought it was funny to spit into the air through a gap in his teeth, and when the others hid under the blankets, he would fart.

On Christmas morning they were allowed into the parlor, musty-smelling but very clean because it was kept closed, except for Sundays, or when the priest visited, or when someone had died and was laid out in a casket supported on two saw horses hidden under a big white silk sheet rented from the undertaker.

The parlor was open, too, for Christmas. Kids opening presents on the floor. Christmas tree weeping needles onto a sheet. A pallid winter sun coming in the window, its beam capturing floating motes of dust.

The smell of mustiness in the parlor . . . and the heavy, sickening smell of flowers. And Grandpapa. Grandpapa . . .

Whenever a random image or sound on the Main triggers his memory in such a way as to carry him back to his grandfather, he always pulls himself back from the brink, away from dangerous memories. Of all the family, he had loved Grandpapa most . . . needed him most. But he had not been able to kiss him goodbye. He had not even been able to cry.

". . . still mad?"

"What?" LaPointe asks, surfacing from reverie. They have rounded the park and are approaching the gate across from his apartment.

"Are you still mad?" Marie-Louise asks again. "You haven't said a word."

"No," he laughs. "I'm not mad. Just thinking."

"About what?"

"Nothing. About being a kid. About my grandfather."

"Your grandfather! *Tabernouche!*"

That is a coincidence. He hasn't heard anyone but himself use that old-fashioned expletive since the death of his mother. "You think I'm too old to have grandparents?"

"Everyone has grandparents. But, my God, they must have been dead for ages."

"Yes. For ages. You know something? I wasn't mad at you this morning. I was sick."

"You?"

"Yes."

She considers this for a while. "That's funny."

"I suppose so."

"Hey, what do you want to do? Let's go somewhere, do something. Okay?"

"I don't really feel like going anywhere."

"Oh? What do you usually do on Sundays?"

"When I'm not working, I sit around in the apartment. Read. Listen to music on the radio. Cook supper for myself. Does that sound dull?"

She shrugs and hums a descending note that means: yes, sort of. Then she squeezes his arm. "I know why you're leading me back to the apartment. You didn't get enough last night, did you?"

He frowns. He wishes she wouldn't talk like a bar slut. He can hardly direct her to the apartment after she has said something like that, so they leave the park and stroll through back streets between Esplanade and the Main. This day of sunshine after weeks of pig weather has brought out the old people and the babies, making it seem almost like summer. In winter, the population of the Main seems to contract at its extremities; the old and the very young stay indoors. But in summer, there are babies in prams, or toddlers in harnesses, their leashes tied to stoop railings, while old, frail-chested men in panama hats walk carefully from porch to porch. And on the Main merchants stand in their open doorways, occasionally stepping out onto the sidewalk and looking up and down the street wistfully, wondering where all the shoppers could be on such a fine day. If one stops and looks in the window, the owner will silently appear beside him, seeming to examine the merchandise with admiration, then he will drift toward the door, as though the magnetism of his body can draw the customer after him.

The weight of her arm through his is pleasant, and whenever they cross a street, he presses it against his side, as though to conduct her safely across. They walk slowly down the Main, window-shopping, and sometimes he exchanges a word or two with people on the street. He notices that she automatically bends her knee to disguise her

205

limp when a youngish man approaches, though she doesn't bother when they are alone.

Around noon they take lunch at a small café, then they go back to the apartment.

For the past hour, Marie-Louise has puttered about, taking a bath, washing her hair, rinsing out some underclothes, trying on various combinations of the clothes she bought yesterday. She does not do domestic chores; the coffee cups go unwashed, the bed unmade. She has tuned the radio to a rock station which serves an unending stream of clatter and grunting, each bit introduced by a disc jockey who babbles with obvious delight in his own sound.

LaPointe finds the music abrasive, but he takes general pleasure in her busy presence. For a time he sits in his chair, reading the Sunday paper, but skipping the do-it-yourself column, which he finds less interesting than it used to be. Later, the paper slides from his lap as he dozes in the afternoon sunlight.

The burr of the doorbell wakes him with a snap. Who in hell? He looks out the window, but cannot see the caller standing under the entranceway. The only cars parked in the street are recognizable as those of neighbors. The doorbell burrs again.

"Yes?" he calls loudly into the old speaking tube. He has used it so seldom that he doubts its functioning.

"Claude?" the tinny membrane asks.

"Moishe?"

"Yes, Moishe."

LaPointe is confused. Moishe has never visited him before. None of the cardplayers has ever been here. How will he explain Marie-Louise?

"Claude?"

"Yes, come in. Come up. I'm on the second floor."

LaPointe turns away from the speaking tube to look over the room, then turns back and says, "Moishe? I'll come down . . ." But it is too late. Moishe has already started up the stairs.

Marie-Louise enters from the bedroom, wearing Lucille's quilted robe. "What is it?"

"Nothing," he says grumpily. "Just a friend."

"Do you want me to stay in the bedroom?"

"Ah, no." He might have suggested it if she hadn't, but when he hears it on her lips, he realizes how childish the idea is. "Turn the radio off, will you?"

There is a knock at the door, and at the same time the rock music roars as Marie-Louise turns the knob the wrong way.

"Sorry!"

"Forget it." He opens the door.

Moishe stands in the doorway, smiling uneasily. "What happened? You dropped something?"

"No, just the radio. Come in."

"Thank you." He takes off his hat as he enters. "Mademoiselle?"

Marie-Louise is standing by the radio, a towel turbaned around her newly washed hair.

LaPointe introduces them, telling Moishe that she is from Trois Rivières also, as if that explained something.

Moishe shakes hands with her, smiling and making a slight European bow.

"Well," LaPointe says with too much energy. "Ah . . . come sit down." He gestures Moishe to the sofa. "Would you like a cup of coffee?"

"No, no, thank you. I can only stay a moment. I was on my way to the shop, and I thought I would drop by. I telephoned earlier, but you didn't answer."

"We took a walk."

"Ah, I don't blame you. A beautiful day, eh, mademoiselle? Particularly after all this pig weather we appreciate it. The feast and famine principle."

She nods without understanding.

"Why did you phone?" LaPointe realizes this sounds unfriendly. He is off balance because of the girl.

"Oh, yes! About the game tomorrow night. The good priest called and said he wouldn't be able to make it. He's down with a cold, maybe a little flu. And I thought maybe you wouldn't want to play three-handed cutthroat."

On the rare occasions when one of them cannot make the game, the others play cutthroat, but it isn't nearly so much fun. LaPointe is usually the absent one, working on a case, or dead tired after a series of late nights.

"What about David?" LaPointe asks. "Does he want to play?"

"Ah, you know David. He always wants to play. He says that without the burden of Martin he will show us how the game is really played!"

"All right, then let's play. Teach him a lesson."

"Good." Moishe smiles at Marie-Louise. "All this talk about pinochle must be dull for you, mademoiselle."

She shrugs. She really hasn't been paying any attention. She has been engrossed in gnawing at a broken bit of thumbnail. For the first time, LaPointe notices that she bites her fingernails. And that her toenails are painted a garish red. He wishes she had gone into the bedroom after all.

"You realize, Claude, this is the first time I have ever visited you?"

"Yes, I know," he answers too quickly.

There is a short silence.

"I'm not surprised that Martin is ill," Moishe says. "He looked a little pallid the other night."

"I didn't notice it." LaPointe cannot think of anything to say to his friend. There is no reason why he should have to explain Marie-Louise to him. It's none of his business. Still . . . "You're sure you won't have some coffee?"

Moishe protects his chest with the backs of his hands. "No, no. Thank you. I must get back to the shop." He rises. "I'm a little behind in work. David is better at finding work than I am at doing it. See you tomorrow night then, Claude. Delighted to make your acquaintance, mademoiselle." He shakes hands at the door and starts down the staircase.

Even before Moishe has reached the front door, Marie-Louise says, "He's funny."

"In what way funny?"

"I don't know. He's polite and nice. That little bow of

208

his. And calling me mademoiselle. And he has a funny accent. Is he a friend of yours?"

LaPointe is looking out the window at Moishe descending the front stoop. "Yes, he's a friend."

"Too bad he has to work on Sundays."

"He's Jewish. Sunday is not his Sabbath. He never works on Saturdays."

Marie-Louise comes to the window and looks down at Moishe, who is walking down the street. "He's Jewish? Gee, he seemed very nice."

LaPointe laughs. "What's that supposed to mean?"

"I don't know. From what the nuns used to say about Jews . . . You know, I don't think I ever met a Jew in person before. Unless some of the men . . ." She shrugs and goes back to the gas fire, where she kneels and scrubs her hair with her fingers to dry it. The side closest to the fire dries quickly and springs back into its frizzy mop. "Let's go somewhere," she says, still scrubbing her hair.

"You bored?"

"Sure. Aren't you?"

"No."

"You ought to get a TV."

"I don't need one."

"Look, I think I'll go out, if you don't want to." She turns her head to dry the other side. "You want to screw before I go?" She continues scrubbing her hair.

She doesn't notice that he is silent for several seconds before he says a definite "No."

"Okay. I don't blame you. You worked hard last night. You know, it was real good for me. I was . . ." She decides not to finish that.

"You were surprised?" he pursues.

"No, not exactly. Older men can be real good. They don't usually blow off too quickly, you know what I mean?"

"Jesus Christ!"

She looks up at him, startled and bewildered. "What the hell's wrong with you?"

"Nothing! Forget it."

But her eyes are angry. "You know, I get sick and

tired of it, the way you always get mad when I talk about
. . . *making love*." Her tone mocks the euphemism. "You
know what's wrong with you? You're just pissed because
someone else *a fait sauter ma cerise* before you could get at
it! That's what's wrong with you!" She rises and limps
strongly into the bedroom, where he can hear her getting
dressed.

Twice she speaks to him from the other room. Once
repeating what she thought was wrong with him, and once
grumbling about anybody who didn't even have a goddamned TV in his pad . . .

He answers neither time. He sits looking out over the
park, where the sun is already paling as the skies become
milky again with overcast.

When she comes back into the living room, she is
wearing the long patchwork dress she bought yesterday. As
she puts on her new coat, she asks coldly, "Well? Coming
with me?"

"Do you have your key?" He is still looking out the
window.

"What?"

"You'll need your key to get back in. Do you have
it?"

"Yes! I've got it!" She slams the door.

He watches her from the window, feeling angry with
himself. What's wrong with him? Why is he fooling around
with a kid like this anyway, like a silly old *fringalet*?
There's only one thing to do; he's got to find her a job and
get her the hell out of his apartment.

Marie-Louise walks huffily down the street, not bothering to flex her knee to conceal the limp, because she
knows he's probably looking down at her and will feel
sorry for her. She is angry about not getting her own way,
but at the same time she is worried about spoiling a good
thing. It's dull and boring, that frumpy apartment, but it's
shelter. He lets her have money. He doesn't ask much of
her. Shouldn't ruin a good thing until you've got something
better. She recalls how the young Greek boy played the
tripoteux with her under the table last night. Perhaps the
old man noticed. Maybe that's why he's so irritable.

Anyway, she'll let him stew about it for a while, then she'll come back to the apartment. He'll be glad enough to see her. They don't get all the young stuff they want, these old guys.

Maybe she'll walk over to the Greek restaurant. See if anyone's around.

Beyond the window, evening has set in, fringing the layers of yeasty cloud. The morning's sunlight was a trick after all, a joke.

The gas fire hisses, and he dozes. He remembers the watery sunlight in the park. It reminded him of Sunday mornings in the parlor of his grandparents' farmhouse. Floating motes of dust trapped in slanting rays of sun. The smell of mustiness . . . and the heavy, sickening smell of flowers.

Grandpapa. . .

A bright winter day with sun streaming in the parlor window, and Grandpapa, thin and insubstantial in the box. All the children had to walk in a line past the coffin. The smell of flowers was thick, sweet. Claude LaPointe's shirt was borrowed, and too small; the tight collar gagged him. The children had been told to take turns looking down into dead Grandpapa's face. The little ones had to stand tiptoe to see over the edge of the coffin, but they did not dare to touch it for balance. You were supposed to kiss Grandpapa goodbye.

Claude didn't want to. He couldn't. He was afraid. But the grownups were in no mood for argument. There were already tensions and angers about who should get what from the farm, and everyone seemed to think that one uncle was grabbing more than his share. And who would take care of Grandmama?

Grandmama didn't cry. She sat in the kitchen on a wooden chair and rocked back and forth. She wrapped her long thin arms around herself and rocked and rocked.

Claude told his mother in confidence that he was afraid he would be sick if he kissed dead Grandpapa.

"Go on now! What's wrong with you? Don't you love your Grandpapa?"

Love him? More than anybody. Claude used to daydream about Grandpapa taking him away from the streets to the farm. Grandpapa never knew about the daydreams; Claude was only one of the press of cousins who used to line up to mutter "Joyous Christmas, Grandpapa."

"Stop it! Stop it right now!" Mother's whisper was tense and angry. "Go kiss your grandfather."

The smooth dusty face was almost white on the side touched by a beam of winter sun. And his cheeks had never been so rosy when he was alive. He smelled like Mother's make-up. He used to smell like tobacco and leather and sweat. Claude closed his eyes tight and leaned over. He made a peck. He missed, but he pretended he had kissed Grandpapa. To avoid hearing the grownups' tight, muttered arguments about furniture and photographs and Grandmama, he went into the summer kitchen with the other kids, who by turns were making shuddering faces and scrubbing their lips hard with the backs of their hands. Claude scrubbed his lips too, so everyone would think he had really kissed Grandpapa, but as he did it he knew he was being a traitor to the living Grandpapa, whom he had never kissed because they were both physically reticent types.

The fat cousin who used to fart under the covers whispered a joke about the make-up, and the girl cousins giggled. His face blank, Claude turned from the window and hit his cousin in the mouth with his fist. Although the cousin was two years older and bigger, he had no chance; Claude was bashing him with all the force of his rage, and fear, and shame, and loss.

Some grownups pulled Claude off the bleeding and howling cousin, and he was shaken around and sent upstairs to be dealt with later, after the priest left.

He sat on the edge of the bed in the grandparents' room. He had never been there before, and it seemed foreign and unfriendly, but he was glad to be alone so he could cry without the others seeing. No tears came. He waited. He opened his mouth and panted out sharp little breaths, hoping to start the crying he needed so badly. No tears would come. A hot ball of something sour in his stomach, but no tears. Others who loved Grandpapa less than Claude could cry. They could afford to let Grandpapa be dead, because they had other people. But Claude . . .

When they came up to punish him, Claude was lost in a daydream about Grandpapa coming to Trois Rivières and taking him away to live on the farm.

That was how he handled it.

It is after midnight. LaPointe has been in bed for over an hour, slipping in and out of light sleep, when he hears the lock turn in the front door. It closes softly, and Marie-Louise tries to tiptoe into the bedroom, but she bumps into something. She suppresses a giggle. There is movement and the rustle of clothes being taken off. She slips in beside him, and cold air comes in with her. He does not move, does not open his eyes. Soon her breathing becomes regular and shallow. She sleepily presses against his back for warmth, her knees cold against the backs of his legs.

He can smell the licorice of ouzo on her breath, and the smell of man's sweat on her.

. . . he can't breathe . . .

. . . he wakes with a start. His face is wet.

He can't understand it. Why are his eyes wet?

He falls back to sleep, and next morning he does not remember the dream.

213

10

Guttmann has arranged the overdue reports in stacks on the little table serving as a desk, leaving just enough room for his typewriter. He has finally made some order and sense out of the mess LaPointe dumped on him; there is a stack for this week's reports, one for last week's, one for the week before, and so on. But largest of all is the pile he mentally calls the Whatever-the-Hell-*This*-Is bunch.

The hissing roar of sandblasting across the street vibrates the cheap ripply glass of the window, causing Guttmann to look up. His eyes meet LaPointe's, which are fixed on him with a frown. Guttmann smiles and nods automatically and returns to his work. But a couple of minutes later he can still feel the Lieutenant's eyes on him, so he looks up again.

"Sir?"

"Is that all you know of that song?"

"What song, sir?"

"The song you keep humming over and over! You keep humming the same little bit!"

"I didn't realize I was humming."

"Well, *I* realize it. And it's sending me up the god-damned wall!"

"Sorry, sir."

LaPointe's grunt suggests that "Sorry" isn't enough. Ever since he came in this morning, he has been emitting dark vibrations and making little murmurs and growls of short temper each time he loses his place in the routine work on his desk. He stands up abruptly, pushing back his swivel chair with the backs of his knees. There is an indented line of white in the plaster from years of the chair banging against it. His thumbs hooked in the back of his belt, he looks out over the Hôtel de Ville, its façade latticed with scaffolding. This morning the noise of the stone-cleaning grates directly upon his nerve ends, like cold air on a bad tooth. And those monotonous zinc clouds!

Guttmann's typewriter clacks on in the rapid, one-word bursts of the experienced bad typist. His memory touches the two nights and a day he has just spent with the girl who lives in his apartment building. He passed Saturday evening in her flat, helping her doctor a head cold. She wore a thick terrycloth robe that did nothing good for her appearance, and she had bouts of sneezing that left her limp and miserable, her face pale and her eyes brimming with tears. But her sense of humor held up, and she found this to be a ridiculous way for them to pass their first date. She got a little high on the hot toddies he made for her, and so did he, because he insisted on keeping her company by drinking one for each of hers. When he looked over her books and records, he discovered that their tastes were absolutely opposite, but their levels of appreciation about the same.

Around midnight, she kicked him out, telling him that she wanted to get a good night's sleep to fight off the cold. He suggested some light exercise might do her a world of good. She laughed and told him she didn't want him to catch her cold. He said he was willing to pay that price, but she said no.

Next morning, he telephoned her from bed. Her cold had broken and she felt well enough to go out. They passed the day visiting galleries and making jokes about the modern junk-art on display. He spent more than he could afford on dinner, and later, in his apartment, they talked about all sorts of things. They seldom agreed on details, but they found similar things funny and the same things important. After they had made love, they lay on their right sides, she coiled in against him, her bottom in his lap. She slept, breathing softly, while he lay awake for a time, sensing the subtle thrill of waves of gentleness emitting from him and enveloping her. A remarkable girl. Not only fun to talk with and great in bed, but really . . . remarkable. . . .

LaPointe turns from the window and looks flatly at Guttmann, who catches the movement and glances up with his habitual smile, which fades as he realizes he has been humming again.

"Sorry."

LaPointe nods curtly.

"By the way, sir, I ran the name Antonio Verdini and the alias Tony Green through ID. They haven't called back yet."

"They won't have anything."

"Maybe not, but I thought I should run it through anyway."

LaPointe sits again before his paper work. "Just like it says in the book," he mutters.

"Yes, sir," Guttmann says, more than a little tired of LaPointe's *cafard* this morning, "just like it says in the book." The book also says that reports of investigations must be turned in within forty-eight hours, and some of this crap on Guttmann's desk is weeks late, and almost all of it is incomplete, a couple of scribbled notes that are almost indecipherable. But Guttmann decides against mentioning that.

LaPointe makes a guttural sound and pushes aside a departmental form packet: green copy, yellow copy, blue copy, pink fucking copy . . .

"I'm going down to Bouvier's shop for a cup of coffee, if anyone wants me. You keep up the good work." He dumps all his unfinished work into Guttmann's in-box.

"Thank you, sir."

The telephone rings, catching LaPointe at the door.

Guttmann answers, rather hoping it is something that will annoy the Lieutenant. He listens awhile, then puts his palm over the mouthpiece. "It's the desk. There's a guy down there asking to speak to you. It's about the Green stabbing."

"What's his name?"

Guttmann takes his hand away and repeats the question. "It's someone who knows you. A Mr. W————." He mentions the name of the wealthiest of the old Anglo families in Montreal. "Is that *the* Mr. W————?"

LaPointe nods.

Guttmann raises his eyebrows in mock surprise. "I didn't know you had Connections in Important Places, sir."

"Yes, well . . . Tell you what. While I'm down with Bouvier, you interview Mr. W————. Tell him you're my assistant and I have every confidence in you. He won't know you're lying."

"But, sir . . ."

"You're here to get experience, aren't you? No better way to learn to swim than by jumping off the dock."

LaPointe leaves, closing the door behind him.

Guttmann clears his throat before saying into the phone, "Send Mr. W———— up, will you?"

"Another cup, Claude?" Dr. Bouvier asks, catching a folder that is slipping from the tip of his high-heaped desk, holding it close to his clear lens to read the title, then tucking it back in toward the bottom.

"No, I don't think I could handle another."

Bouvier laughs ritually and pushes his glasses back up to the bridge of his stubby nose. But they slip down immediately because the dirty adhesive tape with which they are repaired is loose again. He must get them fixed someday. "Did you see the report I sent up on your stabbing? We ran his clothes through the lab and the result was zero."

"I didn't see the report. But I'm not surprised."

"If you didn't come down here to talk about the report, then what? You just come down to improve your mind? Or is the weather getting you down? One of my young men was complaining about the weather this morning, grousing about the way it keeps threatening snow without delivering. He said he wished it would either shit or get off the pot. Now, there's a daunting image for the bareheaded pedestrian. I warned the lad about the dangers of indiscriminate personification, but I doubt that he took it to heart. All right, let's talk then. I suppose you're pissed about that stabbing of yours getting into the papers so soon. I'm sorry about that; but the leak didn't come from this office. Someone up in the Commissioner's shop released it."

"Those assholes."

"Penetrating evaluation, if something of an anatomic synecdoche. But come on, it's not so grave. Just a couple of column inches. No photograph. No details. You still have the advantage of surprise as you walk your way through the case. By the way, how's that stroll coming along?"

LaPointe shrugs. "Nothing much. The victim's turning out to be a real turd, the kind anyone might have wanted to kill."

"I see. You have assholes for bosses and a turd for a victim. There's a certain consistency in that. I hear your Joan ran a name and an alias through ID this morning. Your victim?" Bouvier points his face toward LaPointe, one eye hidden behind the nicotine lens, the other huge and distorted. He is showing off a bit, proving he knows everything that goes on.

"Yes, that's the victim."

"Hm-m. An Italian kid with an Anglo alias. No record of fingerprints. Not a legal immigrant. What does that give us? A sailor who jumped ship?"

"I doubt it."

"Yes. The hands were wrong. No calluses. Any leads to a skill or a craft?"

"No." LaPointe's head rises just as Bouvier's eye is opening wide. They have the same thought at the same moment.

It is Bouvier who expresses it. "Do you think your victim was being laundered?"

"Possible."

There are a couple of small-timers up on the Italian

Main who make their money by "laundering" men for the American organized-crime market. A young man who gets into trouble in Calabria or Sicily can be smuggled into Canada, usually on a Greek ship, and brought into Montreal, where he blends into the polyglot population of the Main while he learns a little English, and while the laundryman makes sure the Italian authorities are not on his tail. These "clean" men are slipped across the border to the States, where they are valuable as enforcers and hit men. Like a clean gun that the police cannot trace through registration, these laundered men have no records, no acquaintances, no fingerprints. And should they become awkward or dangerous to their employers, there is no one to avenge, even to question, their deaths.

It is possible that the good-looking kid who called himself Tony Green was in the process of being laundered when he met his death in that alley.

Dr. Bouvier takes off his glasses, turning his back so that LaPointe doesn't see the eye normally covered by the nicotine lens. He flexes the broken bridge and slips them back on, pinching the skin of his nose to make them stay up better. "All right. Who's active in the laundry business up on your patch?"

Old man Rovelli died six months ago. That leaves Canducci—Alfredo (Candy Al) Canducci.

"Chocolate," LaPointe says to himself.

"What?"

"Chocolate. As in candy. As in Candy Al."

"I assume that makes some subtle sense?"

"The kid had a 'cousin' who rented his room for him. The concierge thought the name had something to do with chocolate."

"And you make that Candy Al Canducci. Interesting. And possible. I'll tell you what—I'll put in a little time on the case. Maybe your friendly family pathologist can come up with one of his 'interesting little insights.' Not that my genius is always appreciated by you street men. I remember once dropping a fresh possibility onto your colleague, Gaspard, when he was satisfied that he had already wrapped up a case. He described my assistance as being as welcome as a fart in a bathysphere. You want some more coffee?"

"No."

Guttmann has made slight rearrangements to receive Mr. Matthew St. John W————. He has moved his chair over to LaPointe's desk, and has seated himself in the Lieutenant's swivel chair. He rises to greet Mr. W————, who looks around the room with some uncertainty.

"Lieutenant LaPointe isn't here?"

"I'm sorry, sir. He's not available just now. I'm his assistant. Perhaps I could help?"

Mr. W———— looks exactly like his photographs in the society section of the Sunday papers—a slim face with fragile bones and veins close to the surface, full head of white hair combed severely back, revealing a high forehead over pale eyes. His dark blue suit is meticulously tailored, and there is not a smudge on the high shine of his narrow, pointed black shoes.

"I had hoped to see Lieutenant LaPointe." His voice is thin and slightly nasal, and its tone is chilly. He surveys the young policeman thoughtfully. He hesitates.

Not wanting to lose him, Guttmann waves a hand at the chair opposite him and says in as offhanded a voice as possible, "I believe you had some assistance to offer in the Green case, sir?"

Mr. W———— frowns, the wrinkles very shallow in his pallid forehead. "The Green case?" he asks.

Guttmann's jaw tightens. He is glad LaPointe isn't there. The victim's name was not mentioned in the newspaper. But the only thing to do is brave it out. "Yes, sir. The young man found in the alley was named Green."

Mr. W———— looks toward the corner of the room, his eyes hooded with thought. "Green," he says, testing the sound. He sighs as he sits on the straight-backed chair, lifting his trousers an inch by the creases. "You know," he says distantly, "I never knew that his name was Green. Green."

Instantly, Guttmann wishes he had somebody with him, a witness or a stenographer.

221

But Mr. W——— has anticipated his thoughts. "Don't worry, young man. I will repeat anything I say to you. What happens to me is not important. What does matter is that everything be handled as quietly as possible. My family . . . I know I could rely on Lieutenant LaPointe to be discreet. But . . ." Mr. W——— smiles politely, indicating that he is sorry, but he has no reason to trust a young man he does not know.

"I wouldn't do anything without consulting the Lieutenant."

"Good. Good." And Mr. W——— seems willing to let the conversation rest there. A thin, polite smile on his lips, he looks past Guttmann's head to the damp, metallic skies beyond the window.

"You . . . ah . . . you say you didn't know his name was Green?" Guttmann prompts, making every effort to keep the excitement he feels from leaking into his voice.

Mr. W——— shakes his head slightly. "No, I didn't. That must seem odd to you." He laughs a little sniff of self-ridicule. "In fact, it seems odd to me . . . now. But you know how these things are. The social moment when you should have exchanged names somehow passes with the thing undone, and later it seems foolish, even impolite, to ask the other person his name. Has that ever happened to you?"

"Sir?" Guttmann is surprised to find the conversational ball suddenly in his court. "Ah, yes, I know exactly what you mean."

Mr. W——— investigates Guttmann's face carefully. "Yes. You have the look of someone who's capable of understanding."

Guttmann clears his throat. "Did you know this Green well?"

"Well enough. Well enough. He was . . . that is to say, he died before we . . ." Mr. W——— sighs, closes his eyes, and presses his fingers into the shallow sockets. "Explanations always seem so bizarre, so inadequate. You see, Green knew about the White Plot and the Ring of Seven."

"Sir?"

"I'd better begin at the beginning. Do you remember the nursery rhyme 'As I was going to St. Ives, I met a man with seven wives'? Of course, you probably never considered the significance of the repeated sevens—the warning passed to the Christian world about the Ring of the Seven and the Jewish White Plot. Not many people have troubled to study the rhyme, to unravel its implications."

"I see."

"That poor young Mr. Green stumbled upon the meaning. And now he's dead. Stabbed in an alley. Tell me, was there a bakery near where he was found?"

Guttmann glances toward the door, trying to think up something he has to go do. "Ah . . . yes, I suppose so. The district has lots of bakeries."

Mr. W——— smiles and nods with self-satisfaction. "I knew it. It's all tied up with the White Plague."

Guttmann nods. "Tied up with the White Plague, is it?"

"Ah! So Lieutenant LaPointe has told you about that, has he? Yes, the White Plague is *their* name for the steady poisoning of the gentile with white foods—flour, bread, sugar, Cream of Wheat . . ."

"Cream of Wheat?"

"That surprises you, doesn't it? I can't blame you. There was a time when we hoped against hope that Cream of Wheat wasn't in on it. But certain evidence has come into our hands. I mustn't tell you more than you need to know. There's no point in endangering you needlessly."

Guttmann leans back in the swivel chair, links his fingers, and puts his palms on the top of his head. His eyes droop, as though with fatigue.

Mr. W——— glances quickly toward the door to make sure no one is listening, then he leans forward and speaks with a confidential rush of words. "You see, the Ring of Seven is directed from Ottawa by the Zionist lobby there. I began to collect evidence against them seven years ago—note the significance of that figure—but only recently has the scope of their plot become . . ."

Guttmann is silent as he drives LaPointe up the Main in his yellow sports car. It is eleven in the morning and the street is congested with off-loading grocery and goods trucks, and with pedestrians who flow out into the street to bypass blocked sidewalks. It is necessary to crawl along and stop frequently. From time to time Guttmann glances at the Lieutenant, and he is sure there are crinkles of amusement around his eyes. But Guttmann is damned if he will give him the satisfaction of bringing it up first.

So it is LaPointe who has to ask, "Did you get a confession out of Mr. W———?"

"Very nearly, sir. Yes."

"Did you learn about Cream of Wheat?"

"What, sir? In what connection would he mention Cream of Wheat?"

"Well, he usually . . ." LaPointe laughs and nods. "You almost got me, son. You heard about Cream of Wheat, all right!" He laughs again.

"You might have warned me, sir."

"Nobody warned me the first time. I was sure I had a walk-in confession."

Guttmann pictures LaPointe being sucked in, leaning forward to catch each word, just as he had done. He has to laugh too. "I suppose this Mr. W——— is harmless enough."

"Look out for that kid!"

"I saw him! Jesus Christ, sir."

"Sorry. Yes, he's harmless enough, I suppose. There was a delicate case some years ago. Your Mr. W——— and a young man were picked up in a public bathroom. The kid was Jewish. Because of W———'s family, the thing was hushed up, and they were both back out on the street before morning. But the fear of scandal did something to the old man."

"And ever since then he comes in each time there's a murder in the papers?"

"Not every murder. Only when the victim is a young male. And only if it's a stabbing."

"Christ, talk about sophomore psychology."

"That truck's backing out!"

"I see him, sir. Are you sure you're comfortable?"

"What do you mean?"

"It must be hard to drive from over there."

"Come on, come on! Let's get going!"

Guttmann waits for the truck to clear, then eases forward. "Yes, that's real sophomore psychology stuff. The need to confess; the stabbing image."

"What are you talking about?"

"Oh, nothing, sir." It seems odd to Guttmann that La-Pointe should know so much about human reactions and the human condition, but at the same time be so uneducated. He doubts that the Lieutenant could define words like "id" and "fugue." He probably recognizes the functioning of these forces and devices without having any names for them.

The worst of the traffic tangle behind them, they continue north on St. Laurent, cresting the hill at the barren little park of Carré Vallières, squeezed in between the Main and St. Dominique. It is a meager little triangle of sooty dirt, no grass, six or seven stunted trees. There are three benches of weathered wood once painted green, where old men play draughts in the summer, and in autumn huddle in their overcoats and stare ahead, or vacantly watch passers-by. For no reason he knows, LaPointe has always associated his retirement with this little square. He pictures himself sitting on one of those benches for an hour or two—always in winter, always with snow on the ground and bright sunshine. The roar of traffic up the Main passes close to the bench he has picked out for himself, and the smell of diesel fumes never leaves the air. From the top of the little rise he will be able to keep an eye on his street, even in retirement.

Once past the park and St. Joseph Street, they are on the Italian Main, where the street loses its cosmopolitan character. Unlike the lower Main, LaPointe's real patch, the quality of the Italian Main is not porous and ever-changing, with languages and people slowly permutating through the arrival and absorption of new tides of immigrants. The upper Main has been Italian for as long as anyone can remember, and its people do not move away to

225

blend into the amorphous Canadian mass. The street and
the people remain Italian.

At a signal from LaPointe, Guttmann pulls over and
parks before a dingy little restaurant bearing the sign:

REPAS PASTO

They get out and cross the street, turning down Rue
Dante, past a barbershop, empty save for the owner who is
enthroned in one of his leather chairs, reading the paper
with the air of a man completely at his ease, a man who
knows he will not be interrupted by customers. Stuck in the
window are sun-faded pictures of vapid young men advertising passé hairstyles. One grins from beneath a flattop,
and another sports that long-sided fashion that used to be
called a "duck's ass." In fact, as LaPointe knows, the only
customers are the barber's relatives, who get their hair cut
for free. The place is a numbers drop.

At the intersection of a narrow street, LaPointe turns
down toward a small bar halfway between Rue Dante and
St. Zotique. It occurs to Guttmann that in this Franco-
Italian district there is something particularly appropriate
about a bar being situated halfway between streets named
Dante and St. Zotique. He mentions this to LaPointe, and
asks if the Lieutenant ever thought of it as a kind of cultural metaphor.

"What?"

"Nothing, sir. Just a thought."

The interior of the bar is overwarm from a large oil
heater, its orange flame dimly billowing behind a mica window. The woman behind the bar is overblown, her chubby
arms clattering with plastic bracelets, her high-piled hairdo
an unnatural blue-black, her eye make-up and lipstick
florid, and the deep V of her spangled blouse revealing the
slopes of flaccid breasts that get most of their shape from
the encasing fabric. She completes a languid yawn before
asking the men what they will have.

LaPointe orders a glass of red, and Guttmann, tugging
off his overcoat in the excessive heat, asks for the same

thing, although he does not particularly care for wine outside meals.

From the back room, beyond a gaudy floral curtain, comes the click of pool balls followed by a curse in Italian and laughter from the other players.

"Who's your friend, Lieutenant?" the barmaid asks as she pours the wine and bestows upon Guttmann a carnivorous leer.

"Is Candy Al back there?" LaPointe asks.

"Where else would he be this time of day?"

"Tell him I want to talk to him."

"That won't be the best news he's had all week." Brushing close by Guttmann, the barmaid goes into the back room, walking with her knees slightly bent to make her broad ass swing invitingly.

"It looks like you've scored," LaPointe says as he sets his empty glass back on the bar. He always drinks off a *coup de rouge* at one go, like the workers of his home city.

"That's wonderful," Guttmann says. "Do you think I'm her first love?"

"One of the first this morning."

LaPointe knows this bar well. It serves two very different kinds of clients. Old Italian men in cloth caps often sit in pairs at the oilcloth-covered tables, talking quietly and drinking the harsh red. When they order, they hold the barmaid by her hip. It is an automatic gesture meaning nothing specific, and the right to hold the barmaid's hip goes, by immutable tradition, to the one who is paying for the drinks.

In summer, the back door is always open, and old men play at bowls on the tarmac alley where there is a thick covering of sand for this purpose. Every twenty minutes or so, a girl brings out a tray of glasses filled with wine. She collects the cork beer coasters from under empty glasses and stacks them at the end of the bar as a count of the wine drunk. The games are played for wine, and very seriously, with slow dignity and with much criticism and praise. Sometimes tipsy old men steal one or two of the coasters and put them into their pockets, not to avoid paying for the wine, but so that the barmaid will have to come looking for them, and when she does, they get a grab of her ass.

In contrast to these good people, the ones who hang out in the poolroom with its jukebox are the young toughs of the neighborhood, who squander their days gambling borrowed money and lying to one another about their sexual conquests and their knife fights. Candy Al Canducci reigns over these wise-cracking punks, who admire his flashy expensive clothes and flashy cheap women. Someday, they too . . .

He occasionally lends them money, or buys rounds of drinks. In return they serve him as flunkies, doing little errands, or standing around looking tough when he makes a personal visit to one of the bars dominated by another boss.

The whole thing is a cut-rate imitation of heavier Family action in north and east Montreal, but it has its share of violence. Occasionally there are border disputes over numbers territories, and there will be a week or two of conflict, single members of one gang beaten up by five or six men from another, with faces and testicles the special targets of pointy-toed shoes. Sometimes there is a nighttime scuffle in a back alley, silent except for panting and the scrape of shoes, and a nasal grunt when the knife goes in.

LaPointe always knows what is happening, but he lets it go so long as no one is involved but themselves. The two things he does not permit are murder and drugs, the one because it gets into the papers and makes his patch look bad, the other just because he does not permit it. If there is a murder, he has a little chat with the bosses, and in the end some informer gives him the killer. It's a tacit understanding they have. Every once in a while, one of the bosses will feel he can stand up to LaPointe. Then things start to go badly for him. His boys begin to get picked up for every minor charge in the book; the police start to hit his numbers drops one after the other; small amounts of narcotics turn up every time LaPointe searches an apartment. The coterie of young toughs around the recalcitrant boss begins to thin out, and each of the bosses knows that with the first sign of weakness his brothers will turn on him and devour his territory. Even the proudest ends with having a little chat with LaPointe, and with turning over the killer he has been sheltering, or pulling back from his little *tentative* into drugs. Of course, there is the usual tough talk about LaPointe waking up some morning dead, but this is just face-saving. The bosses don't really want him gone. The next cop might not let them settle things among themselves, and they might not be able to trust his word, as they can always trust LaPointe's.

While there are these unspoken agreements, there is no protection. From time to time, one of the bosses makes a mistake. And when he does, LaPointe puts him away. They expect nothing else; LaPointe is like Fate—always there, always waiting. The bosses are all Catholics, and this sense of hovering punishment satisfies their need for retribution. The older ones take an odd pride in their cop and in his dogged honesty. You can't buy LaPointe. You can come to an understanding with him, but you can't buy him.

For his part, LaPointe has no delusions about his control on the Italian Main. This is not the Mafia he faces. The Mafia, with its American connections and trade union base, operates in north and east Montreal, where it occasionally becomes visible through sordid shootouts in the Naugahyde-and-chrome bars they infest. It isn't so much LaPointe's presence that prevents the organization from moving onto the Main as it is the district's own character. The Main is too poor to be worth the pain the old cop would give them.

At forty, Candy Al Canducci is the youngest of the local petty bosses; he is flashy in a "B" movie way, wise-mouthed, self-conscious, pushy; he lacks the Old-World dignity of the older bosses, most of whom are good family men who care about their children and take care of the unemployed and aged on their blocks. They're all thieves; but Candy Al is also a punk.

The barmaid's plastic bracelets clatter as she bats the gaudy curtain aside and comes back into the bar. "He doesn't want to see you, Lieutenant. Says he's busy. In conference."

There has been a silence in the back room for the past minute or two, and now there is suppressed laughter with this phrase "in conference."

The barmaid leans against the counter and plants a fist on her hip. She looks steadily at Guttmann as she toys with the crucifix around her neck, tickling her breasts by dragging the cross in and out of the cleavage.

"In conference, eh?" LaPointe asks. "Oh, I see. Well, at least give me another red."

There is a snicker from the back room, and the click of pool balls begins again.

As the barmaid takes her time going around to pour the wine, LaPointe tugs off his overcoat and drops it over a chair. Without waiting for the drink, he slaps the floral curtain aside and enters the poolroom. Guttmann takes a breath and follows him.

The hanging lamp over the pool table makes a high wainscoting of light that decapitates the half-dozen young men standing around the table. They draw back to the walls as LaPointe enters. One of them puts his hand in his pocket. A knife, probably, but mostly a sassy gesture. And one young tough pats the back of his hair into place, as though preparing for a photograph. Guttmann sets his broad body in the doorway as he notices that there is no other exit from the room. He feels a trickle of sweat under his shoulder holster. Seven against two; not much room for movement.

Candy Al Canducci continues playing, pretending not to have noticed the policemen enter. The coat of his closely cut suit hangs open, and his broad paisley tie brushes the green felt as he lines up a shot with taunting care. His pants are so tight that the outlines of his girdle-underwear can be seen.

LaPointe notices that he has changed from looking over a rather difficult shot that would have left him with good position to taking a dogmeat ball hanging on the rim of the pocket. He smiles to himself. Candy Al's cheap sense of theatrics will not permit him to punctuate some bit of lip with a missed shot.

"Let's have a talk, Canducci," LaPointe says, ignoring the ring of young men.

Candy Al brushes the chalk from his fingers before lifting the sharp crease of one trouser leg to squat and line up the straight-in shot. "You want to talk, Canuck? All right, talk. Me, I'm playing pool." He doesn't look up to say this, but continues to examine his shot.

LaPointe shakes his head gravely. "That's too bad."

"What's too bad?"

"The way you're putting yourself in a hard place, Canducci. You're showing off for these asshole punks. First thing you know, you'll be forced to say something stupid. And then I'll have to spank you."

"Spank me? Ho-ho. You?" He rolls an in-cupped hand and looks around his coterie as if to say, Listen to this crap, will you? He draws back the cue to make his shot.

LaPointe reaches out and sweeps the object ball into its pocket. "Game's over."

For the first time, Canducci looks up into LaPointe's eyes. He detests the crinkling smile in them. He walks slowly around the end of the table to face the cop. There is an inward pressure from the ring of punks, and Guttmann glances around to pick out the first two he'd have to drop to keep them off his arms. Canducci's heart is thumping under his yellow silk shirt, as much from anger as from fear. LaPointe was right; if it hadn't been for the audience, he would never have taken this tone; now he has no choice but to play it out.

He stops before LaPointe, tapping the shaft of his cue into his palm. "You know what, Canuck? You take a lot of risks, for an old man."

LaPointe speaks over his shoulder to Guttmann. "There's something for you to learn here, son. This Canducci here and his punks are dangerous men." His eyes do not leave Candy Al's, and they are still crinkled in a smile.

"Better believe it, cop."

"Oh, you're dangerous, all right. Because you're cowards, and cowards are always dangerous when they're in a pack."

Canducci pushes his face toward LaPointe's. "You got a wise mouth, you know that?"

LaPointe closes his eyes and shakes his head sadly. "Canducci, Canducci . . . what can I tell you?" He lifts his palms in a fatalistic shrug.

The next happens so quickly that Guttmann remembers only blurred fragments of motion and the sound of scuffling feet. LaPointe suddenly reaches out with one of the lifted hands, grabbing the dandy by the face and driving him back against the wall in two quick steps. Canducci's head cracks against a pinup of a nude. LaPointe's broad hand masks the face, the palm against the mouth and the fingers splayed across the eyes.

"Freeze!" he barks. "One move, and he loses his eyes!"

To make his point, he presses slightly with his fingertips, and Canducci produces a terrified squeal that is half-muffled by the heel of LaPointe's hand. LaPointe can feel saliva from the twisted mouth against his palm.

"Everyone sit on the floor," LaPointe commands. "Out away from the wall! Sit on your hands, palms up! I want the legs out in front of you! Do what I say, or this asshole will be selling pencils on the street!" Again a slight pressure on the eyes; again a squeal.

The punks exchange glances, no one wanting to be the first to obey. Then Guttmann, with a gesture that surprises LaPointe, grabs one by the arm and slams him up against the wall. The tough sits down with almost comic celerity, and the others follow.

"Sit up straight!" LaPointe orders. "And keep those hands under your asses! I want to hear knuckles crunch!"

This is a trick he learned from an old cop, now dead. When men are sitting on their hands, not only is any quick movement impossible, but they are embarrassed and humbled almost instantly, producing a sense of defeat and the desirable passivity of the prisoner mentality. It is a particularly useful device when you are badly outnumbered.

No one speaks, and for a full minute LaPointe continues to press Canducci's head against the wall, his fingers splayed over the face and eyes. Guttmann doesn't understand the delay. He looks over at the Lieutenant, whose head is hanging down and whose body appears oddly limp. "Sir?" he says uneasily.

LaPointe takes two deep breaths and swallows. The worst of it is over. The vertigo has passed. He straightens up, grabs Canducci's broad paisley tie, and snatches him away from the wall, propelling him ahead toward the gaudy curtain. One more push on the shoulder and Candy Al stumbles into the barroom. LaPointe turns back to the six young men on the floor. "You watch them," he tells Guttmann. "If one of them moves a muscle, slap his face until his ears ring." LaPointe knows exactly what threat would most sting cocky Italian boys.

When he pushes aside the curtain and enters the bar, he finds Candy Al sitting at a table, dabbing at his eyes with a handkerchief. "The Commissioner's going to hear about this," he says without much assurance. "It's a free country! You cops ain't the bosses of everything!"

LaPointe picks up his glass of red from the bar and sips it slowly, not setting down the glass until he feels recovered from the swimming dizziness and the constriction in his chest and upper arms that caught him unawares a minute ago. When the last of the effervescence has fizzed out of his blood, he leans back against the bar and looks down at Canducci, who is carefully touching the edge of his handkerchief to the corner of his eye, then examining the damp spot with tender concern.

"You got your finger in my eye! I wear contacts! That could be dangerous for a guy that wears contacts! Fucking cops." Alone out here without his gang, he reverts to the whining petty thief, alternating between playing it as the movie tough and simpering piteously.

"We're going to talk about a friend of yours," LaPointe says, sitting in the chair opposite Canducci.

"I don't have any friends!"

"That's truer than you know, shithead. The name is Antonio Verdini, alias Tony Green."

"Never heard of him."

"You rented a room for him. The concierge has given evidence."

"Well, this concierge has her head up her ass! I tell you I never met . . . whatever you said his name is."

"Was."

"What?"

"Was. Not is. He's dead. Stabbed in an alley."

The handkerchief is up to Canducci's eyes, so La-Pointe misses the effect of the drop. After a short silence, the Italian says, "So, what's that to me?"

"Maybe twenty years. Stabbing is the kind of action your people go in for. The Commissioner is on my ass for an arrest. With your record, you're dogmeat. And I don't really care if you did it or not. I'll be satisfied just to get you off the street."

"I didn't kill the son of a bitch! I didn't even know he was dead until you told me. Anyway, I got an alibi."

"Oh? For what time?"

"You name it, cop! You name it, and I got an alibi for it." Candy Al dabs at his eyes again. "I think I got a busted blood vessel or something. You're gonna pay for that. Like they say in the lotteries, *un jour ce sera ton tour.*"

LaPointe reaches across the table and pats Canducci's cheek three times, the last tap not gentle. "Are you threatening me?"

Candy Al jerks his head away petulantly. "Where you get off slapping people around? You never heard of police brutality?"

"You'll have twenty years to make your complaint."

"I told you, all my time is covered."

"By them?" LaPointe tips his head toward the poolroom.

"Yeah. That's right. By them."

LaPointe dismisses them with a sharp puff of air. "How long do you think one of those kids, sitting back there with his ass in his hands, could stand up to interrogation by me?"

Canducci's eyes flicker; LaPointe's point is made. "I'm telling you I didn't kill this guy!"

"You mean you *had* him killed?"

"Shit, I don't even know this Verdini!"

"But at least you remember his name now."

234

There is a pause. Canducci considers his situation.

"I don't talk to cops. I think you're holding an empty bag. You got a witness? You got fingerprints? You got the knife? If you had any lever on me, we wouldn't be sitting here. We'd be downtown. You're empty, cop!" Canducci says this last loudly, to be overheard by the boys in the back. He wants them to see how he treats cops.

Candy Al's reasoning is correct, so LaPointe has to take another tack. He shifts in his chair and looks out the window past Canducci's head. For a moment he seems to be absorbed in watching two kids playing in the street, coatless despite the cold. "I hear you've got something going with your boys back there," he says absently.

"What do you mean? What you talking?"

"I'm talking about the rumor that you keep your boys around for pleasure. That you pay them to use you like a woman." LaPointe shrugs. "Your flashy clothes, your silks, you wear a girdle . . . it's easy to see how a rumor like that could spread."

Canducci's face bloats with outrage. "Who's saying this? Give me a name! I'll sink my fingernails into his forehead and snatch his fucking face off!"

LaPointe lifts a hand. "Take it easy. The rumor hasn't started yet."

Canducci is confused. "What the hell you talking about?"

"But by tomorrow night, everyone on the street will be saying that you take it like a woman. I only have to drop a hint here, a wink there."

"Bullshit! Nobody would believe you! I got a doll on my arm every night."

"A smart cover-up. But always a different girl. They never hang around. Maybe because you can't satisfy them."

"Agh, I get tired of them. I need a little variety."

"That's your story. The other bosses would grab up a rumor like that in a second. They'd have big laughs over it. So Candy Al is a *fif!* Some punk would paint words on your car. Pretty soon your boys would drift away, because they don't want people saying they're queers. You'd be alone. People would talk behind their hands when you

235

walked by. They'd whistle at you from across the street."
Every touch is calculated to make the proud Italian wince.

His mind racing, Canducci glares at LaPointe for a
full minute. Yes. A rumor like that would spread like clap
in a nunnery. They'd love it, those shitheads over on Mar-
coni Street. His jaw tightens and he looks down at the floor.
"You'd do that? You'd spread a rumor like that about a
man?"

LaPointe snaps his fingers softly. "Like that."

Candy Al glances toward the poolroom and lowers his
voice. He speaks quickly to get it over with. "All right.
This Verdini? A friend asked me to find a room for him
because his English ain't too good. I found the room. And
that's it. That's all I know. If he got himself killed, that's
tough shit. I got nothing to do with it."

"What's this friend's name?"

"I don't remember. I got lots of friends."

"Just a minute ago you told me you didn't have any
friends."

"Agh!"

LaPointe lets the silence sit on Canducci.

"Look! I'm giving it to you straight, Lieutenant!"

"Lieutenant? What happened to Canuck?"

Canducci shrugs, lifting his hands and dipping his
head. "Agh, I was just pissed. People say things when
they're pissed."

"I see. I want you to say the word 'wop' for me."

"Ah, come on!"

"Say it."

Canducci turns his head and stares at the wall.
"Wop," he says softly.

"Good. Now keep talking about this kid."

"I already told you everything I know!"

After a moment of silence, LaPointe sighs and rises.
"Have it your way, Canducci. But tell me one thing. Those
boys back there? Which one's best?"

"That ain't funny!"

"Your friends will think so." LaPointe slaps his hand
on the bar to summon the barmaid, who disappeared when
she heard how things were going in the poolroom. She has

been around enough to know that it is not wise to witness Candy Al's defeats. She comes from the back room, tugging down her skirt, which is so tight across the hips that it continually rides up.

"What do I owe you?" LaPointe asks.

"Just a minute," Canducci says, raising his hand. "What's your rush? Sit down, why don't you?"

The barmaid looks from one to the other, then returns to the back room.

LaPointe sits down. "That's better. But let's cut the bullshit. I don't have the time. I'll start the story for you. This Green was brought into the country illegally. You were laundering him. You found him a room on the lower Main, away from this district where the immigration authorities might look for him if the Italian officials had sent out a want bulletin. You kept him in walking-around money. You probably arranged for him to learn a little English, because that's part of the laundering process. Now you take it from there."

Canducci looks at LaPointe for a moment. "I'm not admitting any of that, you know."

"Of course not. But let's pretend it's true."

"Okay. Just pretending what you say is true . . . This kid was a sort of distant cousin to me. The same village in Calabria. He was supposed to be a smart kid, and tough. But he gets into a little trouble back in the old country. So next thing you know he's here, and I've promised to find some kind of work for him. As a favor."

LaPointe smiles at the obliquity.

"Okay. So I get him a room, and I get him started learning some English. But I don't see him often. That wouldn't be smart, you dig? But all the time this bastard's needing money. I give him a lot, but he always needs more. He blows it on the holes. I never seen such a crotch hound. I warn him that he's beginning to get a reputation about all the squack he's stabbing, and what the super don't need right now is a reputation. He goes after all kinds. Even old women. He's sort of weird that way, you know? So the only time I visit him is to tell him he shouldn't draw attention to himself. I tell him to take it easy with the holes. But

237

he don't listen, and he asks me for more money. Five will get nine it was a woman that put the knife into him."

"Go on."

"Go on to what? That's all! I warn him, but he don't listen. And you walk in here this morning and tell me he's got himself reamed. He should of listened."

"You don't sound too sorry for your cousin."

"I should be sorry for myself! I'm out a lot of scratch! And for what?"

"Call it a business risk. Okay, give me the names of some of his women."

"Who knows names? Shit, he was on the make day and night. Drag a net down the Main and you'll come up with half a dozen he's rammed. But I can tell you this. He went for weird action. Two at a time. Old women. Gimps. Kids. That sort of thing."

"You said something about his taking English lessons? Who was he taking them from?"

"No idea. I give him a list of ads from the papers. I let him pick for himself. The less I know about what these guys are doing, the better for me."

"What else do you want to tell me?"

"There's nothing else to tell. And listen—" Canducci points a chubby white finger at LaPointe—"there ain't no witnesses here. Anything I might have said, I would deny in court. Right?"

LaPointe nods, his eyes never leaving Candy Al's as he weighs and evaluates the story he just heard. "It could be the way you say. It could also be that the kid got too dangerous for you, drawing attention to himself and always asking you for money. It could be you decided to cut your losses."

"My word of honor!"

LaPointe's lower eyelids droop. "Well, if I have your word of honor . . . what else could I want?" He rises and begins to tug on his overcoat. "If I decide I need more from you, I'll be by. And if you try to leave town, I'll take that as a confession."

Canducci dabs at his eyes once more, then folds his mauve handkerchief carefully into his breast pocket and pats it into place. "It's a crying goddamned shame, you know that?"

"What is?"

"That way this kid gets me into trouble. That's what you get for trying to help a relative."

After LaPointe and Guttmann leave the bar, Canducci sits for a time, thinking about how he will play it. He takes several bills from his wallet. As he saunters into the pool-room where his boys are standing around sheepishly, work-ing their hands to restore circulation, he tucks the money back into the wallet with a flourish. "Sorry about that, boys. My fault. I got a little behind in my payments. These penny-and-nickel cops don't like it when they don't get their payoff on time. Okay, rack 'em up."

They are the only customers in the A-One Café. After serving them the one-plate lunch, the old Chinese has re-turned to his station by the window where, his eyes empty, he looks out on the sooty brick warehouses across the street.

"Well?" LaPointe asks. "How do you like it?"

Guttmann pushes his plate aside and shakes his head. "What was it called?"

"I don't think it has a name."

"I'm not surprised."

There is a certain pride in the Lieutenant's voice when he says, "It's the worst food in Montreal, maybe in all of Canada. That's why you can always come here to talk. There's never anyone else here to disturb you."

"Hm-m!" Guttmann notices that his grunt sounded just like the Lieutenant's grumpy responses.

During the meal, LaPointe has filled him in on what he learned from Candy Al, together with a description of the operation known as laundering.

"And you think this Canducci might have killed Green, or had him killed?"

"It's possible."

Guttmann shakes his head. "With every lead, we turn another suspect. It's worse than not having any suspects. We've got that tramp, the Vet. Then we've got that guy

239

Arnaud, the concierge's friend. Now Canducci, or one of his punks. And it seems that it might have been almost any woman on the Main who isn't under ten or over ninety. And what about the woman you talked to alone? The lesbian who runs a café. Is she a viable?"

Is she a viable? Precisely the kind of space-age jargon that LaPointe detests. But he answers. "I suppose. She had reason, and opportunity. And she's capable of it."

"What does that give us now? Four possibles?"

"Don't forget your Mr. W———. You came close to wringing a confession out of him."

Guttmann feels a flush at the nape of his neck. "Yes, sir. That's right."

LaPointe chuckles. "I'm not ragging you, kid."

"Oh? Is that so, sir?"

"No, you're thinking all right. You're thinking like a good cop. But don't forget that this Green was a turd. Just about everybody he touched would have some reason for wanting him dead. It's not all that surprising that we find a suspect behind every door. But pretty soon it will be over."

"Over? In what way over?"

"The leads are starting to thin out. The talk with Canducci didn't turn another name or address."

"The leads could be thinning out because we've already touched the killer. And passed him by."

"I haven't passed anybody by yet. And there's still the possibility that Carrot will come up with a name or two, maybe a bar he used to go to."

"Carrot?"

"The lesbian."

"But she's a suspect herself."

"All the more reason for her to help us . . . if she's innocent, that is. But I wouldn't bet on closing this case. I have a feeling that pretty soon we're going to open the last door, and find that blank wall."

"And you don't particularly care?"

"Not particularly. Not now that we know the sort of kid the victim was."

Guttmann shakes his head. "I can't buy that."

"I know you can't. But I've got other things to do

240

besides chase around after shadows. I've got the whole neighborhood to look after."

"Tell me something, Lieutenant. If this Green were a nice kid, say a kid who grew up on the Main, wouldn't you try harder?"

"Probably. But a case like this is hard to sort out. When you're tracking a kid like this Green, you meet nothing but dirty types. Almost everyone you meet is guilty. The question is, *what* are they guilty of?"

"Guilty until proven innocent?"

"Lawyers being what they are, probably guilty even then."

"I hope I never think like that."

"Stay on the street for a few years. You will. By the way, you didn't do too badly back in Canducci's bar. We walked in without a warrant, slapped people around, and you handled yourself like a cop. What happened to all this business about civil rights and going by the book?"

Guttmann lifts his hands and lets them drop back onto the table. You can't discuss things with LaPointe. He always cuts both ways. But Guttmann realizes that he has a point. When he handled that tight moment when the boys were resisting the order to sit on their hands, he had felt . . . competent. There is a danger in being around LaPointe too long. Things get less clear; right and wrong start to blend in at the edges.

When he looks up, Guttmann sees a crinkling around LaPointe's eyes. "What is it?"

"I was just thinking about your Mr. W————."

"Honest to God, I'd give a lot if you'd get off that, sir."

"No, I wasn't going to rag you. It just occurred to me that if Mr. W———— ever did kill somebody, all he'd have to do would be to wait until it got into the papers, then come to us with a confession involving Jewish plots and Cream of Wheat. We'd toss him right out."

"That's a comforting thought."

"Oh. By the way, didn't you say something the other night about playing pinochle?"

"Sir?"

241

"Didn't you tell me you used to play pinochle with your grandfather?"

"Ah . . . yes, sir."

"Want to play tonight?"

"Pinochle?"

"That's what we're talking about."

"Wait a minute. I'm sorry, but this just came out of nowhere, sir. You're asking me to play pinochle with you tonight?"

"With me and a couple of friends. The man who usually plays with us is sick. And cutthroat isn't much fun."

Guttmann senses that this offer is a gesture of acceptance. He can't remember anyone in the department having bragged about spending off time with the Lieutenant. And he is free tonight. The girl in his building takes classes on Monday nights and doesn't get back until eleven.

"Yes, sir. I'd like to play. But it's been a while, you know."

"Don't worry about it. Nothing but three old farts. But just in case you're a little rusty, I'll arrange for you to be partners with a very gentle and understanding man. A man named David Mogolevski."

11

The evening of pinochle has gone well—for David.

As usual he dominated play, and as usual he overbid his hand, but the luck of the cards allowed Guttmann to bail him out more times than not, and as partners they won devastatingly.

After a particularly good—and lucky—hand, David asked the young man, "Tell me, have you ever thought of becoming a priest?"

Guttmann admitted that the idea seldom crossed his mind.

"That's good. It would ruin your game."

On one occasion, when not even luck was enough to save David from his wild overbidding, he treated Guttmann to one of his grousing tirades about how difficult it was, even for a pinochle *maven* like himself, to schlep a partner who couldn't pull his own weight. Unlike Father Martin, Guttmann did not permit himself to be martyred to David's peculiar and personal view of sportsmanship. He countered with broad sarcasm, mentioning that the Lieutenant had rightly described David as a gentle and understanding partner.

But David's thick skin is impervious to such attacks. He thrust out his lower lip and nodded absently, accepting that as an accurate enough description of his character.

For his part, Moishe was slow in warming to the young intruder into their game, despite Guttmann's genuine interest in the fabric Moishe had on the loom at that moment. He had been looking forward to one of his rambling philosophic chats with Martin.

Still, so it shouldn't be a total loss, he made a venture toward drawing Guttmann out during their break for sandwiches and wine. "You went to university, right? What did you major in?"

It occurs to LaPointe that he never asked that question. He wasn't all that interested.

"Well, nothing really for the first two years. I changed my major three or four times. I was more looking for professors than for fields."

"That sounds intelligent," Moishe says.

"Finally, I settled down and took the sequence in criminology and penology."

"And what sorts of things does one study under those headings?"

David butts in. "How to steal, naturally. Theft for fun and profit. Theft and the Polish Question."

"Why don't you shut up for a while?" Moishe suggests. "Your mouth could use the rest."

David spreads his face in offended innocence and draws back, then he winks at LaPointe. He has been riding Moishe all night, piquing him here and there, ridiculing his play, when he knew perfectly well that all the cards were against him. But he is a little surprised when his gentle partner snaps back like this.

"So?" Moishe asks Guttmann. "What did you study?"

Guttmann shrugs off the value of his studies, a little embarrassed about them in the presence of LaPointe. "Oh, a little sociology, some psychology as related to the criminal and criminal motives—that sort of thing."

244

"No literature? No theology?"

"Some literature, sure. No theology. Would you pass the mustard, please?"

"Here you are. You know, it's interesting you should have studied criminal motives and all this. Just lately I have been thinking about crime and sin . . . the relationships, the differences."

"Oh boy," David puts in. "Here we go again! Listen! About crime it's all right to think. It's a citizen's duty. But about sin? Moishe, my old friend, AK's like us shouldn't think about sin. It's too late. Our chances have passed us by."

Guttmann laughs. "No, I'm afraid I never think about things like that, Mr. Rappaport."

"You don't?" Moishe asks gloomily, his hopes for a good talk crumbling. "That's strange. When I was a young man thinking was a popular pastime."

"Things change," David says.

"Does that mean they improve?" Moishe asks.

Guttmann glances at his watch. "Hey, I'm sorry, but I've got to be going. I have a date, and I'm already late."

"A date?" David asks. "It's after eleven. What can you do so late?"

"We'll think of something." As soon as he makes this adolescent single-entendre remark, Guttmann feels he has been disloyal to his girl.

Moishe rises. "I'll walk you to your car."

"That isn't necessary, sir."

"You're already late for your date. And you're not familiar with the streets around here. So don't argue. Get your coat."

As they leave, Moishe has already begun with ". . . when you stop to think about it, the differences between sin and crime are greater than the similarities. Take, for instance, the matter of guilt . . ."

As the door closes behind them, David looks at La-Pointe and shakes his head. "Oh, that Moishe. Sin, crime, love, duty, the law, the good, the bad . . . he's interested in everything that's so big it doesn't really matter. A scholar! But in practical things . . ." His lips flap with a puff of air. "That reminds me of something I wanted to talk to you about, Claude. A matter of law."

"I'm not a lawyer."

"I know, I know. But you know something about the law. This may come as a surprise to you, but I am not immortal. I could die. At my age, you have to think about such things. So tell me. What do I have to do to make sure the business goes to Moishe if he should, *cholilleh*, outlive me?"

LaPointe shrugs. "I don't know. Isn't all that handled in your partnership agreement?"

"Well . . . that's the problem. Actually, Moishe and I aren't partners. In the legal sense, I mean. And I have a nephew. I'd hate to see him come along and screw Moishe out of the business. And, believe me, he's capable of it. Of working for a living, he's not capable. But of screwing someone out of something? Of that he is capable."

"I don't understand. What do you mean, you and Moishe aren't partners? I thought he started the business, then later took you on as a partner."

"That's right. But you know Moishe. He's not interested in the business end of business. A beautiful person, but in business a *luftmensh*. So over the years, he sold out to me so that he wouldn't have to be bothered with taxes and records and all that."

"And you're afraid that if you die—"

"—*cholilleh*—"

"—he might not get the business? Well, David, I told you I'm no lawyer. But it seems to me that all you have to do is make out a will."

David sighs deeply. "Yes, I was afraid of that. I hoped it wouldn't be necessary. I'm not a superstitious man, don't get me wrong. But in my opinion a man is just asking for it, if he makes out his will while he's still alive. It's like saying to God, Okay. I'm ready whenever you are. And speaking personally for myself, I'm not ready. If a truck should run over me—okay, that's that. But I'm not going to stand in the middle of the street shouting, Hey! Truck-drivers! I'm ready!"

As LaPointe steps out onto the blustery street, turning up the collar of his overcoat, he meets Moishe, returning from seeing Guttmann to his car. They fall into step and walk along together, as they usually do after games.

"That's a nice young man, Claude."

"He's all right, I suppose. What did you talk about?"

"You."

LaPointe laughs. "Me as a crime? Or me as a sin?"

"Neither one, exactly. We talked about his university studies; how much the things he learned turned out to reflect the real world."

"How did I fit into that?"

"You were the classic example of how the things he learned were *not* like it is in the real world. The things you do and believe are the opposite of everything he wants to do with his life, of everything he believes in. But, oddly enough, he admires you."

"Hm-m! I didn't think he liked me all that much."

"I didn't say he likes you. He admires you. He thinks you're the best of your kind."

"But he can live without the kind."

"That's about it."

They have reached the corner where they usually part with a handshake. But tonight Moishe asks, "Are you in a hurry to go home, Claude?"

LaPointe realizes that Moishe is still hungry for talk; the short walk with Guttmann couldn't have made up for his usual ramblings with Father Martin. For himself, La-Pointe has no desire to get to his apartment. He has known all day what he will find there.

"How about a glass of tea?" Moishe suggests.

"Sure."

They go across the street to a Russian café where tea is served in glasses set in metal holders. Their table is by the window, and they watch late passers-by in the comfortable silence of old friends who no longer have to talk to impress one another, or to define themselves.

"You know," Moishe says idly, "I'm afraid I frightened him off, your young colleague. With a young girl on his mind, the last thing in the world he needed was a long-winded talk about sin and crime." He smiles and shakes his head at himself. "Being a bore is bad enough. Knowing you're boring but going ahead anyway, that's worse."

"Hm-m. I could see you had something stored up."

Moishe fixes his friend with a sidelong look. "What do you mean, I had something stored up?"

"Oh, you know. All through the game you were sending out little feelers; but Father Martin wasn't there to take you up. You know, I sometimes think you work out what you're going to say during the day, while you're cutting away on your fabric. Then you drop these ideas casually during the pinochle game, like they just popped into your head. And poor Martin is fishing around for his first thoughts, while you have everything carefully thought out."

"Guilty! And being guilty I don't mind so much as being transparent!" He laughs. "What chance does the criminal have against you, tell me that."

LaPointe shrugs. "Oh, they manage to muddle along all right."

Moishe nods. "Muddle along. System M: the big Muddle. The major organization principle of all governments. She seemed like a nice girl."

LaPointe frowns. "What?"

"That girl I met in your apartment yesterday. She seemed nice."

LaPointe looks at his friend. "Why do you say that? You know perfectly well she didn't seem nice. She seemed like a street girl, which is all she is."

"Yes, but . . ." Moishe shrugs and turns his attention to the street. After a silence, he says, "Yes, you're right. She did seem like a street girl. But all girls of her age seem nice to me. I know better, but . . . My sister was just her age when we went into the camp. She was very lovely, my sister. Very shy. She never . . . she didn't survive the camp." He stares out the window for a while. Then he says quietly, "I'm not even sure I did. Entirely. You know what I mean?"

LaPointe cannot know what he means; he doesn't answer.

"I guess that's why I imagine that all girls of her age are nice . . . are vulnerable. That's funny. Girls of her age! If she had lived, my sister would be in her early fifties now. I can't picture that. I get older, but she remains twenty in my mind. You know what I mean?"

LaPointe knows exactly what he means; he doesn't answer.

Moishe closes his eyes and shakes his head. "Ach, I don't think I'm up to stumbling around in these parts of my memory. Better to let these things rest. They have been well grieved."

"Well grieved? That's a funny thing to say."

"Why funny, Claude? You think grief is shameful?"

LaPointe shrugs. "I don't think about it at all."

"That's odd. Of course grief is good! The greatest proof that God is not just playing cruel games with us is that He gave us the ability to grieve, and to forget. When one is wounded—I don't mean physically—forgetfulness cauterizes and heals it over, but there would be rancor and hate and bitterness trapped under the scar. Grief is how you drain the wound, so it doesn't poison you. You understand what I mean?"

LaPointe lifts his palms. "No, Moishe. I don't. I'm sorry . . . but I'm not Father Martin. This kind of talk . . ."

"But Claude, this isn't philosophy! Okay, maybe I say things too fancy, too preciously, but what I'm talking about isn't abstract. It's everyday life. It's . . . obvious!"

"Not to me. I don't know what you're talking about when you say grief is good. It has nothing to do with me." LaPointe realizes that his tone is unfriendly, that he is closing the door to the chat Moishe seems to need. But this talk about grief makes him uncomfortable.

Behind his round glasses, Moishe's eyes read LaPointe's face. "I see. Well . . . at least allow me to pay for the tea. That way, I won't regret having bored you. Regret! There's a little trio often confused: Grief, Remorse, Regret! Grief is the gift of the gods; Remorse is the whip of the

249

gods; and Regret . . . ? Regret is nothing. It's what you say in a letter when you can't fill an order in time."

LaPointe looks out the window. He hopes Father Martin will get well soon.

They shake hands on the sidewalk in front of the Russian café, and LaPointe decides to take one last walk down the Main before turning in. He has to put his street to bed.

Even before switching on the green-and-red lamp, he senses in the temperature of the room, in the smell of the still air, the emptiness.

Of course, he knew she would be gone when he came back tonight. He knew it as he lay in bed beside her, smelling the ouzo she had drunk. He knew it as he tried to get back to sleep after that dream . . . what was it? Something about water?

He makes coffee and brings the cup to his armchair. The streetlamps down in the park spill damp yellow light onto the gravel paths. Sometimes it seems the snow will never come.

The silence in the room is dense, irritating. LaPointe tells himself that it's just as well Marie-Louise is gone. She was becoming a nuisance, with that silly, brief laugh of hers. He sniffs derision at himself and reaches for one of his Zolas, not caring which one. He opens the volume at random and begins to read. He has read them through and through, and it no longer matters where he begins or ends. Before long, he is looking through the page, his eyes no longer moving.

Images, some faded, some crisp, project themselves onto his memory in a sequence of their own. A thread of the past comes unraveled, and he tugs it with gentle attention, pulling out people and moments woven so deep into the fabric of the past that they seemed forgotten. The mood of his daydream is not sadness or regret; it is curiosity. Once he has recalled and dealt with a moment or a face, it does not return to his memory. He examines the fragment, then lets it fall from him. He seldom remembers the same thing twice. There isn't time.

Some of the images come from his real life: Trois Rivières, playing in the street as a kid, his grandfather, St.

Joseph's Home, Lucille, the yellow alley cat with the crooked tail, one paw lifted tentatively from the ground.

Other memories, no less vivid, come from his elaborate fantasy of living in the house in Laval with Lucille and the girls. These images are richest in detail: his workshop in the garage with nails up to hold the tools, and black-painted outlines to show which tool goes where. The girls' First Holy Communions, all in white with gifts of silver rosaries and photographs posed for reluctantly and stiffly. He sees the youngest girl—the tomboy, the imp—with her scuffed knee just visible under the thin white communion stocking. . . .

He sniffs and rises. His rinsed-out cup is placed on the drainboard, where it always goes. He cleans the pressure maker and puts it where he always puts it. Then he goes into the bathroom to shave, as he always does, before going to bed. As he swishes down the black whiskers, he notices several long hairs in the bowl. She must have washed her hair before leaving. And she didn't rinse it out carefully. Sloppy twit.

He is sitting on the edge of his bed, pulling off his shoes, when something occurs to him. He pads into the living room and opens the drawer in which he keeps his house money, uncounted and wadded up. There is a bunch of twenties there, some tens. He does not know how much there was in the first place. Perhaps she took some. But that doesn't matter. What matters is that she left some.

He lies on his back in the middle of the bed, looking up at the ceiling glowing from the streetlamp outside the window.

He never realized before how big this bed is.

Guttmann is tapping away on the portable typewriter when LaPointe enters with a grunt of greeting as he hangs his overcoat on the wooden rack.

"I'm beginning to see daylight at the end of the tunnel, sir."

"What are you talking about?"

"These reports."

"Ah. Good boy. You've got a future in the department. That's the important thing—the paper work." La-Pointe picks up a yellow telephone memo from his desk. "What's this?"

"You got a call. I took the message."

"Hm-m." The call was from Carrot. She questioned her clients who went bar crawling with Tony Green; there seemed to be only one place he frequented regularly, the Happy Hour Whisky à Go-Go on Rachel Street. LaPointe knows the place, just one block off the Main. He decides to drop in on his way home that evening. The leads are thinning out; this is the last live one.

"Anything else?" he asks.

"You got a call from upstairs. The Commissioner wants to see you."

"That's wonderful." He sits at his desk and glances over the Morning Report: several car thefts, two muggings, somebody shot in a bar in east Montreal, another mugging, a runaway teen-ager . . . all routine. Nothing interesting, nothing from the Main.

He starts to make out his duty sheet for yesterday. What did he do yesterday? What can you write down? Drank coffee with Bouvier? Talked to Candy Al Canducci? Walked around the streets? Played pinochle? Took a glass of tea with Moishe? Went home to find the bed bigger than I remembered? He turns the green form over and looks at the three-quarters of a page left blank for "Remarks and Suggestions." He suppresses an urge to write: Why don't you shove this form up your ass?

LaPointe is feeling uncertain this morning, and diminished. He had a major *crise* while brushing his teeth. First the fizzing blood, then tight bands of jagged pain gripped his chest and upper arms. He felt himself falling forward into a gray mist in which lights exploded. When it passed, he was on his knees, his forehead on the toilet seat. As he continued brushing his teeth, he joked with himself: I guess you better get a lighter toothbrush, LaPointe.

"Tomorrow's my last day," Guttmann says.

"What?"

"Wednesday I go back to working with Sergeant Gaspard."

"Oh?" It is a noncommittal sound. He has enjoyed showing off his patch and his people to the kid; he has even enjoyed Guttmann's way of braving out his scorn for the shiny new college ideas. But it wouldn't do to seem to miss the boy.

"How did it go last night?" he asks, making conversation to avoid the goddamned paper work.

"Go, sir? Oh, with Jeanne?"

"If that's her name."

Guttmann smiles in memory. "Well, I got there late, of course. And at first she didn't believe me when I told her I was playing pinochle with three men in the back room of an upholstery shop. It sounded phony to me even while I was saying it."

"Does it matter what she thinks?"

Guttmann considers this for a second. "Yes, it does. She's a nice person."

"Ah, I see. Not just a girl. Not just a lay."

"That's the way it started, of course. And God knows I'm not knocking that part of it. But there's more. We sort of fit together. It's hard to explain, because I don't mean that we always agree. Matter of fact, we almost never agree. It's kind of like a mold and a coin, if you know what I mean. They're exact opposites, and they fit together perfectly." There is a slight shift in his tone, and he is now thinking out the relationship aloud, rather than talking to LaPointe. "She's the only person I've ever known who . . . I mean, I don't have to be set up and ready when I talk to her. I just say what I feel like saying, and it doesn't bother me if it comes out wrong, or stupid-sounding. You know what I mean, sir?"

"How did you meet her?"

Guttmann doesn't understand why LaPointe is interested, but he enjoys the uncommon friendly tone of the chat. He has no way of knowing that his leaving tomorrow is what allows the Lieutenant to relax with him, because he won't have to deal with him further. "Well, I told you she lives in my apartment building. We met in the basement."

"Sounds romantic."

Guttmann laughs. "Yeah. There's a bunch of coin-operated washing machines down there. It was late at night, and we were alone, waiting for our washing to get done, so we started talking."

"About what?"

"I don't remember. Soap, maybe. Hell, I don't know."

"Is she pretty?"

"Pretty? Well, yes, I guess so. I mean, obviously *I* find her attractive. That first night in the basement, I wasn't thinking of much other than getting her into bed. But pretty isn't what she is mostly. If I had to pick one thing about her, it would be her nutty sense of humor."

LaPointe sniffs and shakes his head. "That sounds dangerous. I remember when I was a kid on the force, I went on a couple of blind dates set up by friends. And whenever they described my girl as 'a good talker' or 'a kid with a great sense of humor,' that always meant she was a dog. What I usually wanted at the time was a pig, not a dog."

For a second, Guttmann tries to picture the Lieutenant as a young cop going on blind dates. The image won't come into focus.

"I know what you mean," he says. "But you know what's even worse than that?"

"What?"

"When the guy who's set you up can't think of anything to say but that your girl has nice hands. That's when you're really in trouble!"

LaPointe is laughing in agreement when the phone rings. It is the Commissioner's office, and the young lady demanding that LaPointe come up immediately has a snotty, impatient tone.

After announcing on the intercom that Lieutenant La-Pointe is in the outer office, the secretary with the impeding miniskirt sets busily to work, occasionally glancing accusingly at the Lieutenant. When she arrived at the office at eight that morning, the Commissioner was already at work.

The man who isn't a step AHEAD is a step BEHIND.
Resnais' mood was angry and tense, and everyone in

the office was made to feel its sting. The secretary blames LaPointe for her boss's mood.

For the first time, Resnais doesn't come out of his office to greet LaPointe with his bogus handshake and smile. Three clipped words over the intercom request that he be sent in.

When LaPointe enters, Resnais is standing with his back to the window, rocking up on his toes. The gray light of the overcast day glints off the purplish suntan on his head, and there is a lighter tone to his sunlamped bronze around the ears, indicating that his haircut is fresh.

"I sent for you at eight this morning, LaPointe." His tone is crisp.

"Yes. I saw the memo."

"And?"

"I just got in."

"In this shop, we start at eight in the morning."

"I get off the street at one or two in the morning. What time do you usually get home, Commissioner?"

"That's none of your goddamned onions." Even angry, Resnais does not forget to use idioms common to the social level of his French Canadian men. "But I didn't call you up here to chew your ass about coming in late." He has decided to use vulgar expressions to get through to LaPointe.

"Do you mind if I sit down?"

"What? Oh, yes. Go ahead." Resnais sits in his high-backed chair, designed by osteopaths to reduce fatigue. He takes a deep breath and blows it out. Might as well get right to it.

The surgeon who cuts slowly does no kindness to his patient.

He glances at his note pad, open on the immaculate desk beside two sharpened pencils and a stack of blue memo cards. "I assume you know a certain Scheer, Anton P."

"Scheer? Yes, I know him. He's a pimp and a *pissou*."

"He's also a citizen!"

"You're not telling me that Scheer had the balls to complain about me."

"No official complaint has been lodged—and won't

255

be, if I can help it. I warned you about your methods just a couple of days ago. Did you think I was just talking out of my ass?"

LaPointe shrugs.

Resnais looks at his notes. "You ordered him off the street. You denied him the use of a public thoroughfare. Who in hell do you think you are, LaPointe?"

"It was a punishment."

"The police don't punish! The courts punish. But it wasn't enough that you ordered him off the streets, you publicly degraded him, making him take off his clothes and climb into a basement well, with the possible risk of injury. Furthermore, you did this before witnesses—a crowd of witnesses including young women who laughed at him. Public degradation."

"Only his shoelaces."

"What?"

"I only ordered him to take off his shoelaces."

"My report says clothes."

"Your report is wrong."

Resnais takes one of the pencils and makes the correction. He has no doubt at all of LaPointe's honesty. But that is not the point. "It says here that there was another policeman involved. I want his name."

"He just happened to be walking with me. He had no part in it."

LaPointe's matter-of-fact tone irritates Resnais. He slaps the top of his desk. "I won't fucking well have it! I've worked too goddamned hard to build a good community image for this shop! And I don't care if you're the hero of every wet-nosed kid on the force, LaPointe. I won't have that image ruined!"

Anger is a bad weapon, but a great tool.

LaPointe looks at Resnais with the expression of bored patience he assumes when questioning suspects. When the Commissioner has calmed down, he says, "If Scheer didn't lodge a complaint, how do you know about this?"

"That's not your affair."

"Some of his friends got to you, right? Ward bosses?"

It is Resnais' habit to play it straight with his men. "All right. That's correct. A man in municipal politics brought it to my attention. He knows how I've worked to maintain good press for the force. And he didn't want to make this public if he didn't have to."

"Bullshit."

"I don't need insubordination from you."

"Tell me something. Why do you imagine your friend interfered on this pimp's behalf?"

"The man is not my friend. I know him only at the athletic club. But he's a politically potent man who can help the force . . . or hurt it." Resnais smiles bitterly. "I suppose that sounds like ass-kissing to you."

LaPointe shrugs.

Resnais stares at him for a long moment. "What are you trying to tell me?"

"Put it together. Scheer is not the run-of-the-mill pimp. He specializes in very young girls. Either your . . . friend . . . is a client, or he's open to blackmail. Why else would he help a turd like Scheer?"

Resnais considers this for a moment. Then he makes some notes on his pad. Above all, he is a good cop. "You might be right. I'll have that looked into. But nothing alters the fact that you have exposed the department to bad public opinion with your gangster methods. Have you ever thought of them that way? As gangster methods?"

LaPointe has not. But he doesn't care about that. "So you intend to tell your political friend that you gave me a sound ass-chewing and everything will be fine from now on?"

"I will tell him that I privately reprimanded you."

"And he'll pass the word on to Scheer?"

"I suppose so."

"And Scheer will come back out onto the street, sassy-assed and ready to start business again." LaPointe shakes his head slowly. "No, that's not the way it's going to happen, Commissioner. Not on my patch."

"Your patch! LaPointe of the Main! I'm sick up to here of hearing about it. You may think of yourself as *the* cop of *the* street, but you're not the whole force, LaPointe. And that run-down warren of slums is not Montreal!"

LaPointe stares at Resnais. Run-down warren!

For a second, Resnais has the feeling that LaPointe is going to hit him. He knows he went too far, talking about the Main like that. But he has no intention of backing down. "You were telling me that this Scheer wouldn't be allowed to start up business again. What do you think you're going to do, Claude?" It's "Claude" now. Resnais is shifting his forensic line.

LaPointe rises and goes to Resnais' window. He never noticed that the Commissioner looks out on the Hôtel de Ville too, on the scaffolding and sandblasting. It doesn't seem right that they should share the same view. "Well, Commissioner. You can go ahead and tell your friend that you gave me a 'private reprimand.' But you'd better also tell him that if his pimp sets foot on my patch, I'll hurt him."

"I am giving you a direct order to stop your harassment of this citizen."

There is a long silence, during which LaPointe continues to look out the window as though he has not heard.

Resnais pushes his pencils back and forth with his forefinger. Finally, he speaks with a quiet, flat tone. "Well. This is the attitude I expected from you. You don't leave me any alternative. Discharging you will make a real *gibelotte* for me. I won't bullshit you by pretending it's going to be easy. The men will put up a hell of a stink. I won't come out of it smelling like a rose, and the force won't come out of it without bruises. So I'm going to rely on your loyalty to the force to make it easier. Because, you see, Claude, I've come to a decision. One way or another, you're out."

LaPointe leans slightly forward as though to see something down in the street that interests him more than the Commissioner's talk.

"Look at it this way, Claude. You came on the force when you were twenty-one. You've got thirty-two years of service. You can retire on full pay. Now, I'm not asking you to retire right now, this morning. I'd be content if you'd send in a letter of resignation effective, say, in six months. That way no one would relate your leaving to any trouble between us. You would save face, and I wouldn't have the mess of petitions and letters to the papers from the kids. Make up an excuse. Say it's for reasons of health—whatever you want. For my part, I'll see to it you're promoted to captain just before you go. That'll mean you retire on captain's pay."

Resnais swivels in his posture chair to face LaPointe, who is still looking out the window, unmoving. "One way or another, Claude, you're going. If I have to, I'll retire you under the 'good of the department' clause. I warned you to sort yourself out, but you wouldn't listen. You just don't seem to be able to change with the changing times." Resnais turns back to his desk. "I'm not denying that it would go easier on me if you would turn in your resignation voluntarily, but I don't expect you to do it for me. There's never been any love lost between us. You've always resented my drive and success. But there's no point going into that now. I'm asking you to resign quietly for the good of the department, and I honestly believe that you care about the force, in your own way." There is just the right balance between regret and firmness in his voice. Resnais evaluates the effect of the sound as he speaks, and he is pleased with it.

LaPointe takes a deep breath, like a man coming out of a daydream. "Is that all, Commissioner?"

"Yes. I expect your resignation on my desk within the week."

LaPointe sniffs and smiles to himself. He would lose nothing by turning in a resignation effective in six months. He doesn't have six months left.

By the time LaPointe has his hand on the doorknob, Resnais is already looking over his appointment calendar. He is a little behind.

The man who enslaves his minutes liberates his hours.

"Phillipe?" LaPointe says quietly.

Resnais looks up in surprise. This is the first time in the thirty years they have been on the force together that LaPointe has called him by his first name.

LaPointe's right fist is in the air. Slowly, he extends the middle finger.

When he gets back to his office, LaPointe finds Detective Sergeant Gaspard sitting on the edge of his desk, a half-empty paper cup of coffee in his hand.

"What's going on?" LaPointe asks, dropping into his swivel chair and turning it so he can look out the window.

"Nothing much. I was just trying to pump the kid here; see if he is learning the *gamique* under you."

"And?"

"Well, he's at least learned enough to keep his mouth shut. When I asked him how you were coming on the Green case, he said you'd tell me what you wanted me to know."

"Good boy," LaPointe says.

Guttmann doesn't look up from his typing for fear of losing his place, but he nods in agreement with the compliment.

"Well?" Gaspard asks. "I don't want to seem nosy, but it is technically my case, and I haven't had a word from you for a couple of days. And I want to be ready, if this case is what Resnais le Grand wanted to see you about."

Already the rumor has been around the department that Resnais was in a furious mood when he called in La-Pointe.

"No, it wasn't about that," LaPointe says.

Gaspard's raised eyebrows indicate that he is more than willing to hear what it *was* all about, but instead La-Pointe turns back from the window and gives him a quick rundown of progress so far.

"So you figure the kid was being laundered, eh?"

"I'm sure of it."

"And if he was such a big time *sauteux de clôtures* as you say, almost anyone might have put that knife into him—some jealous squack, somebody's lover, somebody's brother—almost anyone."

"That's it."

"You on to anything?"

"We've got suspects falling out of the trees. But most of the leads have healed up now. I've got something I'm looking into tonight; a bar the kid used to go to."

"You expect to turn something there?"

"Not much. Probably twenty more suspects."

"Hungh! Well, keep up the good work. And do your best to bring this one in, will you? I could use another letter of merit. So how's our Joan getting on? Is he as much a pain in the ass to you as he was to me?"

LaPointe shrugs. He has no intention of complimenting the kid in his presence. "Why do you ask? You want him back today?"

"No, not if you can stand to have him a while longer. He cramps my romantic form, hanging around all the time." Gaspard drains the cup, wads it up in his hand, and misses the wastebasket. "Okay, if that's all you've got to tell me about our case, I'll get back to keeping the city safe for the tourists. Just look at that kid type, will you? Now that's what I call style!"

Guttmann growls as Gaspard leaves with a laugh.

LaPointe feels a slight nausea from the ebb of angry adrenalin after his session with the Commissioner. The air in his office is warm and has an already-breathed taste. He wants to get out of here, go where he feels comfortable and alive. "Look, I'm going up on the Main. See what's going on."

"You want me to go with you?"

"No. I lose you tomorrow, and I want this paper work caught up."

"Oh." Guttmann does not try to conceal his deflation.

LaPointe tugs on his overcoat. "I'm just going to make the rounds. Talk to people. This Green thing has taken up too much of my time. I'm getting out of touch." He looks down at the young man behind the stacks of reports. "What do you have on for this evening around seven? A date to wash clothes?"

"No, sir."

"All right. Meet me at the Happy Hour Whisky à Go-Go on Rachel Street. It's our last lead. You might as well see this thing through."

Before it lost its cabaret license, the Happy Hour Whisky à Go-Go was a popular dance hall where girls from the garment shops and men from the loading docks could pick one another up, dance a little, ogle, drink, make arrangements for later on. It was a huge, noisy barn with a turning ball of mirrored surfaces depending from the ceiling, sliding globs of colored light around the walls, over the dancers, and into the orchestra, the amplified instruments of which made the floor vibrate. But once too often, the owner had been careless about letting underage girls in and about making sure his bouncers stopped fights before they got to the bottle-throwing stage, so now dancing is not permitted, and the patronage has shrunk to a handful of people sitting around the U-shaped bar, a glowing island in a vastness of dark, unused space.

At the prow of the bar is a drum stage four feet in diameter on which a go-go dancer slowly grinds her ass, her tempo in no way associated with the beat of the whining, repetitive rock music provided by a turntable behind the bar. The dancer is not young, and she is fat. Bored and dull-eyed, she undulates mechanically, her great bare breasts sloshing about as she slips her thumbs in and out of the pouch of her G-string, tugging it away from her *écu* and letting it snap back in a routine ritual of provocation.

Blue and orange lights glow dimly through the bottles of the back bar, producing most of the illumination, save for a strong narrow beam at the cash register. Ultraviolet lamps around the dancing drum cause the dancer's G-string to glow bright green. She has also applied phosphorescent paint to her nipples, and they glow green too. Standing just inside the door, far from the bar, LaPointe looks over the customers until he picks out Guttmann. From that distance, the back-lit figure of the dancer is almost invisible, save for the phosphorescent triangle of her crotch and the circles of her nipples. As she grinds away, she looks like a man with a goatee, chewing and rolling his eyes.

LaPointe climbs up on a stool beside Guttmann and orders an Armagnac. "What are you drinking?" he asks Guttmann.

"Ouzo."

"Why ouzo?"

Guttmann shrugs. "Because it's a Greek bar, I guess."

"Good thing it isn't an Arab bar. You'd be drinking camel piss." LaPointe looks along the curve of customers. A couple of young men with nothing to do; a virile-looking woman in a cloth coat sitting directly in front of the dancer, staring up with cold fascination and tickling her upper lip with her finger; two soldiers already a little drunk; an old Greek staring disconsolately into his glass; a neatly dressed man in his fifties, suit and tie, a briefcase up on the bar, watching the play of the thumbs in and out of the G-string, his starched collar picking up the ultraviolet light and glowing greenish. All in all, the typical flotsam of outsiders and losers one finds in this kind of bar in the early evenings, or in rundown movie houses in the afternoons.

The fat dancer turns her head as she jiggles from foot to foot and nods once to LaPointe. He does not nod back.

Sitting behind the bar, at the base of the drum, is a girl who attends to the jury-rigged turntable and amplifier. She is fearful of not doing her job right, so she stares at the turning disc, holding her breath, poised to lift the needle and move it to the next selection when the song runs out. She counts the bands to the one she must hit next, mouthing the numbers to herself. Occasionally she lifts her face to look up at the fat dancer. Her eyes brim with admiration and wonder. The lights, the color, and everyone watching. Show business! She appears to be fifteen or sixteen, but her face has no age. It is the bland oval of a seriously retarded child, and its permanent expression is a calm void over which, from time to time, comes a ripple of confusion and doubt.

The tune is nearing its end, and the girl is straining her concentration in preparation for changing the needle without making that horrible rasping noise. The dancer looks down at her and shakes her head. The girl doesn't know what this signal means! She is confused and frightened. She freezes! After an undulating hiss, the record goes on to the next band—the wrong band! The girl snatches her hands away from the machine, recoiling from all responsibility. But the dancer is already coming down from the drum, her great breasts flopping with the last awkward step. She growls at the girl and lifts the needle from the record herself. Then she walks along behind the bar to a back room. In a minute she emerges, wearing clacking bedroom slippers and a gossamer tent of a dressing gown through which the brown, pimpled cymbals of her nipples are visible.

She slides onto the stool next to Guttmann, her sweaty cheek squeaking on the plastic. She smells of sweat and cologne.

"Want to buy me a drink, gunner?" she asks Guttmann.

LaPointe leans forward and speaks across the young man. "He's not a mark. He's with me."

"Sorry, Lieutenant. I mean, how was I to know? You didn't come in together."

With a tip of his head, LaPointe orders her to follow as he takes up his Armagnac and walks away from the bar to a table with bentwood chairs inverted on it. He has three chairs down by the time the woman and Guttmann arrive. The table is small, and Guttmann cannot easily move his knee away from hers. She presses her leg against his to let him know she knows.

"What's the trouble now, Lieutenant?" The tone indicates that she has had run-ins with LaPointe before. She can't imagine why, but the Lieutenant has never liked her. Not even in the old days, when she was working the streets.

LaPointe wastes no time with her. "There's a kid who comes in here. Young, Italian, doesn't have much English. Good-looking. Probably calls himself Tony Green."

"He's in trouble?"

LaPointe stares at her dully. He asks questions; he doesn't answer them.

"Okay, I know the kid you mean," she says quickly, sensing his no-nonsense mood.

"Well?" he says. He has no specific questions, so he makes her do the talking.

"What can I tell you? I don't know much about him.

264

He started coming in here a couple of months ago, sort of regular, you know. At first he can't say diddly shit in English, but now he can talk pretty good. Sometimes he comes alone, sometimes with a couple of pals. . . ." Willing though she is, she runs out of things to say.

"Go on."

What can I say? Ah . . . he usually drinks Strega, if that's any use. Just another cock hanging out. He ain't been in for the last few nights."

"He's dead."

"No shit?" she asks, only mildly interested. "Well, that explains it, then."

"Explains what?"

"Well . . . we had a little appointment set up for last Thursday night. And he didn't show."

"That was the night he was killed."

"Just my luck. Now I'm out the fifty bucks."

"He was going to pay you fifty bucks?" LaPointe asks incredulously. "What for? Six months' worth?"

"No, he didn't want me. He had me the first night or so he was here. He's big on back-door stuff. But he didn't seem interested in a second helping."

"If not you, who then?"

She lifts her chin toward the bar. "He wanted to screw the kid that helps me with the music."

Guttmann glances at LaPointe. "Christ," he says. "A moronic kid?"

"Now wait a minute!" the dancer protests quickly. "You can't hang anything on me. The kid's nineteen. She's got consent. Ask the Lieutenant. She's nineteen, ain't she?"

"Yes, she's nineteen. With the mind of a seven-year-old."

"There you are! And anyway, she seems to like it. She never complains. Just stares off into space all the time it's going on. Look, I got to get back to my public. That butch in the front will pull her goddamned lip off if I'm late. Look, I'd tell you if I knew anything about the Italian kid. You know that, Lieutenant. Shit, the last thing I need is more trouble. But like I said, he was just another cock hanging out for a little *fonne*. Hey, did you notice that ci-

265

vilian in the suit? Now, there's a weirdo for you. You know what he's doing under the bar?"

"*Sacre le camp,*" LaPointe orders.

The dancer tucks down the corners of her mouth and shrugs, making a little farting noise of indifference with her mouth. Then she leaves for the back room, from which she soon appears without the slippers and dressing robe to clamber up onto the drum and stand, bored and impatient, while the retarded girl tries to set the needle down silently. She fails, and there is a screech before the whining music begins. The dancer darts a punitive glance at her, then begins to jiggle from foot to foot, running her thumbs around the belt of her G-string and in and out of the pouch.

The sting of the reprimand slides quickly from the girl's smooth mind, and soon she is lost in rapt fascination, looking up at the woman dancing in the blue and orange light, all eyes on her. Show business.

Guttmann finishes his ouzo at a gulp. "I hate to admit it, but I'm beginning to agree with you."

"You'd better watch that."

"This Green was real shit."

"Yes. Come on. Let's go."

At the door, LaPointe looks back at the dimly lit bar, small in the cavern of the unused dance floor. The man with the goatee is chewing and rolling his eyes.

They walk side by side down Rachel toward the Main, toward the luminous cross that advertises Christianity from the crest of Mont Royal.

"It's still early," Guttmann says. "You want a cup of coffee?"

That's a switch, and LaPointe senses that the young man wants to talk, but he feels too fed up, too tired of it all. "No, thanks. I'll just go home. I'm tired."

They walk on in silence.

"That Green . . ." Guttmann mutters.

"What?"

"I mean, come on. That's *too* sick."

"No sicker than that dancer."

"Sir?"

"The girl is her daughter."

266

Guttmann walks on mechanically, staring ahead, his fists clenched in his overcoat pockets. They cross over St. Laurent, where LaPointe stops to say goodbye. "You have a date with your girl tonight?" he asks.

"Yes, sir. Nothing big. We're just going to sit around and talk about things."

"Like the future?"

"That sort of thing. Will you tell me something, Lieutenant? Does anyone survive a career as a cop and still feel anything but disgust for people?"

"A few do."

"You?"

LaPointe examines the boy's earnest, pained face. "See you in the morning."

"Sure."

12

Two days pass; Guttmann has returned to Detective Sergeant Gaspard to finish out his tour as a Joan. When no new leads open on the Green case, there is talk down in homicide of closing down the investigation.

Pig weather continues to depress spirits and abrade tempers, and a popular rumor circulates on the Main to the effect that Russian and American atomic testing has done irremediable damage to the polar icecap, and the weather will never return to normal.

LaPointe's time and attention is soaked up by typical problems of the Main. Mr. Rothmann's butcher shop is broken into; the newspaper vendor on the corner of Rue Roy is held up for eight dollars and thirty-five cents; and the construction force demolishing a block of row houses to make way for a high-rise parking facility arrives on the site one morning to find that extensive vandalism has ruined work and tools. On a scabby brick wall, the posse of vandals has painted:

On the Rothmann break-in, nothing was stolen and the only damage was to the doorframe and lock. Probably some street tramp or shelterless American draft avoider trying to get out of the damp cold of night. Once again, LaPointe advises Mr. Rothmann to install special police locks, and once again Mr. Rothmann argues that the police ought to pay for them. After all, he's a taxpayer, isn't he?

The holdup of the newspaper vendor is a different matter. LaPointe presses it to a quick finish because he realizes that someone might have been killed. Not the victim; the holdup man.

The paper seller could only give a description of the thief's shoes and legs, and of the gun. Tennis shoes, bell-bottom jeans. A kid. And a black gun with a tiny hole in the barrel. The tiny hole meant the weapon was one of those exact-replica waterguns the Montreal police have made repeated complaints about, to no avail. After all, the people who sell them to kids are taxpayers, aren't they? It's a free country, isn't it?

LaPointe makes two telephone calls and talks with four people on the street. The word is out: the Lieutenant wants this kid, and he wants him right now. If he doesn't have him by noon, the street is going to become a hard place to live on.

Two and a half hours later, LaPointe is sitting in the cramped kitchen of a basement flat with the thief and his parents. The father admits he doesn't know what the hell is wrong with these goddamned kids these days. The mother says she works her fingers to the bone, never sees anything but these four walls, and what thanks does it get you? You carry them under your heart for nine months, you feed them, you send them to Mass, and what does it get you?

The kid sits at the kitchen table, picking at the oilcloth. His eyes lowered, he answers LaPointe's questions in a reluctant monotone. Once he makes the mistake of sassing.

In two steps, LaPointe crosses the room and snatches the kid up by the collar of his imitation-leather jacket.

"What do you think happens if a cop chases you and you flash that goddamned water pistol? Hein? You could be killed for eight lousy bucks!"

There is fear in the kid's eyes; defiance too.

LaPointe drops him back into his chair. What's the use?

It's a first offense. The Lieutenant can make arrangements, can find a job for the kid swabbing out some restaurant on the Main. The boy will pay the newspaper vendor back. He will have no record. But next time . . .

As he leaves, he hears the mother whining about carrying a child under her heart for nine months, and what thanks does she get? Heartache! Nothing but heartache!

There will be a next time.

About the vandalism at the building site, LaPointe does nothing, although this is not the first time it has happened. He goes through the motions, but he does nothing. His sympathy is with the people who are losing their homes and being shipped out to glass-and-cement suburban slums high-rising from muddy "green zones" dotted with emaciated twigs of one-year-old trees tied by rags to supporting sticks.

Corners, whole blocks of row houses are being torn down to make room for commercial buildings. Narrow streets of three-story Victorian brick with lead-sheeted mansard roofs are falling prey to the need to centralize small industry and commerce without threatening land values and the quality of life in the better neighborhoods. The residents of the Main are too poor, too ignorant, too weak politically to protect themselves from the paternal tyranny of city planning committees. The Main is a slum, anyway. Bad plumbing; rats and roaches; inadequate playgrounds. Relocating the immigrants is really for their own good; it helps to break up the language and culture nodes that delay their assimilation into New Montreal: Chicago on the St. Lawrence.

Although LaPointe knows that this blind striking out at the construction sites will change nothing, that the little people of the Main must lose their battle and ultimately their identity, he understands their need to protest, to break something.

More subtle than these dramatic attacks on the Main are the constant erosions from all points on its perimeter. Individuals and organizations have discovered that protecting what is left of old Montreal can be a profitable activity. Under the pretext of preservation, rows of homes are bought up and gutted, leaving only "quaint" shells. Good plumbing and central heating are installed, rooms enlarged, and residences are created for affluent and swinging young lawyers, pairs of career girls, braces of interior decorators. It is fashionable to surprise friends by saying you live on the Main. But these people don't live on the Main; they play house on the Main.

LaPointe sees it all happening. In his bitterest moods he feels that this bubble in his chest is consonant with the rest of it; there wouldn't be much point in surviving the Main.

When he arrives at the office Thursday morning, his temper is ragged. He has picked up word that Scheer is bragging about being back on the street before long. Obviously, the Commissioner has reported to his political acquaintance.

After scanning the Morning Report, he paws about in the three days' worth of back paper work that has accumulated since Guttmann's departure. Then he comes across a memo from Dr. Bouvier asking him to drop down to Forensic Medicine when he has a free moment.

As always, the smells of wax, chemicals, heat, and dust in the basement hall trigger memories of St. Joseph's: *moue, tranches,* the Glory Hole, Our Lady of the Chipped Cheek . . .

When LaPointe enters his office, Bouvier is just drawing a cup of coffee from his urn, his finger crooked into the cup to tell when it is nearly full.

"That you, Claude? Come in and be impressed by one of my flashes of insight, this particular one focused on the case of one Antonio Verdini—alias Green—discovered one night in an alley, his body having acquired a biologically superfluous, and even detrimental, orifice."

LaPointe grunts, in no mood for Bouvier's florid style.

"My ingenious filing system"—Bouvier waves toward his high-heaped desk—"has produced the interesting fact that our Mr. Green's uncommon appetite for ventilation was shared by"—he cocks his head in LaPointe's direction and pauses for effect—"the victims of two other unsolved murder cases."

"Oh?"

"Somehow I had expected more than 'oh?'."

"Which cases, then?"

"Men known to the department, and therefore to God, as H-49854 and H-50567, but to their intimates as Mac-Henry, John Albert, and Pearson, Michael X. This X indicates that his parents gave him no middle name, doubtless in a spirit of orthographic economy." Bouvier holds the two files out to LaPointe and stares proudly at him with one huge eye and one nicotine-colored blank. The Lieutenant scans rapidly, then reads more closely. These are Bouvier's personal files, fuller than the official records because they include clippings from newspapers, relevant additional information, and certain scribbled notes in his large, tangled hand.

One file is six years old, the other two and a half. Both stabbings; both males; both without signs of robbery; both at night on deserted streets.

"Well?" Bouvier gloats.

"Could be coincidences."

"There's a limit to antichance. Notice that both happened on the edges of what you call your patch—although I hear there is some difference of opinion between you and the Risen Cream as to the extent of that realm, and of its monarch's authority."

"What's all this business here?" LaPointe puts one report on Bouvier's desk, keeping his finger on a passage scribbled in the doctor's hand.

Pressing the bridge of his broken glasses to hold them in place, Bouvier leans over, his face close to the page.

273

"Ah! Technical description of the wound. Angle of entry of the weapon."

"Identical in all three cases?"

"No. Not quite."

"Well, then?"

"That's where you discern the touch of genius in me! The angles of entry are not identical. They vary. They vary in direct proportion to the heights of the three men. If you insist on playing the game of coincidence, you have to accept that there were three killers of identical height, and who held a knife in the identical way, and all three of whom were most gifted in the use of a knife. And if you want to stack up coincidences with the abandon of a Victorian novelist, how's this? Pearson, Michael X., made love shortly before his death. Once again, that nasty habit of failing to wash up. A professor at McGill, too! You'd think he'd know better. The other fellow, MacHenry, John Albert, was an American up here on business. There is every reason to believe that he also made love shortly before contributing his personal dust to the Universal Dust. He washed up within an hour of his death. Not a full bath; just the crotch area. There's the American businessman for you! Time is money."

"Can I take these with me?" LaPointe asks rhetorically, already on his way out with the reports.

"But make sure you bring them back. I can't stand having my files in disorder!" Bouvier calls after him.

Read and reread, Bouvier's dossiers rest on LaPointe's desk, covering the unfinished paper work. He links his fingers over his head and leans back in his swivel chair to look at the large-scale city plan of Montreal tacked up on his wall, finger-smudged only in the area of the Main. His eye picks up the places where the three men were found—stabbed, but not robbed. The Green kid . . . there. In that alley almost in the center of the Main district. The American businessman . . . there. On a narrow street off Chateaubriand between Rue Roy and Rue Bousquet, on what LaPointe would call the outer edge of his patch. And that professor from McGill . . . there. Well outside the Main, on Milton Street between Lorne and Shuter, normally a busy area, but probably deserted at . . . what was it? . . . estimated time of death: between 0200 and 0400 hours.

Probably the same killer. Probably the same woman. Jealousy? Over a period of six years? Hardly what you would call a flash of jealous anger. One woman. One killer. Perhaps the woman *was* the killer. And . . . what kind of woman could unite a Canadian professor, an American businessman, and an illegal Italian alien with sperm on his brain?

The freshest of these old cases is thirty months old. All traces would be healed over by now.

He sighs and puts the files into a thick interdepartmental envelope to send them over to Gaspard in homicide. LaPointe can picture Gaspard's anger when he discovers he has inherited a set of killings with a sex link. Just the kind of thing the newspapers salivate over. Unknown Knife Slayer Stalks . . . Police Baffled . . .

All the while he is eating in a cheap café, unaware of what is on his plate, all the while he walks slowly through the Main, putting the street to bed, LaPointe carries the details of the two files in the back of his mind, turning over the sparse references to personal life, looking for bits that match up with what he knows about Tony Green. But nothing. No links. He is standing outside his apartment on Esplanade, looking up at the dark windows of his second-story flat, when he decides to return to the Quartier Général and muck around with late paper work, rather than face a night alone with his coffee and his Zola.

"What in hell are you doing here?"

"Jesus Christ! You startled me, sir."

"You leave something behind?"

Guttmann has been sitting at LaPointe's desk, his mind floating in a debris of problems and daydreams. "No. I just remembered that you have a map of the city on your wall, and I still had my key, so . . ."

"So?"

"It's about that packet of files you left for Sergeant Gaspard."

With a jerk of his thumb, LaPointe evicts Guttmann from his swivel chair and occupies it himself. "I'll bet he was happy to find three closed cases suddenly reopened."

"Oh, yes, sir. He could hardly contain his delight. He was particularly colorful on the subject of Dr. Bouvier. He said he needed that kind of help about as much as starving Pakistanis need Red Cross packages filled with menus."

"Hm-m. But that still doesn't explain what you're doing in my office."

Guttmann goes to the wall map and points out light pencil lines he has drawn on it. "I got this weird idea in the middle of the night."

LaPointe is puddling about in his paper work. "Joans aren't supposed to have ideas. It ruins their typing," he says without looking up.

"As it turned out, it wasn't much of an idea."

"No kidding? Let's hear it."

Guttmann shrugs his shoulders, not eager to share his foolishness. "Oh, it was just grade-school geometry. It occurred to me that we know where each of the three men was killed, and we know where each was going at the time. So, if we extended the lines back on the map . . ."

LaPointe laughs. "The lines would meet on the doorstep of the killer?"

"Something like that. Or if not at the doorstep of the killer, at least on the doorstep of the woman they all made love with. I assume it was one woman, don't you?"

"Either that or a whorehouse."

"Well, either way, it would be one dwelling."

LaPointe looks up at the map on which Guttmann's three lines enclose a vast triangle including the east half of the Main district and a corner of Parc Fontaine. "Well, you've narrowed it down to eastern Canada."

Guttmann realizes how stupid his idea sounds when said aloud. "It was just a wild shot. I knew that any two lines would have to meet somewhere. And I hoped that the third would zap right in there."

"I see." LaPointe moves aside the files Guttmann brought along with him and picks up a splay of unfinished reports. He wants the kid to see he came here to do some work. Not because he was lonely. Not because his bed was too big.

"Can I get you a cup of coffee, sir?"

"If you're getting one for yourself."

While Guttmann is at the machine down the hall, La-Pointe's eyes wander back to the wall map. He makes a nasal puff of derision at the idea that things get solved by geometry and deduction. What you need is an informer, a lot of pressure, a fist.

With a brimming paper cup in each hand, Guttmann has some trouble with the door; he slops some and burns his fingers. "Goddamn it!" He gives the door a kick.

LaPointe glances up. This kid is usually so controlled, so polite. As Guttmann sits in his old chair against the wall, his long legs stretched out in front of him, LaPointe sips his coffee.

"What's your problem?"

"Sir?"

"Trouble with this girl of yours?"

"No, that isn't it. That's turning out to be a really fine thing."

"Oh? How long have you known her? A week?"

"How long does it take?"

LaPointe nods. That is true. He had been sure he wanted to spend his life with Lucille after knowing her for two hours. Of course, it was a year before they had the money to get married.

"No, it isn't the girl," Guttmann continues, looking into his coffee. "It's the force. I'm thinking pretty seriously about quitting." He had wanted to talk to LaPointe about this that evening after they'd been at the go-go joint, but there hadn't been an opportunity. He looks up to see how the Lieutenant is taking the news.

There is no response at all from LaPointe. Perhaps a slight shrug. He never gives advice in this kind of situation; he doesn't want the responsibility.

There is an uncomfortable, interrogative quality to the silence, so LaPointe looks up at the wall map for something to fill it. "What's that northwest–southeast line supposed to be?"

277

Guttmann understands. The Lieutenant doesn't want to talk about it. Well . . . "Ah, let me see. Well, that X is the alley where we found Green."

"I know that."

"And the circle is his apartment—the rooming house with the concierge with the broken lip? So I just drew a line between them and continued it on southeast to see where it would lead. Just an approximation. It cuts through the middles of blocks and such, but it must have been the general direction he came from."

"Yes, but he wasn't going back to his rooming house."

"Sir?"

"He was going to the Happy Hour Whisky à Go-Go, remember? He had a date with that dancer's retarded kid."

Guttmann looks at the map more closely and frowns. "Yeah. That's right!" He takes out his pencil and crosses to the map. Freehand, he sketches in the revised line, and the vast triangle is reduced by a considerable wedge. "That narrows it down a lot."

"Sure. To maybe thirty square blocks and six or eight thousand people. Just for the hell of it, let's take a look at the other lines. What's the one running roughly east-west?"

"That's the McGill professor. The X is where his body was found; the circle is his office on the campus."

"How do you know he was going to his office?"

"Assumption. His apartment was up north. Why would he walk west unless he was going to the campus? Maybe to do some late work. Grade papers, something like that."

"All right. Assume it. Now, what about the other line? The north–south one?"

"That's the American. His body was found right . . . here. And his hotel was downtown, right . . . ah . . . here. So I just extended the line back."

"But he wouldn't have walked south."

"Sure he would. That was the direction to his hotel, and also the best direction to go to find taxis."

"What about his car?"

"Sir?"

"Look in the report. There was something about a

278

rented car. It was found three days later, after the rental agency placed a complaint. Don't you remember? The car was ticketed for overparking. Bouvier made some wiseassed note about the bad luck of getting a parking ticket the same night you get killed."

Guttmann taps his forehead with his knuckle. "Yes! I forgot about that."

"Don't worry about it. One line out of three isn't bad. For a Joan."

"Where was the car parked?"

"It's in the report. Somewhere a few blocks from where they found the body."

Guttmann takes up the folder on MacHenry, John Albert, and leafs quickly through it. He misses what he's looking for and has to flip back. The major reason Dr. Bouvier is able to come up with his little "insights" from time to time is his cross-indexing of information. In the standard departmental files, the murder of MacHenry, the report of the car-rental agency, and the traffic report of the ticketed car would be in separate places; in fact in separate departments. But in Dr. Bouvier's files, they are together. "Here it is!" Guttmann says. "Let's see . . . the rental car . . . recovered by the agency from police garage . . . ah! It was parked near the corner of Rue Mentana and Ruc Napoléon. Let's see what that gives us." He goes to the map again and sketches the new line. Then he turns back to LaPointe. "Now, how about that, Lieutenant?"

The three lines fail to intersect by a triangle half the size of a fingernail. And the center of that triangle is Carré St. Louis, a rundown little park on the edge of the Main.

LaPointe rises and approaches the map. "Could be coincidence."

"Yes, sir."

"We would be looking for a woman somewhere around Carré St. Louis who has made love three times in the past six years. It's just possible that more than one would fit that description."

"Yes, sir."

"Murders aren't solved by drawing lines on maps, you know."

"Yes, sir."

"Hm-m."

Guttmann lets the silence extend awhile before offering, "I'll bet Sergeant Gaspard would let me go with you. I've just about finished his paper work too."

LaPointe taps the pale green rectangle of the square with his thick forefinger. It has been about a week since he wandered through there on his rounds. The night of the Green killing, come to think of it. He pictures the statue of the dying Cremazie.

Pour Mon Drapeau
Je Viens Ici Mourir

The empty pond, its bottom littered. The peace symbol dripping rivulets of paint, like a bleeding swastika. The word LOVE, but the spray can ran out while they were adding FUCK YO . . .

LaPointe nods. "All right. Tomorrow morning we'll take a walk around there." He returns to his desk and finishes his cooling coffee, crushing the cup and tossing it toward the wastebasket. "What does she think about it?"

"Sir?"

"Your girl. What does she think about your decision to leave the department?"

Taken off balance, Guttmann shrugs and wanders back to his chair. "Oh, she wants me to do what I want to do. Maybe . . . maybe I shouldn't have joined up in the first place. I came out of school with the idea that I could do something . . . useful. Social work, maybe. I don't know. I knew how people felt about the police, particularly the young, and I thought . . . Anyway, I realize now I wasn't cut out to be a cop. Maybe I've always known it. Being with you these few days has sort of pushed me over the edge, you know what I mean? I just don't have the stomach for it. I don't want everyone I meet to hate me, or fear me. I don't want to live in a world populated by tramps and losers and whores and punks and junkies. It's just . . . not for me. I'd never be good at it. And nobody

280

likes to be a failure. I've talked it all over with Jeanne; she understands."

"Jeanne?"

"The girl in my building."

"She's *canadienne,* this girl of yours?"

"Didn't I mention that?"

"No."

"Well, she is."

"Hm-m. You've got better taste than I thought. Are you going to drink that coffee?"

"No. Here. You know, this idea about the map was really sort of an excuse to come down here and think things over."

"And now you've decided?"

"Pretty much."

Guttmann sits in silence. LaPointe drinks the coffee as he looks at the wall map with half-closed eyes, then he scrubs his hair with his hand. "Well, I'd better call it a day."

"Can I drop you off, sir?"

"In that toy car of yours?"

"It's the only car I've got."

LaPointe seems to consider this for a moment. "All right. You can drop me off."

Guttmann feels like saying, Thank you very much, sir. But he does not.

13

A clammy mist settles over Carré St. Louis, sweating the statue of Cremazie, sogging litter in the pond, varnishing the gnarled roots that convulse over a surface too cindery and hard-packed to penetrate. Between stunted, leafless trees, there are weathered park benches, all bearing carved graffiti in which vulgar, romantic, and eponymous impulses overlay and defeat one another.

Once a square of town houses around a pleasant park, Carré St. Louis has run to ruin and has been invaded by jangling, alien styles. To the west is a great Victorian pile, its capricious projections and niches bound together by a broad sign all along the front: YOUNG CHINESE MEN'S CHRISTIAN ASSOCIATION. Even the lack of repainting for many years and the hanging mist that broods over the park does not mute its garish, three-foot-high Chinese characters of red and gold. The top of the square is dominated by a grotesquerie, a crenelated castle in old gray stone and new green paint, the home of the Millwright's Union.

What in hell is a millwright, LaPointe wonders. A

man who makes mills? No, that can't be right. He glances at his watch: quarter after eleven; Guttmann is late.

Only to the east of the park is the integrity of the row houses preserved; and even there it is bogus. Behind the façades, the fashionable and artsy have gutted and renovated. Soon this bit of the Main will be undermined and pried loose from the cultural mosaic. The new inhabitants will have the political leverage to get the trees trimmed, the fountain running, the spray-paint peace symbol cleaned off the side of the pool. There will be grass and shrubs and new benches, and there will be an ironwork fence around the park to which residents will have keys.

LaPointe grunts his disgust and looks around to see Guttmann crossing the park with long strides, anxious about being late.

"I couldn't find a parking place," he explains as he approaches. When LaPointe doesn't respond, he continues with, "I'm sorry. Have you been waiting long?"

The Lieutenant blocks the small talk. "You know this square?"

"No, sir." Guttmann looks around. "God, there are a lot of houses. Where do we begin?"

"Let's take a little stroll around."

Guttmann walks beside LaPointe, their slow steps crunching the gravel of the central spine path, as they scan the buildings on both sides.

Guttmann continues along in silence, until it occurs to him to ask, "Sir? What is a millwright?"

LaPointe glances at him sideways with a fatigued expression that says, Don't you know *anything?*

They cross over from the park and walk down the east side of the square, down the row of renovated buildings. LaPointe walks with the long slow steps of the beat-pounder, his fists deep in his overcoat pockets, looking up at each doorway in turn.

"What are we looking for, sir?"

"No idea."

"It's sort of a needle in a haystack, isn't it? It occurred to me on the way over that if one of those lines on the map

284

was just a few degrees off, the woman could live blocks away from here."

"Hm-m. If she still lives here. If it's *one* woman. If. . ."

LaPointe's pace slows slightly as he looks up at the next door. Then he walks on a little more quickly.

"If what, sir?"

"Come on. I'll buy you a cup of coffee."

They take coffee in a little place two blocks east of the square, in one of those self-conscious bohemian cafés frequented by the young. At this time of day it is empty, save for an intense couple in the far corner, a bearded boy who appears to be staggering under the impulse to communicate, a skinny girl in round glasses who is straining to understand. They work very hard at avoiding artifice.

The waitress is a young slattern who tugs a snarl out of her hair with her fingers as she repeats Guttmann's order for two cappuccini. Back at the coffee machine, she stares indifferently out a front window hung with glass beads as she lets steam hiss into the coffee. For once they are in an atmosphere in which Guttmann is more at home than LaPointe, who looks across the table and shakes his head at the young policeman. "You talk about God being on the side of drunks, fools, and kids. I didn't expect anything to come of your silly game of drawing lines on a map. Not one chance in a thousand."

"*Has* something come of it?"

"I'm afraid so. Chances are our woman works, or did work, at that school."

"School, sir?"

"Seventh building from the end of that renovated row. There was a placard on the door—brass. It's a school of sorts. One of those places that teaches French and English to foreigners in a hurry."

Guttmann's expression widens. "And Green was learning English!"

LaPointe nods.

"But wait a minute. What about the American?"

"Could have been learning French. Maybe he wanted to set up a business in Québec."

"And the McGill professor?"

"I don't know. We'll have to see how he fits in. If he does."

"But wait a minute, sir. Even if the school is the contact point, maybe it isn't a teacher. Could be one of the students."

"Over a period of six years?"

"All right. A teacher, then. So what do we do now?"

"We go talk to somebody. See if we can find out which teacher is ours." LaPointe rises.

"Aren't you going to finish your coffee, sir?"

"This swill? Just tip the greasy kid and let's get out of here."

Considering the slop and dregs he has had to drink with the Lieutenant in Chinese, Greek, and Portuguese cafés, Guttmann doubts that it is the quality of the coffee LaPointe is rejecting.

". . . so, out of a total faculty of thirteen, that would make a full-time equivalency of nine or nine and a half, considering that some of my teachers are only part-time, and some are university students training in our techniques of one-to-one intensive language assimilation." Mlle. Montjean lights her cigarette from a marble-and-gold lighter, takes a deep drag, and tilts her head back to jet the uninhaled smoke upward, away from her guests. Then she lightly touches the tip of her tongue between thumb and forefinger, as though to pluck off a bit of tobacco, a residual gesture from some earlier time when she smoked unfiltered cigarettes.

Many things about her put Guttmann in mind of a fashion model: the meticulous, underrolled coiffure, that bounces with her quick, energetic gestures; the assured, almost rehearsed moves and turns; the long slim arms and legs; the perfectly tailored suit that is both functional and feminine. And, like a model, she appears to be aware of herself at every moment, as though she were seeing herself from the outside. Guttmann finds her voice particularly pleasing in its combining of great precision of pronunciation with a low, warm note just above husky. She laughs in exactly the same key as that in which she speaks.

"I suppose that seems quite a large faculty for a little school like ours, Lieutenant, but we specialize in intensive training with a low student-to-teacher ratio. We *submerge* the student in a linguistic culture. The student who is learning French, for instance, doesn't hear a word of English for six hours a day, and he even takes lunch with instructors and other students in a French restaurant. And at night, if he wishes, the student will be taken to French nightclubs, cinema, theatre—all in the company of an instructor. We concentrate on the *music* of the language, you might say. The student learns to *hum* in French, even before he learns the words to the song. Our methods were pioneered at McGill, and indeed some of our student teachers are graduate students from there." Mlle. Montjean suddenly stops and laughs. "I must be sounding like our promotional material."

"A little," LaPointe says. "You have a connection with McGill then?"

"No formal connection. Some of their students get experience and credit by working with us. Oh!" She butts her cigarette hurriedly. "Excuse me just a moment, won't you." She leaves the "conversation island," consisting of deeply padded white leather "comfort forms" around a kidney-shaped, glass-topped coffee table, the whole sunken two steps below the floor level. She goes quickly to her desk overlooking Carré St. Louis, and there she presses the button of a concealed tape recorder and speaks conversationally: "Maggie, remind me tomorrow to get in touch with Dr. Moreland. Subject: Evaluation Procedures for Part-time Students." She releases the button and smiles across at the policemen. "I would have forgotten that completely if I hadn't happened to mention it to you. I've got a brain like a sieve."

This is a social lie and an obvious one. Mlle. Montjean runs her specialized and very expensive school with such great efficiency that she appears to have free time for people who drop in unexpectedly. Even policemen.

287

The school occupies a double building: the façades of two former homes have been gutted and renovated to contain "conversation foyers," "learning environments," and audio-visual support systems on the first two floors, while the mansard-roofed third story houses Mlle. Montjean's living and working quarters. Guttmann is impressed by the way she has folded into her large living room the equipment necessary for running her business. Files are concealed within Victorian court cupboards; her hi-fi system is tied in with her dictation instruments; her business telephones are ceramic French "coffee-grinder" models; her desk is an inlaid feminine escritoire; the "conversation island" would serve equally well for staff meetings or a romantic tête-à-tête. The walls and ceiling are white stucco with attic beams revealed and varnished, and this neutral background helps to blend the improbable, but not offensive, mélange of modern, Victorian, and antique furniture.

In theory it ought not work, this mixture of furniture styles, the stucco walls and dark beams, the Persian carpets, the modern and classical prints on the walls. But any feeling of discord and jumble is avoided by the sense that everything has been selected by one person of firm personality and taste. All the elements are aligned by one coign of vantage, one articulation of preference.

LaPointe doesn't like the place.

"I haven't offered you a drink, have I?" she says, shaking her head as though to imply she would forget it if it weren't attached. "What do you take before lunch? Dubonnet?"

Guttmann says Dubonnet would be fine.

"Lieutenant?" she asks.

"Nothing, thank you." After being shown up to the office apartment by a fussy man of uncertain function, La-Pointe presented his identification card and introduced a question about the faculty of the school. Graciously, indeed overwhelmingly, Mlle. Montjean took up the cue, describing her business with a glibness that had a quality of rote. Even the asides and pauses to light a cigarette seemed considered, rehearsed. She said more than he wanted to know, as though attempting to drown questions with answers.

LaPointe sits back and lets Guttmann be the focus for her talk. This kind of woman—educated, capable, confident of her attraction and gifts—is alien to LaPointe's experience.

Of one thing he is sure; she is hiding something.

"Are you sure I can't tempt you, Lieutenant? I have everything." She gestures toward a bar at the end of the room, near a wide marble fireplace.

"Say, that's a *real* bar," Guttmann says in surprise. "That's fantastic." He rises and goes with her as she crosses to pour out the drinks. It is indeed a real bar, complete with back bar and beveled mirrors, a brass rail, copper fittings, and even a spittoon.

"I like to believe my guests will treat that as a mere decoration," she says, indicating the spittoon.

"Where did you get a turn-of-the-century bar like this?" Guttmann asks.

"Oh, they were tearing down one of those little places up on the Main, and I just bought it." She grins mischievously. "The workmen had a hell of a time getting it up here. The walnut top is one piece. They had to bring it in through the window."

Guttmann tries the bar on for size, putting his stomach against the polished wood and his foot up on the rail. "Fits just fine. I'll bet the neighbors wondered what you were up to here. I mean, a whole bar. Come on!"

"That never occurred to me. I should have had my bed brought in through the window, too. That would really have given them something to gossip about. It's one of those big circular waterbeds." She laughs lightly. Guttmann realizes she is a very attractive woman.

LaPointe's patience with this social nonsense is thin. He rises from the deep cushions of the "conversation island" and joins them at the bar. "I would like a little Armagnac after all, Mlle. Montjean. And I would like to know something about Antonio Verdini, alias Tony Green."

She does not pause in pouring out the Dubonnet, but her voice is unmodulated when she responds, "And *I* would like to know what you're doing here. Why you're interested in my school. And why you're asking these questions." She looks up and smiles at LaPointe. "Armagnac, did you say?"

"Please. Do you mind the questions?"

"I'm not sure." She takes down the Armagnac bottle and looks at it thoughtfully. "Tell me, Lieutenant LaPointe. Would my lawyer be unhappy with me, if I were to answer your questions without his being here?"

"Possibly. How did you know my name?"

"You showed me your identification when you came in."

"You barely glanced at it." There is another thing he does not mention. By habit he holds out his identification card with his thumb over his name. He's been a cop for a long time.

She sets the bottle down and looks directly at him, her eyes shifting from one of his to the other. Then she slowly raises both arms until her palms are level with her ears. In a deep, graveled voice she says, "You got me, Lieutenant. I give up. But don't tell Rocky and the rest of the mob that I ratted."

Both she and Guttmann laugh. A glance from La-Pointe, and she is laughing alone as she pours out the Armagnac. "Say when."

"That's fine. Now, how do you know my name?"

"Don't be so modest. Everyone on the Main knows Lieutenant LaPointe."

"You know the Main?"

"I grew up there. Don't worry about it, Lieutenant. There's no way in the world you could remember me. I left when I was just a kid. Thirteen years old. But I remember you. Of course that was twenty years ago, and you weren't a lieutenant, and your hair was all black, and you were slimmer. But I remember you." There is something harder than amusement in the glitter of her eyes. Then she turns to Guttmann. "What do you think of that? What do you think of a woman giving away her age like that? Here I go admitting that I'm thirty-three, when I know perfectly that I could pass for thirty-two any day . . . if the light wasn't too strong."

"So you come from the street?" LaPointe says, unconvinced.

"Oh, yes, sir. From the deepest depths of the street. My mother was a hooker." She has learned to say that with the same offhandedness as one might use to mention that her mother was a blonde, or a liberal. She evidently likes to drop bombs. But she laughs almost immediately. "Hey, what do you say, gang. Shall we drink at the bar, or go sit in a booth?"

When they have returned to the "conversation island," Mlle. Montjean assumes her most businesslike voice. She tells LaPointe that she wants to know exactly why he is here, asking questions. When she knows that, she will decide whether or not to answer without the advice of counsel.

"Have you any reason to think you might be in trouble?" he asks.

But she is not taking sucker bait like that. She smiles as she sips her aperitif.

LaPointe is not comfortable with her elusive blend of caution and practiced charm. She is so unlike the girls on his patch, though she claims to be one of them. He dislikes being kept off balance by her constant changes of verbal personality. She was the urbane vamp at first, completely castrating the policeman in Guttmann. Then there was that clowning "gun moll" routine under the guise of which she had admitted to being caught off base . . . but to nothing more. LaPointe fears that when he hits her with the fact that Green is dead, her control will be so high that it will mask any surprise she might feel. In that way, she could seem guilty without being so. She might even confuse him by being frank and honest. She is the type for whom honesty is also a ploy.

"So," LaPointe says, looking around at the costly things decorating the apartment, "you're from the Main, are you?"

"*From* is the active word, Lieutenant. I've spent my whole life being *from* the Main."

"Montjean? You say your mother was a hooker named Montjean?"

"No, I didn't say that, Lieutenant. Naturally, I have changed my name."

"From?"

Mlle. Montjean smiles. "Can I offer you another Armagnac? I'm afraid it will have to be a quick one; I have a working lunch coming up. We're involved in something that might interest you, Lieutenant. We're developing an intensive course in Joual. You'd be surprised at the number of people who want to learn the Canadian usages and accents. Salesmen, mostly, and politicians. The kinds of people who make their living by being trusted. Like policemen."

LaPointe finishes his drink and sets the tulip glass carefully on the glass tabletop. "This Antonio Verdini I mentioned . . . ?"

"Yes?" She lifts her eyebrows lazily.

"He's dead. Stabbed in an alley up on the Main."

She looks levelly at LaPointe, not a flutter in her eyelids. After a moment, her gaze falls to the marble-and-gold cigarette lighter, and she stares at it, motionless. Then she takes a cigarette from a carved teak box, lights it, tilts back her head with a bounce of her hair, and jets the uninhaled smoke over the heads of her guests. She delicately plucks an imaginary bit of tobacco from the tip of her tongue.

"Oh?" she asks.

"Presumably you were lovers," LaPointe says matter-of-factly, ignoring Guttmann's quick glance.

Mlle. Montjean shrugs. "We screwed, if that's what you mean." More of that precious bomb-dropping, a kind of counter-attack against LaPointe's ballistic use of Green's death. Her control had been excellent throughout her long pause . . . but there *was* the pause.

"Our information says that he was learning English here," LaPointe continues. "I assume that's right?"

"Yes. One of our Italian-speaking instructors was guiding him through an intensive course in English."

"And that's how you met him?"

"That's how I met him, Lieutenant. Tell me, do I need a lawyer now?"

"Did you kill him?"

"No."

"Then you probably don't need a lawyer. Unless you intend to withhold information, or refuse to assist us in our inquiry."

She taps the ash from her cigarette unnecessarily, gaining time to think. Her control is still good, but for the first time she is troubled.

"You're thinking about the others, of course," LaPointe says.

"What others?"

LaPointe bends on her that melancholy patience he assumes during examination when he lacks the information necessary to lead the conversation.

"All right, Lieutenant. I'll cooperate. But let me ask you something first. Does this have to get into the papers?"

"Not necessarily."

"You see, my school is rather special—expensive, elite. Scandal would ruin it. And it's everything I've worked for. It represents ten years of work. What's more, it represents the ten thousand miles I've managed to walk away from the Main. You understand what I'm saying?"

"I understand. Tell me about the others."

"Well, it couldn't be a coincidence. Mike was killed the same way: stabbed in the street."

"Mike?"

"Michael Pearson. Dr. Michael Pearson. He used to run the Language Learning Center at McGill."

"And you were lovers?"

She smiles thinly. "You *do* run to circumlocution, don't you?"

"And what about the other one. The American?"

Her eyes open with confusion. "What other one?"

"The American. Ah . . ." He looks to Guttmann.

"John Albert MacHenry," Guttmann fills in quickly.

Mlle. Montjean glances from one to the other. "I have no idea what you're talking about. I don't think I ever met anyone by that name. I can assure you that I never . . . screwed . . . your Mr. MacHenry." She reaches over and squeezes LaPointe's arm. "That's just my homey way of saying we were not lovers, Lieutenant."

293

"You seem sure of that, Mlle. Montjean. Do you keep a list?"

Her smile is fixed and her eyes perfectly cold. "As a matter of fact, I do. At least, I keep a diary. And it's a fairly long list, if you will forgive my bragging. I enjoy keeping count. My analyst tells me that it's rather typical behavior in cases like mine. He tells me the reason I use so many men is because I detest them, and by scoring them one after the other I deny them any individuality. He talks like that, my analyst. Like a textbook. And can you guess when he told me all this crap? In bed. After I had scored him too. Later, he sat right there where you're sitting and told me how he understood my need to screw even him. A typical gesture of rejection, he told me. And when I mentioned that he wasn't much of a lay, he tried to laugh it off. But I know I got to him." She grins. "The phony bastard."

"The point of all that being that you don't know this American, this MacHenry?"

"Precisely. Oh, I've had my share of Americans, of course. One should have an American at least once a quarter. It makes Canadians look so good by comparison. And at least once a year, one should have an Englishman. Partially to make even the Americans look good, and partially as penance. Did you know that making love with a Brit shortens one's time in purgatory?" The intercom on her desk buzzes; Mlle. Montjean butts out her cigarette and rises, flattening her skirt with her palms. "That will be my luncheon appointment. I assume I'm free to go to it?"

LaPointe rises. "Yes. But we have more to talk about."

She has crossed to her desk and is taking up a folder of material pertaining to her working lunch. She glances at her calendar. "I'm tied up all afternoon. Are you free tonight, Lieutenant?"

"Yes."

"Say nine o'clock? Here?"

She shakes hands with Guttmann, then offers her hand to LaPointe. "You really don't remember me, do you, Lieutenant?"

"I'm afraid not. Should I?"

Still holding his hand, she smiles a montage of amusement and sadness. "We'll talk about it tonight. Armagnac, isn't it?"

She shows them to the door.

By nine o'clock it is dark in the little park of Carré St. Louis. For the first time in weeks, the wind is from the north and steady. If it remains in that quarter, it will bring the cleansing snow. But its immediate effect is to hone the edge of the damp cold. LaPointe has to fold in the flap of his collar against his throat as he cuts across the deserted park, picking his way carefully over the root-veined path because the dappled light from distant streetlights serves more to confuse than to illuminate.

Suddenly he stops. Save for the hiss of wind through gnarled branches, there is no sound. But he has a tingling in the back of his neck, as though someone were watching him. He looks around through the zebra dapple of black trees and shadows interlaced with the silver of streetlights bordering the park. There is nothing to be seen.

He continues across toward Mlle. Montjean's school, where there are lights behind drawn shades on the first and third floors; probably late students learning French or English in a hurry. His knock is answered by the fussy man he met earlier. Mlle. Montjean is not in, but she is due any minute; she has left instructions that the Lieutenant is to be shown up to her apartment. The nervous man looks LaPointe over, his lips pursed critically. It isn't *his* business who Mlle. Montjean's friends are. *He* doesn't care what his employer does on her own time. But there *are* limits. A policeman, *really*. Oh, well, he'll show him up anyway.

Three lamps light the apartment, pooling three distinct areas. There is a porcelain lamp on the escritoire by the windows overlooking the square; a dim hanging lamp picks out the sunken "conversation island"; and beyond that, over the bar, is a glass ball confected of bits of colored glass and lit from within. The room is centrally heated, the dwindling fire in the fireplace largely decorative. LaPointe takes off his overcoat and makes himself at home to the extent of putting two kiln-dried, steam-cleaned logs on the fire and poking at the embers. He enjoys fiddling with open fires, and he often pictures himself in his daydream home in Laval, turning logs or pushing in burnt-off ends. The bark has begun to crackle and flutter with blue flame when Mlle. Montjean enters, her coat already off, her fur hat in her hand.

"Sorry, Lieutenant. But you know how these things are." She does not mention what things. "Oh, good. I'm glad you've tended the fire. I was afraid it would die out; and I set it especially for you." She ducks under the bar flap and begins to pour out two Armagnacs, light from the ball of glass shining in her carefully done hair. When La-Pointe sits on a bar stool across from her, he realizes that she has been drinking fairly heavily, not beyond control, but perhaps a little beyond caring.

"I hope you didn't have anything big on tonight," she says.

"Nothing very big. A pinochle game I had to postpone, that's all."

"Hey, wow, Lieutenant." She makes two clicking sounds at the side of her cheek. "Pinochle! You really know how to get it on." She lifts her glass. "Salut?"

"Salut."

She finishes half her drink and sets it down on the bar. "That word 'salut' reminds me of a proof we recently had that our aural-oral system of language learning is not without its flaws. We had an Arab student here—a nephew of one of those oil pirates—and he was being preened to take over the world, or learn to surrender in six languages, or whatever the fuck they do. Dumb as a stick! But they were giving him all sorts of special tutoring at McGill—I think his uncle bribed them by buying an atomic laboratory for them, or half of South America, or something like that. . . . I mean, he was *really* stupid. He was so dumb he'd have difficulty making the faculty of a polytechnic in Britain, or getting his Ph.D. in journalism in the States. . . . That line would get a laugh in an academic crowd."

"Would it?"

"You're not much of an audience, LaPointe. And now

I don't even remember what that story was supposed to illustrate."

"Maybe nothing. Maybe you're just playing for time."

"Yes, maybe. How about another drink?"

"I still have this one."

"I think I'll have another." She brings it around the bar and sits beside him. "I had the weirdest experience just now. I was crossing the park, and there was someone there, in the shadows."

"Someone you know?"

"That's just it. I had the feeling I knew him, but . . . I can't explain it. I didn't see him, really. Just sort of a shadow. But I had this eerie feeling that he wanted to talk to me."

"But he didn't?"

"No."

"Then what frightened you?"

She laughs. "Nothing. I was just scared. I warned you it was a weird experience. Am I babbling, or is it my imagination?"

"It's not your imagination. This afternoon you said you knew me. Tell me about that."

As she speaks, she deals with her glass, not with him. "Oh, I was just a kid. You never really noticed me. But for years, you've been . . . important in my life." She puffs out a little laugh of self-derision. "Now *that* sounds heavy, doesn't it? I don't mean you've been important in the sense that I think of you often, because I don't. But I think of you at . . . serious times. It must be embarrassing to have a stranger tell you that she has a rather special vision of you. Is it?"

He lifts his glass and tips his head. "Yes."

"You think I'm drunk?"

He balances his thumb against his little finger. "A little."

"Drunk and disorderly," she says in a distant tone. "I charge you, young woman, with being drunk, and with having a disorderly life—a disorderly mind."

"I doubt that. I think you have a very orderly mind. A very clever one."

"Clever? Yes. Neatly arranged? Yes. But disorderly nevertheless. The front shelves of my mind are all neatly stacked and efficiently arranged. But back in the stacks there is a stew of disorder, chaos, and do you know what else?"

"No. What?"

"Just a pinch of self-pity."

They both laugh.

"*Now* how about another drink?" She goes around the bar to refill her glass.

"No, thanks . . . all right. Yes. And tell me, with that self-pity you talk about, is there some hate?"

"Tons and tons, Lieutenant. But . . ." She points at him quickly, as though she just caught him slipping a card from his sleeve. "But not enough to kill." She laughs drily. "You know something, sir? I have a feeling we may spend a lot of this night talking about two different things."

"Not all of it."

"A threat?"

He shrugs. "So, tons and tons of hate. Do you hate me for not remembering you?"

"N-n-no. No, I don't blame or hate you. You were a central figure, a star actor on the Main. I had an aisle seat near the back. I spent my time staring at the one actor, so naturally I remember him. You—if you ever bothered to look out at the audience—wouldn't see them as individuals. No, not hate. Take two parts disappointment, mix in one part resentment, one part dented vanity, dilute with years of indifference, and that's what I feel. Not hate."

"You said your mother was a hooker on the street. What was her name?"

She laughs without anything being funny. "Her name was Dery."

LaPointe's memory rolls and brings up an image of twenty years ago. Yo-Yo Dery, a kind of whore you don't see around anymore. Loud, life-embracing, fun to be with, she would sometimes go with factory workers who didn't have much money, and for free, if they were good *mecs* and she liked them. Carefree and mischievous, she earned a reputation as a clown and a hellcat when, right in the middle of the dance floor of a crowded cabaret (the place where the Happy Hour Whisky à Go-Go now is), she settled a dispute with another hooker who claimed that Yo-Yo's red hair was dyed. She lifted her skirt, dropped her drawers, and proved that her red hair was natural.

"You remember her, don't you," Mlle. Montjean says, seeing his eye read the past.

"Yes. I remember her."

"But not me?"

Yes, come to think of it. Yo-Yo had a daughter. He talked to her once or twice in Yo-Yo's flat. After Lucille's death, when the need to make love got annoying, he went with street girls occasionally, always paying his way, although as a cop he could have got it free. Yo-Yo and he made love three or four times over the years. Yes, that's right. Yo-Yo had a little girl. A shy little girl.

Then he recalls how Yo-Yo died. She killed herself. She sent the kid to stay with a neighbor, and she killed herself. It astonished everybody on the Main. Yo-Yo Dery? The one who's always laughing? No! The one who proved she was a redhead? Suicide? But why?

LaPointe made the break-in. Rags stuffed in the crack under the door. He had to shatter a window with a beer bottle. Yo-Yo had slipped sideways onto the kitchen floor, her cheek resting on the bristles of a broom. There were cards laid out on the table. She had turned on the gas, and started playing solitaire.

Funny how details come back. There was a black queen on a black king. She had been cheating.

But what became of the kid? Vaguely, he recalls something about a neighbor keeping the girl until the social workers came around.

"Do you remember why they called her Yo-Yo?" Mlle. Montjean asks, almost dreamily.

He remembers. Like a Yo-Yo, up and down, up and down.

Mlle. Montjean turns the stem of her tulip glass, revolving it between her thumb and finger. "She was good to me, you know that? Presents. Clothes. We went to the park every Sunday when it wasn't too cold. She really tried to be good to me."

"That would be like her."

"Oh, sure. The good-hearted whore. A real Robert Service type. In a way, I always knew what she did for a living, even when I was four or five. That is . . . there were always men around the flat, and they left money. What I didn't know at that age was that it wasn't the same in everyone else's house. But when I was old enough to go to school, the other kids straightened me out soon enough. They used to chant at me: 'Redhead, Redhead'—I can still hear those two singsong notes, like a French ambulance. I didn't understand why they chanted that, and why they giggled. My hair has always been brown. You see. I didn't know about Yo-Yo's epic proof in the dance hall. But all the other kids did."

This is not what LaPointe came here to listen to, and he doesn't want the burden of problems he did not cause and cannot help. "Oh, well," he says, making a gesture toward the expensive apartment, "you've come a long way from all that."

She looks at him sideways through her shoulder-length, rolled-under hair. "You sound like my analyst," she accuses.

"The one you take to bed?"

"The one I screw," she corrects. "What is it? Why are you shaking your head?"

"It must be the fashion to use the ugliest words for making love. I met a girl just recently who found the nicer words funny, and couldn't help laughing at them."

"I say screw because I mean screw. It's the *mot juste.* When I'm with a man, we don't 'go to bed,' and we certainly don't 'make love.' We screw. And what's more, they don't screw me. *I screw them.*"

"As in, Screw you, mister!"

Mlle. Montjean laughs. "Now you *really* sound like my analyst. How about another Armagnac?"

"No, thanks."

She carries her glass to the divan before the fireplace,

where she sits staring silently for a short time before beginning to speak, more to herself than to him. "It's funny, but I never despised the men Yo-Yo brought home—mostly good *mecs*, laughing, a little drunk, clumsy. Yo-Yo used to come in to tuck me in and kiss me good night. Then she'd close the door slowly because the hinges creaked. She had a way of waving to me with her fingertips, just before the door closed. I remember the light on the wall, a big trapezoid of yellow getting narrower until the door clicked shut, and there was only a thin line of light from the crack. Her bedroom was next to mine. I could hear her laughing. And I could hear the men. The squeak of the bedsprings. And the men grunting. They always seemed to grunt when they came." She looks over at LaPointe out of the corner of her eye and she half smiles. "You never grunted, Lieutenant. I'll say that much for you."

He lifts his empty glass in acceptance of the compliment, and immediately feels the stupidity of the gesture. "And you didn't resent me?"

"Because you screwed Yo-Yo? Hey, notice the difference? Men screwed Yo-Yo; I screw men. Deep significance there. Or maybe shallow. Or maybe none at all. No, I didn't resent you, Lieutenant! Goodness gracious, no! I could hardly have resented you."

"Why not?"

"Because you were my father," she says atonally. Then, "Hey, want another drink?"

LaPointe takes the shot in silence and doesn't speak until she has crossed to the bar and is refilling her glass. "That was cute. That 'want another drink?' part was particularly cute."

"Yeah, but kind of hokey."

"Of course you know that I was not . . ."

"Don't panic, Lieutenant. I know perfectly well that I don't owe the Gift of Life to any squirt from you—grunted or ungrunted. My father was Anonymous." She has a bit of trouble saying the word; the drink is beginning to close down on her. "You know the famous poet, Anonymous. He's in all the collections—mostly toward the front. Hey?

Aren't you just dying to know how come you're my father?"

She stands behind the bar, leaning over her glass, the ball of colored light tinting her hair, her face in the shadow. LaPointe is unable to see the expression in her unlit eyes. At a certain point, he turns away and watches the fire dwindle.

She uses a clowning, melodramatic style behind which she can hide, and occasionally her voice broadly italicizes words to prove she isn't taken in by the sentimentality that hurts.

"You see, children, it all began when I was very, very young and suffering from a case of innocence. I overheard Yo-Yo talking to some hooker she had up to the apartment for drinks. The subject was one Officer LaPointe, our beat cop, blue of uniform and blue of eye. Some yahoo had given Yo-Yo trouble, and the brave LaPointe had duly bashed him. You remember the incident?"

He shakes his head. In those days, that was not so uncommon an event that he would be likely to remember it.

"Well, bash you did, sir. *You Protected My Mother.* And the next Sunday, when she was taking me for a walk in the park, she pointed your apartment out to me. *This Was the House of the Man Who Protected My Mother.* And there were other times when she had good things to say about you. I didn't know then that she was praising you for paying for your nookie when, as a cop, you didn't have to.

"Well, sir, it was about that time that I went off to school and discovered that other kids had daddies. Before that, I had never thought about it. Living alone with Yo-Yo was simply how one lived. I neither had a daddy nor lacked one. Then the teasing about being a redhead began. And little boys wanted me to go behind the bushes and pull down my pants to show them my red hair. I couldn't understand. You see, I didn't have *any* hair, let alone red.

"So life went along, and went along, and went along. Then when I was about ten or eleven, the *Great Myth* began. One day after school, I was crying with anger and

302

frustration and there was a ring of kids around me, chanting 'Redhead, wet to bed . . . Redhead, wet to bed!' And I screamed at them to cut it out, or else! Or else what, one of them asked, logically enough. And another asked why I didn't run home and tell my father on them. And everyone laughed—we have to save the children, Lieutenant; they're our hope for the future—so I suddenly blurted out that I would too tell my father, if they didn't leave me alone! And they said I didn't have a father. And I said that I did too! Sergeant LaPointe was my father! And he would bash any son of a bitch who gave me trouble!"

There is a thud and a tinkle of glass, then silence.

"Oops. I have knocked over my glass in my efforts to decorate my fable with . . . whatever. How graceless of me."

LaPointe keeps his eyes on the fire. It would be unfair to look at her just then. He hears her walking behind the bar, the crisp crunch of glass under her shoes. He hears the squeak of the cork in the Armagnac bottle. When she speaks again, she has assumed a gruff, comic tone.

"Well, sir, that was the winter when I had a father . . . or, to be more exact, a *dad-dy*. You screwed Yo-Yo two times that winter, and both times I was awake when you came to the flat, and you chatted nonsense with me before she put me to bed. Your uniform smelled like wool, which wasn't so strange, considering the fact that it was made of wool. But it smelled good to me . . . like my blanket. Like the blanket I pressed against my nose when I sucked my thumb. At ten, I still sucked my thumb. But I've given that up in favor of cigarettes. Thumb-sucking causes lung cancer.

"And every day that winter, on my way home from school, I made a big loop out of my way so I could pass your apartment on Esplanade. I used to stand there, sometimes in the snow—grab the image of a little girl standing in the snow! Doesn't it just rip you up?—and I would look up at the windows of your apartment on the third floor. By the way, your apartment *is* on the third floor, isn't it?"

"Yes," he lies.

"I knew it. Infallible instinct. I knew you would live

303

on the top floor, looking out over the world. Hey, wouldn't it be funny if all those afternoons I had been looking up at the wrong apartment? Wouldn't that be an ironic blast?"

He nods.

After a silence, she puffs out a sigh. "Thank God that's out of me! Pal, you have no idea what a zonker it was when you walked in here this afternoon. Talk about ghosts! I didn't really have an appointment tonight. I was walking up on the Main—the first time in years. I dropped in at a bar or two and had Armagnac, because that was your drink. And I walked around the old streets, over past your apartment, trying to decide if I should unload all this crap on you. And finally I decided that I wouldn't. I decided to keep it to myself. *Sic transit* all claims to being mistress of my fate."

LaPointe has nothing to say.

"Well!" She brings him an Armagnac he doesn't want and sits on the divan beside him. "Presumably you didn't come here to hear all this psychological vomit. What can I do for you, Lieutenant?"

It isn't an easy change to make, and LaPointe sips his drink slowly before he begins. "There have been three men killed . . . probably by the same person."

"And a neurotic man-hater seems a likely suspect?"

He ignores this. "Two of them trace to you. When was the last time you saw Antonio Verdini?"

"I checked that little fact in my diary. I thought you might ask. By the way, I'll let you read my diary if you want. I suppose you'll want the names of the men I've screwed. In case the killer was one of them. Maybe jealousy, or something like that. Although I can't imagine why any of them would be jealous. After all, my door's been open to just about anyone who knocked. I view my body as something of a public convenience."

LaPointe doesn't want to get mired again in her self-pity; he holds to the line of questioning. "When was the last time you and Verdini made love?"

"A week ago tonight. He didn't leave until about midnight. It was a longish number. He was showing off his endurance, which, by the way, was something—"

"All right." LaPointe cuts her off. He doesn't care about that. "That checks. He was killed that night, shortly after he left here."

"Hey . . . maybe I can put you on to something. He might have been just boasting, but he said he had to leave early because he was going to screw some dancer . . . no. No, a dancer's kid. That was it."

"I know about that. He never got there."

"Too bad for the kid. He was a good plumber."

LaPointe regards her flatly. "Why don't we just stick to the questions and answers, Mlle. Montjean?"

"My hearty attitude toward sex doesn't impress you, Lieutenant?"

"It impresses me. But it doesn't convince me."

"Hey! Wow! The wisdom of the streets! Mind if I take a note on that?"

"Do you want your ass spanked?"

"Whatever turns you on, Daddy!" she snaps back. She's an experienced emotional in-fighter.

He settles his patient, fatigued eyes on her for a moment before continuing. "All right. Now, this professor at McGill. Tell me about him."

She chuckles. "You hold your cool pretty well, La-Pointe. Of course, you've got the advantage of being sober. And you've got another edge. Indifference is a mighty weapon."

"Let's just hear about the McGill professor."

"Mike Pearson? He was in charge of the Language Learning Center. That's where I got my idea of setting up this school. The high-saturation methods we use here were developed by Pearson. I took my M.A. under him . . . literally."

"Meaning that you and he—"

"Whenever we got a chance. Even while I was a student. The first time was on his desk. He got semen on papers he was grading. Do you know the root of the word 'seminar'? He was my first *conquest*. Think of it, Lieutenant! I was a virgin until I was twenty-four. A technical virgin, that is. Before that, I was what you might call manually self-sufficient. My analyst has given me some textbook crap about protracted virginity being common in cases of sexually traumatic events in childhood. He went on to say that it was typical that the first man should be a teacher—a father figure, an authority figure. Like a cop, I guess. That anus of an analyst always plays doctor after we've screwed. It's his way of taking an ethical shower. Think of it! A virgin at twenty-four! But I've made up for it since."

"Would your diary tell me the last time you and this Pearson were together?"

"I can tell you that myself. Mike's stabbing was in the papers. He was killed not twenty minutes after leaving here."

"Why didn't you inform the police?"

"Well, what was the point of getting involved? Mike was married. Why did the wife have to know where he spent his last night? I didn't dream his getting killed had anything to do with me. I thought he was mugged, or something like that."

"And that's why you didn't inform the police? Consideration for the wife?"

"All right, there was the reputation of the school too. It would have been messy PR. Say! Wait a minute! Why wasn't there anything in the papers about Tony's death?"

"There was."

"I didn't see it."

"His name wasn't mentioned. We didn't know it at the time. But I wonder if you would have called us, if you had known about the Verdini stabbing."

She has emptied her glass, and now she reaches automatically for his untouched one. He frowns, afraid she will get too drunk before the questioning is over. "Yes, I think I would have. Not out of civic duty, or any of that shit. But because I would have been scared, like I've been scared all afternoon, ever since you told me about it." She grins, the alcohol rising in her. "You see? That proves I didn't kill them. If I were the killer, I wouldn't be scared."

"No. But you might tell me you were."

"Ah-ha! The foxy mind of the fuzz! But you can take my word for it, Lieutenant. I don't go around stabbing men. I make *them* stab *me*." She wobbles her head in a blurred nod. "And there, Sigmund, you have a flash of revelation."

LaPointe has opened his notebook. "You say you don't know anything about the third man? The American named MacHenry?"

She shakes her head profoundly. "Nope. You see, there are *some* men in Montreal whom I have not yet screwed. But I'll get around to them. Never fear."

"I don't want you to drink anymore."

She looks at him incredulously. "What . . . did . . . you . . . say?"

"I don't want you to drink anymore until the questioning is over."

"You don't want . . . ! Well, fuck you, Lieutenant!" She glares at him, then, in the wash of anger and drunkenness, her manner trembles and dissolves. "Or . . . better yet . . . fuck *me*, Lieutenant. Why don't you screw me, LaPointe? I want to be screwed, for a change."

"Come on, cut it out."

"No, really! Making it with you may be just what I need. A psychic watershed. The final daddy!" She slides over to him and searches his eyes. There is a knowing leer in her expression, curiously confounded with the pleading of a child. Her hand closes over his leg and penis. He lifts her hand away by the wrist and stands up.

"You're drunk, Mlle. Montjean."

"And you're a coward, Lieutenant . . . Whatever-yournameis! I'll admit I'm drunk, if you'll admit you're a coward. A deal?"

LaPointe reaches into his inside coat pocket and takes out a photograph he picked up from Dr. Bouvier that afternoon. He holds it out to her. "This man."

She waves it away with a broad, vague gesture. She is hurt, embarrassed, drunk.

"It may not be a good likeness. It's a post-mortem shot. Would it help you to place the man if I told you he was killed about two and a half years ago?"

Like a petulant child forced to perform a chore, she snatches the photograph and looks at it.

The shock doesn't shatter her; it voids her. All spirit leaks out of her. She wants to drop the photograph, but she can't let go of it. LaPointe has to reach out and take it back.

As she puts her barriers back together, she saws her lower lip lightly between her teeth. A very deep breath is let out slowly between pursed lips.

"But his name wasn't MacHenry. It was Davidson. Cliff Davidson."

"Perhaps that was the name he told you."

"You mean he didn't even give me his right name?"

"Evidently not."

"The son of a bitch." More soft wonder in this than anger.

"Why son of a bitch?"

She closes her eyes and shakes her head heavily. She is tired, worn out, sick of all this.

"Why son of a bitch?" he repeats.

She rises slowly and goes to the bar—to get distance, not a drink. She leans her elbows on the polished walnut and stares at the array of bottles in the back bar, shining in the many colors of the glass ball light. Her back to him, she speaks in a drone. "Clifford Davidson was the giddying and grand romance in my life, officer. We were betrothed, each unto each. He came up to Canada to set up some kind of manufacturing operation in Quebec City, and he came here to learn Joual. He already spoke fair French, but he was one of your smarter cookies. He knew it would be a tremendous in for him if he, an American, could speak Joual French. The *canadien* workers and businessmen would eat it up."

"And you met him."

"And I met him. Yes. An exchange of glances, a brush of hands, a comparison of favorite composers, a matching up of plumbing. Love."

"Go on."

"Go on? Whither? *Quo vadis, pater?* Want to know a secret? That Latin I drop every once in a while? That's just an affection. It's all I got out of Ste. Catherine's Academy: a little Latin I no longer remember, and the grooming injunction that all proper girls keep their knees together, which advice I have long ignored. My knees have become absolute strangers. There's always some man coming between them. And how is *that* for an earthy little pun?"

"You and this Davidson fell in love. Go on."

"Ah, yes! Back to the interrogation. Right you go, Lieutenant! Well, let's see. Cliff and I had a glorious month together in gay, cosmopolitan Montreal. As I recall, marriage was mentioned. Then one day . . . poof! He disappeared like that fabled poofbird that flies in ever-smaller circles until it disappears up its own anus . . . poof!"

"Can you tell me the last time you saw him?"

"For that we shall need the trusty diary." She descends from the bar stool uncertainly and crosses to her desk, not unsteadily, but much too steadily. *"Voilà.* My gallery of rogues." She brandishes the diary for LaPointe to see. "Ah-ha. I see you have been nipping at the Armagnac, Lieutenant. You're having a little trouble staying in focus, aren't you, you sly old dog." With large gestures she pages through the book. "No, not him. No, not him either . . . although he wasn't bad. My, my, that was a night to set the waterbed a-sloshing! Come out of that book, Cliff Davidson. I know you're in there! Ah! Now let's see. The last night. Hm-m-m. I see it was a night of plans. And of love. And also . . . the night of September the eighteenth."

LaPointe glances at his notebook and closes it.

"That was the night he was stabbed?" she asks.

"Yes."

"Fancy that. Three men make love to me and end up stabbed. And to think that some guys worry about VD! I assume he was married? This MacHenry-Davidson?"

"Yes."

"A little wifey tucked away in Albany or somewhere. How quaint. You've got to hand it to these Americans. They're fantastic businessmen."

"Oh?"

"Oh, yes! Fantastic. Naturally, I never charged him for his language lessons."

LaPointe is silent for a time before asking, "May I take the diary with me?"

"Take the goddamned thing!" she screams, and she hurls it across the room at him.

It flutters open in the air and falls to the rug not halfway to him. Feckless display.

He leaves it lying on the rug. He'll get it as he goes.

When she has calmed down, she says dully, "That was a stupid thing to do."

"True."

"I'm sorry. Come on, have a nightcap with me. Proof of paternal forgiveness?"

"All right."

They sit side by side at the bar, sipping their drinks in silence, both looking ahead at the back bar. She sighs and asks, "Tell me truthfully. Aren't you a little sorry for me?"

"Yes, I am."

"Yeah. Me too. And I'm sorry for Tony. And I'm sorry for Mike. I'm even sorry for poor old Yo-Yo."

"Do you always call her that?"

"Didn't everybody?"

"I never did."

"You wouldn't," she says bitterly.

"You never call her Mother?"

She lays her hand on his shoulder and rests her cheek against her knuckles, letting him support her. "Never out loud. Never when I'm sober. You want to know something, Lieutenant? I hate you. I really hate you for not being . . . *there.*"

She feels him nod.

"Now, you're sure . . ." She yawns deeply. ". . . you're absolutely sure you don't want to screw me?"

His eyes crinkle. "Yes, I'm sure."

"That's good. Because I'm really sleepy." She takes her cheek from his shoulder and stands up. "I think I'll go to bed. If you've finished with your questions, that is."

LaPointe rises and collects his overcoat. "If I have more questions, I'll come back." He picks up the diary from the floor of the "conversation island," and she accompanies him to the door.

"This memory trip back to the Main has been heavy,

310

Lieutenant. Heavy and rough. I sure hope I never see you again."

"For your sake, I hope it works out that way."

"You still think I might have killed those men?"

He shrugs as he tugs on his overcoat.

"LaPointe? Will you kiss me good night? You don't have to tuck me in."

He kisses her on the forehead, their only contact his hands on her shoulders.

"Very chaste indeed," she says. "And now you're off. *Quo vadis, pater?*"

"What does that mean?"

"Just some of that phony Latin I told you about."

"I see. Well, good night, Mlle. Montjean."

"Good night, Lieutenant LaPointe."

14

From horizon to horizon the sky is streaming southward over the city. The membrane of layer-inversion has ruptured, and the pig weather is rushing through the gap, wisps and flags of torn cloud scudding beneath the higher roiling mass, all swept before a persistent north wind down off the Laurentians. Children look up at the tide of yeasty froth and have the giddying sensation that the sky is still, and the earth is rushing north.

The wind has held through the night, and by evening there will be snow. Tomorrow, taut skies of ardent blue will scintillate over snow drifts in the parks. At last it is over, this pig weather.

LaPointe stands at the window of his office, watching the sky flee south. The door opens behind him and Guttmann's head appears. "I got it, sir."

"Good. Come in. What are you carrying there?"

"Sir? Oh, just a cup of coffee."

"For me?"

"Ah . . . yes?"

"Good. Pass it over. Aren't you having any?"

"I guess not, sir. I've been drinking too much coffee lately."

"Hm-m. What did you find out?"

"I did what you told me; I checked with McGill and found that Mlle. Montjean attended on a full scholarship."

"I see." This is only part of the answer LaPointe is looking for. As he walked through back streets of the Main toward his apartment last night, he was pestered with the question of how a girl from the streets, a chippy's daughter, managed to get the schooling that transformed her into a sophisticated, if bent and tormented, young woman. If she had been Jewish or Chinese, he would understand, but the French Canadian culture does not contain this instinctive awe for education. "How did she come by the scholarship?"

"Well, she was an intelligent student. Did well in entrance tests. Super IQ. And to a certain degree, the scholarship was a foregone conclusion."

"How come?"

"She attended Ste. Catherine's Academy. I remember the Ste. Kate girls from when I was in college. They're prepped specifically for the entrance exams. Most of them get scholarships. Not that that's any saving of money for their parents. It costs more to send a girl to Ste. Kate's than to any university in the world."

"I see."

"You want me to check out Ste. Catherine's?"

"No, I'll do it." LaPointe wads up the coffee cup and misses the wastebasket with it.

Guttmann pulls his old bentwood chair from the wall and sits on it backwards, his chin on his arms. "How did it go last night? Did it turn out to be true that she never met the American, MacHenry?"

"No. She met him." LaPointe involuntarily lays his hand over the five-year diary he has been scanning with a feeling of reluctance, invasion.

"Then why did she deny it?"

"He gave her a phony name. She probably read about his death in the papers without knowing who it was."

314

"How about that? She's quite a . . . quite a woman, isn't she?"

"In what way?"

"Well, you know. The way she's got it all together. Her business, her life. All under control. I admire that. And the way she talks about sex—frank, healthy, not coy, not embarrassed. She's got it all put together."

"You'd make a great social worker, son; the way you can size people up at a glance."

"We'll have a chance to find out about that." Guttmann rubs the tip of his nose with his thumb knuckle. "I've . . . ah . . . sent in my resignation, effective in two months." He glances up to see what effect this news has on the Lieutenant.

None.

"Jeanne and I talked it over all last night. We've decided that I'm not cut out to be a cop."

"Does that mean you've got too much of something? Or too little?"

"Both, I guess. If I'm going to help people, me, I want to do it from their side of the fence."

LaPointe smiles at the "me, I" construction. His French was better when they met . . . but more bogus. "From the way you talk it sounds like you and your Jeanne are getting married."

"You know, that's a funny thing, sir. We've never actually talked about marriage. We've talked about how children should be brought up. We've talked about how when you design a house you should put the bathroom above the kitchen to save on plumbing. But never actually about marriage. And now it's sort of too late to propose to her. We've sort of passed that moment and gone on to bigger things." Guttmann smiles comfortably and shakes his head over the way their romance is going. People in love always imagine they're interesting. He rises from his chair. "Well, sir. I've got to get going. I report this afternoon out at St. Jean de Dieu. I'll be doing my last two months on the east side."

"Be careful. It can be rough for a Roundhead out there."

315

Guttmann tucks down the corners of his mouth and shrugs. "After being around you, maybe I can pass." If the chair weren't in the way, he might shake hands with the Lieutenant.

But the chair is in the way.

"Well, see you around, sir."

LaPointe nods. "Yes, see you around."

A few minutes after Guttmann leaves, it occurs to La-Pointe that he never learned the kid's first name.

"Lieutenant LaPointe?" Sister Marie-Thérèse enters the waiting room with a crisp rustle of her blue habit. She shakes hands firmly, realizing that uncertain pressures are vulnerable to interpretation. "You surprise me, Lieutenant. I expected an army officer." She smiles at him interrogatively, with the poise that is the signature of Ste. Catherine girls.

"I'm police, Sister."

"Ah." Meaning nothing.

As LaPointe explains that he is interested in one of their ex-students, Sister Marie-Thérèse listens politely, her face a mask of bland benevolence framed by a wide-winged wimple of perfect whiteness.

"I see," she says when he has finished. "Well, of course Ste. Catherine's is always eager to be a good citizen of Montreal, but I am afraid, Lieutenant, that our rules forbid any disclosure of our students' affairs. I am sure you understand." Her manner is gentle, her intention adamant.

"It isn't the young lady we're interested in. Not directly."

"Nevertheless . . ." She shows her palms, revealing herself to be helpless in the face of absolute rules.

"I considered getting a warrant, Sister. But since there were no criminal charges against the young lady, I thought it might be better to avoid what the newspapers might consider a nasty business."

The smile does not desert the nun's lips, but she lowers her eyes and blinks once. There are no wrinkles in her dry, almost powdery forehead. The face shows no signs of age, and none of youth.

"Still," LaPointe says, taking up his overcoat, "I understand your position. I'll come back tomorrow."

She lifts a hand toward his arm, but she does not touch him. "You say that Mlle. Montjean is not implicated in anything . . . unpleasant?"

"I said that she was not facing criminal charges."

"I see. Well, perhaps Ste. Catherine's could serve her best by cooperating with you. Will you follow me, please, Lieutenant?"

As they pass along a dark-paneled hall, he walks through air set in motion by the nun's habit, and he picks up a faint scent of soap and bread. He wonders if there is a Glory Hole here, and little girls working off punishment *tranches* by holding out their arms until their shoulders throb. He supposes not. Punishment at Ste. Catherine's would be a subtler matter, modern, kindly, and epulotic. Theirs would be a beautifully appointed little chapel, and their Virgin would not have a chip out of her cheek, would not be cross-eyed.

Two teen-aged girls dash around a corner, but arrest their run with comic abruptness when they see Sister Marie-Thérèse, and assume a sedate walk, side by side in their identical blue uniforms with SCA embroidered on bibs that bulge slightly with developing, unexplained breasts. In passing, they mutter, "Good morning, Sister." The nun nods her head, her expression neutral. But as the girls pass LaPointe they make identical tight-jawed grimaces and suck air in through their lower teeth. They'll get it later for running in the halls. Young ladies do not run. Not at Ste. Catherine's.

The Sister opens a tall oak door and stands aside to allow LaPointe to enter her office first. She does not close the door after them. As principal, she often has to meet male parents without the company of another nun, but never in rooms with closed doors.

The whole atmosphere of Ste. Catherine's Academy vibrates with sex unperformed.

With a businesslike rustle of her long skirts, she passes behind her desk and opens a middle file drawer. "You say Mlle. Montjean came to us twenty years ago?"

"About that. I don't know the exact date."

"That would be before I held my present position." She looks up from leafing through the files. "Although it certainly would not be before I came here." A careful denial that she is claiming youth. "In fact, Lieutenant, I am a Ste. Catherine girl myself."

"Oh?"

"Yes. Except for my girlhood and my years at university, I have lived all my life here. I was a teacher long before they made me principal." A slight accent on "made." An elevation to which she had not aspired, and for which she was unworthy. "It's odd that I don't remember a Mlle. Montjean."

Of course. He had forgot. "Her name was Dery when she was here."

"Dery? Claire Dery?" The tone suggests it is impossible that Claire Dery could be in trouble with the police.

"Her first name may have been Claire."

Sister Marie-Thérèse's fingers stop moving through the file folders. "You don't *know* her first name, Lieutenant?"

"No."

"I see." She does not see. She lifts out a file but does not offer it. "Now, what exactly is the information you require?"

"General background."

Her knuckles whiten as she grips the file more tightly. She has a right to know, after all. A duty to know. It's her responsibility to the school. Personally, she has no curiosity about scandal.

LaPointe settles his melancholy eyes on her face.

She compresses her lips.

He starts to rise.

"Perhaps you would like to read through the file yourself." She thrusts it toward him. "But it cannot leave the school, you understand."

The folder is bound with brown cord, and it opens automatically to the page of greatest interest to Ste. Catherine's. The information LaPointe seeks is there, in the record of fees and payments.

318

". . . I was sure you saw me last night in Carré St. Louis."

"No, I didn't."

"But you stopped suddenly and turned around, as though you had seen me."

"Oh, yes, I remember. I just had one of those feelings that someone was watching me."

"But *she* saw me. When she was crossing the park, I am sure she saw me."

"She mentioned that she saw someone. But she didn't recognize you."

"How could she? We have never met."

They sit diagonally opposite one another in comfortably dilapidated chairs in the bow window niche of a second-floor apartment in a brick row house on Rue de Bullion, two streets off the Main. Below them, the street is filled with a greenish gloaming, the last light of day captured and held close to the surface of the ground, causing objects in the street to be clearer than are rooftops and chimney pots. As they talk, the light leaks away; the gray clouds tumbling swiftly over the city darken and disappear; and the room behind them gradually recedes into gloom.

LaPointe has never been in the apartment before, but he has the impression that it is tidy, and characterless. They don't look at one another; their eyes wander over the scene beyond the window, where, across the street to the left, a billboard featuring a mindless smiling girl in a short tartan skirt enjoins people to smoke EXPRESS "A." Directly beneath them is a vacant lot strewn with broken bricks from houses being torn down to make way for a factory. There is a painted message of protest on the naked brick wall: 17 PEOPLE LIVED HERE. The protest will do no good; history is against the people.

In the vacant lot, half a dozen children play a game involving running and falling down, playing dead. An older girl stands against the denuded side of the next house to be demolished, watching the kids play. Her posture is grave. She is too old to run and fall down dead; she is still too young to go with men to the bars. She watches the kids, half wanting to be one of them again, half ready to be something else, to go somewhere else.

"Will you take something, Claude? A glass of schnapps maybe?"

"Please."

Moishe rises from the chair and goes into the gloom of the living room. "I've been waiting for you here all day. Once you traced your way to Claire . . ." He lifts a glass in each hand, a gesture expressive of inevitability. "I suppose you went to Ste. Catherine's Academy?"

"Yes."

"And of course you found my name in the records of payment."

"Yes."

Moishe gives a glass to LaPointe and sits down before lifting his drink. "Peace, Claude."

"Peace."

They sip their schnapps in silence. One of the kids down in the vacant lot has turned his ankle on a broken brick and is down on the hard-packed dirt. The others gather around him. The girl still stands apart.

"I'm crazy, of course," Moishe says at last.

LaPointe shrugs his shoulders.

"Oh, yes. Crazy. Crazy is not a medical term, Claude; it's a social term. I am not insane, but I *am* crazy. Society has systems and rules that it relies on for protection, for comfort . . . for camouflage. If somebody acts against the rules, society admits of only two possibilities. Either the outsider has acted for gain, or he has not acted for gain. If he has acted for gain, he is a criminal. If he has broken their rules with no thought of gain, he is crazy. The criminal they understand; his motives are their motives, even if his tactics are a little more . . . brusque. The crazy man they do not understand. Him they fear. Him they lock up, seal off. Whether they are locking him in, or locking themselves out—that's a matter of point of view." Moishe draws a long sigh, then he chuckles. "David would shake his head, eh? Even now, even at the end, Moishe the *luftmensh* looks for philosophy where there is only narrative. Poor David! What will he do without the pinochle games?"

320

LaPointe doesn't respond.

"I've caused you a lot of trouble, haven't I, Claude? I'm sorry. I tried to confess twice; I tried to save you the trouble. I went to your apartment Sunday for that purpose, but that young girl was there, and I could hardly . . . Then again after the game, when we were in the Russian café. I wanted to tell you; I wanted to explain; but it's so complicated. I only got as far as mentioning my sister. You remember?"

"I remember."

"She was very pretty, my sister." Moishe's voice is hushed and husky. "Delicate. Almost painfully shy. She would blush at anything. Once I asked her why she was so shy in company. She said she was embarrassed. Embarrassed at what, I asked. At my blushing, she said. Claude, *that* is shy. To be shy about being shy, *that's* shy. She . . . they put her into a special barracks in the camp. It was . . . this barracks was for the use of . . ."

"You don't have to tell me all this, Moishe."

"I know. But some things I want to tell you. Some things I want to explain . . . to say out loud for once. In classic drama, when a man has stepped on the inevitable treadmill of fate, he has no right to escape, to avoid punishment. But he does have a right to explain, to complain. Oedipus does not have the right to make a deal with the gods, but he has a right to bitch." Moishe sips his schnapps. "When the word reached me through the camp grapevine that my sister was in the special barracks, do you know what my first reaction was? It was: oh, no! Not her! She's too shy!"

LaPointe closes his eyes. He is tired to the marrow.

After a pause, Moishe continues. "She had red hair, my sister. Did you know that redheaded people blush more than others? They do. They do."

LaPointe looks over at his friend. The finger-stained round glasses are circles of bright gray reflecting the boiling sky. The eyes are invisible. "And Yo-Yo Dery had red hair too."

"Yes. Exactly. What a policeman you would have made."

"You went with Yo-Yo?"

"Only once. In all my life, that was my only experience with a woman. Think of that, Claude. I am sixty-two years old, and I have had only one physical experience with a woman. Of course, in my youth I was studious . . . very religious. Then in early manhood other things absorbed my attention. Politics. Philosophy. Oh, there were one or two girls who attracted me. And a couple of times one thing led to another and I was very close to it. But something always went wrong. A stranger happening along the path. No place to go. Once, in a field, a sudden rainstorm . . .

"Then there were the years in the camp. And after that, I was here, trying to start up my little business. Oh, I don't know. Something happens to you in the camps. First you lose your self-respect, then your appetites, eventually your mind. By clever forensics and selective forgetfulness, one can regain his self-respect. But when the appetites are gone . . . ? And the mind . . . ?

"So, with one thing and another, I end up a sixty-two-year-old man with only one experience of love. And it really *was* an experience of love, Claude. Not on her part, of course. But on mine."

"But you couldn't have been Claire Montjean's father. You weren't even in Canada—"

"No, no. By the time I met Françoise, she was experienced enough to avoid having children."

"Françoise was Yo-Yo's real name?"

Moishe nods, his light-filled glasses blinking. "I hated that nickname. Naturally."

"And you only made love once?"

"Once only. And that by accident, really. I used to see her pass the shop. With men usually. Always laughing. I knew all about her; the whole street knew. But there was the red hair . . . and something about her eyes. She reminded me of my sister. That seems funny, doesn't it? Someone like Françoise—hearty, loud, always having fun—reminding me of a girl so shy she blushed because she blushed? Sounds ridiculous. But not really. There was something very fragile in Françoise. Something inside her

was broken. The noise she chose to make when it hurt was
. . . laughter. But the pain was there, for those who would
see it. I suppose that's why she killed herself at last.

"And the men, Claude! The men who used her like a
public toilet! The men for whom she was nothing but friction and heat and a little lubrication! None of them bothered to see her pain. One after the other, they used her.
They queued up. As though she were . . . in a special barracks. They sinned against love, these men. Society has no
laws concerning crimes against love. Justice cries out
against it, but the Law is silent on the matter."

"Are you talking about the mother now, or about the
daughter?"

"What? What? Both, I guess. Yes . . . both."

"You said you made love to . . . Françoise by accident?"

"Not by intent, anyway. I used to see her walking by
the shopwindow—that was back when David was only my
employee, before we became partners—and she was always
so pert and energetic, always a smile for everybody. You
remember, don't you? You went with her yourself, I believe."

"Yes, I did. But—"

"Please. I'm not accusing. You were not like the others. There is a gentleness in you. Pain and gentleness. I'm
not accusing. I'm only saying that you had a chance to
know how full of life she was, how kind."

"Yes."

"So, well. One summer evening I was standing in front
of the shop, taking the air. There was not so much work as
there is now. We had not been 'discovered' by the interior
decorators. I was standing there, and she came by. Alone
for once. Somehow, I could tell she was feeling blue . . .
had the *cafard*. I said, Good evening. She stopped. We
talked about this and that . . . about nothing. It was one of
those long, soft evenings that make you feel good, but a
little melancholy, like sometimes wine does. Somehow I got
the courage to ask her to take supper with me at a restaurant. I said it in a joking way, to make it easy for her to say
no. But she accepted, just like that. So we had supper to-

gether. We talked, and we drank a bottle of wine. She told me about being a child on the Main. About men taking her to bed when she was only fifteen. She joked about it, of course, but she wasn't joking. And after supper, I walked her home. A warm evening, couples strolling. And all this time, I wasn't thinking about going to bed with her. I couldn't think of that. After all, she reminded me of my sister.

"When we got to her place, she invited me up. I didn't want to go home early on such an evening, to sit here alone and look out this window, so I accepted. And when we got into her apartment, she kissed her little girl good night, and she went into her bedroom and started undressing. Just like that. She undressed with the door open, and all the time she continued to chat with me about this and that. She had been sad that night, she had needed to talk; and now she was offering me what she had in return for giving her dinner and listening to her stories. How could I reject her?

"No! No!" Moishe's hands grip the arms of his chair. "This is no time for lying to myself. Maybe not wanting to reject her had something to do with it, but not much. She was undressed and I was looking at her body . . . her red hair. And I wanted her. She had told me stories about sleeping with men to get enough money for food, and now she was willing to sleep with me for giving her a dinner. I wanted to prove to her that I was not like those other men! I wanted to leave her alone! As a gesture of love. But she was nude, and it had been a gentle evening with wine, and . . . I wanted her. . . .

"And . . . one week later . . . she committed suicide."

"But, Moishe . . ."

"Oh, I know! I know, Claude! It had nothing to do with me. I wasn't that important in her life. A coincidence; I know that. But I felt I had to do something. I had failed to show that I was not like the other men. And now I had to do something, to show that I had affection. Then I thought of the daughter."

"So you arranged to have the girl taken into Ste. Catherine's. How did you find the money?"

324

"That's when I began to sell out the business to David. Bit by bit, as she needed money for school, for clothes, for vacations, I arranged for a summer in Europe, and later for a loan to start her language school."

"And all this time you never talked to the girl? Never let her know what you were doing for her?"

"That wouldn't have been right. I wanted to do something. A gesture of love. If I had accepted the daughter's gratitude, even affection maybe, then it would not have been a pure gesture of love. It would have been payment for value received. It was a sort of game—staying in the background, looking after her, taking pride in her accomplishments. And she has turned out to be a wonderful woman. Hasn't she, Claude?"

LaPointe's voice has become fogged over. He clears his throat. "Yes."

"When you think of it, it's ironic that you have met her, while I have not. But I know what a wonderful woman she has become. Look what she is doing for others! A school to teach people how to communicate. What could be more important? And she is a loving person. A little too loving, I'm afraid. Men take advantage of her. Oh, I know that she has had many lovers. I know. I have kept an eye on her. In my day, or yours, to have lovers would have been the mark of a bad girl. But it's different now. Young people aren't afraid to express their love. Still . . . still . . . there are some men who take a girl's body without loving her. These people sin. They defile.

"I used to go to Carré St. Louis often at night and keep an eye on her. I came to recognize the men. When I could, I checked up on the ones who visited often. That was a game too, checking up on them. It's amazing how much you can find out by asking a little question here, a little question there. Especially if you look like me—mild, unassuming. Most of the men were all right. Not good enough for her, maybe. But that's how a father always thinks. But some of them . . . some of them were sinning against her. Taking her love. Taking advantage of her gentleness, of her need for love. The first one was that university professor. A teacher! A teacher taking advantage of an innocent student fresh from convent school! Think of that. And a married man! Would you believe it, Claude, I saw him come to her school again and again for more than a year before it occurred to me that he was taking her love . . . her body. Inexperienced as I am, I thought he was interested in her school!

"Then there was that American. He had a wife in the United States. And from the first day, he was lying to her. Did you know that he used a false name with her?"

"Yes, I learned that."

"And finally there was this Antonio Verdini. When I found out about his reputation on the Main . . ."

"He was a bad one."

"An animal! Worse! Animals don't pretend. Animals don't rape. That's what it is, you know, when a man takes the body of a woman without feeling gentleness or love for her. Rape. Those three men raped her!"

The room is quite dark now; a ghost of gloaming still haunts the vacant lot where children play at falling down dead, and the lone girl watches soberly.

On the billboard, the woman in a short tartan skirt smiles provocatively. She'll give you everything she has, if you will smoke EXPRESS "A."

While Moishe sits unmoving, calming his fury, La-Pointe's mind is flooded with scraps and fragments. He recalls Moishe's wonderful skill with a knife when cutting fabric. David once said what a surgeon he would have made, and Father Martin made a weak joke about appendices being made of damask. LaPointe remembers the long discussions about sin and crime, and about sins against love. Moishe was trying to explain. Then a terribly unkind image leaks into LaPointe's mind. He wonders if, when he made love to Yo-Yo, Moishe grunted.

"Tell me about her," Moishe says quietly.

It takes LaPointe a second to find the track. "About Mlle. Montjean?"

"Yes. One of my daydreams has always been that I meet her somehow and we spend a few hours talking about this and that . . . not revealing anything to her, of course, but finding out how she thinks, what values she holds, her

326

plans, hopes, outlook, *Weltanschauung*." Moishe smiles wanly. "It doesn't look as though that will happen now. So why don't you tell me about her. She's an intelligent girl, eh?"

"Yes, she seems to be. She speaks Latin."

"And did you find her sensitive . . . open to people?"

"Yes."

"I knew she would be! I knew she would take that quality from her mother. And happy? Is she happy?"

LaPointe realizes what trash it would make of all that Moishe has done, if the girl is not happy.

"Yes," LaPointe says. "She's happy. Why shouldn't she be? She has everything she could want. Education. Success. You've given her everything."

"That's good. That's good." The sky is dark and is no longer reflected in Moishe's glasses. His eyes soften. "She is happy." For a time he warms himself with that thought. Then he sighs and lifts his head, as though waking. "Don't worry about it, Claude."

"About what?"

"This business, it must be awkward for you. Painful. After all, we are friends. But you won't have to arrest me. I will handle everything. A thousand times when I was in the camp, I cursed myself for letting them take me. I regretted that I hadn't killed my body before they could degrade and soil my mind. So, after I got out, I managed to purchase some . . . medicine. You would be surprised how many people who have survived the camps have—hidden somewhere—such medicine. Not that they intend to use it. No, they hope and expect that they will never have to use it. But it is a great comfort to know it is there. To know that you will never again have to surrender yourself to indignities.

"I shall take this medicine soon. You won't have the embarrassment of having to arrest me."

After a silence, LaPointe asks, "Do you want me to stay with you?"

Moishe is tempted. It would be a comfort. But: "No, Claude. You just go do your rounds of the Main. Put the street to bed like a good beat cop. I'll sit here awhile.

327

Maybe have another glass of schnapps. There's only a little left. Why should it go to waste?"

LaPointe sets down his empty glass and rises. He doesn't dare follow his impulse to touch Moishe. Moishe has it under control now. Sentiment might hurt him. LaPointe presses his fists deep into his overcoat pockets, grinding his knuckles against his revolver.

"What will become of her?" Moishe asks.

LaPointe follows his glance down to the adolescent girl standing alone with her back against the scabby brick wall. "What becomes of them, Claude?"

LaPointe leaves the room, softly closing the door behind him.

It is snowing on the Main, and the shops are closing; metal grids clatter down over display windows, doors are locked, one or two lights are left on in the back as deterrents to theft.

The sidewalks are thick with people, pressing, tangling, fluxing, their necks pulled into collars, their eyes squinting against the snow. At street corners and narrow places there are blockages in the pedestrian swarm, and they are pressed unwillingly against one another, threading or shouldering their way through the nuisance of these faceless and unimportant others, the wad.

Plump snowflakes the size of communion wafers slant through the garish neon of nosh bars, fish shops, saloons, cafés. People try to protect their packages from being soaked through; women put newspaper tents over their hair; those wearing glasses tilt their heads down so they can see over the top. Friends meet at bus stops and grumble: the goddamned snow; won't be able to get to work tomorrow. It was too good to last, the pig weather.

Snow crosshatches through the headlights of trucks grinding past the deserted park of Carré Vallières, at the top of the rise that separates the lower Main from the Italian Main. LaPointe sits on a bench, alone in the barren triangle of sooty dirt and stunted trees he has always associated with his retirement. Huddled in his great shapeless coat, the dark and the snow insulating and protecting him, the Lieutenant weeps.

The scar tissue over his emotions has ruptured, and his grief is pouring out. He does not sob; the tears simply flow from his eyes, and his face is wet with them.

LaPointe is grieving. For his grandfather, for Lucille, for Moishe. But principally . . . for himself. For himself.

For himself he grieves that his grandfather left him without support and comfort. For himself he grieves that Lucille died and took his ability to love with her. For himself he grieves the loss of Moishe, his last friend. At last, he pities the poor old bastard that he is, with this bubble in his chest that is going to take him away from a life he never quite got around to living. He is sorry for the poor old bastard who never had the courage to grieve his losses, and to survive them.

He slumps in the soporific pleasure of it. It feels so good to let the pressure leak away, to surrender finally. He knows, of course, that his life and force are draining out with the grief. His strength has always come from his bitterness, his reserve, his indifference. When the weeping is finished, he will be empty . . . and old.

But it feels so good to let go. Just . . . to let it all go.

At first the snow melts as it touches the sidewalk outside Chez Pete's Place, but as the slush builds up, it begins to insulate, and the large flakes remain longer before they decompose.

Inside, a dejected group of *bommes* sit around the center table, drinking their wine slowly so they won't have to buy another bottle before the proprietor makes them go out into the weather. Dirtyshirt Red glowers with disgust at two men sitting at a back table. He sneers to the ragged man sitting beside him, drinking a double red from a beer mug.

"Wouldn't ya know it? The only guy who'll drink with that potlickin' blowhard son of a bitch is a nut case!"

His mate glances over at the table and growls agreement with any slander against the Vet, that stuck-up shitlicker with his cozy kip off somewhere.

At the back table, a bottle of muscatel between them, sit the Vet and the Knife Grinder. They are together because they had enough money between them to buy the bottle. They have seen one another on the Main, of course, but they have never talked before.

"It's beginning," the Knife Grinder says, staring at the floor. "The snow. I warned everyone that it was coming, but no one would listen."

"Can you believe it?" the Vet answers. "They just caved it in! These goddamned kids come when I wasn't there, and they caved it in. Just for the hell of it."

"People fall in the snow, you know," the Knife Grinder responds. "They slip off roofs! Happens alla time, but nobody cares!"

The Vet nods. "They come and dragged off the roof. Then they caved in the sides. No reason. Just for the hell of it."

The Knife Grinder squints hard and tries to remember. "There was somebody . . . somebody important. And he told me there wouldn't be any snow this year. But he was lying!"

"What can you do?" the Vet asks. "I'll never find another one. They just . . . caved it in, you know? Just for fun."

They are both staring at the same spot on the floor. A kind of sharing.

In close to buildings, where pedestrian feet have not ground it to slush, the snow has built up to a depth of three inches. The wind is still strong, and it blows flakes almost horizontally across the window of Le Shalom Restaurant and Coffee Shop. Inside, where damp coats steam and puddles of melt-water make the tiles dangerous, the Chinese waitress barks orders to the long-suffering Greek cook, and tells customers to hold their water; has she got more than two hands?

Two girls sit in a booth near the counter. They are giggling and excited because a romance is beginning. One girl pushes the other with her elbow and says, "Ask him." The other presses her hand over her mouth and shakes her

330

head, her eyes sparkling. "Not *me*. *You* ask him!" She dares a quick look at the two grinning Hungarian boys in the next booth. "Go on!" the first girl insists, stifling her giggle. "No, *you* ask him!"

The Chinese waitress has found time to grab a cigarette. She mutters to herself, "For Christ's sake, *somebody* ask him!"

Four young women from the garment factory walk briskly down St. Laurent, laughing and kidding one another about boyfriends. One tries to catch a snowflake on her tongue; another starts a bawdy folk song about a lute player who will fix your spinet for you like it's never been fixed before, if you have a fresh new *écu* to give him for the lesson. They link arms and walk four abreast with long energetic strides as they sing at the top of their voices. They overtake an old Chasidic Jew with *peyiss*, his *shtreimel* level on his head, his long black overcoat collecting snowflakes. Playfully, they split, two on each side, and link arms with the startled man who is pulled along at a pace alien to his dignified step. "Buy us a drink, father! What do you say?" one of them shouts, and the others laugh. The old man stops, and the girls continue on, linking up four abreast again, their butts tweaking merrily along. He shakes his head, confused but not displeased. Youth. Youth. He looks up to check the street sign, as he always does before turning down toward the house he has lived in for twenty-two years.

Snow slants against the darkened window of a fish shop in which there is a glass tank, its sides green with algae. A lone carp glides back and forth in narcotized despair.

The long wooden stoop of LaPointe's apartment building is blanketed with six inches of untrodden snow. He holds the rail and half pulls himself up each step, tired, empty. Because his head is down, he sees first her feet, then her battered shopping bag.

"Hello," she says.

331

He passes her without a word and opens the front door. She follows him into the vestibule, lit only by a fifteen-watt bulb. He leans against the banister and looks at her, his eyes hooded.

She shrugs, her lips compressed in a flat half grin. The expression says, Well, here I am. That's the way it goes.

LaPointe rubs his whiskered cheek. What's the use of this? He doesn't need this. He is empty at last, and at peace. He wants to finish it off easily, cocooned in his routine, his chair by the window, his coffee, his Zola. It's not as though she would stay. The first time she finds a handsome Greek boy to buy her ouzo and dance with her, she'll be gone again. And probably she'll come sniffing back when he gets tired of her. What is she after all? A stupid twit the age of his daughters, the age of his wife. And worst of all, he would have to tell her about this thing in his chest. It wouldn't be fair to let her wake up some morning and reach over to touch him. And find him . . .

No, it's better not to want anything, need anything. There's no point in opening yourself up to hurt. It's stupid. Stupid.

"How about a cup of coffee?" he asked.

Bestselling Books for Today's Reader

____ **THE CAPTAINS**   05644-8/$3.50
Brotherhood of War #2
W.E.B. Griffin

____ **SHIKE: TIME OF THE DRAGONS**   07517-5/$3.95
Robert Shea

____ **SHIKE II: LAST OF THE ZINJA** 07518-3/$3.95
Robert Shea

____ **BITTERLEAF**   07360-1/$3.95
Lisa Gregory

____ **THE ULTIMATE GAME**   06524-2/$3.50
Ralph Glendinning

____ **THE WOMEN'S ROOM**   06896-9/$3.95
Marilyn French

____ **RIVINGTON STREET**   07149-8/$3.95
Meredith Tax

____ **SARINA**   07366-0/$3.50
Francine Rivers

____ **EIGHT MILLION WAYS TO DIE** 07257-5/$2.95
Lawrence Block

____ **SYBELLE**   07128-5/$3.95
Roberta Gellis

____ **THE CHILDREN OF THE ISLAND** 07129-3/$2.95
T.M. Wright

____ **FOREVER, VICTORIA**   07444-6/$3.50
Dorothy Garlock

____ **LIVE FOR LOVE**   07385-7/$3.95
Shana Carrol

Prices may be slightly higher in Canada.

Available at your local bookstore or return this form to:

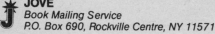

JOVE
Book Mailing Service
P.O. Box 690, Rockville Centre, NY 11571

Please send me the titles checked above. I enclose _____ Include 75¢ for postage
and handling if one book is ordered; 25¢ per book for two or more not to exceed
$1.75. California, Illinois, New York and Tennessee residents please add sales tax.

NAME_____

ADDRESS_____

CITY_____STATE/ZIP_____

(allow six weeks for delivery)   **SK23**

More Bestsellers from Berkley
The books you've been hearing about and want to read

___	**SEMPER FI, MAC**	06253-8 — $3.95
	Henry Berry	
___	**VALIANT HEARTS**	05969-3 — $3.50
	Evan H. Rhodes	
___	**DUNE**	06434-4 — $3.95
	Frank Herbert	
___	**DOG TRAINING MY WAY**	05960-X — $2.95
	Barbara Woodhouse	
___	**LICENSE RENEWED**	06397-6 — $3.50
	John Gardner	
___	**ELRIC OF MELNIBONÉ**	06044-6 — $2.50
	Michael Moorcook	
___	**DEATH BEAM**	07123-5 — $3.95
	Robert Moss	
___	**THE WHITE PLAGUE**	06555-3 — $3.95
	Frank Herbert	
___	**THE KILLING ZONE: MY LIFE IN THE VIET NAM**	06534-0 — $3.50
	Frederick Downs	
___	**THE MATCH TRICK**	06415-8 — $3.50
	Don Zacharia	
___	**A WOMAN OF DESTINY**	06476-X — $3.95
	Orson Scott Card	
___	**REAP THE SAVAGE WIND**	06536-7 — $3.95
	Ellen Tanner Marsh	

Prices may be slightly higher in Canada.